THE FIGUREHEAD

PAUL DEAN COKER

COASTWISE COMMUNICATIONS
TEMPLETON, CA

COASTWISE COMMUNICATIONS

A Division of The Coastwise Group
1449 Whippoorwill Lane
Templeton, CA 93465
1-805-434-2413
Web Address: www.thecoastwisegroup.com

ISBN 1-886178-03-8

Library of Congress Control Number 2006930500

First Edition - Printed in the United States of America

The Ballad "Kilkelly" - used by permission - Peter Jones, songwriter.
The Drawing "Figurehead" – used by permission – Estate of Bones Lehman.

Typeset:
Titles – FELIX TITLING
Text – California FB

This book is printed on acid free paper.

Cover Design by JEM Design, Atascadero, CA
Editorial Services by First Impressions, Atascadero, CA
Book Design by Paul Dean Coker

For
Valerie Maxine Schneider

My *Maxine*

In Memory of
Charles "Rick" Rickerich

Naval Architect

CONTENTS

PREFACE

I met, or should say—discovered—my first two spies at age seventeen, while a senior in high school. Aside from my amazement that these people worked for intelligence agencies, I was stunned to discover them in small towns in Michigan and Indiana. I was not supposed to know what they were doing, nor do I have any reason to believe they knew I knew what they were doing.

Later in life I learned more about the amount of money spent and the geopolitical logic of spying and realized I shouldn't have been surprised at all. This is even truer after Sept. 11, 2001. Spying amongst ourselves will be pervasive.

Also, later in life, I occasioned to know an arms dealer, a highly placed senator and several other colorful East Coast characters. A couple decades of yachting afforded the opportunity to sail with some interesting mates.

This story, however, isn't specifically about them, or me. This story is a celebration of the Irish peace process and the widely recognized and exemplary Belfast Agreement, also known as the Good Friday Agreement.

This story is about people from both sides of the "pond" who engaged in a Herculean effort to do everything possible to discover the things that make us a society rather than a fractured and brutal collection of misfits.

The basis of diplomatic achievement, like the Belfast Agreement, comes when our *viewpoint* is broad and the *context* of our relationships is understood. These are the two main principles I believe led to this agreement—viewpoint and context. These are the soundest underpinnings of diplomacy.

Thus, the Belfast Agreement and the process followed to accomplish it is a model—a model we should all understand. It is a model to emulate when we ultimately face the great settling of our ideological and geopolitical differences all around the world.

Paul Dean Coker

ACKNOWLEDGEMENTS

Jeanette Morris was first mate on this cruise, editing and offering invaluable suggestions. Her insight and experience certainly enabled this passage. Judy Coker, sister, teacher, and adventurer offered continual support from Kyoto, Japan. Kathy Gervasi, sailor, boat restorer, and great friend read the story and sometimes found herself at the tiller.

Although this is a work of fiction, those on board this passage are both composites and interpretations of people I've sailed with—including the mysterious, secretive, and irascible!

Finally, the real "Bones," Bones Lehmann, drew the "Figurehead" in 1937. A copy of the drawing was mounted in and sailed aboard the *Old Bird*, a 37 ft. Atkin ketch that Kathy Gervasi and I restored in 1980 while graduate students at the University of Notre Dame.

THE FIGUREHEAD

PROLOGUE

DECEMBER 2004

Isn't it strange, thought Carter. *The sun has shown on this atoll since it rose from the bottom of the sea, yet I've been insensible, worse—oblivious—to its existence. I've been thinking the sun only rose on the Big Lake . . .*

≋≋≋

Carter Phillips contemplated the aquamarine reflection of the Maldivian sky from the low aspect of a brightly colored beach chair. The halcyon firmament colored the water. A light morning breeze carried flower-blossom aroma from a nearby grove.

Inhaling the fragrant air, Carter extended his arm, holding a sketch pad lifted from his lap. He studied the sketch, looking between the drawing and the scene before him.

Not far offshore his sailboat swung on her mooring. Looking past his sketch pad, the young architect studied the angle of her mainsail boom. He kept her topping lift snug, hiking the boom up a couple degrees at the stern, giving the vessel a proud comportment. She floated idly in the tropical sea, protected by a crescent reef.

A barely discernable change in the whitish-blue of the water near shore caught his attention.

That's odd, he thought.

Craning his neck forward, he noticed an unusual silver-green color spread across the shallows. He looked to the sky to see if a cloud was forming, thinking he might be seeing a reflection. The sky was clear.

Sitting upright in the chair, looking up and down the palm-speckled beach, Carter saw no one else in sight, no one to affirm the strange transformation.

Abheem Solih's three-legged dog ran from behind a nearby palm, kicking and scattering sand as if its missing hind leg had been superfluous after all. Carter smiled at the bizarre sight. He liked the pitiable creature whom Abheem, Martha's handyman, named Sir Tom, short for Sir Thomas Lipton. Carter was unable to decide whether the name was a tribute to or a mockery of the English who governed the Maldives during the early decades of Abheem's life.

Aside from Sir Tom, Carter was alone. He checked the time; it was 9:45 A.M. The women, guided by Hundali Nadeem, were in Male on a shopping trip. They had stayed overnight in the Maldivian capital and would return this evening in accordance with the ferry schedule.

Patrick was out fishing for tuna; at least that's what Carter assumed when he saw the Irishman's vadhu dhoni missing from its spot on the beach. Fishing was his close friend's new pastime, Martha had informed Carter soon after his arrival in the Maldives. It began, she explained, when Patrick built a small dhoni under *kissaru wadin's* critical eye. Dhonies were Arabic sailboats, the lines of which invoked an ancient appearance such as in Homer's Odyssey.

Patrick often sailed his dhoni to the outside edges of the atoll to hook big tuna. Then, as would an untended child, he squealed gleefully as his catch towed him around in circles, the little dhoni skidding across the surface like a toboggan. The Nantucket Sleigh Ride, as Patrick called it, always ended badly for the fish when it became dinner in Hundali's hammered copper pan.

Looking back out to sea, surprised by what he saw, Carter dropped his sketch book and pushed himself up from the low-slung chair. Gasping audibly, he realized that in the time he had turned away, the tide had fallen drastically.

That's not right . . .

His heart began beating faster, adrenalin seeping into his blood.

He reached for his field glasses hanging on the back of the chair, bringing them quickly to his eyes. The tide dropped farther, then farther.

He swung to the north and looked up the beach.

Holy Christ, what the . . .

He turned rapidly and looked to the south.

This can't be . . .

The water was receding at an unbelievable rate.

Screwing the binoculars to his disbelieving eyes, he saw small fish and minnows, suddenly stranded, flopping around on bare sand.

This isn't possible . . .

Carter left the thought dangling and searched the horizon for Patrick. Panicked over his whereabouts, he spotted the dhoni, its lateen rig peeking above the horizon past the edge of the shallow atoll. Carter guessed Patrick was a half-mile out. He swung the glasses toward his sloop. She seemed fine—sitting steadily on her waterline.

Wouldn't Ibriham Shaahir have mentioned a tide this extreme?

Shaahir was *kissara wadin*, the local boat builder. Patrick befriended the "curved carpenter," the literal interpretation of *kissara wadin*, when he, Martha and Bones first arrived on the atoll nearly four years earlier.

Carter looked back toward the small grouping of bungalows and thought of the tourists who arrived the night before. He wondered where they were. Maybe they were sleeping in, suffering jet lag. Abheem was supposed to prepare breakfast in Hundali's absence.

Where's Abheem? He'll know about this tide.

Turning back toward the beach, Carter was shocked at the scene before him now. His sloop, moored in twelve feet of water, lay on her side on bare sand! The water was gone! The bay looked like an empty lake bottom.

Horrified, Carter unconsciously yelled, "No!" and raced onto the dry flats, running toward his boat. She lay two hundred yards beyond what moments earlier had been the low tide line. Dodging stranded fish and benthic organisms, he ran as if there were something he could do about his sloop's predicament.

Beyond his beached yacht, Carter saw a strange interruption on the horizon line out near the edge of the crescent atoll. He stopped running. He reached for his field glasses, squinting his eyes, trying hard to focus. He thought he saw a foaming surge of water rising above the distant horizon.

What on earth...

Carter's face paled while through the binoculars he witnessed a mounting flood of roily water climbing over the barrier reef. He spotted Patrick O'Clery, his dhoni coming about as if he too finally realized the danger.

He's not going to make it; he's going to be hit...

Carter's heart hammered in his chest. He instantly realized what was bearing down on Patrick.

A tsunami!

Taking the field glasses from his eyes, the tsunami looked farther away, still cresting the edge of the atoll. There were a few seconds, perhaps a minute, to act, to run, to do something. He turned and sprinted inland.

The tourists... I've got to find Abheem....

Splashing back over the tidal flats, Carter ran toward the bungalows, looking for refuge on high ground. Oddly, considering the situation, he remembered reading a cruising guide: "The highest elevation on the Maldives is only 2.4 meters above sea level. . . ."

He did a quick calculation.

Eight feet!

The irrefutable equation spoke volumes. It defined the coming destruction: absolute and unstoppable. There would be no safe place to run, no way to escape!

Carter scanned the island for high ground, but as the equation defined, there was none to be found. He looked for trees, trying to spot the center of the thickest grove, his feet flying beneath him, jarring his vision.

From behind the main bungalow, Abheem Solih suddenly appeared. He looked out into the harbor and spotted Carter's yacht, lying on her side. A blank, questioning look widened his coconut-brown eyes. He turned toward Carter who frantically sprinted toward him.

"Mister Caahter, sir, what's going on, Mister Caahter?"

Carter realized Abheem, like himself, had never seen what they were seeing now.

Carter wailed, "Tsunami! Wake the tourists, Abheem, run for high ground—into the trees!"

Carter's admonitions confused Abheem and he froze, unable to react. A second or two passed.

The black-skinned Maldivian finally stirred, but instead of running to warn the tourists, he turned to the beach. He bellowed for Sir Tom, shouting the dog's name until his three-legged friend came running toward him.

Carter yelled again, "Abheem, wake the tourists, wake the tourists . . ."

Abheem continued ignoring him, crouching instead to sweep the dog into his frail, black arms. Sir Tom vigorously licked Abheem's face.

Abheem's purpose finally dawned upon Carter. The old native did indeed recognize the deadly circumstance. He was not, however, going to run for the tourists—rather, he ran for the thing he cared about most. Carter thought again of Patrick, and the women in Male.

With Sir Tom safely in hand, Abheem turned back toward high ground.

"Mister Caahter, sir, Mister Caahter," he called out. "Please Mister Caahter, wait . . ."

Carter paused a moment and Abheem caught up with him. With fear and futility pouring from his dark narrow face, the old Maldivian handed Sir Tom to Carter, pleading with him to save his small companion's life.

Sir Tom squirmed and yelped in Carter's arms, struggling to remain with his ancient master. Abheem turned toward the bungalows, looking back one last time. He spoke to the dog in Dhivehi, issuing a command that calmed the frightened creature. Changing to English he spoke to Carter.

"I'm too old, Mister Caahter, sir. Take him. You run fast Mister Caahter, sir, take him and run to the grove, please! I'll wake the tourists . . . go, now, hurry please, Mister Caahter."

Carter looked at the dog and then Abheem; what could he do? He looked again toward the sea, wondering about Patrick. All he saw was a mounding wave tumbling forward across the flats at an ungodly speed.

By the time he turned back toward Abheem, the Maldivian was making his way to the bungalows yelling crazily in Dhivehi. Carter assumed whatever it was he was shouting meant "run for your life," which is exactly what Carter Phillips, Sir Tom clutched under his arm, began doing.

Carter sprinted across a lawn, through a garden, then between two bungalows. Sir Tom, sensing his rescue, stopped squirming and rode obediently. Leaping a low border fence, the twosome dove headlong into a thicket.

Once inside the grove, Carter sped toward a tree with multiple branches forming a crude ladder. Reaching with his free arm he grabbed a branch and launched himself upward and into a V-shaped crotch. Sir Tom yelped in distress, but his bark was obliterated by the sound of shattering bungalows as the tsunami bore down upon them.

Carter looked for something bigger, stronger, but it was too late. A wall of water struck him with incomprehensible force, knocking him nearly senseless. As if shot from a cannon, he launched explosively through the branches of the thickly vegetated grove. Together, the living flotsam of man and dog tumbled in the wave that raked the sunken atoll.

Despite the brutal punishment, Carter held fast to Sir Tom. There was little else he could do considering the force of the wave that carried them away. He was unsure if the dog was alive.

Suddenly, the vegetation became sparse and Carter looked ahead to see the open ocean. Fear struck deeply as he contemplated being swept out to sea. He panicked and grabbed for a passing branch, not realizing the force of his movement. He felt a snap.

My arm or the branch?

Distinguishing which had broken was impossible. He continued tumbling forward, the water pushing him relentlessly along his destined course.

Then the tsunami's force began dissipating as if all its energy was suddenly drawn away as punishment for its terrible deed. Carter sensed the calming. He considered that his calamity may soon end and he might actually survive. After all, he thought, it was a wave; it functioned by rules, by laws of physics. The worst, he figured, was over.

Within a few seconds the water stretched out flat and paused in place. Carter was able to stand up; the water was only waist deep. Dazed and wobbly, he looked around. It was like the moment of a changing tide in New England.

The water began moving the opposite direction. Recovering his wits, it dawned on Carter what was going to happen next—the water would recede slowly at first, then faster and faster.

Physics.

He tried to switch Sir Tom to his other arm. A fiery pain shot through his free appendage. His arm was broken. He tried to raise it and saw a small bone protruding through the flesh of his forearm. The sight of torn flesh and exposed bone made him nauseated. He nearly fainted. Staggering a moment, he looked away from the wound and worked to steady himself in the rapid current of water.

Then, following the dictates of physics, Carter was pushed back toward the grove, carried by the force of the sea. He struggled to remain standing but the speed increased steadily. From the corner of his eye he saw three human bodies floating face down in the swirling debris. He looked away, knowing there was nothing he could do except to try to avoid joining them.

Keeping Sir Tom and himself alive became Carter's focused goal, yet every couple of seconds he thought of Patrick—was he one of the three? He should have checked—then he realized he couldn't even stand upright, let alone navigate in the tumultuous current.

Pain and confusion finally overwhelmed him. He collapsed and fell backward, struggling to keep Sir Tom's head above water. The receding wave dragged them back into the grove. This time, the tree branches, stripped of soft vegetation, stabbed and tore at the sodden pair.

With his free hand, Carter absentmindedly reached for a cluster of protruding limbs rising from the muddied water. An excruciating pain shot through his arm the instant his fractured appendage bumped against a branch. He withdrew it and automatically reached with his other hand to grab hold, causing him to lose his grip on Sir Tom.

Realizing his mistake, he struggled to retrieve the dog by letting go of the branch. To his horror he discovered he was entangled in vegetation. He writhed violently, trying to set himself free, but his feet swept out from under him. Stretched out horizontally, one arm useless, the other flailing wildly, he desperately tried to right himself.

Suddenly, from behind, a door torn from a demolished bungalow struck the back of his head. Carter's eyes rolled upwards and everything went black.

The force of the blow tore Carter free and he floated face up directly into another cluster of upright branches on a leafless tree.

Sir Tom frantically paddled to the door, scrambling aboard as it floated past Carter. The door, with the dog on board, lodged in branches a few feet downstream. For a moment, everything was still; the water moved quietly beneath the entangled Carter, back where it came from.

The three legged creature broke the stillness, pacing anxiously, barking a futile message in the direction of his uncomprehending new master.

The water level began dropping. Within a couple of minutes, Carter was laying contorted, snagged horizontally in the dripping branches. His feet were in the quickly receding water, his arms and legs akimbo.

From his vantage point on the door, Sir Tom cocked his head and appeared to study Carter's predicament. After a few moments, the scrawny canine leapt back into the water and swam to the buckled body of the injured sailor. Climbing first onto Carter's leg, and then up his torso, Sir Tom sniffed and licked Carter's pale and muddied face. Sir Tom seemed to sense Carter's distress and perched himself like a parrot on the battered sailor's shoulder. There the canine sentinel remained—looking up at the sky, looking out over the atoll, watching in the distance for whatever things animals conjure in their tiny minds.

≋≋≋

Carter regained consciousness. "You're alive, Sir Tom, good boy—you're alive!"

He looked over the dog. Sir Tom appeared unharmed. He looked over himself. He was shocked to discover his own miserable condition. Shifting his eyes upward, not wanting to gaze upon his awful situation, Carter looked into a clear, calm sky. It had been unaffected by the tsunami. He noted, however, the fragrant aroma that embraced him earlier was gone, replaced with the smell of displaced mud and tropical detritus.

Lowering his head again, he looked out across the horizon to see if he could spot Patrick. He wondered if the old Irishman survived. Then he thought of the floating bodies once again.

Carter felt numb and disconnected from his body. His head lay at a slight angle and he was grateful he could see the distant horizon. The tsunami had ended and all that remained were spindly branches of a once luscious grove. As he feared, the devastation of Martha and Patrick's resort was complete; it had literally disappeared. He worried again over Patrick's survival.

Unable to turn his head more than a few degrees either way, he checked the horizon for his sloop. She was nowhere in sight. He attempted to shift in place, to look behind himself, but was unable to move. He was sinking into despair when a thought occurred that lifted his spirits.

She may still be afloat. She might be behind me, out of sight. Perhaps Patrick is too!

He closed his eyes, took a deep breath just to feel something inside him move, and allowed it to exhaust from his lungs. There was no pain and for that he was grateful. Sir Tom responded to the movement with more licking, and for that, too, he was grateful.

Carter closed his eyes, thinking he might rest a few moments, then reconsider his situation. Instead, he began fading into a hazy, semi-consciousness. He knew he was badly injured, he knew the resort was destroyed, and he knew his yacht had gone missing. What he didn't know—what he wondered now—was whether Patrick O' Clery survived?

As Carter Phillips hung suspended a couple feet above a ravaged landscape surrounded by a docile sea, memories of the old Irishman blossomed in the stricken sailor's mind. He allowed the thoughts to grow, to expand and push away his misery. The memories brought relief, a way to forget his present condition, a way to survive until, and if, he was discovered . . .

BOOK I

MARBLEHEAD HARBOR

Roger Williams

c. 1603-1683

There goes many a ship to the sea, with many hundred souls in one ship, whose weal and woe is common, and is a true picture of a commonwealth or a human combination or society. It hath fallen out sometimes that both Papist and Protestant, Jews and Turks may be embarked in one ship; upon which supposal I affirm that all the liberty of conscience that ever I pleaded turns upon these two hinges – that none of the Papists or Protestants, Jews or Turks be forced to come to the ship's prayers or worship, nor compelled from their own particular prayers or worship, if they practice any.

Letter to the Town of Providence – January 1655

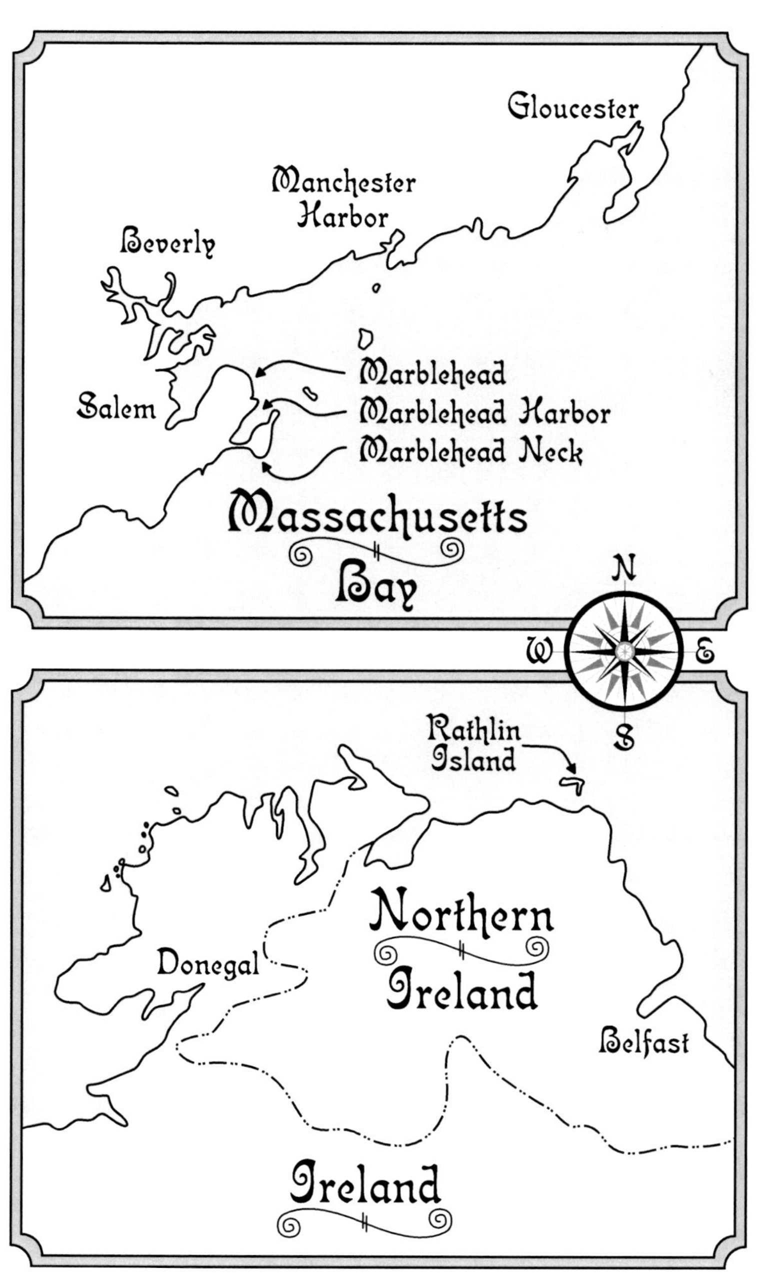

Gloucester
Manchester Harbor
Beverly
Marblehead
Salem
Marblehead Harbor
Marblehead Neck
Massachusetts Bay
N
W
E
S
Rathlin Island
Northern Ireland
Donegal
Belfast
Ireland

CHAPTER 1

PATRICK O'CLERY

Carter Phillips was anxious to return north. His winter in Florida, pleasant as it may have been, had reached its tolerable end. He longed to rejoin *Maxine*, his wooden boat, but more than a boat, his home.

The previous summer, Carter had sailed *Maxine* in the Gulf of Maine, arriving eventually in Marblehead where he left her on the hard. An excellent adventure considering most of his sailing had been on the Great Lakes in icy waters and for incredibly short seasons. The coast of New England presented a great mystery to Carter, he being a Midwesterner, born and raised in Michigan. He was convinced that his last season was merely a glimpse of the experiences New England waters held.

Upon arriving in Boston that day in March, Carter decided to stay and have a look around. After a couple days, he'd move on up to Marblehead and his waiting *Maxine*. Weary after a day of exploring the city, Carter searched the *Boston Globe* for a movie—something to relax his mind. After selecting a film, he departed his hotel. From the edge of the Italian district, not far from the waterfront, he headed deep into the glass and steel canyon locals called "The Hub."

The walk proved surprising as Carter passed the Old South Meeting House. It was there, he discovered, Sam Adams signaled the start of the Boston Tea Party. Farther along, he strode past the site of the Boston Massacre.

The theatre was *not* in a particularly picturesque location: above it a parking facility and below it the subway. Boston was built on top of itself beginning long ago on backwater swamps and waterways. On the day of Carter's exploration, Boston looked nothing as it did when the Colonials defended Bunker Hill.

The movie turned out not to be what Carter expected. He expected an adventure, and instead, after about 20 minutes, the movie evolved into a surprisingly warm love story, imbued with pathos. The storyline was clever and surrealistic in its representation of love—love lost by a tear in the fabric of time; time portrayed as fluid, like Dali's clocks. As Carter watched he began noticing an older man sitting across the aisle. He was alone—as was Carter.

The man viewed the film intently and that caught Carter's attention. Carter's curiosity was piqued not only by the story, but by the old man's peculiar intensity. Taking glimpses between scenes, Carter noticed his face bore a series of contorted expressions, the effects of the film becoming obvious even in the dark cavernous space.

Carter glanced elsewhere around the theatre. No one else seemed quite so moved, nor had anyone else noticed the old man. Curiously, Carter watched as the elderly viewer imbibed with unbridled thirst; every aspect of the old man's attention focused on the film. Even in the dark the old fellow's comportment told Carter that the scenes of love, full and intense, lost yet desperately desired, were sweeping the ancient viewer to another place, another time.

Carter's own imagination was getting ahead of itself, and he concluded, perhaps a bit presumptuously, that the old man probably once knew a deep love like that of the characters in the movie. Carter figured he was connecting to it, infected by it. It explained his demeanor, and maybe, his solitude.

As the film neared its end, Carter realized he had become ridiculously compelled to help or do something to soothe the pain he assumed welled in the old man's heart. Carter was certain he could discern a dazed appearance on the face of the stranger. The old man kept glancing around the theatre as if to look for support, something to hold on to like the lifelines of a boat in a storm.

As the credits trailed off and the moment of the unavoidable return to ordinary existence approached, the old man again looked desperately around the emptying theatre. Carter watched his agonizing search. The fellow wiped his wrinkled eyes as they darted from one departing moviegoer to the next. Carter was sure no one saw what he saw: the anguish, the sadness.

Carter's eyes never moved from the old man. He too was filled with a strange emotion, and although he didn't fully realize it, he and the old man had slipped into empathetic phase, a spatial dimension where they were together in sentiment.

After a few seconds, the old man appeared to abandon his hope of someone throwing him a lifeline, and pulling him from his personal sea of sadness. He gave up and rose from the seat.

Except for the two of them the theatre was now empty. Carter believed the old man hadn't noticed him. As the man turned slowly, his internal dialogue escaped his lips in the silent, dimly lit surroundings. He verbalized his thoughts unabashedly as age often allows.

His words remained indiscernible. In fact, Carter thought they might have been foreign. But he took them, again perhaps presumptuously, to be an utterance of despair reserved solely for the old and forsaken.

The old man paused at the edge of the aisle. He behaved like someone not wanting to let go, not willing to let go—not this time. Perhaps he let go before. Perhaps he regretted it. Whatever happened on the screen to cause this effect, it was clear the old man did not want it to end. He was engaged in a silent battle to keep hold of what Carter assumed he'd already lost somewhere in time.

Carter rose from his seat, the movement catching the old man by surprise. Raising tired graying eyes, the old man looked at the younger one, suddenly realizing there was a witness. Unable to ignore the old man's apparent sorrow. Carter decided to speak up and say something.

What can I say? He hesitated. Was he certain about his assumptions? Had he been swept away by empathy? After all, he too was alone. Without being conscious of it, had he raced forward in time, placing himself as a lonely old man in the body of a stranger in a strange theatre in a strange town?

He didn't know the answers to his questions, but it was time to do something. Carter gestured a handshake and spoke quite awkwardly, "I'm not from around here."

The old man looked up at him, eyeing him just a moment then raising his hand and replying with an Irish brogue, very distinct and surprisingly rich. "Aye laddie – where would ya be from then skippah?"

Carter paused an instant, almost as if he hadn't actually expected a reply.

"I'm from the Lakes," he muttered.

He realized that sounded odd too.

"I'm from the Great Lakes," he added, noticing the old man's coat lying on the theatre seat nearby. He reached for it and helped the old Irishman place it over his shoulders.

"Gary," the old fellow said, then paused a moment. "I was third mate on a freightah haulin' steel to Gary, Indiana—just aftah the war. I know wheah yer from laddie. I know the Lakes."

Carter smiled in reply. He breathed easier. He was affected by the sound of old man's voice. It was kind and penetrating.

Without further introduction, for plenty had been said under the awkward circumstance, the two sailors walked up the aisle, stepped through the theatre doors, and out into the cold Bostonian night.

CHAPTER 2

ON HER BED OF WATER

"Wheah yer stayin', skippah?"

"The North End."

The old man nodded and spoke again.

"Theah's a place ta get coffee neah the Orange Line, but laddie, if you ahn't from 'round heah, the first thin' you need ta' undahstand is regulah in these pahts comes with cream and two sugahs."

Carter listened with interest to Patrick's Irish East Coast accent as together, but with Patrick one step ahead, they proceeded toward the Orange Line.

≋≋≋

Patrick took Carter to a seafood diner, a plethora of aluminum and chrome with glaring fluorescent light streaming onto the street. It stood bright against its dim neighbors like the beacon of a lighthouse. Inside, the tables were covered in red-checked tablecloths, and they sat down together on tall stools facing a red and gray Formica counter.

Carter's mind cleared a bit as he studied the menu, relieved to be ascending from the strangely emotional circumstance that delivered him to his new acquaintance. He decided to order a "regulah" coffee and examine the menu.

Carter smiled at the server when she set his coffee on the counter. Patrick O'Clery smiled at her too. The Lake sailor watched the old man from the corner of his eye, curious to see how he behaved. Then he glanced around the diner, taking in its contents. Crème colored walls, decorated with an array of nautical memorabilia. Swordfish jaws and colorful lobster buoys hung next to sports banners extolling the greatness of both the Patriots and the Celtics. Photos of hurricane floods and boats strewn along a shore covered one wall, and a large faded photograph of Tall Ships in Boston Harbor covered another.

Carter realized then that this was a foreign place, not like Chicago or Detroit. They were home to him. Boston was not home; it was strange yet vibrant, and perhaps dangerous. It held secrets, he suspected. Big secrets, he figured. The salt air smelled different from the air back home. The people talked different. They put "R's" where they shouldn't, and dropped them where they ought not to.

Carter smelled the steaming clams and heard the crack of "lobstah" shells in the hands of people wearing silly looking plastic bibs that drew no notice from the Irishman sipping coffee next to him. If he ate lobster, would he require a bib too? He turned to Patrick, as if asking for guidance.

The old man appeared calm, not at all agitated or distraught as he had in the theatre. Carter puzzled at the quick transformation. Patrick O'Clery appeared entirely at home in the seafood diner. When he noticed Carter looking at him, he began to speak. Patrick, as he insisted Carter address him, began by explaining that at sea, on board merchant ships from Ireland to Indonesia, he was a teller of great yarns.

Carter listened with interest. He was a good listener, prepared with a question, knowing most people will talk freely with a little prodding. His new acquaintance was no exception. In fact, the old man quickly assumed the posture of storyteller as he surreptitiously consumed an entire pot of steamers.

"The mates liked me stories more thahn work," he said, then laughed aloud as he pulled the skin from the neck of a steamer. A second later he dipped it in a bowl of hot clam juice, "...to wash away the sand," he explained.

Carter winced as Patrick dropped the steamer into his mouth. He had never seen anything so grotesque. In time, Patrick would express with friendly incredulity, his amazement that Carter had grown to be twenty-eight years old, called himself a sailor, and had never seen, much less eaten, whole clams.

"No suh," Patrick uttered, "hahd steamahs since I was a wee lad. Cahn't see how ya suhvived till now, skippah."

Carter considered whether he should try one of the odd-looking delicacies. Patrick smiled and continued his discourse.

"A spieler of notoriety, laddie, thaht's what I was. Amongst the crews of the merchant fleet thaht sailed paast Boston light, fer inta the world beyond, laddie, I was famous fer me stories."

However, on land these many years, Patrick simply told a tale or two when an innocent, such as Carter, found himself trapped in the net of an old man's lonely circumstance.

During their time in the diner, bellies to the Formica counter, Patrick O'Clery made no apologies for his emotional reaction to the film or even acknowledged it occurred. Instead, his demeanor transformed pleasantly and his aged face, topographic in its convolutions, took on the appearance of one who just recognized, and seized, an opportunity. In a textured, melodic voice, Patrick proceeded to tell Carter the first of many fascinating tales of the sea.

≋≋≋

It was getting late. Carter needed to return to his room. He inquired about helping Patrick home and the old Irishman firmly declined.

"I live in Maahblehead, Caahtah. I've been stayin' with mates heah in Bahston fer a couple days, headin' baack t'morrow, skippah."

Carter registered surprise that Patrick hadn't mentioned living in Marblehead earlier in the evening. Paper emerged from Patrick's coat. He wrote down an address and phone number and invited Carter to visit when he arrived in Marblehead to commission *Maxine*. Then with gestures of friendliness atypical of the region, he persuaded Carter to make the effort. He had something to show him. He spoke with intrigue in his voice, a crafty sparkle in his eye.

Patrick's friendliness was fresh and unexpected and made Carter suspicious. He worked to overcome his apprehension. He recalled spending the previous summer sailing *Maxine* from Maine to Rhode Island and no one extending a particularly welcoming hand. He took the slip of paper anyway and nodded his agreement.

≋≋≋

Carter remained in Boston two more days, torn between continuing his exploration and returning hastily to *Maxine*, the home he missed all winter. He could imagine the smell of the old wood down below and the glossy varnished trim of her main saloon. He thought for a moment of the feel of her rolling beneath his feet at her mooring. Carter loved dropping his eyes to the floor as he sat in her settee reading in the light of a brass oil lamp, imagining the water beneath her. He lived on water in the white ceiling and brown trim of her cabin, secure within her painted planks, framed all around in glassy mahogany and golden teak.

Boston will still be here, he concluded.

Before checking out, Carter started to call Patrick O'Clery whom he assumed would be back in Marblehead. He paused after punching in the first digits of Patrick's number. He was reticent, even reluctant, but being an outsider was frustrating. He could use a friend.

Carter proceeded to push the last buttons and wondered why his new acquaintance was so friendly, so different. Why did Patrick make Carter feel welcome when most New Englanders took only cursory notice of his existence? He pressed the final button and listened to the ringing on the other end.

Perhaps the very fact that I'm not from anywhere near here is why I am being invited. Sometimes people carry baggage; sometimes a friend with no strings attached can be a valuable friend indeed.

The instant before he heard Patrick's voice he remembered Patrick saying he had something to show him. He remembered the sly glint in the old man's eyes.

Patrick answered simply. "Aye."

"Hello, Patrick O'Clery—this is Carter Phillips, we met in Boston, a couple days ago. I'm headed for Marblehead and thought we could get together for a cup of coffee . . . regulah!"

≋≋≋

The train from Boston, running along the North Shore, wound a serpentine thread through old and mossy communities. The Atlantic Ocean made ignoble appearances as the train sped along.

About the time Carter hoped to arrive in Marblehead, he discovered the tracks ended far short of his goal at a wretched place called Wonderland, so named for the nearby dog racetrack. After waiting an hour to board a bus, he learned from an unhappy woman that it would be another forty-five minutes before they reached Marblehead. She was annoyed by his friendly banter.

His head bobbed painfully as the bus hit pothole after pothole. As the seemingly endless trip proceeded, the bus would slow to a crawl and then speed up as it wound its way along roads whose origins were cart trails.

Carter gazed outside his window along an appalling stretch of urban detritus and contemplated life ashore. The communities the route pierced could have been a dream, or more correctly, a nightmare. Slowly, to his great relief, the landscape began to change.

The triple-story factory housing gave way to nicer homes, gaining in size and substance. Tree-lined streets, framed cottages with shake shingles, and dormered gambrel roofs became the common view. Often they bore a shake-shingle façade on the sides with narrow horizontal planking on the front.

Not like the Midwest.

Carter often made mental notes of landscape and buildings alike. He visually measured and registered curious shapes and sizes of the things that made up his view. His skills at observation were keen—the results of architecture studies at the University of Notre Dame.

"Learn to see, really see, like a painter or photographer . . ." his instructors advised.

Carter had been a conscientious student. His professors liked him. He became an ardent practitioner of seeing—really seeing. Consequently, he earned degrees in both architecture and landscape architecture, but in great measure forsook their practice for a life aboard boats.

This obsession with boats blossomed while in graduate school, much to the chagrin of his mentor, an architect from Great Britain, originally from Belfast. Carter recalled his much-admired mentor and realized he did not have an Irish accent. This discrepancy gnawed at Carter now. He remembered distinct descriptions his professor gave of his family's estate in Belfast. Still, the professor's accent was distinctly British.

In his years at Notre Dame, Carter never thought much about Ireland or Northern Ireland or Great Britain. He rarely thought of the "troubles" as the conflict between them was often called. For that matter, he never even knew if his professor was Catholic or Protestant.

The motion of the bus jolted Carter back to New England as it crawled past saltbox houses mixed with an occasional Victorian. Finally he spewed forth from the chrome leviathan and stepped into a dense, picturesque community, the place where he left his sailboat for the winter.

Carter paused to allow the tension gripping his neck and shoulders to escape his body. He drew a deep breath of sea air, for he could smell it, even though he stood a number of blocks away from the shore and could not see it. He loved it. He breathed in more, as if to fuel up. Then, he began walking towards the town center. He strode with the step of a man returning to a woman after an interminable absence, and this was true. For Carter Phillips, this woman was a yacht, and her name was *Maxine*.

Carter was destined to remain on foot for the summer. He owned an automobile, but it was stored in Maine. He quickly learned that Marblehead on foot was bigger than Marblehead by car. Walking to his waiting home took a while. He wouldn't have ordinarily minded except he couldn't restrain his excitement at seeing his sailboat again.

Carter strode quickly past places and things he ordinarily would have paused to investigate. He was heading to Little Harbor, a protected inlet on the north side of Marblehead Harbor and *Maxine's* winter haven. As it finally came into view, his excitement heightened. It was this way every year, every time he returned to *Maxine* after a long winter ashore.

Eight winters and counting.

The sea air continued filling his lungs and a pleasurable, albeit nervous joy came over him as he saw the boats on the hard up ahead. *Maxine* stood cramped among a bevy of yachts all tucked together as tight as the mechanical lift machine could place them. Most had canvas covers to protect them from winter rain and snow. They were weather-worn and dirty from the polluted air that found its way up the industrial seaboard. However, *Maxine* was in there somewhere and *Maxine* meant home. Even obscured from view, tucked under her canvas cover, his first glimpse was an emotional one.

Carter poked his head into the yard office and spoke with the manager who maintained the cool demeanor Carter came to expect from the locals. He asked to use a yard ladder and the manager grudgingly agreed. Moments later Carter boarded his yacht, loosening lines that held her canvas down, slipping the ladder underneath.

He crawled into the covered cockpit. She was dark under the canvas, and cold. She had the smell of an idle boat, but that would change, he thought, as he gazed up and down the deck to see how she fared the winter.

The canvas was tight and close to her deck so he couldn't crawl forward. She looked secure and he checked for wear marks caused by flapping canvas rubbing against his home all winter. Placing his hands on the varnished wood of the companionway hatch, he slowly pushed the hatch along its brass tracks and sniffed the air rising from below.

The smell was cold but familiar, soon to be warm again as he regained his life aboard. He would fire up her coal stove as soon as he removed her cover. He would pour a cup of water into the through-deck stovepipe casting that kept the deck from catching fire from the heat. Each time he burned coal he filled the deck casting repeatedly. The ritual was one of many things making life aboard different from life on shore.

He dropped down below and looked about in the dim light penetrating her portholes. Everything lay just as he left her.

She wouldn't seem welcoming to a landsman.

It was true; at first glance she looked a mess. To allow *Maxine* to breathe during the winter, Carter left open her empty compartments; the cabin sole was lifted to air the bilge and stacks of gear rose from the settees. Her running rigging hung coiled along lines led fore and aft through her main saloon.

Carter inched his way forward to continue his inspection. He smelled for mildew. He ran fingers over her varnished trim to feel for cracking. Her smell met approval and her varnish felt smooth to his touch.

Finally, Carter climbed the companionway ladder, crossed the cockpit, and slipped out from under the cover. As he emerged, he realized the sun had begun fading in the west. He turned and looked east into Little Harbor. Cold, blue-gray wind blew down from

Manchester by the Sea. The wind filled the inlet with ripples turning the water dark and declaring the end of the day.

Carter would sleep on board despite the disarray. It would be cold but he would be out of the elements. Besides, he hadn't noticed any hotels along the streets he had taken to wend his way to Little Harbor. In a week or two, after long hours and days of toil, *Maxine* would be snug, warm, and floating on her bed of water.

CHAPTER 3

SCHOONAH ABUILDIN'

Carter slept uncomfortably, woke up early, and was happy all the same. Crawling out of his sleeping bag he climbed into stiff, cold clothing. Shivering in the dim light, he studied *Maxine's* bright woodwork and sculpted cockpit coaming as if it were his first time. She was gorgeous. *Maxine* was classic, she was designed during a period most would agree was the greatest in yachting.

Sliding the companionway hatch open, Carter climbed topside to see the first light streak over the Atlantic. He climbed down onto the hard and stretched. After a couple seconds, with great strides, he headed back into the village. He strode past sturdy dwellings displaying small signs explaining who built them—names like Jeremiah Lee, Jonathan Glover, and Benjamin Watson. The buildings' ages were remarkable. He remembered visiting the Abbot Public Library the season before and learning the granite outcropping misnamed Marblehead became home for settlers in 1629.

"Maahbleheaders was fishermen and boatmen, laddie, 'twas by necessity, don't ya know," Patrick had explained at the diner. "This heah was a frontier, at least ta the Europeans who pushed aside Native 'mericans already occupyin' the land. Who'da figgered those early settlahs would one day revolt; thaht they would shove a vastly superior force from theah shore; thaht a fightin' navy would spring ta life just a quartah mile down the cobblestone road from wheah ya left yer pretty *Maxine* fer the wintah, eh skippah?"

To Carter, as a Midwesterner, life in America started after the American Revolution. With the exception of Plymouth Rock and Thanksgiving Day traditions, schoolchildren where he came from in Michigan knew little about the people who lived as colonials in New England.

≋≋≋

The brown and gray landscape lay in every direction as he paced along the gentle hills and winding streets towards the neighborhood the locals called "Old Town." There he planned to drink coffee, warm up, and plan his day. He looked about but saw no distant views because buildings blocked them. He walked briskly through the visually constrained landscape so full of houses there were yellow traffic signs that read, "Thickly Settled." Carter registered this unusual street sign, having never seen one before.

Early morning fog was prominent and the horn at Marblehead Light sounded. Its thick, somber tone reminded him that the sea was often dangerous, and at times like this, when he was cold and the weather gray, he thought of fishermen lost in storms.

With a shudder accompanying the thought, Carter jogged across a cobblestone lane. He looked down State Street towards Tucker's Wharf. In the distance he could see the stately mansions across the harbor on Marblehead Neck. Below the ostentatious dwellings, rolling quietly from motion generated far out at sea, were no fewer than a thousand moorings. Lobster pots bobbed lazily in the mist that hovered over the water.

It was early in the season, but already a forest of masts rose from boats on moorings. Yacht club launches were commencing to move about in the harbor taking people to and from the mostly fiberglass craft. Like water spiders skidding across the surface of a creek in Michigan, the launches of the great yacht clubs harked back to the days of a harbor filled with famous wooden boats.

Carter continued walking toward the aroma of fresh-brewed coffee and baked goods. It came from an ancient building and above the door a sign read "The Marblehead Roasting Company." Exactly what Carter hoped for stood before him: a warm woody place with people eating scones and reading the *Boston Globe*. This, too, would become home. All live-aboards take claim to landside places. They often seek refuge from the confines of a small cabin closing in a bit too tightly.

Carter stepped inside and walked up to the counter. An attractive black haired woman said good morning.

"I'll have a coffee."

"Regular?"

Remembering Patrick's advice that regular came with cream and two sugars he smiled and replied, "Actually, I'll have a double decaf latte."

The waitress turned to fetch a cup while Carter studied the pastries in the finely built display case. The joinery caught his eye. He recognized the work of a boat carpenter.

"I'll have a scone, too."

The waitress complied and Carter reached in his pocket to pay for his order. He slipped a five across the counter.

"Please, keep the change and thank you, I slept aboard a very cold boat last night. I'm in real need of something hot."

The young, fair-skinned waitress courteously acknowledged his comment and his tip and her politeness made Carter wonder if she was a local.

Carter took a sip of his latte and looked around. He noticed an entire corner of the shop gave way to the purpose of its name. An elaborate device poured forth, roasted, and rotated coffee beans continuously while tended by an intense, distant looking man. Carter took him to be the owner.

A glimpse of daylight shone through a nearby window. Carter circled and then settled into an oversized padded armchair.

He bit into his raisin scone made in the New England style and proceeded to satisfy his wanting appetite. He sipped the steaming hot coffee and set the oversized mug on an end table. A copy of the *Globe* lay abandoned by an earlier patron—he picked it up and glanced at the headlines.

For a few minutes the studious architect read the affairs of the outside world. He scanned the litany of troubles and conflicts that pockmarked the voluminous first section. He skimmed the international news, then focused on the metro section; a scandal involving a selectman in Newton; a liberal arts college in Framingham expanding classroom capacity; perennial notifications of road construction, reminding him of the bus trip from Boston.

Carter reached for his scone, crumpling his paper in his lap, and as he did he noticed a headline partially hidden in a fold. All he could see was "...arrested in IRA weapon... " This caught his interest. Using both hands to straighten out the paper he read the hidden text.

"Three Arrested in Local IRA Weapon Plot."

What the hell . . . this can't be true.

He looked up from the paper and surveyed the scene around him, wondering if one of the accused might be having coffee there at that moment. An older gentleman sat alone at a table, deep in thought. Two stately middle-aged women held their cups quite properly and talked in whispers. At the counter stood a man dressed in boatyard garb, khaki top to bottom with a long billed cap.

Boston may be filled with Irish terrorists, but Marblehead doesn't look like an axis of political intrigue.

Carter sipped again and moved on to the entertainment section. Suddenly, the sound of toppling glass startled him.

"Oh, I'm sorry! Please let me—"

Looking up he saw the waitress and the khaki-dressed yard worker in the midst of a coffee spill. The yard worker, who faced the counter, jerked back and adroitly wiped coffee from his shirt and pants. Carter could see the hot coffee spilling down the face of the counter.

"What the hell have you done?"

Hot words spewed forth and people in the room turned curiously toward the mishap.

"Damn woman, can't you be freakin' careful? I swear you're gonna get my freakin' ass sued!"

Curiously, the hot words weren't coming from the patron who silently wiped himself dry. Rather, the epithets poured forth from the coffee roaster who continued to dress down the waitress in a nasty tirade.

"What the hell is it gonna take? Those useless shits at the agency said you'd work out fine!"

Taken aback and slightly annoyed at the man's response, Carter could only stare in disbelief. The roaster's reaction seemed far beyond necessary. He watched for an instant longer and then returned to his paper, hoping the fracas would die away quickly. Instead the angry man's anxiety rose higher.

"God damn it! Gimme the rag, this shit's wreckin' the freakin' counter!"

The sullen-faced man's raving caused Carter's own adrenalin to notch up. He glanced at the distraught face of the beset waitress. Her oppressor ranted on; spitting inauspicious words far too severe for the situation.

Man, this guy is going over the top.

Carter rose from his seat. The patron at the counter, the victim of the mishap, suddenly spoke, causing Carter to pause. The patron's voice reported with depth and thickness, reshaping the character of the event.

"Thaht's enough, Mr. O'Neil, enough I say!"

Carter realized it wasn't a yard worker at all; he recognized him immediately—it was Patrick O'Clery!

"The lassie meant no haahm, caused no haahm, so just calm ye down a mark, Mr. O'Neil, calm ye down!"

O'Neil, apparently the shop owner, rose from wiping the counter and turned on Patrick with a glare. Carter thought he detected a movement, as if the coffee roaster contemplated giving Patrick a shove. In response, to Carter's amazement, Patrick stepped forward, not backward, and spoke with daring calm. "Yer cahfee's the finest in the village laddie, tis an honah to be bathed in it." Then in an instantaneous transition, Patrick chuckled aloud in a most peculiar manner. Carter realized, as Mr. O'Neil surely did as well, it wasn't the chuckle of a man unsure of his position. Quite the opposite, it was the mirth of a wholly confident, superior being.

The peculiar transformation disarmed the shop owner. O'Neil stepped backward a half pace, backing down, or at least pausing to consider the outcome of an impudent reply.

Patrick stopped smiling and his eyes focused sharply under a tightly-creased brow. He lifted his cap from his head; a gray-red ponytail fell from under it. He tossed the cap onto the counter without breaking eye contact with the furious Mr. O'Neil. His frame braced. They stared at each other another long second. Then Patrick glanced past the owner at the rotating tray of the roasting machine and boomed aloud gregariously, "Will those beans burn if not tended, Mr. O'Neil? We wouldn't want thaht to happen, now would we, laddie?"

Mr. O'Neil couldn't resist turning to check his coffee beans. They did need tending. He glanced back at Patrick.

"I'll not sucker punch ya, Mr. O'Neil, ya needn't worry."

The disgruntled coffee roaster made a waning gesture of annoyance then shot a look of derision towards the waitress.

Carter watched as the disturbance dissipated. He stood motionless for an instant, not knowing what to do. He questioned whether Patrick had recognized him. Should he say hello? Should he turn away?

Still Carter paused. Did he know Patrick O'Clery; well, yes, but then again, no. The scene before him certainly made him unsure. Patrick's calculated daring did not remind him of the emotive old man he had met in the theatre in Boston. His bearing now seemed upright, ominous, even violent, as he faced off the angry Mr. O'Neil.

Carter watched as Patrick lifted his hat from the counter and spoke quietly to the waitress as he fit his ponytail back beneath it. Then Patrick turned and looked straight at Carter and winked.

Holy Christ, Patrick must have known I was here all along.

The old man lifted a fresh cup of coffee off the counter and stepped toward Carter. The familiar kindness Carter recognized from their encounter in Boston beamed in Patrick's glowing smile. Patrick's transformation was instantaneous—a characteristic that could be good or bad, sometimes real bad, Carter thought. The old man walked directly over to Carter, sat down in a chair close to him and said in a wily yet kindly voice, "Welcome to Maahblehead, skippah!"

≋≋≋

An hour steamed by and a sea story recounted before Patrick asked Carter if he remembered he had something to show him.

Without waiting for an answer, Patrick was on his feet with Carter following quickly behind. As they departed, Patrick glanced over and nodded at the waitress, apparently speaking volumes though never opening his mouth. She smiled back, apparently answering whatever silent message Patrick had sent. Carter noticed her look of calm defiance. It flowed from her gleaming eyes and attractive features. She looked confident and resolute. He wondered exactly what Patrick whispered in her ear during their earlier encounter.

Carter looked back at Patrick now smiling at him. Patrick's brow raised in that way of old men who notice younger ones staring at pretty girls. Carter shrugged in admission. She was attractive, he was alone, what could he say? Without speaking they turned and walked out the coffee shop door.

Once on the cobblestone street, the two sailors walked into the narrow ways of Old Town, heading south, walking briskly through the dissipating fog. Crocker Park fell away to port as they strode along. The distinct smell of salt water, thick in the air, rushed into Carter's lungs. The sound of motor launches became more distinct as they paced closer to the harbor. Carter caught glimpses of bright orange starfish clinging to old wooden piles exposed by the fallen tide. He worked to keep up with Patrick. Carter could see the old fellow was excited about revealing his surprise.

As they came down a slight incline, turning southeasterly toward the water, Patrick motioned ahead to an old shed tucked between an apartment house and a sail loft. Sheathed in weather-worn boards with a shake shingle roof, it looked New England in every aspect; the very image a tourist would send by postcard to his friends in the Midwest.

As they got closer, Carter smiled inwardly, gazing at the flotsam and jetsam decorating every wall and window of the colorful, scrappy old building. It reminded him of bizarre crabs that stick everything they can find to their shells to create camouflage.

A driveway lay next to the shed, paved with a thick layer of crushed clamshells, the custom of the area. It emitted whiteness that stood proud next to the gray weathered shed. From Patrick and Carter's position on the road, descending and turning as they walked, Carter couldn't make out where the driveway led. As they came nearer, he could see it was a lane serving both the shed and the sail loft next to it. A tall barn-wood fence obscured the view of the yard behind the shed, and Carter could see great hinges that allowed the barn-wood to be parted when necessary to move large objects in or out.

Straight to the windowless plank door Patrick strode. He reached in the pocket of his khakis for a set of keys attached to a foam rubber float adorned by a worn-out boatyard logo.

This guy's been on the water a while.

Carter queued up behind the exuberant Irishman. Patrick fidgeted with the rusty padlock hanging from a latch that was green with verdigris while Carter cast his eyes about the front of the building.

The rickety structure was set back four or five feet from the paved lane passing in front of it. In the tiny but crowded space there were stacks of lobster traps, yellow nylon line old enough to be the original stuff, broken oars, a dried-out plywood row boat filled with lumber, mechanisms of indistinct purpose and every other curious object a life within fifty yards of shore would lead one to collect. The smell of wood preservative rose from the lobster traps and hung in the morning fog that continued dissipating.

As Patrick rattled the lock, Carter kept glancing from side to side, studying the rest of the items nailed to, hung on, tied around, or leaning against the busy façade. He noticed hand scrawled marks with dates going back to the early 1930s.

Suddenly realizing what they were, Carter swung around to see the elevation of the shed compared to the fallen tide at the boat ramp lying at the end of the lane. The marks and dates were high-tide lines from hurricanes and Carter tried to imagine the scene where roaring winds drove water to those elevations, shoving buildings from their foundations and casting yachts ashore as if they were toys.

Carter had never experienced a hurricane; it was just a word to him. It reminded him he was merely a visitor in New England, an outsider from a distant place.

Patrick released a sound that heralded his success and turned to see Carter taking in the busy scene.

"Ya nevah know when ya might be needin' somethin' on boahd thaht don't come handy down at the variety store skippah."

Carter was standing close to Patrick and saw the words roll from under his mustache. He saw with wonderment details of Patrick's face as if for the first time. It was a bit gaunt but not weary, his facial hairs were sparse and in need of trimming. They retained a tinge of red from his youth. He was discovering his new friend a little at a time.

Carter blinked back to the present, nodded, and the two stepped into the darkened shed.

The building's contents were much like the exterior, Carter noted, as he followed Patrick through a dimly lit aisle. Carter was broader at the shoulders and stood a few inches taller than Patrick, who was slender and lithe. Carter needed to turn sideways to slip through stacks of objects cast about on both sides.

The place was a veritable chandlery packed into a space the size of a big living room. Stuffed in every dusty corner lay boat hardware, bronze deck fittings, teak and mahogany, brass lamps, deck prisms and boxes of charts. The ceiling was open-framed, and hanging from the rafters were coiled lines with varnished blocks on metal beckets.

Carter was enthralled, but above all else he loved the smell of the place. He breathed in the aroma of boats. His eyes absorbed the sights. He could taste the residual of varnish in the air as he obediently followed Patrick. He also noticed that despite the initial impression of chaos, the shed enjoyed a rudimentary organization. Tools had homes and cabinets lined one wall. A workbench along the opposite wall held vices, clamps, and bottles of glue set out in working order.

The shed stretched deeper into the lot than the front revealed. As Patrick led him along, they stepped into a second larger room and through a set of hinged doors through which objects of great size could be moved. Presently, the room held an array of large power tools, including an enormous band saw, a table saw, joiner, planer, and power sander. Along one of the walls in this room, Carter noticed a Whitehall, a finely designed rowing boat sitting on sawhorses and the smell of fresh paint explained why it was there. Then Patrick spoke.

"Well, skippah, heah's what I've hahd the mind to show ya," and with a grin causing his face to widen broadly he pushed aside a sliding metal door.

Bright light met Carter as the noisy rollers crawled over their tracks. The opening glowed from sunlight burning through the morning fog, causing him to squint. He raised his hand to his brow to shadow his eyes. There before him, supported by a great cradle of steel, was a wooden schooner. A schooner abuildin'!

"Laddie," said Patrick with exuberance. "May I introduce ya ta *Red Shoes*!"

CHAPTER 4

THE PURSER'S QUARTERS

During the ensuing discovery of *Red Shoes*, Carter happened to mention his chilly situation on board *Maxine*. Patrick insisted he consider spending a couple nights at the B&B where he kept rooms.

"'T'would be a wee bit more comfortable laddie, and surely yer lady *Maxine* will fergive ya this brief indulgence," said Patrick. "She'll haav ya all summah long!"

Patrick jotted down the address and Carter, reluctant once again to accept favors yet willing to sleep in a warm bed, set out to find it.

Departing the boat shop, Carter chugged up the grade like a steam launch headed for a regatta. He caught a glimpse of the harbor as he left Crocker Park to starboard. Patrick, in giving directions explained, "She's not faar beyond Tuckah's Whaaf. If ya blink you'll miss 'er, skippah, and if you go to faar, you'll run aground at Fort Sewall.

"Keep yer head up, laddie," Patrick added, "and you'll see a boat hull swingin' ovah the doorway. Thaht would be a wee gift I made Maatha, Maatha O'Donnell," he repeated. "She's the ownah. And by the way laddie, don't mind Maatha. She makes a crusty first impression. Just tell 'er I sent ya and yer the skippah of *Maxine*. Thaht'll be all the callin' caahd ya need."

Carter paused a moment. *Did he say card or cod?*

"Oh, and by the way skippah, Maatha's fey, don't ya know." Patrick paused, then added, "Thaht means she believes in the occult theah, laddie—Salem witches and all thaht mystical stuff, eh. Pay no nevah mind."

Carter considered the idea ridiculous. Then he reminded himself that in Salem, only a mile or two away, and for whatever incomprehensible reason, men persecuted and murdered innocent women not all that long ago.

Setting the thought aside and proceeding toward the B&B, Carter walked northeast along Front Street. As he walked he noticed a stinging sensation on the heel of his left foot. The deck shoes he purchased at Faneuil Hall the Sunday before were stiff, not broken in. He became anxious to reach his destination.

Then up ahead, just as Patrick described, there was indeed a boat hull mounted perpendicular over the doorway of one of the town's ancient homes. A wrought iron brace held it from above allowing it to swing freely in the breeze.

Only in Marblehead.

The Purser's Quarters, Martha O'Donnell's bed & breakfast, had its moniker carved on a name board like those found aboard yachts. The difference was the varnished teakwood and gilded letters hung above an antique doorframe instead of main mast shrouds.

Carter studied the sign for a second. Next to the name board, a small plaque was mounted, like the one Carter noticed on many houses in the village. "The Isaac Thomas Residence—Ship Purser," the plaque read. It went on to point out, "Built in 1735."

Everything about the B&B, from roof peak to foundation appeared weather worn and a bit out of kilter. Yet, despite its unevenness, it looked sturdy and appeared fixed to the ground. Carter gained the impression the house and ground had become one.

At the age of two hundred sixty five, that may well be the case, he considered.

Then the architect in Carter cast his eyes about the building and examined its details. He figured it had more coats of paint than he had years of life. The paint was so thick it gave the appearance of roundness to all the trim and fittings. Where it peeled, it exposed layer after layer of colors Carter could count like rings on a tree. The window glass was old and wavy and had a deep green tint. There was moss and mold growing in shady crevices and some of the nails wept brown.

Carter stepped up to the door, gently rapped the brass knocker, and waited. No one answered. He knocked again. Still no one came. He stepped forward and put his ear to the weathered door, certain he heard a television. He knocked louder and waited again; no response. Becoming frustrated, he stepped back and studied the front façade as if to will it to respond.

The old house stared back at him with a complacent look. The chalky whitewashed siding and sorry-eyed windows saw no purpose in indulging an anxious stranger.

Vexed, Carter stepped forward again, gave the brass knocker another hardy rap, and thought maybe he should walk to a nearby phone and give a call to the number Patrick had jotted down. The heel of his foot stung; he wanted off it for a while, and he didn't want to add walking distance to an already lengthy trip from town. Besides, he walked a long way seeing only houses, and figured a pay phone would be clear back at Tucker's Wharf.

The soreness in his shoe prompted one last try. Again—no answer.

Maybe Martha's hard of hearing.

Patrick hadn't said.

Resigned to leave, Carter stepped back from the stoop and at that instant the door handle turned and began shaking noisily. The thick paint and warped attitude of the centuries-old framework appeared to be holding tight to the door. It gave Carter the feeling the house was alive and annoyed by the intrusion.

A couple audible epithets issued from a coarse female voice within. "Open up old gul, open or I'll haav ta get thaht damn pry bar again . . ."

The shaking and pulling continued a moment longer, and then as if to accept its fate, or avoid the pry bar, the ornery cottage gave in. A cloud of cigarette smoke met Carter, and Martha O'Donnell, matron of the Purser's Quarters, shuffled forward.

"Cahn I help you young man?" she said, shooting a wary glance toward Carter. She was dressed in a night robe, a white flannel gown with flower designs embroidered in yellow, red and green.

Aside from her spectacled, aging face ringed with gray hair set in a 1950s movie-actress style, Carter couldn't help notice the cigarette precariously hanging from her lips. It bobbed vigorously and slightly impaired her speech as she greeted him with the squint of the eye common to smokers and skeptics alike.

Carter told Martha exactly what Patrick advised and it produced the predicted result. Within a minute's time he was invited to come inside and sit—and she would get some ointment for his foot.

Carter glanced sideways at her. Surprised, he began to say "How did you know about my . . ." and checked his remark mid-sentence. Martha quickly, unabashedly, broke in, cigarette bobbing in her lips.

"I'm a nurse, well, perhaps a nursemaid ya might say."

The explanation didn't exactly fit the situation and Carter recalled Patrick's warning about her being fey. "She sees things," Patrick had cautioned.

Carter obediently followed Martha as she led him through the door into the great room. He gazed about a colonial parlor that, like the coffee shop, enjoyed fine wood joinery and was crammed full of antiques and nautical memorabilia.

At first glance, Carter thought the room looked like the interior of a yacht. Along one wall a small library stood, built in the fashion one would find on a classic yacht when libraries and harpsichords might have graced the main saloon. The shelves were crowded with books. There was a fiddle along the edge of each shelf, placed there to keep the books in-board while the yacht was heeling. Considering this was not a yacht, Carter puzzled at the detail. Additionally, there were several drawers and compartments, and near the base of the shelves stood a small writing table and a drop - down circular stool for sitting; the sort of detail one might find on a boat where space is at a premium.

Probably the most dramatic, if not peculiar detail of the room, however, was the queen-sized bed jutting from one wall—Martha's bed, as it would turn out. She had given over her master bedroom to the purpose of the B&B. Carter took in the scene and found it a bit odd being in the great room and Martha's bedroom at the same time. Martha apparently did not. She left Carter standing there without explanation and disappeared down a hall for a moment, returning with a jar of salve.

"Haav a seat theah, young man." Martha motioned to an over stuffed chair, using her cigarette as a pointer. "I'm goin' to apply some ointment to thaht theah wounded foot," pointing at his left shoe. Apparently, she "sensed" that it was his left because he had not explained as much.

"No, well, thank you, but that's not...I'm okay, Mrs...uh..."

Carter suddenly realized he couldn't remember her last name; moreover, he thought it entirely strange to bare his foot to a perfect stranger.

"Maatha, young man, Maatha, and I'll haav no arguing. Yoah foot hurts and I cahn make it feel bettah, don't ya know; and what did yoah parents name you young man?" Martha's sternness transformed into kindness as she crouched to begin her treatment.

"I'm Carter, ma'am—Carter Phillips."

The matron of the Purser's Quarters looked up from the aspect of a shoe salesman and smiled.

"Caahtah, I like thaht name—Mistah Caahtah Phillips."

Martha continued her treatment and Carter remained compliant. It made him feel peculiar but Martha showed no signs of caring how he might have felt. Eventually, Carter relaxed and began to appreciate the procedure. As Martha rubbed ointment into his foot, the Lake sailor gazed around the room asking questions as he always did.

"That chart, Martha, there above the dresser, is that Ireland?"

"The Northern haalf, Caahtah."

"Are you from Ireland, Martha?"

"No Caahtah, I was born and raised right heah in Massachusetts. Irish on deah Mothah's side, English on Fathah's."

For a moment Carter wondered if the Northern Ireland conflict generated any household enmity. Carter's curiosity was piqued but he restricted his questions and decided to let them lie. The "Irish troubles," as he noticed it referred to that morning in the *Boston Globe*, was over 800 years old and apparently it was more than an academic or household debate. The idea that people in his midst, recalling his recent days in Boston, were still smuggling guns and money into Northern Ireland struck him as unbelievable. What persona would a covert gun smuggler assume—a construction worker, a businessperson, a student at Boston College? He rejected each prospect out of hand, feeling strange. He brushed aside the thoughts and looked down once again at the white hair of the woman holding his injured foot in her hand and concluded there was no need for answers to those particular questions. He was simply an observer. Carter had always figured that if conflict ever came his way, he would remain aloof, study its facets and move on.

"The othah foot now, Caahtah."

"Oh no, that's okay, Martha..."

"Caahtah, be a good lad, I cahn't do half my job."

Carter figured he may as well be polite and slipped the right shoe off. While Martha removed his sock she explained she worked most of her adult life as a private nurse for a wealthy spinster, heir to a textile fortune, out on Marblehead Neck. Her husband, a merchant marine, died at sea many years ago.

"I'm sorry to hear that, Martha."

Martha didn't acknowledge Carters sympathy. She deliberately changed subjects and spoke heartily of her bed and breakfast. She even told of a gaggle of girlfriends who all believed in witchcraft.

"Really, Martha? I suppose that's kind of a tradition around here, Salem being so close and all."

"Moah than kinda, Caahtah, but don't you mind my ramblin's young lad, nevah you mind. Pahtrick thinks it's all a bunch of gob-shite."

Soon the treatment ended and Carter felt deeply refreshed, Martha's evident friendliness affecting him greatly. She persuaded him to stay at her bed and breakfast until *Maxine*, a name she said she also liked, was ready to launch.

Carter agreed, and with that decided, they stepped through a door at the back of the kitchen opening into a foyer. Inside the foyer, there was an entrance from the outside on the left and a narrow staircase to the right. Carter followed the flowing robe up the stairs and arrived at a loft with a small but inviting sitting area. Immense, ancient, hand-hewn wooden beams held up the ceiling. Small windows carved into the thick walls allowed light to play on the beams, creating an appealing geometry.

The furnishings were old and some, possibly valuable, Carter thought as the smell of age emitted from them, fighting gallantly against the grayish lace of cigarette smoke Martha trailed behind her. The ceiling with its exposed beams hung lower than those in modern houses, and Martha's thin but tallish stature filled the space. She motioned with her cigarette to a doorway, shorter than usual, and said it led to the bedroom and farther into a bath. Carter walked towards it, bent to open it, and peeked in.

Upon inspection he looked back and gave Martha a nod. He liked the place and he liked Martha too.

That's two. Two people who have welcomed me to Marblehead.

Squinting slightly from the backlight, Carter watched Martha return his nod with what he took to be a smile. It was hidden by her shadow, but apparent all the same.

The tour now concluded, the flowing robe turned and descended the narrow stairs. Carter paused for a moment to be alone in his temporary quarters, to determine if they welcomed him too. He decided with a smile they did. He bounded down the stairs on fresh feet and stepped out the foyer door. Moments later he was headed toward Little Harbor and his waiting *Maxine*.

CHAPTER 5

AN EXCEPTING ACCEPTANCE

Within a couple days of moving into the Purser's Quarters and hanging around the boat shop, Martha and Patrick had taken Carter in like family. More than once he stopped to ponder why. New Englanders were family oriented, he could see, but perhaps this trait, so accentuated in their society, made someone like Carter feel rejected, or, at best, kept at arms length. It was as if they were determined to preserve their bloodlines, as if outsiders threatened their ethnicity.

So, why were Patrick and Martha exceptions? It was hard for Carter to say. At first, he thought it was probably a shared passion for wooden boats. When wooden boat lovers found each other, their mutual passion usually resulted in a certain level of camaraderie. Yet this didn't fully explain Patrick's overt friendliness, and definitely not Martha's. Another thing Carter realized, as he laid out his tools and began work commissioning *Maxine*, was that he hadn't been introduced to any of Patrick's friends and relatives.

There were some exceptions—the "Red Shoes Irregulars," for example, the cadre of old timers who monitored every step of *Red Shoes'* construction. But Patrick didn't treat them like friends or even confidants except the one he called Bones. Bones enjoyed a high status.

"Mostly they aah a distraction," Patrick would whisper. Nevertheless, their age and perhaps their experience commanded a modicum of respect. Patrick was old, but they were older, and Carter recognized in Patrick the character of a man who respects his elders, a man who maintains strong loyalties in matters of tradition.

Carter observed right away that there were a couple of other young men staying at the Purser's Quarters. They were about his age he figured, and like he, they were lean and athletic. On close scrutiny, however, they appeared gaunt, lacking color, where he was fuller in stature and his features rounded in comparison. He also took note of their separate entrance to the B&B on the opposite side of the house.

These other guests appeared not to enjoy the same privileges as Carter. For example, they didn't breakfast with Martha each morning as did Carter. He noticed that Patrick and Martha interacted with the men from time to time. Martha, he figured, had business with them. Patrick just seemed to know them.

Carter kept expecting to see tourists check into the B&B, but since it was only March, and seeing none, he concluded it was too early in the season. Carter thought he and the other tenants, including Patrick, made the place feel more like a boarding house than a bed and breakfast. Despite the bevy of men wandering around, Carter noticed Martha mostly ignored them and spent most of her time reading in her great room.

"Mothah was a librarian, Caahtah. These books are her legacy, a gift foah me to enjoy any time, any day. In fact, while you stay heah you may enjoy them too. You do read, Caahtah?"

"Oh yes Martha, I have a far smaller library on *Maxine*, but I practically live at the library in whatever town she sails me to."

It was interesting, Carter thought, as he watched her reading one evening while perusing her book collection, that Martha and Patrick appeared to be friends even though they kept a distance. He wondered what their relationship was, if any, beyond being long time Marbleheaders and coincidentally, living in the Purser's Quarters. It crossed Carter's mind again that his quick acceptance into this colorful trio of sailor, matron, and "schoonah" could have something to do with the fact that he was an outsider. As an outsider, Martha and Patrick both may be viewing him as a friend primarily because he carried no knowledge of their lives.

This idea of being an unconditional friend had come up before, about five years earlier. A man in Florida who befriended Carter and with whom he sailed turned out to be an arms dealer. He had formed a considerable relationship with the man and his schooner, *Angeline*, before he eventually discovered the man's real occupation. The incident taught the inquisitive Carter something important. Not all questions should be spoken; not all are appropriate to ask. All the same, he came to realize his friendship with the arms dealer arose largely because Carter knew nothing about his other life, that is, the world of arms dealing. It was an extraordinary situation.

Patrick and Martha seemed extraordinary too. To Carter, Patrick was born in the aisle of a theatre and his verifiable existence extended forward from the laying of *Red Shoes'* keel. Anything taking place before that was open speculation. Martha's existence was verified only by the trail of white smoke following her around the B&B and by a collection of books of recognizable distinction.

≋≋≋

As *Maxine's* commissioning proceeded, Carter found himself splitting time equally between *Maxine* and *Red Shoes*, and Patrick did the same.

Without contract or agreement, Carter welcomed the opportunity to become Patrick's shipmate, working together, anticipating each other's needs, responding without a word—just a glance and a movement. He noticed they rarely asked for each other's help; rather, they watched each other like sailors in a gale, knowing full well their lives depended on their eyes, ears, and most of all, their mates.

None of this shipmate camaraderie suited the Red Shoes Irregulars, however. It didn't do for an outsider to suddenly show up in their midst. From the vantage point of well-worn lawn chairs, they quickly pointed out that Patrick spent too much time on *Maxine* and not enough on *Red Shoes*.

Luckily for Patrick, by early afternoon the restless Irregulars, that is, all but Bones, shuffled off to Tucker's Wharf. There they could work unabated at their jobs of finding fault.

The Irregular named Bones tended to be around more than the others. Patrick even assigned Bones tasks to complete if Patrick left the shop to run an errand. Carter figured Bones' continual attendance was attributable to his obviously bad knees. Even though he didn't appear crippled, Bones stayed in one place. His almost constant presence resulted in more interaction with Patrick, who while kindly mocking the others, appeared to hold genuine respect for Bones.

≋≋≋

Carter's initial rush to get *Maxine* in the water subsided as he found equal pleasure in helping Patrick with *Red Shoes*. He spent time with Martha, too, and decided not to hastily depart the Purser's Quarters.

Martha insisted Carter use her kitchen and refrigerator and would shop for groceries for him if he made a list. She drove a red Ford Escort around town; hands in the "ten-two position," shoulders hunched forward a couple degrees.

Carter formed habits quickly and laid claim to places landside with a purpose. He habitually sought morning coffee at the Marblehead Roasting Company, despite the reprehensible owner. The coffee was good and the young woman at the counter attracted his eye. He ate lunch at the old armament at Sewall Point as long as the weather held fair. He spent evenings on the water exploring the boats in the vast, mysterious harbor. His working hours remained devoted to *Maxine* and the gestating *Red Shoes*.

In time, Sewall Point became a favorite place for the same reasons Marbleheaders built a fort there 200 years earlier. It commanded a panoramic view of the harbor. There was a picnic table on a precipice above a granite rock outcropping where Carter and Patrick often sat to eat lunch. They shared stories of cruises and worked out details of their respective projects aboard *Red Shoes* and *Maxine*.

It was Tuesday and lunchtime at Sewall Point and the two sailors sat at the perpetually damp and weathered table. They contentedly ate lobster rolls sent along by Martha. A light breeze sailed across the harbor, rushing towards the Neck. When the breeze blew on through, Carter glanced at Patrick and speculated they were thinking the same thing: judging the wind, considering its direction, gauging its force, making sail trim in their minds as if they were on board at that moment.

Carter was tempted to speak up and ask Patrick about the night they met. He was curious why Patrick appeared so affected by the film. He didn't though, reminding himself of the lessons he learned in his relationship to the arms dealer. Eventually, Carter figured, the mystery would unveil itself and so he kept the flame of curiosity under control.

They were finishing their lunch when one of the men Carter recognized from the other side of the B&B approached on foot. Patrick noticed him, too. When the man got close, he spoke directly to Patrick in a tongue Carter could not understand. This surprised Carter, and he realized for the first time Patrick understood and probably spoke a foreign language, Gaelic, if that was the right guess.

Carter studied the other man. Despite the language difference he detected the inflection of urgency in his voice. After a brief exchange hidden from Carter by the foreign tongue, Patrick turned and explained that wood just arrived at the boat shed and needed unloading. Patrick then turned back to the Irishman, made a few gestures, and sent him away. As he departed, Patrick cried after him, "Be theah shortly, and nothin's ta be off loaded till I arrive."

This instruction Patrick gave in English, as if to inform Carter of the goings on. The Irishman, who seemed to understand English perfectly well, departed, leaving Carter wondering why they spoke in Gaelic in the first place. As the man turned and headed back down the lane, Carter noted his hard, deliberate step—like a man on a mission.

Carter looked over at his messmate to see what he was going to do next. Patrick, who stood to converse with the messenger, returned to the table, drew his long red-gray hair behind his head and wound it up under his cap. He looked out across Marblehead Neck in the direction of the East Harbor Yacht Club and explained that he needed to head back to the shop. Carter quickly offered to help unload the lumber but Patrick would have nothing to do with it.

"Subject those ahchitect's hands to slivahs and scrapes, skippah!" he replied with humor and jest. "Shamus there will do the hard work as he owes me ah favah or two, laddie," he insisted. "I just need to supahvise. What ya could do fer me though, is step round to *Maxine* and haav a look about. I am thinkin' I left my jacket on 'er cradle when we got ta workin' yestahday aftahnoon. I couldn't find it this mornin' when I set out from Maatha's." Then, with a smile almost completely hidden behind the red-tinged mustache, Patrick turned and walked after the Irishman who was still waiting at the bottom of the hill.

Carter turned back to his lunch, finished the last bite of lobster roll and looked out across the sunny harbor toward the Neck. Feeling an urge to lie back and relish the warmth of the early spring sun, Carter decided he would head over to *Maxine* to look for Patrick's jacket later on. He found a gentle slope perfectly framing a view of the harbor and propped his backpack against a rock.

He gazed out over the sparkling water as a couple of boats dodged lobster pots, making way to the harbor entrance. He breathed in the warming salt air and slumped gently on the pack, letting his mind wander to his home waters of Lake Michigan, the

"Big Lake" as people called it. Carter knew of no place on Lake Michigan that resembled Marblehead. All the Great Lakes, and Carter had traveled them extensively, were different from the East Coast waters.

A siren blaring at the bow of the Marblehead Harbor Patrol boat jolted Carter back to Sewall Point. He sat up to see what was going on. Lifting his binoculars, Carter spotted the patrol boat bearing down on a speedboat that chose, at an inopportune time, to leave a hefty wake as it pulled away from a fuel dock. Boats and masts rolled as Carter scanned the scene of the crime.

Gazing through the glasses, Carter suddenly noticed Patrick motor by at the helm of an inflatable dinghy about twenty yards or so behind the patrol boat. Patrick appeared to ignore the crime scene and drove the boat on in the direction of the East Harbor Yacht Club. At the bow of the inflatable sat the Irishman who came for Patrick only a short while earlier. Carter looked at his chronometer. Only thirty minutes transpired since the two left to walk back to the boat shed. That trip on foot was a good twenty minutes.

How could they have done a job like that so fast?

He continued watching the two Irishmen through the glasses, feeling like he was spying. Disturbed by the inappropriateness of his observation, he stuffed the glasses back in their cover, laid them on his belly and decided to mind his own business. He returned to his daydream of the Big Lake.

CHAPTER 6

MORNINGS WITH MARTHA

Wednesday morning Carter sat at the breakfast table and listened while Martha made left-leaning remarks about political figures. He enjoyed listening to her ramblings because she was brash and opinionated—something he felt he couldn't be for fear of rejection by a community where people were not particularly accepting. He also smiled because he figured she had never pronounced an *r* correctly in her entire life, nor placed one in its proper location.

"Caahtah," she said, in this case skipping the *r* altogether, "Theah's a caahton of milk to poor on thaht cereal so help yer'self and I'm headin' ovah to Salem, don't ya know. I'll pick up anythin' you might aask for on my way home. Just make me a list."

Since his arrival at the Purser's Quarters, Martha had prepared breakfast for Carter with the ardor of a mother duck attending her young. He enjoyed everything except the instant coffee. It sat waiting for him each morning in an inexpensive ceramic pot in the kitchen. Being a self-anointed coffee connoisseur, Carter ordinarily wouldn't allow instant coffee to pass under his youthful mustache.

However, for the purpose of social edification and the particular desire to be accepted, he drank submissively. He held the small cup in large hands, his brown, curious eyes carefully gauging how much he could leave unnoticed when the meal ended. This trick, however, left him apprehensive that after breakfast Martha might come dashing by the Marblehead Roasting Company in her red Ford Escort and notice him sitting there drinking a tall latte.

In Carter's effort to reciprocate the friendship Martha extended, he offered to do the dishes, sweep up or do odd jobs. She would rarely accept, since she knew his hurry to get to the boatyard and commence work aboard his or Patrick's boat.

This particular morning he managed to persuade her to allow him to carry out the wastebasket. When he did, a discarded section of the paper lying in the basket caught his attention. He began reading as he made his way along the crushed seashell path leading behind the B&B. A small headline peeking out behind a crumpled bread wrapper read "Skipper sentenced in IRA gun-running." When he arrived at the dumpster, he propped the trash basket on the edge and tore the article from the soiled remainder.

> DUBLIN, Ireland – An Irish ship's captain who admitted transporting arms from Libya for the Irish Republican Army today was sentenced in a Dublin Court to three years imprisonment.
>
> Judge Liam Flynn sentenced the skipper, Adrian O'Hanlon, to eight years in prison, and then suspended five years of the sentence.
>
> O'Hanlon and four other Irish nationals aboard the 'Blackthorn II' were taken into custody off the coast of France on Oct. 30 1997. French customs agents found 150 tons of arms, including surface-to-air missiles, guns, and explosives on the Panamanian-registered freighter.

> O'Hanlon, 52, along with the others, jumped bail in France then fled. O'Hanlon was apprehended in Belfast and has been in custody for a year. The others remain at large. In February, a French court found all five guilty in absentia and sentenced them to seven years for arms smuggling.
>
> Authorities have said the weapons were loaded at the Libyan port of Tripoli, a country openly accused of promoting terrorism through the sale of arms and other forms of support including harboring terrorist training camps.
>
> The IRA has been fighting to drive the British from Northern Ireland.

Carter finished reading the brief, disturbing article on his return trip to the side door of the B&B. This was the second article about the IRA in recent days.

He replaced the container in its home under the kitchen counter, folded the paper, and slipped it in his shirt pocket. He did this by habit. He often inserted things like the article, things that caught his attention, into *Maxine's* logbook. It helped fill out his record of travels on board and brought memories to the forefront when he reviewed the logs years later.

Carter stood up and found Martha watching him. Her look was motherly, Carter thought, and reminded him of his own mother. A queer thought suddenly popped into Carter's mind and out his mouth.

"Why don't the other boarders eat breakfast with us, Martha?"

Martha's cigarette bobbed as she spoke straight away in a short pointed reply. "The othahs, Caahtah, aah flyin' coach."

Carter expected more explanation but Martha changed the subject in that way people do when one has pried where they shouldn't.

≋≋≋

As Carter sipped hot coffee from his adopted berth near the window of the Marblehead Roasting Company, he roughed out a day's activity on board *Maxine*, leaving time in case Patrick needed something done.

Red Shoes was nearing completion. Patrick explained he had begun abuildin' over four years ago. He got up a head of steam about two years ago and would be "...laahnchin' 'er by the fall, laddie, in time to shake 'er down and maybe cruise the Cape and Islands afore settin' 'er back on the hard."

"Will she be finished down below?" Carter inquired.

"She don't need to be Bristol fashion first season, laddie," he declared, "just needs to have a swing stove and a hammock rigged fer sleepin', skippah."

That was all he had to say on the subject. Carter hoped more detail would come later.

Red Shoes' laminated spars were receiving their final shaping and finishing by Bones, a task he carried out sitting down. Carter noticed Bones worked slowly and methodically, hour after hour. He scooted along the spars in a chair Patrick rigged with casters mounted on two by fours. The simple arrangement enabled Bones to move back and forth without standing up frequently. His pipe, as ancient as its smoker, followed him everywhere, clenched tightly between his teeth. Carter noted it hardly ever exhausted smoke.

Patrick rarely asked Carter to do mast shaping or any of the other tedious or time-consuming work on *Red Shoes.* He realized Carter was anxious to get *Maxine* floating again. Rather, he utilized Carter's relative youth and eagerness to chase around town fetching hardware, fittings, gaskets, and knobs. Carter was quick to agree, as his curiosity about unseen parts of Marblehead remained an itch in need of scratching. Patrick was apologetic about sending Carter on so many missions, but Carter rebuffed his apologies and reassured him that he needed all sorts of little things to get *Maxine* underway as well.

One of the first jaunts into the village took Carter near Abbott Public Library. He considered this fortuitous since he intended to stop there anyway. Considering he might stay around Marblehead for a while, he wanted to get familiar with the place. On this trip, he simply peeked in the door, checked for hours, and inquired about a borrowing card. Turning to leave, Carter spotted a bank of new computers along one wall. The reference desk attendant explained a computer software company donated them; and yes, they were available for use; and yes, including Internet access. He registered this opportunity and resolved to visit again soon.

Soon Carter charted a nicely woven course around town, passing by the best coffee shops, eateries, hardware stores, and chandleries. He liked the Old Town area best and made excuses to walk through it whenever possible.

Patrick, Carter noted, insisted he patronize particular suppliers with whom he apparently had credit because he never sent Carter out with cash. He simply told him what he wanted and with whom to deal. As soon as the vendor knew whom the item was for, no further questions were asked. Occasionally, the vendor would explain the purchase evened a previous favor or another vague explanation that clearly suggested no further discussion of the matter was necessary or appropriate. When that occurred, Carter figured it was none of his business and left well enough alone.

≋≋≋

Breakfast on Thursday was exactly like breakfast on Wednesday and Tuesday before that. This suited Carter fine. He found it pleasing to spend time with Martha and as each day went by, he gained mastery of the art of drinking less instant coffee without her noticing, or so he thought.

Aside from serving breakfast, Martha lounged habitually in bed, reading and keeping the television on at the same time, the television serving as her companion. Reading was a virtue inherited from her mother, Martha explained. Carter noticed she gave pause each time the subject of her mother came up. Apparently her mother, Miread, had read aloud to Martha as a child. Many of the books Miread read to her daughter still occupied space on shelves throughout the house. An enormous collection of Irish poetry enjoyed prominent positions.

"Poetry is taken in the brain, like music, Caahtah. Unlike lit'ratuah, which might be read once or twice before it becomes stale, poetry can be enjoyed ovah and ovah again, like a song sung all the days of one's life."

Her mother imparted this wisdom to her long ago and Carter realized that Martha appeared pleased to pass Miread's words on to him, almost as if he were a son. He paused when that thought came to him, wondering why he postulated that phrase "almost as if he were a son." It occurred to Carter that he may have unconsciously revealed the reason she had accepted him so readily. It was apparent Martha had no children because all mothers talk of their children, even if they are no longer living. Was he becoming a surrogate son? Was this okay?

Carter stayed the thought, unprepared for that level of involvement. Yet somewhere in his soul, the idea pleased him. He lived alone now; his parents were gone, they had passed away within a short time of each other, four years earlier. It seemed longer. The idea that Martha might adopt him, even if only for a short time, that is, until *Maxine* sailed on to distant ports, held a certain appeal.

CHAPTER 7

AN AMERICAN INNOVATION

Yellow oilskins, or at least their modern incarnation, dashed in and out of the Marblehead Roasting Company. Carter watched them come and go from the dry station of his over-stuffed chair. A hot buttered scone sat nicely atop Martha's eggs, and all he could do was hope she didn't dash by in the red Escort and spot him double dipping. He raised the *Globe* a little higher as if to hide from passing cars.

The rain outside was tolerable, but the wind made work aboard *Maxine* impractical. The forecast indicated changing conditions by late morning. He could be back on the job by early afternoon. Besides, it was Friday and he didn't care to rush about. After coffee he thought he'd stop by *Red Shoes*, and if Patrick had no particular need of his assistance, he'd make his way over to the Abbot Public library. Carter was interested in logging on to one of the computers to cruise the Internet. He had set up an e-mail account while in Florida, and had been too busy since he came North to check it.

A yellow-clad figure came through the doorway, hidden partially under a sou'wester, giving him the look made famous by frozen seafood packages. It was Patrick, and his appearance saved Carter a walk down to the boat shop in the pouring rain. Patrick reported that his plans for the morning would keep him away from the shop for a few hours.

"The weathah will be clearin' out early, laddie," he predicted. "I'm thinkin' I'll be takin' mess at the Fort 'round noontime, skippah," his way of inviting Carter to join him.

"I'll see you there," Carter replied. "I'm going to the library, then maybe I'll walk by the boat shop and see how Bones is doing; see if he needs anything to keep working."

"Thaht would be fine, laddie," he returned. "Poor old bugger cahn't get around like he used to. It's his knees, don't ya know, cahn't fault him fer thaht. He'll work till he cahn't work no more, thaht Bones will, skippah. He's not like thaht othah bunch, he's cut from better timbah. They're a tired crew, the Irregulahs, and their fate has left 'em high on the hard o' life, laddie. They're not good fer much, but Bones, now he's a different case. He's all theah topside. His mind's as cleah as a view from the crosstrees."

"Has Bones been around for a while?" Carter asked. "I mean, here in Marblehead," he quickly added.

"Well, of course Bones Matheson's been 'round a while, laddie, he's 90 years old! I'm gettin' so I cahn't remember 'im not bein' 'round."

Carter took this to mean Bones was from Marblehead originally. He thought back to the times he might have heard Bones speak more than a word or a sentence. He definitely carried an accent, but not an Irish brogue. Bones, Carter could see, exhibited aplomb. The others were all too quick to criticize in unpropitious tones of voice. Bones was different. He contributed when he spoke, never dominating conversation by will or force. When Bones spoke, Patrick always paused, if only for an instant. It was either his way of acknowledging he heard Bones, or he was commencing serious consideration of whatever Bones had to say.

"Lookee heah, laddie," Patrick said slyly. "I've somethin' to show ya," and he reached under his oilskin and produced one of those big wallets usually attached to a belt loop by a chain. In this instance, it was attached by a hemp lanyard, braided at both ends with a bronze snap shackle.

"Yer an ahchitect, right, skippah? I'll bet you've drawn a pretty picture or two haavn't ya laddie, ya know, houses and buildings and trees and the like, right?"

From a leather fold in the dark brown wallet he drew out a laminated piece of plastic about three by four inches in size. Between the plastic there was a white slip of paper and he held it slightly askew so Carter couldn't see it directly.

"Maatha went down to the office store one day and hahd this made fer me. She nevah made a big deal out of it, just handed it to me a while back; said it was a present."

Carter watched Patrick grip it like a precious document, maybe a birth certificate, or a will. He stared into Patrick's eyes for an instant and saw that look again, the special look, the transformation.

After a ritual moment, Patrick handed over the plastic for Carter to view. He watched as Carter clasped it carefully in his hands. The architect leaned back in his chair and held it toward the natural light entering through the window. Carter's deep brown eyes studied the pen and ink drawing, his scrunched brow revealing his studious nature.

This is grand, Carter thought, *extraordinary!*

He looked closer. The sketch was drawn in the hand of olden artists who worked between the time of wood blocks and lithographs, usually with a quill tipped pen. The tiny drawing was of an older boy leaning against a bollard on an unknown wharf. The lad gazed longingly at the bare breasts of a figurehead mounted on the bow of a fully rigged sailing ship tied to the wharf. The ships bowsprit rose high at an angle above the woman who looked dispassionately toward the sea. The jutting sprit and the bow of the vessel dwarfed the young man. Through the opening between the youth and the figurehead lay a detailed scene of sailing ships and masts and sea gulls flying amongst carefully rendered pen and ink clouds.

Carter heard Patrick say, "I got the original laddie. She'll be mounted in *Red Shoes* come 'er laahnchin," but Carter didn't fully register the remark as he was lost in the depth of the scene.

As an accomplished draftsman, Carter responded to the soul of the picture and wondered at its maker. In script so small he could barely read it he saw the one word title, "Figurehead," and next to it the signature— "B. Matheson, 1937."

"Bones drew this?" Carter exclaimed.

"Aye laddie, thaht he did," and Patrick retrieved the sketch from Carter, carefully replacing it in his oversized wallet.

≋≋≋

Dashing through drizzling windswept streets, Carter ducked into the Abbot Public Library. There he quickly discovered he was not the only one seeking refuge from the rainy weather. The library was busy, with only one computer available. He sat down and logged on.

After checking and responding to e-mails he decided to search the Internet for information about the ship that was smuggling arms he read about in the *Boston Globe.* Reaching into his pocket, Carter found the newspaper clipping. He unfolded and pressed the clipping flat on the desk. He entered the vessel's name and registry.

Ten "hits" later Carter knew just about everything one would want to know about the freighter, *Blackthorn II*, including the year her keel was laid, 1964; who built her, the Belfast Ship Building Company; gross tonnage, ownership records, and even her disposition when the French released her after the smuggling incident in 1997.

Carter's curiosity was drawing like a Genoa jib in a building breeze. It occurred to him that the Internet could enable him to track articles and follow leads all through the history of this particular event. The thrill of the hunt gripped him.

After a while Carter paused searching and checked his chronometer. He realized it was time to pack up, stop by the deli, and make way for Sewall Point and lunch with Patrick. He shoved the article back into his shirt pocket and swore this time he would remember to put it in *Maxine's* log that very afternoon.

≋≋≋

Carefully placing his cup of chowder on the always-damp park bench at Sewall Point, Patrick swallowed a drink of soda he called "tawnic," looked across the harbor and began to speak.

"The schoonah, laddie," Patrick paused, looked Carter's way, then repeated, "the schoonah, don't ya know, was refined nice and pretty by 'mericans."

He took several more spoonfuls of chowder and glanced again towards Carter in a manner Carter thought to be the look of a friendly embrace.

"The schoonah, laddie, bein' a fore and ahft rig, did somethin' all the boats before it couldn't do haalf as well."

Carter listened. He detected Patrick was about to explain why, of the many sail plans a modern sailor might choose, he chose the beautiful but antiquated schooner as the sail plan for *Red Shoes*.

"You see, skippah, sailin' ships of old couldn't point high into the wind; they couldn't make way in the direction the wind was comin'." He spooned the chowder and went on. "Since cloth was first hung from sticks, all 'round the globe, and you do know, laddie, I've been 'round 'er a couple times," he added for emphasis, not really boasting, "boats were pushed to wheah they were goin'.

"This arrangement worked fine fer hundreds of yeahs as boats began travelin' all 'round the world, explorin' . . . , exploitin' . . . whatever you've the mind to call it, laddie. The world changed when trades began blowin' the big rigs about."

Carter shifted on the damp bench and continued listening.

"The 'mericans laddie, they were a different breed from the rest of the world at the time the schoonah' came ta age. They were buildin' something big. The country was just born and they hahd thrown the bloody British out on theah arses. And, by the way, skippah, thaht's one thing we Irish can relate to. We been tryin' to kick 'em out fer eight hundred yeahs and we're not rid of 'em yet."

Carter's attention perked. It was the diversion he came to expect in Patrick's stories. Carter's mind raced forward with questions about the Irish. He nearly spoke up but thought again, had doubts, and kept quiet.

Patrick's story returned to schooners and Carter regretted not asking his questions. Are you from Northern Ireland, Patrick? Do you hate the British? Isn't there a solution to the conflict? Will more people kill and be killed?

Carter turned towards Marblehead Light as Patrick continued. He raised his binoculars and fixed on a double-ended wooden cutter. He had seen her a couple minutes before, breaking the horizon line further offshore. Now she was making way toward the mouth of the harbor, and as she came closer, Carter began to think he recognized her.

A second later Patrick's voice played through "...and thaht laddie, is one of the reasons I'm abuildin' *Red Shoes*: tradition, an honorable and impahtant historical tradition."

Carter realized he missed something, pretended he hadn't, and continued watching the cutter as it made its way through a maze of lobster pots.

"The othah reason is thaht it is simply the most beautiful sail plan to grace this planet's oceans. 'Tis the ultimate combination of beauty and efficiency, skippah." Patrick concluded.

Carter acknowledged the end of the story with a nod and continued watching the cutter as a crew of three hands tended sails and made ready to take up a mooring as the vessel circled in front of the East Harbor Yacht Club. She was a stately yacht, straight from the North Sea, heavily built, probably fifty, maybe sixty years old, with a tall wooden stick towering over the boats in the harbor around it. Carter guessed she was about sixty-five feet on deck.

A burly-looking, middle-aged man stepped clear of the finely finished pilothouse. He stood near the stern chewing steadily on a cigar as he watched the proficient crew at work. The cigar man stood by, holding the aft stay without making a gesture or issuing an order.

"Patrick?" Carter inquired, "Do you know that boat down there? I've seen her around, but can't place where."

Carter handed him the glasses.

Patrick shuffled on the bench to look.

The vessel was rounding up to a mooring.

Patrick raised the glasses and paused for an instant before saying, "Oh yeah, *Holger Dansk*, thaht's a shippy Scandinavian boat, Aage Neilson design. Shame the ownah, a very fine sailorman, died a couple yeahs baack. Now his poor widow and 'er maid live aboard each summah. It's sad "Happy Dancer" nevah leaves the moorin'. Yet I admire the wife, bein' true to the boat and all. She loved 'er sailorman and bein' aboard must keep his spirit alive, poor lassie."

Carter knew *Holger Dansk*, having given her a thorough inspection during one of his evening surveys of the harbor.

"No, not that boat, Patrick." He realized Patrick must have been looking about a point to starboard of the cutter. "I'm talking about the double ender approaching the mooring, just to port of *Holger Dansk*."

Patrick appeared to Carter to play dumb for a moment, taking too long to answer a simple question. Then he said, "Oh, you mean the cutter *theah*, laddie. Okay let me see." He moved the glasses around the area in front of the yacht club longer than obviously necessary to find it.

Finally, Carter noticed the glasses stop their search. He knew Patrick spotted the vessel and was expecting him to speak. Instead Patrick pulled his eyes away from the lenses. He bent his head to the side and wiped a strand of his long, red-gray hair from his brow with a sawdust-covered sleeve. For an instant their eyes met.

Patrick quickly looked back into the glasses, but it was too late. In that brief exchange of glances the familiar outpouring of emotion was revealed once again, then instantly withdrawn.

Carter was taken aback. He turned his own eyes towards the boat trying to conceal his discovery and wonderment. The wind blew a puff of air up the granite rocks from below. It hit Carter's face and cleared his thinking for an instant. He regained his composure and glanced back at Patrick who was once again peering through the glasses.

Patrick was studying the scene, erect and alert, like a pointer on a bird. Still, Carter suspected Patrick was gazing through the glasses in large measure to avoid looking at him. After another minute Patrick finally spoke. "You're askin' about *Gael Na-Mara*," and the words poured from his lips like an Irish poem. It entered Carter's brain like music, like Martha's dear mother spoke of poetry. The tone of his voice was warm, more endearing than usual.

Carter couldn't tell if Patrick was aware of the change. Perhaps he simply couldn't restrain it and didn't really care, knowing somehow Carter would not have the poor judgment to ask about it, to probe where he hadn't been invited.

Patrick repeated the boat's name, "*Gael na Mara*," and Carter knew in that instant Patrick was in his Gaelic mind, his inner dialogue spoken in a tongue Carter could only imagine. Patrick was for this moment an Irishman, pure of blood, locked in his heritage. Carter heard the passion and the sorrow of his Irish ancestors and all the oppression heaped upon them. From his lips, in that miniscule moment, came the wail of the great hunger and the following migration so vast and unparalleled in modern times. The few words spoke volumes and caused an indefinable change in the sea air surrounding them as they stood atop their great perch. It was as if for an instant they were enveloped in a green mist, transported through space and time, looking out over a rugged windswept cliff on the coast of Ireland.

Patrick spoke again and said resolutely, "Woman of the Sea." It was his English voice now, and the man standing beside Carter was Patrick of Marblehead again, Patrick of *Red Shoes*. The illusion now dissipated, they stood together once more at Sewall Point, the vastness of Marblehead Harbor stretching out before them.

CHAPTER 8

"BEVAHLY"

Carter and Patrick left Sewall Point after watching *Gael na Mara* tie up to a visitor's mooring. They parted in opposite directions. Patrick returned to his boat shed and Carter strode directly to Little Harbor.

Climbing aboard *Maxine*, Carter went below and withdrew her log from the shelf above the chart table. From his pocket he pulled the O'Hanlon article and placed it in the log. He made his normal daily entry then slipped it back between Chapman and Dutton.

The remaining hours of the afternoon Carter spent diligently working. The work cleared his mind, freshened his attitude and before long he became aware it was time to clean up. He had agreed to have supper with Martha at her favorite restaurant in nearby Beverly.

While washing for dinner, Carter recalled shying away from the invitation, but Martha was persistent. He detected a modicum of urgency in her invitation. To the reticent Carter, the invitation seemed more like an appeal. She strained to convince him he would love the food. She claimed she just received a deposit from her first tourist couple for Memorial weekend. She'd buy, she insisted.

All this appeared unlike the usually flannel-robed Martha who typically devoted evenings to reading in her great room with the television as her companion. All things considered, he decided he could muster the mettle to have dinner with her at the restaurant she so lavishly described.

≋≋≋

Martha chattered more than usual as she drove the red Escort through twists and turns in route to "Bevahly." Carter found it best to sit back and surrender control to the driver, her cigarette leading the way, bobbing like a blind person's cane.

As she drove, she poured forth colorful and unverifiable portions of local history while Carter listened attentively. She told him about places colonists gathered and conspired against the king, and the real reason behind the Salem witch-hunt. Finally, Martha pulled up to a seafood diner and into an angled parking space. With a lurching stop, rocking them both forward in their seat, she proclaimed their arrival.

"Heah we aah, Caahtah—best red snappah this side o' Bahston."

The diner was last in a row of buildings that included a marine electronics shop, brass boutique, and an insurance company offering "Boat Insurance" in gold letters printed under the broker's name.

Judging from their reception at the door, Carter quickly surmised Martha was a regular. A hostess in a white dress and apron, whose name tag proclaimed her Dorothy, greeted them with garrulous banter and a furtive glance when she noticed Martha's young male escort.

Dorothy led them to a table and as they passed through the noisy dining room, Carter smelled fried fish and vinegar. There was a certain familiarity about the place. He smiled when it dawned on him it was exactly like the diner Patrick took him to in Boston.

After being seated, a big plastic covered menu was placed in Carter's hands. He stroked his trim brown mustache unconsciously as he focused on the long list of dinner specials.

≋≋≋

Martha watched Carter from over the top of her menu. He was a handsome lad, she thought, trim but not skinny, a well proportioned face with high cheek bones. She nearly giggled when he stroked his mustache—an accoutrement she figured he believed made him look older. After a recollection of her husband and a speculative thought about what a son might have looked like had they conceived one, Martha snapped back to the present.

Dorothy stood ready with her pencil poised. Martha looked up and explained to the waitress that she would have her regular.

"Red snappah," she announced. "With extra lemon slices and a stuffed quahog on the side."

≋≋≋

Martha insisted Carter take his time, but the very manner in which she did so suggested he should hurry up and order the same. So he did. Carter didn't know what a stuffed quahog was, but ordered it anyway.

With this essential task completed, Martha enjoyed Carter's full attention. Without further small talk she began to tell him about a gathering, earlier that day, of several of her friends of the spiritual persuasion. As she spoke, Carter began to suspect she needed to get something off her mind, and he soon realized the acceptance of the proffered "red snappah" dinner was going to obligate him to her confidence. He bravely acquiesced, thinking for a moment that in a way, this was a very endearing offer. He should be honored by her trust.

It seemed she and her "friends"—Carter read "coven"—gathered to conduct some "spiritual business" wherein they all pitched in to hire a fortune teller.

The waitress dashed by the table and set two stuffed quahogs, "stuffies" as he would learn to call them, on the table with lemon slices and Tabasco sauce, then flitted on her way.

Carter looked at the dish before him, sniffed it, and looked up at Martha for guidance. She was preoccupied with telling her story. In time, Carter was able to watch and followed suit as Martha squeezed the lemon over the "stuffie" and hammered Tabasco sauce on top of it. Carter didn't think it looked like much more than a mound of bread crumb dressing stuffed in a giant clam shell. Martha later explained the shell was a quahog shell, a clam species unique to Narragansett Bay. Carter tasted it and found it to his liking, and was happy he didn't have to wear a bib to eat it.

Martha talked on, describing the afternoon's events which began as the seer, a Slavic-looking woman named Madame Russalka, met with each of them individually, of all places, in Carter's sitting room.

Carter looked up quizzically when she explained the geography of the event.

"Oh, I hoped you wouldn't mind..." she quickly added, "...we hahd to use it. Madame Russalka walked each of the rooms downsteahs, touchin', smellin', and listenin' to each room's spirit. When she floated up to your sittin' room, I could see she got very excited."

Carter wondered if she meant the floating part literally and his curiosity rose with the mounting suspense of Martha's delivery. He was feeling a bit captured by the aura of the presentation.

"My last gulfriend stepped from the room lookin' pleased at huhr reading, but then it was my turn."

The white-dressed waitress interrupted, delivering two plates of red snapper and said to Carter, "Heah we aah, handsome."

"Catch of the day for you, Maatha deah?" and winked at Martha, her eyes darting from Martha back to Carter before dashing back through the swinging doors to the kitchen.

Martha was undeterred from her story and spoke again the instant the waitress was out of ear shot.

"When I walked through the door, Madame Russalka was on huhr feet lowerin' a curtain thaht daarkened the room. Ya know the windows aah small in theah to begin with. As she turned, our eyes met and with very little humah she aasked me to be seated, pointin' at a chair opposite huhr. I was troubled by huhr serious voice, and caught myself lookin' back at the door, thinkin' of all my giddy friends who just reported delightful results from our guest speakah.

"Now I've already said I'm not new to the workin' of mystics, mind ya. Howevah, when Madame Russalka took my hand in huhrs, she was tremblin' like a hen on the choppin' block. I didn't know exactly what she hahd done or said to all those othah women, but I hahd a terrible feelin' I wasn't goin' to be walkin' out of thaht room laughin' and tellin' jokes about how I'd be winnin' the lottery.

"Suddenly she spoke in what I thought was a kind of Mediterranean accent, maybe Greek or Turkish or somethin' like thaht." Martha made another look from side to side. "Then she told me thaht I should plahnt three trees on the south side of my house, and thaht I must do it immediately. It was a matter of great urgency; much was at stake and I must not fail to comply."

"Plant three trees?" Carter said. The words fell out before he could restrain his incredulity. Martha continued.

"Madame Russalka said, 'Dats right, you must do r-r-right avay—today, tomorrow, bettah today. Tomorrow okay, but no later, understand?'"

Martha abruptly ceased her oration.

Carter didn't know what to say. Then, almost without thinking, he asked, "What kind of trees?"

Martha was clearly exasperated and whispered across the table as if she were about to reveal a government secret. "You won't believe what she told me, Caahtah!"

"Plant . . . feeg . . . tr-r-rees." Martha mimicked the seer, spacing out each word as Madame Russalka delivered them. She looked at Carter for a long moment, waiting for him to speak.

Carter was totally baffled and replied rather loudly, "What the hell kind of fortune is that!"

"If I knew, I wouldn't be so damned upset now, would I?" Carter took no offense; damn was in common usage by Martha.

"But thaht's not all. Not knowin' exactly what to think or say, I aasked our deah Madame Russalka how I was supposed to keep fig trees alive durin' the wintah in this climate," Martha replied.

Almost as mysteriously as Madame Russalka's fortune seemed to Martha, Carter just as mysteriously remembered a friend whose Italian grandmother used to grow fig trees in Michigan. Martha could have been knocked over with a feather when Carter mechanically spoke up and explained that it was easy.

"You dig a long rectangular hole, well below the frost line and wide enough so as not to compress the branches too much, kind of the size of a grave. Then you carefully dig up the trees in the late fall after they become dormant, wrap them in burlap bags, place each tree on its side in the grave-shaped hole, and cover them first with peat and then with soil. In the early spring, as soon as the ground thaws, you dig them out, and plant them once again in the lawn."

Martha was flabbergasted and he surprised even himself with the detail of his recollection. When she regained her composure, she spoke up.

"See, I knew it! The fact thaht you knew all thaht about fig trees must haav somethin' to do with why she picked your room. This must haav somethin' to do with you as well as me," she concluded.

"Wait a minute," Carter protested, "can't we keep me out of your business with Madame Russalka? I mean, no offense intended, but I'm not sure I believe this kind of stuff."

"It's just odd, don't you think, thaht you seem to be tied into this mystery somehow? Aftah all, you aah the one who knows how to grow fig trees, right?"

Martha beseeched him with her eyes.

"Well, I'll tell you what I will do. As long as I don't have to have a reading with Madame Russalka, I'll help you plant them just for the heck of it. We'll do it together as soon as we can find some 'feeg tr-r-rees.'"

"Maybe we should do thaht, Caahtah. Maybe we should." Martha's voice was tired but she seemed relieved.

"Theah's just one thing Caahtah, somethin' I want you to think about. It's been my experience thaht the important paht of a message from beyond may not be the spoken message at all. Sometimes the important message is obscured. It might come as a riddle, or in this case, Caahtah..." and her cigarette stopped bobbing. That alone gave her a somber demeanor. "...it may have come as a numbah," she paused, and with a grave, serious tone that spoke both solemnity and foreboding she said, "and thaht numbah would be three."

Carter leaned back in his chair and set his fork down. Thinking about Madame Russalka's edict he realized there were threes of things all over the place in Marblehead: three "feeg tr-r-rees," three new friends, Patrick, Martha and Bones, and from what he could tell, three mysterious Irishmen – the boarders on the other side of the wall at the Purser's Quarters.

≋≋≋

It was nearing sunset when Martha and Carter arrived back at the B&B. He left Martha, assuring her once again there was no harm in planting three fig trees. He told her he'd help if she looked around for a greenhouse that could supply them.

Martha seemed tired and he wrestled with the perennially ornery door for her, holding her hand as she stepped onto the stone stoop. Her hand felt delicate and frail compared to the hand that massaged his foot the first day they met. When she stepped across the threshold into the ancient dwelling, she turned and thanked him for joining her.

Carter departed the B&B, shaking his head in wonder over the "spiritual side" of his evening, and walked directly down to Patrick's boat shop. The harbor appeared golden in the evening sun. Lights sprinkling the yacht club lawns on Marblehead Neck blinked on forming a charming necklace around the water's edge. The music of a dance band wafted across the water and the vessels on moorings swayed in rhythm. It was going to be a beautiful evening on the water.

Patrick continued working on *Red Shoes* as Carter approached. He was assisted by two sturdy lads Carter didn't immediately recognize. He wondered if they might be new boarders. Carter spoke up and asked Patrick's permission to take the Whitehall for a sunset row around the harbor. Patrick gave an affirmative nod. Carter was pleased at the lack of interest the request drew because he was, very pointedly, on a mission. A mission he would not have admitted, if asked.

A few minutes later he stepped carefully into the beautifully crafted wooden row boat and placed the sweeps in their locks. As he shoved off, he began thinking about his new friends.

Are these people strange, he wondered? *Or are they simply painted with stronger colors than most?*

He considered the two possibilities.

Maybe they wouldn't have appeared so strange in times past when witchcraft prevailed and wooden boat building was commonplace.

Above all else, Carter felt a huge distension of curiosity, particularly regarding Patrick. He had a growing, burning need to know what elicited Patrick's emotional reaction at the sight of *Gael na Mara.* Since Carter had perceived in Patrick an unwillingness to divulge his secret, there remained only observation and deduction as a means of discovery. He felt a momentary tug of moral self-doubt as an obscure voice spoke inside him. *Is what you are about to do observation – or spying?*

The obscure voice surrendered to the greater allure of curiosity and he set course across the harbor—a course leading straight to the mysterious "Woman of the Sea."

CHAPTER 9

GAEL NA MARA

Carter had a simple theory: the dim light of sunset is the best time to study boats. "Not for purchasing one, of course," he had said to Patrick, "only to enjoy their design qualities unfettered by imperfections made obvious during the day. It's like blurring ones eyes and seeing the spirit, not merely the detail, of the boat," he explained to his Irish friend, who understood spirits and mystical things better than Carter realized.

"All o' Ireland is filled with 'em." Patrick had said in reply, humorously pointing out that "our landlady's one o' those mystical thin's, too, don't ya know, skippah."

Along the course he laid for the cutter, despite the urgency of his mission, Carter paused to examine a Fife sloop, a sistership to *Maxine*. As he pulled around the sloop's bow, he was startled by the harbor police boat. The hard bottom inflatable came out of nowhere firing up its blue flashing lights. It gave a quick, resounding blast of its siren only yards ahead of the Whitehall.

The sound shot into Carter's ears like a cannon, catching him by surprise. Adrenalin spurted into his blood. Carter turned and watched as the patrol boat leapt forward in pursuit of a small inboard speeding across the harbor on a joy ride.

He decided to put the adrenalin to work as he pulled the Whitehall back onto his intended course. Then an odd feeling of déjà vu suddenly came over him. He attributed it to the adrenalin. He suddenly stopped pulling on the sweeps, turned, and looked back at the patrol boat. In an instant, his mind reconstructed a scene he observed earlier in the week as he sat daydreaming atop Sewall Point. The same type of occurrence interrupted his daydream then. It was a harbor patrol boat doing similar duty.

As he recalled the event in his mind's eye, he remembered seeing Patrick slip across the water beyond the patrol boat in his inflatable with one of the young Irishmen at the bow. Then, just as unexpectedly, he recalled another detail that eluded his conscience mind at the time. When he noticed Patrick speeding along out beyond the patrol boat, Carter had looked briefly ahead of Patrick to see if he could spot his destination.

As Carter's mind played back the scene he swept out ahead on the course Patrick was steering and there she was—*Gael na Mara*!

He knew he had seen the beautiful vessel before.

Carter's mind held the recollection long enough to remember seeing *Gael na Mara* sitting quietly on the same mooring she returned to just that afternoon. He remembered thinking, *she's fantastic, I'll have to have a look at her some evening.*

Although the boat lay ahead on Patrick's course, it never occurred to Carter, at least at the time, that Patrick was speeding towards her. He thought Patrick was headed for the East Harbor Yacht Club or some other destination in that same direction.

Now Carter was convinced that was exactly where he had seen the cutter before. Furthermore, he now thought Patrick and the young Irishmen must have had business to conduct on board her. This was all making sense, at least to a point. However, it was also suspicious and raised several questions.

He slipped the sweeps back into the water and rowed on toward his destination. As he did, the impending coolness hovering over the blackening water's surface began touching his skin. He wished he brought a jacket.

Rowing harder to make heat, another thought crept into his mind. Patrick had been called away from lunch to supervise the unloading of mahogany for *Red Shoes*, Carter recollected. Only about thirty minutes transpired before the two Irishmen were out on the water. That's when Carter watched them go by, attracted first by the harbor patrol boat. Even then Carter couldn't believe Patrick and the Irishman had enough time to unload lumber before he noticed them speeding across the harbor.

With a troubling sensation roiling in his stomach, Carter admitted to himself that it appeared Patrick might not have been entirely truthful about his reason for departing during their lunch on Sewall Point. However, there was no way of actually determining if that was the case, at least not at that moment. Then Carter remembered Patrick asking him to retrieve his coat on board *Maxine*. Carter became suspicious that this request, too, was merely a ploy to get him to leave Sewall Point and go around to Little Harbor, entirely out of sight of Marblehead Harbor. Had Carter rushed to perform that simple favor instead of laying down to take a rest, day dreaming about the Big Lake, he would not have seen Patrick on his trip across the harbor to wherever it was he was going.

Carter tried to stop himself from forming a scenario of deception but the pieces seemed to fit. The obvious question then was why Patrick wanted to conceal his activities from Carter?

Carter increased the pace of his rowing. He wondered if he was reacting more suspiciously than warranted. Even though Carter felt he had become a close friend of Patrick's, he reminded himself that basically, he was an acquaintance of recent origin.

The Whitehall picked up speed and glided across the sparkling water. Carter quelled his suspicions, concluding he was getting ahead of himself, perhaps exhibiting a touch of paranoia. Patrick certainly didn't owe Carter any explanation for his activities. The most likely explanation was that Patrick simply tried to make Carter comfortable by giving the reason he did for leaving early during lunch that afternoon. It really was none of Carter's concern. Maybe something else came up and Patrick only needed to spend a minute with the people delivering the lumber. Then he had ran off to handle some other business.

Gael na Mara reentered Carter's mind and the pendulum of logic swung the other way. He asked himself again why Patrick seemed so affected by her presence.

≋≋≋

Gael na Mara was no longer on the visitor mooring outboard the East Harbor Yacht Club's dock. She had moved to the harbor entrance, probably while he and Martha supped in Beverly. He altered his course in that direction.

Ink-black waters of the harbor surrounded the Whitehall as lobster pots and mooring pennants continued to interrupt her progress. *Gael na Mara* stood a good distance away and the sparkling lights surrounding the inner harbor were beginning to fade.

Carter pulled the Whitehall forward with ease and when he looked over his shoulder to check his course, he could see the cutter's sweeping sheer off in the distance.

The cool evening breeze increased and blew gently from the harbor entrance. The smell of the salty sea invigorated Carter, making him glad to be on the water. Wavelets broke gently against the Whitehall as she glided across the surface. The sound of her bow parting the water entered his right ear as he looked over his shoulder to maintain course.

Marblehead Harbor opened directly to the northeast and the harbor entrance was susceptible to motion from the open water beyond. Carter felt the swell roll the Whitehall beneath him. As he closed in, the blackness of night got blacker. He pulled the last few strokes towards *Gael na Mara*. Her white hull seemed bluish gray in the dim light; however, her lines remained vivid. The cutter's pilothouse stood proud above the cabin trunk, and through large windows he could see tiny red lights on a modern instrument panel.

He thought they looked incongruous with the classic lines of the vessel.

He approached first, out of habit and tradition, on her starboard side about twenty yards off so he could gain full view of her profile. He shipped oars and coasted silently.

When he pulled about ten yards ahead he could see her nearly plumb bow and the great mast rising from the sweeping decks. As he gazed at the mysterious yacht, a warm spark of excitement, or perhaps apprehension, crept into his heaving chest.

Little of her cabin trunk was discernable from his low aspect, and to Carter that was an advantage since her sheer line appeared accentuated from this perspective. This afforded him a gratifying opportunity to study the subtleties of her design. It also kept him out of view of the portholes dotting her low, curving cabin sides. He stroked silently, bringing the Whitehall in closer.

He gave the cockpit wide berth. If someone was on board they probably couldn't see him any better than he could see them. He preferred lingering unnoticed. He questioned himself again; was he studying the boat design or was he creeping around . . . spying. He had to admit he really wanted to know how, or why, this boat was important to Patrick. Who was the cigar man he saw on board, the one that seemed in charge? Who were the young crewmembers he observed moving about the deck earlier that day?

He pulled around the cutter's bow and studied her mast as it rose to the sky in the moonless night. Carter could only make out the top of the mast by the blackness it cast amongst the stars. Carter began rowing a complete circle around *Gael na Mara*, coming closer as he neared her port quarter.

Her hull dominated his viewpoint and from his low angle it was as if there was no cabin trunk at all. He felt invisible to anyone on board. Of course, discovery would be immediate if someone did step out on deck. There he sat, in full view and obviously intent on creeping about. He continued nervously.

As he finally neared her stern, his circumnavigation complete, the pilothouse once again stood proud against the lines of her sheer. For an instant, Carter saw the little red lights at the instrument panel blink out and back on. It puzzled him. Did an object on deck interrupt the lights, or did someone moving about in the pitch-black compartment cause them to disappear?

He remained steady on his course, not stirring the sweeps, just letting them ride silently above the waterline as he continued coasting. He realized he was holding his breath, so he quietly exhaled the salt air and tried to relax. Still, he did not want to be conspicuous in case someone was on board; nor did he want to draw attention and, thusly, bring someone on deck either.

He saw the blackness come over the lights again, and this time, he caught the faintest glimpse of a body, a body holding something across its chest like a boat hook or broom handle.

The darkness obscured Carter's vision. He strained his eyes and watched for movement. He saw none. Yet he could have sworn a person continued standing in the dark of the pilothouse holding an object across his chest, like a hunter resting his firearm or a soldier standing guard.

Carter glimpsed away for an instant and noticed that the breeze, in conjunction with the tidal current, had set him towards the cutter. Excitement crept from his stomach to his bowels and he wished he were close to shore so he could relieve himself. This predicament added measurably to his growing anxiety, but his closing proximity snapped him back to attention. If he didn't take action soon he would be too near *Gael na Mara* to be able to move his sweep and resume pulling without smacking the water loudly, or worse yet, bumping up against her topsides.

Still, Carter remained frozen in position, continuing to drift closer to her stern, while peering unabashedly into the pilothouse trying to discern the blue-black image inside. A chill suddenly clawed at his chest and it dawned on Carter he was losing heat by sitting still in the cool breeze. His nose suddenly felt stuffy, the night air colder and metallic smelling.

He looked again at the pilothouse and realized either his eyes were playing tricks or there *was* a man fixed against the faint glow of the red instrument lights. Carter convulsed involuntarily at the sight. It seemed as if the ethereal man was staring directly back at him. Carter thought he could feel his eyes on him and a surge of deep anxiety washed over him. That same instant Carter realized the object that lay across his chest, held prominently so Carter could see it, *was* a rifle.

Carter lowered his port sweep into the rolling water and drew a long pull that stayed the set of the tide and moved his craft past *Gael Na Mara's* stern. He gripped tight to the handles of the oars in an ineffective attempt to control the shivering that began unexpectedly, caused by the anxiety rising from deep within his chest. He wondered if he was visibly shaking. If he was, he wanted to conceal it from the occupant of the pilothouse.

The loss of body heat and the unexpected surge of adrenalin cast a peculiar blueness over his situation. He thought of the deadly weapon, poised at the ready, held by a hand prepared to use it. It completely stripped any innocence from his dubious evening sojourn. For all practical purposes, he had been caught—caught snooping around. He began rowing away from *Gael na Mara*, the physical exertion restoring the precious heat in the center of his chest.

It's late, it's dark, someone probably was on board, and some people are entirely at home with firearms.

He kept telling himself there was nothing that suspicious about his encounter—yet something wasn't right and whatever that something was eluded him or perhaps it chose not to reveal itself. There were people watching and listening who thought he had seen too much already.

CHAPTER 10

THE SEASON BEGINS

Maxine rose from her cradle in the great straps of the lift machine. Carter watched with apprehension despite his familiarity with the maneuver. Fully rigged and painted glossy white, she cut a magnificent image as her wine glass hull crawled towards the haul out well. Carter followed alongside as *Maxine* moved across the pavement. Nervously he darted ahead and checked the depth of the water in the haul out well.

Launching *Maxine*, which drew 7 foot 4 inches, required high tide so she would have water under her keel. Even though the tide changed slowly, so did the yard hands that moved her.

Finally, the vessel hung out over the water and the lift operator waited patiently as the gentle swing she developed on her trip across the hard dissipated. The hissing sound of hydraulics announced her descent.

Carter moved quickly from side to side and inspected *Maxine's* through-hull fittings, the rudder, and her zincs. Slowly she sank past his view.

When level with the hard, her descent was stayed a moment while a plank was laid across to her rail so a hand could go on board and manage her lines. This done, *Maxine* eased into the water after a long winter on land and was returned to the sea.

Carter watched attentively as a worker on *Maxine's* deck tossed up her lines to waiting hands all around. To Carter's surprise, Patrick snatched one of the lines from mid-air, glanced his way and issued a brief, gleaming smile. Carter forgot Patrick was stopping by. He had a way of being on hand at the right moment. This time, though, Patrick's comportment told Carter something more was afoot. Patrick nodded a signal causing Carter to turn all the way around.

There, leaning against a bollard, looking mightily reminiscent of the young man in the "Figurehead," stood Bones. The old man looked spry, his pipe erect, like the bowsprit of the great ship in Bones' own drawing. The ancient sailor nodded an approving gesture.

"He insisted on comin' along, laddie. Haasn't been down to watch a laahnchin' fer better'n ten yeahs. Looks just like hisself in thaht drawren, eh, skippah," he whispered and laughed. "He was determined to come and see yer fine lassie meet the watah. Poor buggah, he'll not see many more like *Maxine.* I thought I ought ta bring 'im down."

When Carter heard those last words he looked at Patrick. Patrick's brow was slightly crooked.

Red Shoes better be launched soon!

In short time, *Maxine* lay secure alongside the service float. Carter ran back to *Maxine's* cradle and grabbed a folding chair stowed in the pile of stuff that was the backbone of *Maxine's* winter cover. He quickly returned and placed it on the hard above the service float.

Patrick, who silently read his intention, helped Bones walk slowly from the bollard and sat him down to rest. Carter noted the care Patrick imparted upon the old man. He thought to himself that the two standing together made Patrick appear almost youthful.

By now, *Maxine* proffered few surprises at launching. Carter emphatically believed *Maxine* was a lucky ship. As *Maxine's* owner, constantly within her immediate zone of influence, Carter felt lucky too. His great vessel's luck was an aura that surrounded her as if it were hers to possess. It formed a capsule of good fortune. The aura made *Maxine* seem alive. It transformed her into a warm-blooded companion.

When Carter thought about this phenomenon, it occurred to him that his friendship with his new messmate, Patrick, enjoyed similar attributes. It meant good fortune, too.

Carter waited a few minutes to monitor the intake of water in the bilge. He checked its rate and watched as it rose above the capacity of the bilge pump. Patrick leaned over to make the same analysis for himself. They looked at each other with mutually doubting eyes and Carter decided to kick over *Maxine's* "iron ginney," her diesel engine installed by a previous owner.

Carter had taken an extra precaution two years earlier by rigging her cooling water intake with a y-valve that, when thrown, drew water from the bilge. This arrangement added greatly to her capacity to drain the bilge and reduced her dependency on the laboring electric pump. It had the added benefit of charging the batteries at the same time the electric pump was draining them.

Patrick, impressed by this simple and effective back-up scheme, decided on the spot to do the same on *Red Shoes*. Carter smiled inwardly with a measure of pride.

Eventually, Carter and Patrick motored *Maxine* out of the slip and made her secure at a mooring nearby. With everything working properly, Carter took five minutes and entered the morning's activity in his logbook. He glanced at the O'Hanlon article taped to the page above his entries. It reminded him of things he wanted to do at the library when *Maxine* was secure.

Carter returned topside and glanced over all objects on deck one last time. He convinced himself his beautiful lady was safe in her element, and decided to return by dinghy to Little Harbor.

Upon reaching the hard, the two sailors helped the waiting Bones climb into the dinghy and made him fast amidships. With Patrick at the bow, the trio shoved off and steamed jauntily back into

Marblehead Harbor. As the trio rounded Sewall Point, Carter set a course that would take them past Tucker's Wharf and eventually on toward the boat ramp near Patrick's shed.

Carter caught an unexpected glimpse of *Gael na Mara* in the distance. She looked magnificent at her mooring. In the excitement of the launch, Carter forgot about her, and about his visit to inspect her the previous evening. A pang of anxiety overtook him as he recalled his uncertain, almost dreamlike encounter with the dark specter in her pilothouse only twelve hours earlier. The sea air rushed across his face and his mouth went dry as he remembered what he was certain was a gun. His palm began to sweat as he involuntarily tightened his grip on the outboard motor's tiller. Carter caught himself giving the motor more gas. Had he been imagining things? Was there any significance in what he had seen?

Patrick sat leaning forward slightly at the bow to bring down the dinghy's nose as they skimmed along the calm harbor surface. He too, it seemed to Carter, was gazing at the North Sea cutter as it rolled gently at the entrance of the harbor.

Carter watched for a telltale sign that would confirm his suspicion and got it as Patrick kept looking *Gael na Mara's* direction while they veered to starboard moving farther into the inner sanctum of the harbor.

Patrick continued looking another moment or two, and then suddenly shifted his gaze ahead of the dinghy, as if remembering what he was supposed to be doing—watching for lobster pots!

The sea air blew in Carter's face and the smell once again reminded him of clams and other benthic organisms unknown in his home waters of the Great Lakes. The pungent odor restored his spirit and brought him back to the present. He decided to stop thinking about the mysterious gunman on board the Irish cutter. The sea air pulled good memories and feelings down from high reaches. He allowed the thoughts of the blackness of last night to dissipate as the sailors sped toward the boat ramp.

Finally, as he maneuvered into the boat ramp, Carter told himself he and Patrick were going to have to talk more about *Gael na Mara.* For now, the reason for her presence in the harbor and the purpose of those on board would remain a mystery.

≋≋≋

Gripping hold of Bones to help him from the dinghy made him seem more real. Until that moment, Bones might have only been a caricature, a representation of a salty New England seaman. Feeling his arm and steadying his shoulder made him flesh and blood—a living soul.

Bones was thick and barrel-chested, but his legs were frail and weak. He wore a Greek fisherman's cap that was tattered and filled with sawdust, making it look almost gray in the morning light. His lips were big, his nose pronounced, and he had bushy eyebrows with dark round eyes beneath them. They revealed, even at a glance, the depth of the things they had seen in his ninety years.

Bones' breath, in conjunction with his unlit pipe, emitted a smoky aroma that over time became a signature. Carter quickly recognized it whenever he came into proximity of the old seaman.

"Thanks for coming down to *Maxine's* launching," Carter said.

"Thaht's a fine boat, Caahtah," Bone's deep voice proclaimed. "Thaht's a fine boat, son."

He shifted his pipe from one side of his mouth to the other. Then, with a look in his eye that spoke pleasure and approval, Bones turned on his own volition, shunning help from Carter or Patrick, and shuffled up the cobblestone lane toward the boat shed. Patrick and Carter followed dutifully, both instinctively ready to assist their aged superior if the necessity arose.

CHAPTER 11

THE RED SHOES "IRREGULAHS"

The full contingent of "Red Shoes Irregulahs" shifted their lawn chairs with exaggerated displeasure as Bones, Patrick and Carter made their way into the boat yard.

The Irregulars looked anxious and made gestures with heads and hands. Empty coffee cups lay crushed alongside a box of half-eaten crullers. The "Irregulahs" had been in their positions, waiting for something to criticize, far too long. With a thick Marblehead accent, one spoke up.

"Dead and cold in my grave I'll be afore I see this schoonah down the ways."

"I knew a fellah down Quincy way, took so long abuildin' a double endah he fell ovah dead afore she sawr a coat of vahnish, let alone a drop of watah," another added.

"Kids sold it to a salvah for the price of the iron in her keel," a third pointed out, his voice filled with indignation.

Bones and Patrick ignored them and went about their work. Carter tried to ignore them, but couldn't help but notice the look of derision escaping from the corner of at least one of the Irregulars' crinkled eyes. It seemed headed his way. It was hard to tell because the whole contingent maintained a chiseled, cranky look, not to mention an aloofness characteristic of the locals in general. Carter was an outsider, and just in case he thought being in Marblehead two weeks changed that, they would be happy to point out it did not.

The most annoying of their comments, their claim that Carter spoke with a funny accent, struck Carter as deliberate ridicule. The blue-blooded aspect of their observation, which Carter took more deleteriously than he probably should have, made him incredulous.

I don't have an accent, he ruminated. However, he found it best to pass over the slight without rejoinder. Ironically, letting the accusation go unchallenged was but another signal confirming Carter came from somewhere else. He observed that Marbleheaders, and New Englanders in general, do not step lightly away from confrontation.

"In Maahblehead, son," Patrick explained with fatherly affinity—having picked up on Carter's feeling of rejection—"if you cahn't trace yer linage back at least fourteen generations yer an outsidah. These aah people whose ancestry is a mattah of great pride. If ya try to take it away, laddie, ya got what we got in Ireland, don't ya know."

Carter's attention perked at the reference to Ireland, noting it was the second time Patrick brought up the topic directly.

"Me, laddie, I'm doubly bound cause I'm both Irish and a Maahbleheader. But like you, I don't haav fourteen generations of New Englanders behind me neithah," Patrick explained. "Well ya know, skippah, if it weren't thaht ya cahn't throw a stick and not hit an Irishman 'round heah, I'd haav got the same treatment as you when I first arrived."

≋≋≋

The Irregulars appeared to calm down measurably once they vented. As the dust settled, they too settled back into their well-worn chairs. Life returned to normal. Carter could see in their attitude they didn't like disturbance. They lived for the regularity of their watch at the helm of *Red Shoes'* construction.

Carter pondered how bad things would be for him when the Irregulars discovered Patrick missing for four days. This would surely send them into paroxysms. He felt little sympathy for their coming plight, however, since Patrick had agreed to run up to Gloucester with him on a shakedown cruise.

Patrick had hesitantly asked if Bones could crew. Carter in turn paused, thinking about his responsibilities as captain and the question of bringing an elderly man aboard a yacht on a shakedown.

"He's a good helmsman, laddie, and keeps a truer course thahn most, don't ya know," Patrick added. It was as if he read Carter's mind. Still, Carter paused, hoping not to have to answer without further consideration. Patrick, seeing this hesitation interjected, "But think it ovah, skippah, no haahm done if you decide othahwise."

≋≋≋

Sunday morning Carter woke with a stuffed-up nose and a discernable scratch in his throat. He lay cocooned in his bed staring up at the rough-hewn beams. His symptoms, he hoped, were only the result of spending last evening with Martha in her smoky great-room.

As he lay in bed, he pondered the enigma of Martha and her inclination toward the occult. He rolled under a great stuffed quilt she placed over him during the night without his knowing she had done so. As he tossed about trying to get comfortable, his eyes caught a glimpse of a tall glass of water on the bedside stand and along side it two white lozenges on a small paper doily. Next to it sat a box of tissues.

She must have placed these here when she brought the quilt.

As with his bruised foot, Martha foresaw his needs and contrived a remedy. Carter remembered Patrick's earlier warning, "She's fey, don't ya know, she sees thin's . . ."

For a moment, Carter reconsidered whether he was comfortable with Martha entering his room without him knowing it. He shrugged it off as merely another aspect of Martha's habits as a nurse. Then he thought, maybe it was more than that, maybe he was becoming family. This occurred to him before and it made sense considering she appeared devoid of family—at least she hadn't mentioned any—and that topic usually comes up quickly in conversation.

Finally, his nostrils stuffed and throat scratchy, he sat up in bed, took the pills, drank the water and fell back into the warmth of the quilt. *Blast! Catching a cold is the last thing I want to do.*

A couple days of hard work commissioning *Maxine* lay ahead. The plan was to get her out to sea and shake her down as soon as possible. The run up to Gloucester was in the offing. With the prospect of a cold slowing him down, he decided right then to bring Bones along. An experienced hand at the tiller could spell Carter and he figured Patrick and Bones could handle *Maxine* if he catnapped from time to time. He dozed in the comforting thought of Patrick and Bones and *Maxine* on the open water, but it wasn't long before the back of his throat burned in a way that reminded him it wasn't the cigarette smoke from the night before. To add to his misery, a low pressure system brought morning rain and played havoc with his head. Wind from the northeast buffeted the old house though it held sturdily as if to say defiantly "send more."

Tossing over again, Carter looked out the small window at the foot of the bed and saw a gray-blue morning sky distorted morbidly by the imperfections of the rippled pane of ancient glass. The time had come to get up.

Carter began to extract himself from the bed, searching for warm clothing. He gazed about the cold, poorly heated room. He groped for pants and socks and stood upright as he slipped them on. He pulled a sweatshirt over his aching head while floundering around for his deck shoes. As he stepped into his shoes, Carter remembered getting a chill during his investigation of *Gael na Mara* night before last. It might explain his cold. As he thought of that night, he realized again that something *was* suspicious about the North Sea cutter and he felt an overwhelming desire to understand why Patrick appeared connected to it; why it was moored in Marblehead Harbor. Why, if it were merely a pleasure craft, as its outward appearance suggested, did the crew guard it with a firearm in a harmless place like Marblehead?

CHAPTER 12

REMEMBERING MIREAD

Adequately dressed for Martha's breakfast table, yet feeling quite puny, Carter moved toward the stairwell. As he began his descent, he looked out the rain-streaked window to the gray world outside. His vacant stare became suddenly focused when two figures in bright yellow rain gear interrupted the otherwise gloomy scene. As they stepped briskly away from the B&B, Carter recognized Patrick's familiar sou'wester. The other figure, in a hooded slicker, he could not identify.

At first he assumed Patrick's companion might be one of the young Irishmen. However, there was something different about this fellow; he was lower to the ground and broader at the shoulders. He rocked from side to side as he pushed ahead.

Fresh off the boat, Carter thought. *Doesn't have his land legs yet.*

Suddenly a spasm of anxiety came over Carter as he spotted thick, curling blue smoke rolling over the top of the stranger's hood. Then with only seconds before they disappeared, Carter noticed the stranger's hand reach to his mouth. He lowered a cigar lodged firmly between his first two fingers. Carter couldn't believe what he saw. It happened so quickly. Now the yellow figures were gone. Only the grayness of windblown rain remained in the view through the rippling, antique glass.

Carter stood frozen at the top of the steps, staring into the grayness as if to reconstitute the scene for further study.

Am I seeing things? Was that Patrick keeping step with the skipper of Gael na Mara? Surely it was, he concluded.

He remembered the black specter on board the mysterious cutter, the gun across its chest. His mind reeled with incongruous thoughts and protestations.

Something strange is going on. Patrick knows the cigar man! There they were. What were they up to?

Revisiting an earlier suspicion, Carter again placed Patrick in route to *Gael na Mara* along with the young Irishman who retrieved him from Sewall Point. Thinking back, he remembered the young Irish stranger seemed out of breath and in an agitated state when he approached. That detail caught Carter's attention. It didn't support the story Patrick made up about a wood delivery. Now, seeing Patrick together with the skipper of *Gael na Mara* convinced him the delivery story *must* have been a cover-up. It was a ruse to hide their real intentions.

Slow down there, Carter, you're jumping to conclusions without evidence.

Carter's anxiety dropped a notch as he considered other possibilities, the simplest being that they were old shipmates. It was entirely arguable that they were heading this moment to the Marblehead Roasting Company for a cup of java and to exchange a couple sea stories. Carter's suspicions would make a jolly tale if discovered by the suspects. Still, there was no doubt whatsoever, that Patrick enjoyed, or suffered, some kind of attachment to *Gael na Mara.* Which—Carter couldn't say.

If you're that curious stop being suspicious and ask Patrick straight away who the guy is.

He thought another moment.

It may be that Martha knows. Maybe he bunked at the B&B last night. I'll ask her at breakfast.

≋≋≋

Carter stepped into Martha's kitchen and was caught off guard by another surprise. Sitting on the dining table, along with Martha's typical breakfast, were three conspicuous additions: a cranberry scone perched neatly on a large paper doily, a neatly folded copy of the *Boston Globe*, and finally, a take-out coffee cup, prominently displaying the logo of the Marblehead Roasting Company!

"Mornin' Caahtah."

Martha stood turned away from him, clad in an aqua-blue dress rather than her signature robe. This alone startled Carter; more evidence she had already been out of the house.

Carter gulped.

Busted! How did she know? I've always kept such a low profile and never once did I see her drive by.

"Good morning, Martha." He tried hard not to sound as guilty as he felt.

She didn't pause from her task at the stove.

"Nasty day out theah, Caahtah," Martha professed. "In your condition ya ought 'ta stay out o' the weathah and get plenty o' rest."

His caregiver turned to greet him face to face. She carried to the table a white ceramic plate of fried bacon and eggs. Carter swore he saw a smile of contentment surface from beneath her aged lips, playful mirth lurking just below the surface.

Carter pulled out a chair and sat while Martha flowed around behind him, setting the dish on the table in front of him.

"Theah you aah, Caahtah."

To Carter's relief, Martha spoke kindly, with a tinge of forgiveness. He hesitated, but then proceeded to open the plastic lid on the coffee cup to reveal a latte made up from his own list of particulars. He wondered how she knew those as well.

Martha then sat beside him at her place at the table and lifted a cup of instant coffee to her lips. As she did, Carter detected the tiniest sea change in her composure. The playful mirth dissipated and he studied her transformation. His breakfast companion proceeded to eat as if nothing were amiss, buttering her toasted white bread with fragile spotted hands. Yet, something was amiss, of that Carter became certain. He decided after a moment of silent observation that perhaps he should speak.

"Martha," he proceeded to say, "Thanks for the blanket this morning. It felt good to wake in the warmth of that quilt."

He spoke gratefully, hoping an appreciative demeanor would begin a discourse that would reveal the reason for her transformed mood. The matron remained silent and acknowledged the gratitude in a glance toward Carter. He went on to ask, "Did you make the quilt?"

"'Twas a gift, Caahtah. 'Twas a gift from my mothah. She made it foah me. 'Twas a special gift to go in my cedar chest thaht fathah built when I was still very young."

Then it came.

A tear formed in the corner of Martha's wrinkled eye.

Carter watched.

It welled in the folds of her aging skin and appeared to smooth the coarseness of her being, revealing the good and passionate person Carter believed Martha to be.

The tear emitted a suffused light that softened the ordinary image of her bobbing cigarette and vigorous chatter. It proved to Carter how much a friend she had become, and conversely, by its mere existence, the friend he had become to her—a friend who would understand a tear shed at breakfast on a gloomy day.

Then, just as the sparkling droplet spilled forth, she reached to claim it with a handkerchief drawn from a pocket in her aqua-blue dress.

Carter paused, unsure what to do. He looked at her again as her chin quivered, and realized that despite his empathy and friendship, Martha felt compelled to restrain whatever was struggling to emerge. With all her might she held it back. He wondered what to say, and remained quiet.

Martha placed the hand holding her handkerchief across her lap with proper etiquette. She lifted her coffee cup slowly to her lips in stately form, little finger poised in space like the women from out on the Neck. Although it oscillated a discernable amount during its ascent, she sipped a drink and the china cup steadied in her hand. Lowering the cup, she appeared slightly more in control. She then looked into Carter's waiting eyes and spoke.

"She died this day, Caahtah; 'tis the anniversary of huhr pahssing. I've lost huhr and cahn't bring huhr baack: I cahn't face this day without thinkin' about huhr."

Carter reached for Martha's trembling, frail hand as her china cup reached the table. He held it in his own youthful fingers, unsure of what else to do. Her other hand, with handkerchief in tow, rose to her lips. She turned slightly away from Carter and cried a gasping cry she could no longer contain.

Carter sat silently. He continued holding her hand. Time felt suspended while Martha struggled to regain composure. Silent moments passed with memories and feelings swirling in the air. Carter thought for a moment of both his parents, remembering for an instant that he too was alone in the world. He held her hand tighter although this exertion came unconsciously.

Then Martha slowly regained her composure, exhibiting for Carter the greatness of strength only age and experience can bring forth. Carter recognized the sea change and decided to speak.

"Martha, can I do something? Can I take you to her resting place? Maybe we can stop at the florist and . . ."

Now Martha reversed her hands' position in his as she mustered strength to explain an important fact. In a solemn voice, she replied. "Caahtah, theah is no grave."

She paused a second, then, in a voice that laid bare a heart full of dreadful anguish she explained. "Thaht's the reason I find this so hard to set right. Mothah was lost at sea, Caahtah, my deah, she was lost . . ." Her voice quivered and failed. Carter believed whatever she couldn't bring herself to say would bring more tears and his sad prediction proved correct.

Carter continued holding Martha's hand as he would the tiller of *Maxine* on a stormy passage, steadily, calmly, but expectant of long service. As Martha wept for the loss of her mother, it took Carter great effort to resist asking questions. He was desperate to know what happened, when it happened, and why it happened.

He remained silent.

In time, Martha depleted her sorrow and he could tell she was returning to the ordinary existence of her breakfast table. Martha's devotion to her mother and the brief interlude of mourning affected Carter deeply. It added yet another thread to the fabric of their friendship. In a few minutes, normalcy prevailed and Carter once again considered asking more detail, to water the thirst of his curiosity.

Before speaking, he reconsidered and decided only a male would do such a thing at a time like that. Yet, he was a male, true enough, and he came up with an alternative. He would ask Patrick for the story in all its detail another time. He smiled inwardly at his cleverness.

With this course charted securely in his mind, he completed his breakfast. He was about to excuse himself when he remembered something he intended to ask Martha about Patrick.

"Martha," he queried, "Who was the sailor headed to town with Patrick this morning? I caught a glimpse of them as I came downstairs, but couldn't make out who it was."

Martha spoke in her normal voice, her coarse and earthy Marblehead voice and said, "A shipmate of Patrick's, Caahtah, a fellah he knows from 'cross the pond whose yacht is in the harbah," she explained without much drama. "Seems he hahd an urge to spend a night ashore and for thaht privilege I separated him from a bit of his purse, thaht is, in exchange for a room thaht wasn't rockin' and a showah big enough to turn around in, don't ya know."

Prying no further for the moment, Carter excused himself from the table, explaining to Martha that he would abide by her advice and stay out of the weather this day.

With the *Globe* under his arm and latte re-heated, he headed up the steep creaking stairs. Climbing tired him and when he got to the top he sank into a chair almost as good as the one he coveted at the Marblehead Roasting Company. Opening the morning paper, he began searching about for a distraction from his malady. He found it in the metropolitan section with a headline that read, "FBI finds rockets in IRA homes."

> BOSTON (AP) – The FBI said yesterday it has seized radar and missile parts from Irish Republican Army members who are accused of developing rockets to shoot down British helicopters over Northern Ireland.
>
> Three of the alleged IRA technical experts were arrested on March 7, in Massachusetts and California on federal charges of conspiring to injure and destroy property of a foreign government. An arrest warrant was issued for a fourth suspect, now in hiding in Ireland.
>
> Investigators say the four were working for the Provisional IRA, the guerrilla wing of the nationalist group fighting to end British rule in Northern Ireland.
>
> Following the arrests, the FBI seized radar parts and rockets "in various stages of development or manufacture" during raids Wednesday and Thursday in Massachusetts, New Hampshire, and Pennsylvania, said Lawrence G. Bertrand, special agent in charge of the FBI's Boston office.
>
> Among items confiscated in the raids on two apartments in Bethlehem, PA., were 6 foot long missile launching tubes and a videotape showing one of the men

> under investigation firing a rocket, the FBI said.
>
> A raid on a house in Nashua, NH, yielded technical documents on missiles and British helicopters. Enough radar parts and electronic gear to fill a station wagon were seized in a house in Rehoboth, Massachusetts, the FBI said.
>
> At a news conference yesterday in Boston, Bertrand said those arrested apparently were close to developing a mobile, radar guided missile that could lock onto aircraft, but there was no evidence they had built the weapon. Such a weapon would add significant firepower to the Provisional IRA's campaign against the British.
>
> Arrested were Robert Clark Johnston, 41, of Nashua, NH; Conrad Herald O'Conner, 27, a citizen of the Republic of Ireland who has been living in Bethlehem, PA since April; and Patricia Ann Reedley, 25, of Sunnyvale, CA.
>
> Still at large is Patrick Damon McKinley, an Irish citizen whom the FBI called the Provisional IRA's top technical expert.

Carter groaned in exasperation. This was the same trio he read about at the Marblehead Roasting Company his first day in town. He tore the troubling article from the paper, folded it and stuffed it in his pocket.

Into the log book.

Shaking his head with disgust, he blew his nose on tissue he extracted from the box Martha set near his bedside. He leaned forward, pulled the quilt from the bed, and wrapped it around himself. He sunk back into the chair, noticing the aroma of cedar wood coming from the quilt, something he hadn't picked up earlier when he awakened. It worked through his stuffed nose making him think about the quilt's maker.

Photographs of Miread adorned Martha's great room; photos of a proud mother holding Martha as a baby, standing next to Martha's father by an old black car. They looked so young, younger than Carter was now. It was hard to imagine the baby was Martha, his enigmatic friend.

Becoming sleepy, his eyes rolled slowly over the surface of the quilt. He began dozing off, imagining Miread's hands passing the needle back and forth, hours upon hours. It made him think of the sea. He imagined the feeling of *Maxine* climbing and descending, the constant push and pull of her tiller in his hand. In his transcendent state, he gazed upon the sparkling sea, as Miread surely gazed upon the sparkling eyes of her child. With these thoughts flowing in his mind, acting as a remedy to his cold's harsh symptoms, he fell asleep.

CHAPTER 13

CLAIRE SMILES

Sinus cold, foul weather, and promises to Martha aside, Carter experienced difficulty staying indoors. By 11:00 A.M. the dark and thickly plastered walls were closing in. He descended upon Martha's great-room where he found her reading a horticulture magazine in bed, the television blaring.

When he noticed what she was reading he remembered his promise—to help plant three "feeg tr-r-rees." He also realized they had not accomplished the project in the time frame Madame Russalka stipulated. Carter considered the bad luck this oversight might bring and ruefully pondered his unexpected illness.

Blowing his nose, he broached the subject of the ritual plantings with Martha. Together they would plant the trees he promised, as soon as she acquired the seedlings. Then he recalled Martha's numerical interpretation of the palm reading.

"Three," he remembered her saying. ". . .thaht numbah would be three."

Carter's head was thick with congestion, and, coincidently, three seconds was as long as he could think, so he drew no conclusions. Instead, he began browsing through Martha's book collection, tissue at the ready to wipe his dripping nose.

As his eyes passed over the library shelves, he stumbled upon a sailing adventure entitled *The Riddle of the Sands.* He read the preface. It explained that a man named Robert Erskine Childers wrote the book in 1903. Childers, a clerk in the British House of Commons and an Englishman by birth, became an advocate of Irish home rule. This idealistic stance eventually got him shot, ironically, by an Irish Free State firing squad after the failed Easter Uprising of 1916.

Carter looked up from his reading and noticed Martha watching him from the corner of her eye. He looked back down and finished the preface. He glanced up again and Martha's eyes dropped to the magazine in her lap. He wondered why she was watching him and, for a second, thought perhaps the book he held was one she would not want to loan him. Nevertheless, intrigued by the title, he asked permission and she assented with a nod and slightly forced smile.

Content with his selection and book under arm, he plodded back upstairs to his loft. His cold annoyed him terribly and he wiped his tender nose. He dropped despondently into his bedside armchair, covered his lap with Miread's quilt, and began to read.

By 3:00 P.M. he was a third of the way through the story and all the way through a bowl of chowder Martha had prepared. Childers' book, a fictitious account of two young British adventurers sailing a sloop in the North Sea and happening upon a dangerous conspiracy, reminded Carter he ought to curb his own irrepressible curiosity. But the trouble curiosity aroused for the story's main characters, Davies and Caruthers, seemed unlikely to occur in his sedate life, so he set the thought aside.

By 3:30 P.M., even though well entertained by the rainy day adventure, Carter became anxious to escape his surroundings and step outdoors. He struggled with the urge, knowing he promised Martha to stay indoors for the entire day. He definitely felt poorly; his throat sore, eyes burning prodigiously. In a climax of frustration, he rose from his chair and checked the weather through his glass port hole to the world.

Doesn't look too bad. He donned a heavy wool sweater, yellow slicker, and a long-billed cap. Then he picked up his pocket field glasses to take along in case he spotted a boat to study from on shore. Shoving a ten-dollar bill in the pocket of his slicker, he descended the stairs, and slipped outdoors.

The driving rain had receded to a mist and everything shone wet. The cool air stung his sensitive nose. He had second thoughts, then defiantly parted the B&B and paced down Front Street. The sullen lake sailor laid a course to a destination he figured would make him feel better: the Marblehead Roasting Company. He needed to "be up on deck," for a short while.

He strode along silently and mused over the early morning sighting of Patrick with the cigar man. This train of thought dissipated suddenly, when a sneeze rated Force 7 on the Beauford Scale shook him to his core.

I should be in bed.

As he entered the warmth of the coffee house, he wheezed and sniffed beneath a handkerchief and realized he could barely smell the roasting coffee beans. Instinctively, he looked behind the counter, hoping for the familiar face of the young waitress. She was an attractive sight and each day began with a wistful glance at her pretty face. She was at the counter so he smiled, greeting her pleasantly. Next, he looked over at the idle roasting machine to see if the pit bull of a roaster, Mr. O'Neil, was on duty. The roaster's station stood vacant and Carter figured the insipient crank had the day off.

As he stepped closer to the counter, his attention, and his frame of mind, returned to the young waitress. She turned away and he caught himself watching her from behind, studying her jet-black hair and shapely lines. The hapless sailor was looking at her in the way of sailors who haven't seen port in a long while. He blinked away desire, wiped his running nose and reached for the money he had pushed into his slicker pocket.

To his amazement, when his eyes turned up from looking at scones stacked neatly in the glass case, the young waitress stood silently staring at him. When their eyes met, she smiled; not just an ordinary smile, she smiled a smile meant solely for him.

Their eyes remained fixed for a daring moment. He smiled back then broke eye contact, glancing towards the baked goods once more. His mind, however, remained focused only on her.

He looked back after another second and voiced his selection. She continued smiling. She meant to make contact. Carter was ecstatic and decided on the spot that he liked her smile very much. He also decided Mr. O'Neil's absence from the establishment was the precipitate reason for the smile, and that was fine, too.

Suddenly, in the midst of this pleasant realization, he remembered what he must look like—*a tramp steamer at best.* Regardless, and to Carter's extreme delight, the young waitress continued to smile, looking directly into his eyes. She waited for him to speak.

Pausing another moment, then cocking her head slightly to the side she said, "You didn't come in this morning. I think your mother came by and ordered your latte and took it home to you, didn't she?"

She spoke to him in a most friendly manner and he nodded silently in the affirmative, and then quickly corrected her.

"Oh . . . but she's not my mother," and felt the way he said it seemed harsh and added, "well she's kind of a mother, a mother away from home...sort of a mother."

The waitress smiled and spoke again.

"I know your order by heart you know; you have the same thing everyday. Your mother, or stepmother, or whoever the dear woman is, described you to me. I knew exactly what to give her."

Carter smiled inwardly, thinking of Martha's breakfast table. *It wasn't entirely witchcraft after all!* Then he thought, *perhaps two women conspiring to affect the lives of men may well be a working definition.*

Carter observed the pretty waitress didn't have an accent. As rich and diverse as accents were in New England, he sometimes longed to hear his own, that is, no accent at all.

Snapping back to the present, Carter proceeded to thank the waitress for her attentiveness. He did not call her by name, however, because he did not want her to know, for some ridiculous reason, that he had taken the time to figure it out.

She simply smiled, asked rather humorously—playfully even—what he would be having, and turned to prepare it without waiting for his dulled senses to respond.

≋≋≋

Despite the pleasure of imbibing in his latte, after a half-hour he became restless in his misery. He resigned to returning to the Purser's Quarters. Perhaps there he would resume reading *The Riddle of the Sands*.

Gathering his slicker and hat he looked one last time behind the counter. Claire busily cleaned her workstation, seemingly oblivious of his intended departure, apparently intent on closing. He lacked the energy and motivation to engage in further social discourse and headed toward the door.

"See you tomorrow morning, Carter."

It was a bright, unexpected farewell. The sound of her voice reinstated his well-being for an instant, and without thinking, he automatically replied.

"See you tomorrow, Claire."

He passed through the door of the coffee shop, nearly missing the first step down. After walking about a block, he suddenly realized they addressed each other by first names. As this dawned upon him, he felt a rush of exhilaration. He raised his downhearted footsteps an inch or two higher and strode towards the B&B.

As Carter approached the doorstep of the ornery cottage he stopped and gazed out into the harbor. He couldn't resist the urge to look in the direction of *Gael na Mara.* He lifted his field glasses and scanned the area.

Gael na Mara was gone!

Panning the entire entry of the harbor, it became clear she was nowhere in sight. Carter dashed across the cobblestone street and looked again—but the Irish cutter had disappeared! Did this mean he missed his opportunity to find out Patrick's attachment to the boat? Would he never know the link between the two?

He turned back toward the B&B and looked at the cottage as if he expected someone to emerge who could explain the mystery; explain where she went! No one did. He drew the glasses back to his eyes and quickly panned the harbor from the causeway going out onto the Neck to the harbor entrance. He could see no cutter.

After several minutes, Carter decided he should end this surveillance. *Gael na Mara* was gone. Maybe she would return. Why should he be so concerned? He suddenly felt exhausted and walked laboriously to his side of the B&B.

Stepping inside, he slowly climbed the creaking stairs to his loft. Without disrobing he fell back into the warmth of the crumpled quilt. Within seconds he drifted into the agitated sleep of a body invaded by a virus.

CHAPTER 14

GLOUCESTER MEN

Martha, the caregiver, warned Carter about his condition.

"I've got a bad feelin', Caahtah. I think you aahn't rid of the infection and it cahn't be ignored." Then she went a step further. "Heah son, take these," and she handed Carter a medicine bottle with no label. He paused, looking at it for a second.

"They aah antibiotics, Caahtah. It's okay, they'll help ya cleah up the infection. Take them three times a day and finish the entire bottle."

Martha's instructions were spoken like a doctor. He wondered where she got the pills and why there wasn't a label. He agreed, however, that his symptoms warranted treatment or he'd be sick for weeks instead of days.

Carter took the medicine and decided he would slip down to the boat shop to discuss his plans to sail to Gloucester with Patrick and Bones.

≋≋≋

"Aye, well theah ya be, laddie." Patrick was looking down over the rail of *Red Shoes*. "Bones and I was staahtin' ta think ya might o' cast off without us, theah, skippah."

Carter blew his nose, shrugged, and with polite jest said, "I've been cruising the North Sea on the *Dulcibella*, don't you know."

"Spyin' on Germans, eh, laddie," Patrick replied and Bones looked up too.

Carter then realized his friends knew the story. They probably knew it very well since the author, Erskine Childers, was a prominent figure in Northern Ireland.

"I cahn see the look in yer eye theah, laddie, yer ready to go to sea. Bones and I haav been waitin' fer the call to bring our sea chests on board. Neithah of us been to Gloucestah by boat since 'fore the Halloween Gale in '91. Now thaht was some foul weathah, eh, Bones," Patrick queried.

"Thaht was a bahd blow, Caahtah, a buggah of a bahd blow," Bones said. "People died, the bleedin' sea got away with murdah." With obvious antipathy, he tried to wash the sad fact away with a sip of hot coffee.

Carter thought for a moment, *1991 . . . the Halloween Gale*, then it came to him. "Wasn't that the Perfect Storm?" he asked.

"Nevah liked thaht name, skippah," Patrick replied sharply. He paused a moment, then continued in a kinder voice. "Now I'm not sayin' the whole affair with the movie and all was a bahd thin', don't ya know. I suppose some good come of it by makin' people undahstand what the cost of theah seafood dinners really is, of what men from Gloucestah been facin' since 1623, son."

"Not to mention theah bloomin' wives and little nippers," Bones added with a furrowed brow that suggested he knew how it felt to lose someone at sea. A deep utterance exhaled from the old man's lips and out beyond his pipe.

Carter already knew Patrick's tendency to be strongly affected by films, so he decided to ask a question.

"Patrick, was it the film or was it the storm on the film that bothered you most?"

"Laddie, I'll tell you what bothered me most, but first let me explain thaht Hollywood cahn't come close to portayin' the wind and the motion of a vessel in storms on the North Atlantic."

Bones added from the side, "Heah, heah."

"Now, skippah, what bothered me most was watchin' those window boards gettin' blown out of those fishermen's hands when they tried to covah the windows on the bridge o' the *Andrea Gail*, torn away by wind so strong and so wild you'd haav thought it was alive! Why you'd a thought it was the devil's hands come up from below, tearin' the last prospects of survival away from those lost souls!"

Patrick shuddered as he spoke. Carter began to discern the singular look that appeared in Patrick's eyes, the look Carter had seen before. It was passion, Irish passion perhaps, and he wasn't sure if it was good or bad. He swore at himself for bringing it on and tried to think of a way to pull his friend back.

Bones intervened.

"Pahtrick, my boy." Bones said, now using the familial reference. He spoke in a fatherly way with the reserve of a man who'd bore witness to more life than most would ever know. "The devil don't exist out theah in thaht bleedin' watah or thaht bleedin' wind! The devil's in people's minds and in theah hearts," the old man said. "Doin' wrong and bein' cruel—thaht's the devil playin' merry hell; people behavin' like Lord Muck, pushin' people 'round, tellin' 'em how ta live theah lives. Thaht's the devil's work."

Carter wondered if Bones was expressing his opinion of British rule in Northern Ireland. The peculiar thing was, it sounded as if there were a tinge of English accent in Bones' voice. From what he knew, Bones was not Irish, and with a name like Matheson, he might well be English. If he was, why would he be criticizing his countrymen?

"Those mates were just too bloody full o' themselves. They got carried away by desperate thoughts and they went down like ten thousand othahs lost from Gloucestah evah since the blightah's staarted pissin' on thaht rock and callin' it home."

Carter was taken by Bones solemnity, like someone who had seen so many lives pass before him he'd become hardened to the precariousness of life. The old seaman seemed less concerned with how people died than how people lived. Bones continued speaking, but steered a slightly different course.

"Now I can say those fisherman in the movie, keepin' in mind the movie chaps were only guessin' 'bout the goin's on from talkin' to othah fisherman, they should 'ave hahd them covah boards wrapped 'round 'em and ready to go the minute thaht damned storm kicked up!" he reproached. "Those mates needed to be bettah at bein' alive and they woulda been more likely to stay alive."

Patrick nodded in agreement and Carter watched as they spoke the debate of shore men—thinking and figuring what they would have done if they had been there. As they debated, the look Carter noticed in Patrick's eyes a few moments earlier faded away. His inclination to become passionate, "the Irish in him," could not so easily exist in the barrenness of rational thought.

The conversation returned to the shakedown and the three sailors unrolled a chart Patrick produced from a storage bin.

"Hand me them spline weights theah laddie and we'll anchor 'er down. Then reach ovah theah fer the shop light. Thaht's right, hang it ovah the chaaht so's we cahn see it good an cleah, skippah."

From another location Bones produced a divider, protractor, and parallel, placing them on the chart for ready use.

"A pencil theah laddie, a pencil from thaht drawrer."

Carter handed a pencil to Patrick and the work commenced. Considering the shakedown would only take them off shore for a long day, that is, unless something broke or the weather took a turn, the crew of *Maxine* agonized over every detail. Carter watched Bones, whose pipe was working vigorously in his teeth more than Carter had noticed before. He also observed how Bones and Patrick worked together, as if they were the left and right hand of some great sailing entity. Soon a course to Gloucester harbor was struck across the opened chart.

Carter's energy began to wane. He had a long walk back to the B&B and wanted to stop by the coffee shop to see if the roaster had left for the day. He hoped for the smile he was deprived of that morning.

Sensing Carter's fatigue, or perhaps his desire, Patrick spoke up. "Well now, theah ya be, laddie," he happily pronounced. "A course laid fer Gloucestah town just as pretty as a gul waitin' on shoah eh, skippah?"

"Thank you both," Carter replied.

"Thank you, Caahtah." answered Bones. "When aah ya figurin' on settin' sail?"

Carter thought for a moment.

"We'll shove off at 6:00 A.M. on Saturday, weather permitting," he announced with captain-like authority.

In the back of his mind he was concerned about shoving off this early in the season. He still suffered the remnant of his cold and very likely, an infection. Riskiest of all, he would be ignoring Martha's warning. Martha, as he had seen, was all-knowing. However, he reminded himself that they were going to be near shore most of the time. They'd only be on the water for a long day. With these factors given weight, he mentally affirmed his decision and began, instead, to think of Claire.

≋≋≋

It was 3:30 P.M. as he stepped into the Marblehead Roasting Company. Carter held great hopes the roaster, whom he assumed arrived early and left early, would be gone. He was and Carter's fatigue waned momentarily. He paced across to the counter where Claire was busily engaged in her late afternoon ritual of cleaning her workstation. With a certain reserve, so as not to exhibit his enthusiasm, he simply said, "Good afternoon, Claire."

Surprised, she turned, paused momentarily then allowed a tiny smile to escape her lips. An awkward silence subsisted as Carter realized it was odd to order the same thing late in the afternoon as he did in the morning. Claire spoke up.

"Afternoon is tea time, Carter. Would you like a cup of Chai tea?"

Carter never considered tea, Chai or otherwise, thinking java was the only proper drink taken in such establishments. He didn't think about it long.

"Sure."

Claire turned lightly on her feet and went to work.

Carter hadn't glanced at the *Boston Globe* that morning and noticed the local section lying open on a nearby table. He began reading it, but looked up when Claire spoke again.

"Would you like a shortbread cookie, Carter?"

Again without hesitation, or a particular liking for shortbread cookies, he jauntily said, "Yes, thank you, sounds great."

The lake sailor hoped his cold symptoms weren't causing him to look as unappealing as before. He wiped his nose while Claire turned away. He repositioned his long billed cap, checked his cheeks for a five o'clock shadow, and convinced himself he looked nearly normal.

Glancing down once again at the newspaper, a headline jumped out. "Engineer Suspected of IRA Plot Released to Parents' Custody".

> BOSTON (AP) – A judge yesterday ordered a 41-year-old engineer released to his parent's custody after his mother said she knew nothing of her son's alleged help in designing weapons for the IRA.
>
> Robert Clark Johnston was arrested last week, as were two other people, on federal charges he took part in an alleged IRA plot to design rockets that would shoot down British helicopters in Northern Ireland.

> In setting conditions for Johnston's release, U.S. Magistrate Richard Moore said the suspect used his expertise "to aid a group committed to violence." In that regard, the judge called him "extremely dangerous to other human beings on this planet."
>
> In releasing Johnston to his retired parents, Joyce and Henry, who lived in Rehoboth, Massachusetts, the judge ordered Johnson to stay in New England and to be accompanied by at least one parent at all times; in effect, under house arrest.
>
> In other developments, Patricia Ann Reedley, an electrical engineering student from Sunnyvale, Calif., who allegedly agreed to act as a courier between Johnston and Conrad Herald O'Conner, a citizen of the Republic of Ireland, was also arrested and being held in Pennsylvania. She is free on $10,000 bail after a hearing in San Francisco, and has been ordered to appear in Boston for trial.

Two things struck Carter. First, the article itself, the continuing saga of three would-be terrorists—a numeral and incident that began to haunt him; and second, the peculiar fact that the newspaper lay open to the page containing the article, and someone had made a small but discernable pen mark by it!

He looked around the room as if he would see whomever made the mark. A second later he realized the paper had probably been on the table since morning.

"Here you are, Carter."

"Oh, thank you."

His mind raced and adrenalin moved him beyond the low level of energy the virus imposed. He quickly added, "Can you join me, Claire?" Claire looked at him and did not speak. It was then he realized his proposition might not be appropriate, especially if the cranky Mr. O'Neil were to return.

Claire smiled and Carter's hopes rose. However, as he suspected, she declined. "My employer would certainly disapprove. He's a bit autocratic, in case you haven't noticed."

Claire's reply surprised Carter. Not that she turned him down; that might be expected. Rather, he was surprised by her use of the word "autocratic." Not the type of word spoken by coffee shop waitresses, even though it described Mr. O'Neil precisely. It was an uncommon word, although not completely arcane. It was the kind of word a political science professor would use.

"Well, perhaps you would join me for coffee sometime after hours, or would coffee be the right thing, considering you're around it all day long?"

Claire smiled once again and lingered at the counter in a way Carter thought he was reading too much into. She tilted her head in a feminine gesture and queried him directly, "Are you asking me out on a date, Carter?"

Her candor was surprising and delightful. He hadn't been thinking in those terms, at least consciously. He cast a quick glance at her ring finger and finding it bare replied, "Well...yes, yes I am."

The enigmatic waitress, or academic, or potential dinner date, crossed her arms in a show of mock defiance. She shifted her weight in a way that gave her the appearance of evaluating Carter like an art piece at an auction house in Boston. Her appraisal complete, she returned an answer Carter thought most encouraging.

"Well, you're right about coffee, Carter. What else might you have in mind?"

Carter thought hard. He suddenly realized he knew little of entertainment in the area. He didn't have a car, and at this thought he laughed to himself, thinking perhaps Martha could be their chaperone in her red Ford Escort.

"How about wine and cheese on *Maxine*?"

Claire looked puzzled at the reference to another woman, and he quickly added, "She's my sailboat. She's on a mooring in the harbor."

"Well," she said in a tone of mock jealously, "another woman in your life. Perhaps it would be imprudent of me to intervene," smiling at her purposeful jest.

"Think of *Maxine* not as a rival, but rather a floating seaside café where drink and conversation is her purpose for being." It was an awkward but earnest attempt at cleverness.

"Indeed, Carter, if that is the case, if I have no rivals, I would be interested in seeing if your allegorical yacht is as fine a café as you suggest."

Now Carter smiled. Then he thought of that word, allegorical. *Not exactly common either.*

Carter explained to Claire about the shakedown cruise to Gloucester. He asked if they could arrange a date upon his return, a request she enthusiastically granted and he enthusiastically affirmed.

≋≋≋

The euphoria Carter was experiencing eventually faded. Feeling exhausted once again, now from the prospect of female companionship, Carter initiated his departure. Rather than exit directly, however, he picked up the opened *Boston Globe* and tore out the article about the three accused zealots. He carefully included the mark someone made on the edge of the column.

When he finished, he turned to see Claire. She was watching him tear out the article. She wasn't smiling, then she did when his eyes met hers. He smiled back and nodded, then placed the article in his shirt pocket and left the coffee shop to walk the cobblestone lane back to the Purser's Quarters.

What will Martha think of Claire? He reminded himself that they already met and conspired to bring him comfort. Then he thought about whether Patrick knew Claire, or knew her well. He remembered the details of his first visit to the Marblehead Roasting

Company and Patrick's behavior as he confronted the oppressive Mr. O'Neil. He recalled Patrick speaking purposefully to Claire after the incident. He could only guess what Patrick might have said. Whatever it was caused a striking change in her demeanor.

Carter's thoughts shifted to the newspaper article. He considered whether the threesome in the *Globe* were freedom fighters or naïve puppets in a plan that would result in death and sorrow for dozens who may or may not be "legitimate" targets of war.

Was British occupation analogous to the oppressive Mr. O'Neil, he wondered. *Is oppression and the legitimacy of revolt a matter of scale, timing or place—in this case Ireland? Could terrorism be justified under circumstances of cruel oppression?*

The B&B came into sight and Carter paused his internal query to cast a quick glimpse across the harbor. *Gael na Mara*, his purpose in looking, could not be seen.

Returning to the question of justifiable terrorism, he decided terror could never be justified. Still, when he saw the look on Claire's face that morning at the café, and Patrick's readiness to fight, he couldn't help but think oppressed people had a right to fight back and fight back hard.

When Carter finally lumbered up the creaking steps to his loft, he concluded that wanton murder, the killing of innocents, can not be justified under any circumstance. With this line of thinking resolved, he felt the strain of the day. He dropped into his armchair and dozed off. When he awoke an hour later a dinner of filet of sole in lemon sauce, steamed asparagus, and rice pudding awaited him. Milk mixed with coffee syrup stood in a glass along side. He thought about the fact that he never heard the good witch, ascend or descend the creaky stairway.

CHAPTER 15

THE BLUE GREATNESS

At breakfast, Martha sat quietly, listening as Carter outlined the cruise he planned for *Maxine*. When she occasioned a comment, she offered advice in the way of provisions, clothing, and first aid supplies—all things familiar to her. Carter detected from her expert suggestions that Martha had been on cruises more than once, although she had never said so. Then her demeanor changed slightly.

"Caahtah, my son, I'm worried about thaht cold."

"I'm feeling much better, Martha, I'm pretty sure it's clearing up."

He wasn't certain of that at all and suspected he couldn't actually hide things from an all-knowing witch.

"I cahn see your doin' a little bettah, Caahtah, but I'm believin' a few more days ashore would cleah your lungs of thaht infection and you'd enjoy yourself all the more, don't ya know," she offered. She paused to allow him to consider her words. After a few silent moments passed she continued.

"You'll not think I'm just a curmudgeon, Caahtah, if I say I've got a bit of a feelin' inside me. I've hahd this kind of feelin' before.

It's like I've always been able to know when my charges were in need of cayah, when they were sick, sometimes afore even they knew it."

Carter thought of Miread's quilt and the medicine mysteriously appearing by his bedside, coincidental with the arrival of his cold symptoms. He remained silent a moment longer, considering the idea of a postponement, knowing Martha's proclivity for seeing things. *She makes a point. I should heed her warnings...at least make sure I'm feeling good before shoving off.*

Then Carter's thoughts swung, picturing Claire in his mind's eye. It dawned on him how much he wanted the young waitress aboard *Maxine*, to speak once again with a female who spoke with no accent. Then Carter thought of Patrick and Bones and their excitement the day before—the joy in their eyes as they charted *Maxine's* course. He didn't want to let them down.

"I'm not sure I mentioned that I have a good crew, Martha. Did I tell you Patrick and Bones will be on board; you know Bones don't you?" He wondered if he ever had seen them together and believed he had not.

Martha suddenly went white. Her reaction wasn't what Carter expected. She seemed genuinely shocked and her coffee cup quivered at her lips. She worked to contain her expression and within a second she steadied the cup, her little finger protruding in proper style, as if to help steady her will. She lowered the cup and spoke.

"Caahtah," she said hesitantly, "I assumed you would be sailin' with Pahtrick. The way things haav been goin' I could see you and he were becomin' mates. I've been figurin' theah was no way Patrick would miss the chance to get on board your yacht," she went on. "The man has a way of findin' himself a berth on boats like a tick finds its way on a quahogger's dog. But Bones, Caahtah," she implored. "He's ninety yeahs old. He shouldn't be headed off shoah in a sailin' yacht, why...why he's too old!"

Carter saw a glassy-eyed look of alarm emerge from behind her spectacles. She paused only a second and proclaimed, "He should be lickin' ice cream and playin' cribbage down at Tuckah's Wharf like the rest of thaht bunch thaht tags along behind Pahtrick."

Martha's directness surprised Carter. It took a second for him to realize, again, he was in the land of directness, a place where people spoke their minds. However, he was concerned, too. He had been reluctant to allow Bones to crew. He had given the possibility a lot of thought starting with the fact that Bones would actually be more like a passenger than a crewman. In addition, the cruise was nothing more than a long day of sailing up to Gloucester. To a lesser extent, Carter relied on Patrick's judgment that there wouldn't be many more cruises for the old sailorman. He sensed Patrick's fear that Bones might not see the launching of *Red Shoes*.

"Martha, I guess you do know Bones...do you know him well?" Carter asked.

"Yes, Caahtah, yes—I know Bones Matheson." She paused, took a short breath and continued. "He's been one of my charges, too, so to speak." Martha said. "Even though I worked for the heiress on the Neck, theah haav been many othahs, thaht is, people 'round town thaht I kept an eye out for, to help 'em along when the weathah turned against them," she explained.

"And Bones is one of those?"

"Yes," Martha replied curtly. She seemed about to clam up. There was a peculiar tone in her voice and Carter wondered how far to take the discussion. He pressed a little further.

"Patrick says he'll do fine and I've seen him show a lot of determination..."

"Caahtah," she stopped him. "I'm sure you aah a fine skippah...and I'm sure *Maxine* is a seaworthy yacht," she said emphatically, the coarseness of her voice coming through, "but Bones, Caahtah, Bones is an old man, a very old man. Cahn't you see thaht, don't you know what thaht means?"

Carter looked down at his coffee. He contemplated the situation for a moment he spoke again.

"I understand what you're saying, Martha, but may I ask a few more questions?"

Martha breathed in a deep breath, released the tight grip on her coffee cup, sat upright in her chair, and nodded.

"A moment ago I asked if you knew Bones and you explained you did by way of telling me he had been, or still is, one of your charges."

"Yes, Caahtah, thaht's correct."

"Do you still see him on a regular basis?"

"Well...yes and no, Caahtah." Her reply was hesitant, as if perhaps she kept an eye on Bones, but Bones didn't believe he needed being kept after. Carter sensed a spirit of independence in Bones, but on the other hand, New Englanders as a whole were staunchly independent.

"Do you think, and I'm asking your professional opinion now, Martha, because I share your concern and I want to do the right thing. Do you think Bones still has the capacity to make decisions? Is he becoming senile or given to bad judgments?"

Martha paused, cognizant of the purpose and direction of Carter's inquiry.

"Well, no, Caahtah. Bones is as cleah-headed as any one of us, probably more thahn most," she said in a tone suggesting she realized the rationale of the question. Her demeanor indicated she also realized that by admitting the truth it made her appeal less compelling.

Martha looked torn. "Caahtah, if Bones knew for an instant thaht I was tryin' to keep him on land he'd haav a fit! I'm just worried Caahtah, thaht's all. What more cahn I say? He's been 'round heah so long. He's defied thaht damnable sea. He's survived where so many haven't and I just want him to remain dry and safe and not be lost..."

Her bottom lip quivered. Carter remembered Miread and realized Martha must be thinking of her, too.

Martha began to cry quietly and he placed his arm around her and drew her close. He felt her frail shoulders, her head against his chest and her sorrow reaching through him in the warmth of her being. Carter held his adopted mother, his special friend, in his arms.

"Martha, I'm going to give this more thought. I'll speak with Patrick and Bones and if you wish, I'll explain your feelings."

"No, Caahtah, you mustn't do thaht. It wouldn't be right." Martha implored, looking up at him. "There's no stoppin' thaht man from goin' to sea. Not *thaht* old man. 'Tis I who must remain on the hard...," and Carter believed she spoke to herself, though the words issued towards him. Again, to herself she said, "I'll keep watch. Everythin' will be all right." Then, looking again up at Carter, the matron of the Purser's Quarters spoke clearly, "Perhaps my feelin's got the bettah of me, Caahtah. Please don't say anythin' to Bones."

With this return of strength and resolve, Carter released his comforting arms from around Martha's shoulders. She looked back into his eyes and spoke.

"One last thing, Caahtah. The fig seedlin's came yestahday. Cahn we plant them afore ya sail to Gloucestah? I think I'd feel a lot bettah if we did thaht, Caahtah," the fragile woman implored.

With a nod in the affirmative, and the belief that complying with Madame Russalka would be a good thing, Carter took his leave. He walked to the landing of the stairs. As he ascended, he thought he heard Martha begin to cry again, very softly, a constrained whimper. He paused, wondering if he should attempt once again to console her. He decided it was inappropriate to interfere or to try and fix the unfixable.

≋≋≋

By 7:30 A.M. Carter set out down Front Street as sailors had for hundreds of years. His excitement grew with each step, the sea air stinging his still tender lungs. For Carter Phillips, an entire winter on land was about to dissolve away into the blue wavelets upon the blue waves upon the blue greatness of the sea.

Understanding that Patrick and Bones loved sailing as much as he, it pleased Carter to know he would take them out on the water for the first time this season, to feel the wind and smell the sea air.

Despite the dimming recollection of Martha's apprehension, he knew they would treasure time aboard *Maxine*.

Carter revisited Martha's feelings. She was right to worry about Bones, and Patrick, too. They were old men, well past their prime if measured by the coarseness of their skin or the imperfection of their eyesight. However, in the bright sunlight of morning, the day rising all around, the thought of mishap or tragedy gave way to a rush of excitement he could barely contain.

Carter opened the door of the Marblehead Roasting Company and smelled the luscious aroma of coffee roasting inside. Ironically, this meant the inimical Mr. O'Neil was tending the roasting machine. Moving to the counter, he received a cursory, restrained greeting from Claire. She seemed a different person in the proximity of the oppressive Mr. O'Neil. *Why did she put up with him.* Then he thought about jobs, and money and the things people need to do.

Departing the coffee house disappointed, he arrived at the boat shop and greeted his crew. A happy crew they were, ready to ship their sea chests and load provisions. Looking more like bright-eyed sea scouts than crusty old salts, Patrick and Bones went to work on a list Carter outlined on a scrap of paper. When he drew the list from his pocket, he remembered the newspaper article about the suspected terrorists he tore out the afternoon before. He reminded himself to tape it into his log on board *Maxine*.

By 3:00 P.M. all manner of provisions, spare gear, and positive intentions were packed in a borrowed rusty pick-up truck parked behind the wooden gate inside the yard next to *Red Shoes*. The great schooner stood watch over the proceedings like the afterguard on a J-Boat, keenly observing every move, watching for correctness and efficiency, all knowing in the effort at hand. Her day was not long off and just as if she were a living, breathing being, Carter looked directly at her and nodded his thanks for her forbearance. He thanked her profusely for granting the use of her builders to help shakedown his beautiful *Maxine*.

With all items checked off his list, he bade good-bye to his shipmates, reminding them, as if he needed to, to be at Tucker's Wharf with the truckload of provisions at 5:00 A.M. and expect to shove off by 6:00. With mock authority, Carter proclaimed, "Anyone not on board and at their station when we let slip the mooring pennant will be left ashore!"

With this edict playfully issued he turned, left the boat yard and began his quest for Chai tea.

≋≋≋

Upon full enjoyment of his tea and Claire's alluring smile, Carter told her he would call again upon his return.

"Bon voyage."

He savored the sound of her voice.

Departing, Carter buoyantly sauntered toward the B&B but by the time he arrived his chest was sore and congested again. He felt uneasy and fatigue broke through his demeanor as he greeted Martha. Attempting to cover his condition, he insisted they plant the three fig trees.

Later, as dusk settled over the village, Carter and Martha stood together outside the B&B in the cool evening air, exhausted from a busy day. Weak of breath in his lungs, he leaned against a shovel and looked across the freshly turned soil at the three fig trees planted neatly in a row. He regarded the broadly grinning face of Martha as she wiped her dirty hands on an apron tied over her ankle length dress. They looked at each other and smiled. Good fortune would prevail, presuming that is why Madame Russalka gave the directive.

As Carter stretched and rubbed his lower back, now stiff from digging, he took in a quantity of sea air. Leaning back as he stretched, his eyes rose into the evening sky. He looked toward the north over the shake-shingled roof of the B&B. A few dim stars hid amongst leafless tree branches moving lightly in the breeze.

Something strange caught his eye.

One of the shadowy stems stood erect amongst the other moving branches. He looked again, straining in the dim light. It was perfectly straight and it wasn't a stem. It was an antenna! He looked down and over toward Martha. She had already stepped away and was entering the front door. She disappeared before he could ask any questions. He wanted to know why a single-sideband radio antenna stood swaying on the roof of the Purser's Quarters. He gazed back up and took note that it was a make-shift arrangement, a simple fiberglass whip, same as the one found on *Maxine.* The type of antenna anyone could put up and take down in a hurry.

Did Gael na Mara have a single-sideband radio on board, he wondered? He thought of his nighttime rendezvous with the North Sea cutter and couldn't recall. Now she was gone from the harbor.

This wasn't the only question gnawing at him, however. He wanted to know where *Gael na Mara* came from, who the cigar man was, why the rifle-toting guard was on board and most of all, would she be returning?

Something was going on with that boat and its crew, and Patrick too, Carter concluded. He didn't want to believe such a strange idea. Maybe it was nothing. Then again, maybe it was, maybe it was something he wasn't supposed to be noticing. Something they thought he wouldn't notice, they being Patrick, the young Irishmen, the cigar man and, and who else...Bones and Martha? Were they part of the mystery, too?

Carter undressed and slipped beneath Miread's quilt. The aroma of cedar had a calming effect. Still, he began to think about the crew of the *Dulcibella* and the way they discovered the riddle of the sands. He contemplated the danger their curiosity had caused them. He believed he should try and contain his own. It was essential that he rest well tonight. He wasn't well and both he and Martha knew it.

CHAPTER 16

UNDER WAY

In spite of his fatigue and the absolute necessity for rest, the excitement of the day kept Carter from falling directly to sleep. The cool temperature of the leaky boarding house bothered his chest, making it hard for him to breathe. He drank eucalyptus tea prescribed by Martha, then tossed about restlessly under Miread's quilt.

Around midnight, the hapless sailor sat up and listened to NOAA weather radio—again. He became anxious about the report, as he had previously. The wind howled outside his loft. He hoped it would blow on through the region and expend its energy. A shakedown is best commenced in light air.

For the last of couple days, he watched as the low-pressure system that exacerbated his cold moved offshore. A high-pressure system over the Great Lakes and Canada dropped toward the east coast. Being unfamiliar with the effects of the coastline, Carter was uncertain how the system would behave when it arrived. The system could be clear and pleasant if it picked up southerly air, or conversely, it would be blistering cold and windy if the northern air pressed down from Canada. This early in the spring, it seemed to Carter, it could go either way.

He dozed anxiously through the night, never entering deep sleep. The fact that he knew this made him more anxious, causing more stress, causing further loss of sleep. Eventually, he rolled over in his bed and stared at the glaring red numerals. They read 4:00 A.M. It became apparent he might as well get up.

≋≋≋

Carter quickly gathered together the last items he needed, walked quietly down the creaking stairs, and stepped into Martha's darkened kitchen. An unsolicited surprise awaited him—breakfast thoughtfully prepared by Martha. He needed only to heat water and add it to instant cereal and instant coffee already placed in their bowl and cup. Next to the setting was an old-fashioned rubber water bottle. On it was a note that read—

> Carter, I'm thinking you haven't one of these on board Maxine. You never know when you might need one, especially with that congestion in your chest. Anyway, it's cold offshore, so please, be careful.

The note was signed "M," and he noticed her handwriting was coarse, like her voice.

Carter took up the pencil that lay next to the note and added, "Will do, thanks, and see you in four days. P.S. Don't worry about those old sailormen, not much can happen between here and there."

≋≋≋

This did not mollify Martha when she read the note. She knew better, she'd been offshore more than the young Lake sailor could have known or imagined, though she appreciated his good intentions.

≋≋≋

The wind had barely abated during the dawn hours and a cold, chilly gust greeted Carter as he stepped from the side door of the Purser's Quarters. He shivered slightly and thought about what he was going to do to stay warm once under way.

He looked out over the waiting harbor and saw masts gently swaying in the breeze. Carter could distinguish dark blue ripples in the water crossing the harbor as gusts dropped down from the hills along the village. One thing he learned on the Big Lake: sailing was a constant heat loss scenario in anything but the balmiest weather.

Patrick, Bones, and the borrowed pick-up truck stood waiting at Tucker's Wharf when Carter arrived. He took one look at them and noted with envy that they likely slept fine all night. With the energy and innocence of youth, the aged sailors moved their provisions and gear down onto the float. The tide was low and the smell of pilings coated with tar and sea-life filled their lungs.

As Carter hoisted gear aboard the inflatable dinghy, he took note of the raggedy old fiddle case Patrick carefully swung over his shoulder. It sported a braided chord laced with wood beads and tiny brass bells. It surprised Carter that Patrick hadn't mentioned being a fiddler. Patrick must have noticed him staring at the case and said, "A little something for the foremast jacks, laddie. Keeps 'em on theah toes and workin' hard fer not much pay, skippah." Laughing gleefully, Patrick slung the fiddle case down to Carter along with his weathered canvas sea bag.

This should be interesting. Smiling inwardly he would reveal, at some later point, the guitar he kept stowed in a pipe berth aft the captain's quarters of *Maxine.*

With the dinghy engine sputtering in the cold dark morning and all gear carefully loaded, the crew of Marblehead salts and a skipper from the Big Lake motored out to the waiting *Maxine.*

Carter glanced around the harbor again, thinking for a second that he might see *Gael na Mara.* He did not. He did have plenty to think about, however, so he set the enigmatic vessel free from its mooring in his mind and imagined it sailing away, perhaps never to be seen again.

Carter brought the dinghy along side *Maxine's* starboard rail and climbed aboard to release the life-line gate. Patrick and Bones, with the diffidence of topmast hands, hoisted the gear aboard while Carter moved it quickly aft to the open cockpit and out of the way.

Once the gear was aboard, Patrick leaped on deck as if he had been sprung from a medieval catapult. Bones, however, presented a different problem. Even on level ground, Bones' knees were hardly able to sustain his bulk. There was no way he could simply climb aboard from the rocking dinghy tied alongside *Maxine*. Furthermore, there was no way Carter and Patrick were going to merely grip his wrists and pull him aboard. That would be neither safe nor dignified.

Carter motioned to Patrick who immediately divined Carter's plan. Within minutes, a boson's chair hung rigged on the main halyard. Then, just as he had done a hundred times, Bones buckled himself in.

Carter operated the winch. Patrick tailed the line. They took up the slack and watched as Bones' Greek fisherman's cap slowly rose above the rail. Moments later they swung him onto the deck and the shakedown officially began.

≋≋≋

Patrick had already been on board and knew where things were. He knew how to access the engine compartment, operate the single-sideband radio, locate the first-aid kit and other emergency gear, including the flare gun.

Bones climbed below on the companionway ladder, despite his knees. Getting back up would be a chore, but he'd be able to pull himself up using the teak hand-holds positioned on each side of the hatch.

After a tour below and a look at the chart, Bones headed topside. Patrick reached automatically for the ship's log that lay on the chart table. Without thinking about propriety, he opened it.

Carter was watching to see that Bones ascended the ladder safely and then turned to discover Patrick reading from the open log. Carter glanced at the page Patrick was reading. The page held the article about O'Hanlon, the captain of the gun running freighter! Touching his chest Carter remembered another article in his shirt pocket that needed to be taped in the log, the one with the mysterious pencil mark that someone else placed on it.

Patrick looked up at Carter with vexed eyes. "I...I just opened it automatically, laddie., Been in the habit so long, skippah... ."

Patrick stopped speaking, but didn't stop looking at Carter. Carter paused awkwardly, then interjected, "Right, no problem. I'll take over and make our departing entry. If you'll go topside and make ready the main halyard and jib sheets, I'll pass the number three jib through the forward hatch. It's breezy—so we'll start out small and work our way up."

Patrick looked again at the page lying open, but said nothing. Carter formed the impression he was having a very difficult time not pointing out the unusual practice of taping newspaper articles in a ship's log—particularly articles about Irish gun runners.

Carter didn't respond.

Finally, Patrick spoke again.

"Thaht's a strange thin' to find in a log book, laddie." He flipped a few more pages and saw other recent inclusions, all about Irish terrorists.

"I keep all sorts of entries in my log," Carter replied. "I know it's not a proper practice, but *Maxine* is a pleasure craft and the log is my diary, a personal scrap book."

Patrick got Carter's message that the log was none of his business. "Right you aah, skippah, I overstepped my bounds and wasn't thinkin' anythin' but the way I use ta work on the bridge of the ol' freightahs." He clamped the book closed. "Heah you go, skippah, take yer log and I'll tell ya 'bout O'Hanlon when I sailed with 'im in '68 on a route from Belfast, 'round Gibraltar. Of course, he wasn't a captain baack then. I'll get topside, skippah and we'll get this pleasure craaft undah way."

Carter sat at his chart table and reopened the log as Patrick climbed the companionway ladder. Half way up Patrick stopped.

"Caahtah, you should know... O'Hanlon's not a bahd man. He was doin' what he thought right. I know it reads bahdly, the way it t'was reported theah, but, laddie, the killin' thaht's been goin' on ovah theah fer centuries now—theah's reasons, don't ya know. Ya need ta realize theah's armed British soldiers and Unionist gangs o' murdahers everywheah ya go. Catholics and the true sons of Ireland need t' protect themselves, skippah."

Carter didn't look up immediately. For a second he didn't know what to say. He hoped Patrick wouldn't detect his shock at the remark. Nevertheless, as the captain of *Maxine*, he felt compelled to speak and looked up from his work.

"We can discuss this once we're underway. I'd be interested in your viewpoint. I've many questions about Ireland; we're taught so little of it back home." He looked back at his log and placing his pen on the paper to write he signaled a discomfited end to the exchange.

Upon completing his log entry, Carter joined his crew topside. He asked Bones to man the helm. The windy air swirled through the chilly cockpit. He looked around and studied the clear pre-dawn sky. It was breezier than he wanted, but not enough to delay shoving off.

Patrick was forward, hanking on the number three jib, the mainsail all ready to hoist. Seagulls darted about and the cold air of the salt-water harbor was burning Carter's sensitive chest. He shuddered as the coolness penetrated his jacket, shaking off the chill as best he could.

He started the diesel engine and leaned overboard to check that cooling water was exhausting out the stern. The bitter metallic smell greeted his nose and caused him to sneeze with such force it hurt. He stood upright to recover, wiping his nose with a handkerchief. He noticed a tiny speck of blood and thought again of Martha's warning. Adjusting the idle speed he looked up and saw Patrick standing next to him. Carter wondered if he had by chance noticed the blood.

"Gonna be breezy out theah, skippah." Patrick looked out in the direction of Children's Island. "Wind's comin' down from the north—gonna be a cold one and if it don't baack ta the west we're gonna be beatin' a fair amount."

Carter nodded in agreement, the assessment being entirely correct. *Not exactly what I would have asked for, but better than windless fog and rain. Damned well better than a nor'easter.*

The three sailors stepped aft and Carter briefed them on his procedures for getting *Maxine* underway. The old salts could have written a book about such matters, had they been men of letters, but they listened intently as proper crew would.

Bones remained at the helm and Patrick went forward to let slip the mooring pennant. Carter, after sending the dinghy aft on its painter, took up position on the starboard quarterdeck where he could see *Maxine's* entire length. On his command, Patrick released the pennant and sent it overboard. Without a word, Bones engaged the gear box and eased the accelerator forward.

Carter's bridled excitement escaped. He suddenly felt like the master of the world as he announced their departure with three sharp blasts of an air horn Bones handed up to him.

Maxine rushed forward from her winter idleness. Carter glanced back at Bones, his pipe jammed in his mouth at a slightly protuberant angle, his bushy eyebrows blowing in the cold morning wind. He looked forward to see Patrick grinning beneath his red mustache. His pony tail escaped from under his long-billed cap and danced about in the crisp wind. He took up position at the mainmast halyard. There was no reason to hoist sails until they were out of Marblehead Harbor. Carter decided to take her out past Children's Island before he raised the main. This would give the engine a little sea time.

Patrick apparently knew the operating plan without explanation, having already arrived at the same conclusion. Bones appeared utterly at home at the helm. Patrick stood patiently, looking forward alongside the mast. He made hand signals to Bones as he spotted lobster pots and Bones, erect on his spindly legs, made minor course changes. For once, Carter noticed smoke coming from Bones' pipe, his white teeth gripping the stem. Carter chuckled at the picturesque sight.

Carter studied the entire scene. He looked repeatedly over *Maxine's* standing rigging as the cold north wind blew. He pondered conditions outside Marblehead Harbor and thought about the fact that they'd have to take *Maxine* farther offshore than he intended or would prefer. In fact, initially, she would head straight for Ireland.

That's no direction for a shakedown. It would be better to hug the shore just in case something did go wrong.

He looked at his crew again and saw no concern whatsoever in their comportment. They were ready for anything and they faced the sea with ease and excitement.

Ten minutes later *Maxine* emerged from Marblehead Harbor, passing guest moorings where *Gael na Mara* once swung on her pennant. The green can at the harbor entrance fell away to starboard. Carter watched it move aft and looked up to see the lighthouse on the end of Marblehead Neck.

Bones changed course a couple points and increased *Maxine's* engine revolutions. The wind blew against her port bow and Carter could see his own breath in the bright light of sunrise. The sky was orange on the northeast horizon and a sprinkling of small fishing boats moved out towards their grounds. Children's Island lay dead ahead.

Carter thought about hoisting sails, but decided to wait until *Maxine* crawled farther out near Children's Channel where there would be more sea room. He was being overly cautious, but wasn't that the point of a shakedown? If something did go wrong, or, if several things went wrong in a row, which is how things usually go wrong on a boat, he'd be blown up against the Neck in minutes.

The wind speed indicator vacillated between fourteen and sixteen knots, occasionally gusting to twenty. Figuring in the wind chill factor and his lack of sleep, he felt apprehensive, concerned about Martha's warnings. He couldn't remember taking her prescribed antibiotics at breakfast.

As soon as we are sailing, I'll go below and make a pot of tea.

He looked at his crew. They stood impervious to the cold and it annoyed Carter that it bothered him so. He resolved to buck up and ignore it.

≋≋≋

Within twenty-five yards of the bell, Bones pushed the tiller to starboard and *Maxine* turned northward. After another hundred yards, he rounded directly up into the wind. Carter gave a nod and Patrick released the mainsail tie downs. The great white cloth sprawled forth onto the deck. Patrick glanced at Carter, main halyard in hand. Carter nodded and Patrick began pulling the huge sail skyward.

When the sail reached three quarters up the carved wooden track, he pulled a winch handle from a pocket mounted on the mast. He began cranking with steady round strokes. The white cloud of fabric stretched open like the wing of a great butterfly emerging from its chrysalis.

When it completed its travel to the top of the towering mast, Patrick cleated-off the halyard and paused to inspect his work. The wooden sloop crept forward, still under engine power. Bones kept her balanced near the wind, releasing, then bringing up the sheet, adjusting it attentively while gently manipulating the tiller.

Patrick was forward in an instant and released the tie-downs holding the jib. Carter picked up the starboard jib sheet and brought it around the bronze cockpit winch. He took up the slack, waiting for Patrick to step back up onto the cabin trunk.

This time, positioning on the port side of the mast, Patrick began yanking down vigorously on the halyard and the jib screamed aloft. It flailed wildly until Carter took up additional slack. Bones allowed her to fall off the wind a half point again and the jib swung clear on the starboard side, allowing Carter to bring up on the sheet.

Carter looked forward and aloft and made a fine adjustment on the winch. Patrick looked aft from the bow pulpit where he slung himself after cleating-off the jib halyard, watching Carter's and *Maxine's* every move. Carter, in turn, cleated-off the sheet after he trimmed the jib sail.

With this done, he glanced back at Bones who eased the tension on both the tiller and the main sheet. The great vessel, driven by the hard, cold air, heeled over a couple degrees and plowed forward. Bones backed her engine down to idle, disengaged the gear box and pulled out on the engine stop. The iron ginny fell silent. Carter nodded with approval.

Wind through the rigging, though cold and blowing gustily, sang its timeless song. Water gurgled at *Maxine's* waterline. The dawn sky was crystalline orange-blue and Carter's beautiful craft sailed once again, ending her wintering over.

CHAPTER 17

THE MONARCH

In the ready room of the United States Coast Guard Cutter *Monarch*, lying 15 nautical miles north-northeast of Cape Ann, a computer screen cast a blue iridescent glow over a youthful face. An encoded message flashed across the monitor. The text read:

"Begin message . . . GNM transmitted Red Haired Boy its position at 22:00 GMT, 22 MAR 98...lying in Manchester Harbor, triple explicative exchanged...GNM awaiting instructions...Red Haired Boy and Tillerman made contact while Tillerman was on shore...Red Haired Boy and Figurehead have departed watch zone 11:00 GMT, 23 MAR 98...standing by...End Message."

BOOK II

MASSACHUSETTS BAY

T. S. ELIOT
c. 1885-1965

Between the idea
And the reality
Between the motion
And the act
Falls the shadow

The Hollow Man - 1925

CHAPTER 18

THE ABSENCE OF HEAT

Bones fell off the north wind a point allowing *Maxine* to reach without strain. Carter considered taking in a reef on the mainsail. After several minutes on this point the wind speed indicator leveled around fourteen knots and the gusting subsided. *Maxine* began loping over the water. Her bow penetrated the blue - green sea and then lifted several feet before dropping again. She gained a cadenced stride. The entire crew began to feel her rhythm.

The feel of *Maxine* riding the sea and the cold, dense wind thrusting against her snow white sails pleased Carter immensely. He walked forward on the high side of the slanting deck and inspected rigging and fittings. The wind blew against his back and sucked heat from around his exposed neck. He could still see his breath. Despite the cold, he took his time and checked off items to monitor like an inspector on an automobile assembly line back home in Michigan. Everything looked perfect in the bright morning sun.

His inspection complete, Carter stepped back into the cockpit and indicated to Bones that he wished to take the helm to see how she felt. On a reach, she could balance out and sail herself. If anything, she would have a weather helm, an inclination to turn into the wind rather than away from it, if the wheel was left untended.

Bones nodded at the skipper's request and surrendered the carved wooden tiller. He then slid across the cockpit bench, forward on the high side, taking up a position against the cabin trunk to break the wind.

Carter called out his heading and speed so that Patrick, who had gone below, could plot it on the chart.

On a reach the shore would recede quickly, yet they would gain little way towards Gloucester. For the time being, however, this point of sail served the primary purpose of the shakedown. Carter cared only about pulling into the fishing port before nightfall.

The shoreline became a thin line on the western horizon while Carter remained on the reach. He contemplated sailing her higher into the wind, thereby heading more directly toward Gloucester. Instead, he deliberately held back to allow *Maxine's* planking time to work. He wanted her caulking to swell so it would close her seams.

The crew of the Fife sloop began to ease into the unique state of mind that only sailors know. It was hypnotic, accentuated only by the unending rising and falling of the vessel's bow. Carter concluded it could only be more perfect if another fifteen degrees of heat burned down from the sun.

The stretch between Marblehead Harbor and Gloucester Harbor is about eighteen nautical miles. Carter estimated that they would be covering more—like forty, or perhaps fifty miles over ground before the day ended. At an average speed of five knots, it looked like eight or ten hours under way before they'd tie up in Gloucester.

On a shakedown cruise in blowing cold, the sun low on the horizon, this amount of time took on a different, less desirable dimension. Carter loathed to admit it, but the cold wind bothered his lungs. He remembered Martha's prophetic plea to delay the trip a few more days.

Continuing his evaluation of *Maxine's* condition, he asked Patrick to take the helm while he dropped below. There he listened to the sound of *Maxine's* bilge pump, satisfied it was not working too hard. Still, he remained anxious to inspect her bilge so he lifted a couple sections of cabin sole. He needed to be certain the strain wasn't opening her planking. Eventually, when they came about, he'd conduct the same inspection on the other tack.

Upon close inspection of the bilge, Carter could see small rivulets of water running aft through limber holes in the floors. He judged it typical and unavoidable, at least until she soaked in the water for a month. She'd eventually swell up tight and the battery operated bilge pump would only occasionally kick on.

With this settled, he stood up from the bilge, feeling unexpectedly dizzy. The sensation struck him as not entirely foreign; Carter knew it to happen when one's head is rotated completely beyond its normal position. This was especially true in the motion of a heaving sea. However, when Carter steadied, a chill went through him and the dizziness remained, making him feel very odd—overtly disoriented. It was as if he wasn't inside himself any longer. The feeling stuck to him when he tried to shake it off and he didn't like the sensation. It wasn't right; it shouldn't persist.

In addition to inspecting the bilge, he intended to heat up water for tea. As he bent over to open a compartment in the galley, dizziness overwhelmed him again. He reached for the tea pot. This time it came with nausea.

He immediately closed and latched the compartment.

Heading up top he breathed in gulps of fresh air, straining to regain his ordinary mind. Surely this was just a momentary event; it would pass as soon as he stood erect for a few minutes. He decided to relieve Patrick at the helm and send him below to heat the water.

As Carter climbed the companionway ladder, another rush of strangeness raced through him; this time in an undeniable fury of illness he could barely contain. This wasn't right although he couldn't say why. He couldn't figure it out and became obsessed trying. It was like nothing else on earth mattered. He relentlessly searched the corners of his mind for a reason, an explanation for the dreadful malaise.

Carter's mind swirled with inner thoughts, mixed with dizziness and nausea, far more chaotic than anything he had experienced before. It could hardly be called thinking; it was more like random firings of neurons that set off images and ideas falling short of logic.

In an instant the imperative of vomiting arose from the cacophony of distorted thoughts. Carter broke into the open cockpit and nearly threw himself to the rail to let loose his breakfast; but he didn't. A visage of his sanity apparently remained, allowing him to control his outward being. It was like play acting, behaving physically as if nothing were awry. He had to maintain control. Throwing up was not an option and the fear of doing so was horribly strange. In all the years he sailed, he never once vomited, never experienced anything more than the lethargic, unpleasant "mal de mere" of motion sickness.

Turning back towards the cockpit, he noticed Bones looking into the northwest. Patrick stared toward the southeast, eyeing a trawler steaming southward, almost out of sight. Carter could register these things in his mind, but the chaos that became his thoughts raged on, directionless expressions of sickness and desperation.

Carter determined with some effort that Bones and Patrick weren't taking notice of him; perhaps not seeing or recognizing his inexplicable episode. He resolved to act normal even if he didn't feel normal. Despite the urge to scream for order, project his bile to the sea, or clamber for the high ground of ordinary existence, he was not going to reveal his horrid malady to the old salts. It was pride, stubborn pride.

Between worsening feelings of impending doom and freezing chills that doused his inner heat, Carter's pride held fast. He couldn't reveal his uncontrollable situation to his crew. Not this crew. Not Bones and Patrick, the builders of *Red Shoes*, sailors of freighters.

Amidst the ringing in his ears and his convulsing stomach, tiny, barely discernable voices screamed reproaches. They chided him for hiding his situation from his mates; it would only make things worse!

The voices receded and his pride held its position. To a degree, it gave him a footing. It formed a place that didn't spin like everything else in his head. It offered a point to strive for—a means to survive for the next few moments until he could figure out what was wrong.

Moving slowly, as if each motion had a discernable beginning, middle and end, he strenuously did what he always preached to visiting landsmen: stand on the high side of the vessel, face into the wind and stare fixedly on the horizon line. He did this very well, considering how great the urge was to puke or scream or run. Neither of the old salts took notice and for this Carter was thankful.

Carter's plan worked in as much as he slowly regained his balance. The dizziness itself diminished slightly as he stood facing the cold wind on deck. However, a lingering sense of doom remained. He kept thinking negative, black, perilous thoughts. He couldn't control them; he was losing control of his mind and this scared him. He feared losing control beyond any other fear.

Finally, the chilling north wind became unbearable against his chalk-white face. He shook inside his jacket. Despite the cold and intangible fear, he was certain that going below would make him dizzy and nauseous again, so he stayed up top.

At a point he felt able to move, he turned to Patrick, and without speaking or revealing his pale face he relieved Patrick at the helm. Patrick acknowledged the transfer, crossed the cockpit, and spoke to Bones.

Carter couldn't make out what he said, nor did he care. His internal dialogue was spinning wildly out of control. It was not allowing for exterior stimulus. Strangest of all was the bizarre feeling that he was out of his mind—and out of his body!

With tiller in hand and *Maxine* clawing ahead unaffected by his plight, Carter tried once again to shake the unnerving thoughts from the webbing of his brain.

He watched ethereally as Bones rose and with Patrick lending a hand, climbed down below. The ancient seaman disappeared out of sight. Patrick soon followed.

Carter was relieved to be alone in the cockpit though he was uncertain he actually stood on deck. He inexplicably felt removed from the immediate scene, almost as if hovering above and behind *Maxine's* stern pulpit. He felt as though he were flying like a kite, jerking wildly on a string.

Carter wrapped his coat around him closer, trying to hop up and down to build body heat. For a second he thought he was all right. Outwardly he succeeded, yet inwardly his mind continued reeling.

Carter's inner dialogue gave way to something beyond language. Inexplicably, he began to groan aloud. The groaning turned to wailing. Worsening even more, he made a roaring sound, like the growl of a great lion in slow motion. The growl scared him and his mind began losing its connection to his body. It happened in a way unknown to him, in a way he couldn't have imagined possible. His vision dimmed and blurred.

He gripped Maxine's tiller in an effort to remain on board. He thought he was passing out and then he feared worse—that he would be thrown out into the wind where the roar would fade and the great boat would sail away. It was a horrid, irrational thought, but he couldn't separate rational from irrational any longer. Every thought seemed horrid. Something was dangerously wrong and he knew it, yet he didn't know it; he felt it, then he couldn't feel it.

Should he say something to Patrick or Bones? Was he losing his grip on the boat; was he actually seeing it from beyond the stern?

Ghastly and abnormal ideas jagged through his misfiring mind. Cold wind raged around his freezing body. His hands were ghost-white and his convulsing chest heaved. Carter stared at the knot meter. It read fourteen knots yet he thought he was in a wild maelstrom, a shrieking hurricane.

What in the hell is happening to me?

He didn't think the cry came out his mouth. The cry came out his ears, no, his chest; no, his eyes were crying. *Stop—stop the crying!*

His connection to his inner dialogue broke and the lion, no, the whale, no--he couldn't control the roar.

Whales don't roar!

But he was roaring with fear; his thoughts and movements were disconnected. The connection was ahead of him, out on the bow—no beyond the bow.

He must remain focused on the bow, he must watch the luffing of the jib; reach for his connection, he must restore his connection, the connection with the roar.

The tiller, like a cold blue snake, froze in his hand. He couldn't disconnect the snake from his hand. The snake consumed his arm. Another roar emitted from his exploding chest. It cried for fear, for help, for an explanation.

What the hell is happening—damn it! What the hell...!

≋≋≋

When the roar actually did escape his mouth, it projected forward with bellowing intensity. It reached the companionway hatch and reverberated through the saloon like a freight train clamoring through a tunnel.

Carter stood frozen at the helm, his body temperature dropping rapidly. He was going into shock; he was on the precipice of total shut down; his deep inner chemistry failing to produce heat.

In a very short time he knew he would self-extinguish. The remaining heat that was his life would rise above the deck and blow away behind *Maxine's* stern. It would swirl only a few seconds in exchange with the chilling molecules of an uncaring north wind.

Maxine galloped on.

He would die.

It couldn't happen this way; he stood on deck, not in the water, not like Miread.

Carter's eyes, though unconnected with reality and his brain unable to connect with motor functions, watched vacantly as Bones flew up the companionway hatch. He saw him leap out onto the deck, his pipe shooting from his mouth, sparkling red ashes spilling from the bowl as it crashed onto the cockpit floor. He watched him launch forward despite his crippled knees.

≋≋≋

At the same instant, Bones bellowed for Patrick, who was passing water in the head, out of earshot. An instant later Patrick, too, sprung on deck and directly reckoned the situation.

Bones held Carter close to his barrel chest and took the helm. Both sailors knew now what had happened. They cursed themselves for allowing it. This was trouble, serious trouble. Carter was succumbing to hypothermia; he was slipping into shock.

Bones knew all the things that needed to happen and he knew they needed to happen fast. Carter would continue to lose body heat until they came up with a way to infuse it back inside him. A body suffering from hypothermia cannot regain its own heat once it drops below a certain threshold.

Patrick and Bones could only guess where Carter was on the continuum. Shock brought with it all kinds of uncertainties. Dangerous uncertainties if not immediately checked.

Maxine bounded ahead in mindless pursuit of an unnamed point lying opposite the direction they needed to be going under the circumstances. They didn't have time to bring her about. Despite the perception by Carter that the whole incident happened in minutes, the fact of the matter was they had already clawed offshore for several hours.

Looking quickly around the horizon, neither Bones nor Patrick saw another vessel in sight. They were on their own. As soon as they gained control of the situation, they would tack and point *Maxine* towards land; but for the moment, Carter's wooden home plunged blindly ahead.

≋≋≋

"Pahtrick, let's get 'im below! Now!"

Bones released the tiller to see what *Maxine* would do. The vessel balanced. However, she was heeled over under full sail and the wind blew steadily and hard—not a good scenario. Since no other vessel could be seen, the coast literally clear, Bones made his decision. *Maxine* would cooperate, she'd sail herself for a short time.

Patrick nodded agreement without words exchanged.

With arms gripping Carter, who wavered between catatonic and convulsive, Bones moved toward the companionway hatch. Patrick checked the horizon again to see that they wouldn't collide with another vessel. It was vacant in every direction. He reversed himself and backed down the companionway ladder to receive Carter from down below.

≋≋≋

In the few moments it took Bones to get Carter turned around and started down the companionway, Patrick reached quickly into *Maxine's* nav station and flipped on the single-sideband radio. He considered sending a distress signal to the Coast Guard, then reconsidered and flipped the switch off.

Patrick winced at the possibility of being responsible for Carter's death. He reached again for the switch, propelled by the fear of being held accountable to Martha or Bones, or for that matter, himself. His mind played ruefully over the years of anguish they suffered because he failed to save Miread. It didn't matter that Bones and Martha both insisted it wasn't his fault. No matter what they said, he felt guilty, and the prospect of hell being his eternal destiny flashed through his mind. Many would argue that's where he belonged, he and Connor O'Donnell both.

He'll likely be in hell—the buggah. Sure that's wheah I'll likely meet 'im next.

He missed his half-brother at times like this. They fit together like hand and glove. He wondered what Connor would have grown to become had he lived beyond his twenty-first year. Thankfully, he died for the cause. Still, losing Connor was different from losing Miread. Miread's death should not have happened, not as it did anyway.

Patrick decided to make the call. He flipped the on switch and pressed the mic button. He was about to speak when Bones bellowed, "Ready below!"

Patrick abandoned the microphone. He stepped back under the open hatch and braced himself to receive the semi-conscious, incoherent captain. As they brought Carter below, *Maxine* sailed swiftly towards Ireland. She sailed like a ghost ship; no human at her helm.

CHAPTER 19

FROZEN IN STASIS

"This way, Caahtah, attaboy theah, laddie," Patrick instructed. He spoke calmly into the uncomprehending ears of the captain of *Maxine*. "Let's move into yer quarters, skippah, and get ya waarmed up a bit."

Carter's clammy white face and frightened eyes stared back at Patrick. He acquiesced mindlessly to the old seaman's direction as they moved together toward the captain's quarters. Carter moved in fits and starts. Patrick glanced back toward the companionway hatch in time to see Bones slowly, painfully, working his way down the ladder.

"Got a wee bit cold up theah, did ya laddie," Patrick said. He opened the door to Carter's quarters. Speaking without expecting an answer, he could see confusion and panic in Carter's eyes.

"Pahtrick," Bones called from the galley, "I'll staaht hot watah, but figure it to be a while 'fore the boy can take anythin' internally. Get 'im into blankets or a bleedin' sleepin' bag if he's got one. One of us haas got to strip down and get in theah wif 'im."

Patrick knew the drill and began clearing Carter's bunk. Carter shuffled mindlessly in the tight quarters. His shaking and convulsing deepened and Patrick didn't like what he saw.

He spoke aloud to Bones.

"We'd bettah get movin' Bones, the boy needs heat right away. Haav ya got the watah staahted out theah?"

≋≋≋

Bones rummaged through the galley compartments, frustrated not knowing where things were. He found a coffee pot and pan, drew water and placed them on the stove. Finally, he ignited the burners.

Intermittently he looked aloft through the companionway hatch. He checked the draw of the mainsail and decided *Maxine* was stable.

Despite her stability, no one at the tiller was precarious at best and down right dangerous at worst. A quiet rage rose within Bones as he thought of his decrepitude, his inability to leap up top and bring *Maxine* quickly about. She should be sailing in the opposite direction, back towards shore.

≋≋≋

Patrick found a sleeping bag, spread it out on the bunk and turned quickly to Carter. The frozen captain shook uncontrollably.

"Heah we go, laddie. Let's get you out o' thaht jacket . . ." Suddenly Carter jolted. Anxiety and fear spewed from the youth. He pulled away from Patrick, crashing into the door of the cabin.

"It's okay theah, skippah, we've got to get ya out of yer clothes now, laddie, you'll be waarm soon son, ya got to work with me now, heah we go . . ." Patrick coaxed the jacket from around Carter's shoulders. He embraced his frozen charge, not solely to provide heat, but to infuse trust as well.

"Bones theah, Bones!" Patrick called through the now closed door. "Gonna need ya in heah, Bones."

"Comin' Pahtrick . . . just found a bloomin' hot watah bottle, it'll be a bit 'fore the watah is ready fer service," came the muffled reply.

"Now the pants theah, laddie, heah, let me help ya." Patrick moved quickly to undress the shivering body.

"Bones, theah, let's switch places. Ya got more heat in ya. How 'bout ya take the first watch?"

"Be right theah," the old man reported, relieved at the prospect of getting off his throbbing legs.

Patrick stripped Carter down to his under shorts. The blue whiteness of the lad's uncomprehending face startled the old seaman. He realized there was no way Carter could pull himself out of this condition. They needed to move quickly to reverse the heat loss.

Patrick placed his hand on Carter's pallid skin, guiding him toward the bunk. The deathly appearance of his charge once again drew up the memory of the night Connor died. He choked on the recollection. Remorse and guilt began to engulf him.

Perhaps when Carter was back in his right mind, he would talk to him, explain some things. Not everything of course, just a thing or two. He might help Carter see the circumstances he faced in Northern Ireland, particularly as a descendent of a Gaelic tribe older than the United States itself. His past was full of dangerous choices and calamitous outcomes. Carter should be able to understand that.

If he could do this, if he could talk to Carter in this way, maybe his mind could get some rest. Patrick needed that rest, and he could trust Carter, he decided; he needed to trust him. Someone needed to believe what he did all those years meant something. Through Carter, if the lad would listen, would understand, he could gain redemption.

≋≋≋

Bones entered the tiny cabin and Patrick stood out of the way as the ninety-year-old man stripped naked to his briefs and socks. He quickly laid his long underwear on top of his outer clothing and observed that Carter hadn't worn this extra protection.

"Move ovah theah, Caahtah, my boy," Bones said. He could see Carter was barely able to discern what was taking place. He climbed into the sleeping bag. His burly abdomen shook involuntarily at the touch of the icy, quivering flesh of the young man who could have been his grandson.

After the initial shock of Carter's cold skin, Bones looked up to see Patrick, who stood watching pensively in the shadow of the dimly lit cabin.

"Pahtrick, old chap," Bones said patiently, "best tend the watah and get this bleedin' vessel headed the propaah direction, don't ya know."

Maxine's motion shook Patrick from his fixation. He broke from his trance and followed his senior's advice.

≋≋≋

Quickly moving back into the galley, Patrick stepped through the cabin door and regained his present thoughts. Formulating his next steps, he left the terrible memories their present circumstance aroused for another time. Patrick switched rapidly from emotion to reason. The ability came from seventy years in a volatile reality; the inescapable reality into which he was born.

Glancing skyward through the companionway hatch he checked the mainsail. He could afford another couple minutes before going on deck and bringing the sloop about. He used this precious time to look quickly beneath the pots of water and check their burning flames.

Fire! Of all the bleedin' thin's to be addin' to an already precarious situation.

Upon close inspection, Patrick could see the stove was clean and well maintained. He trusted the flames would remain in their bounds. He judged they would do their work unattended so he reached again for the microphone mounted on the front of the single-sideband radio.

Suddenly, with an explosive crash, *Maxine* lunged upward with rancorous force. The sound of the collision was deafening in the otherwise silent cabin.

The motion threw Patrick forward from the galley towards the settees in the main saloon. Pots of near boiling water came straight after him as they fell from the gimbaled stove. He slammed down hard, hitting his shoulder against the edge of the settee and again on the floor when he hit the cabin sole.

Maxine groaned loudly as every plank in her hull carried the forces of the collision aft to her stern. Her mast shook wildly, yanking dangerously on her bronze fittings and stainless steel stays. Then, almost instantly, she came to a halt, seemingly dead in the water; frozen in stasis.

In the captain's quarters, Bones rose on his elbow. He fought against Carter who began wailing incoherently. Bones struggled to slip free from the sleeping bag in a desperate attempt to figure out what happened. He worked against Carter like a rescuer attempting to save a drowning victim. Carter, though absent of heat, was full of adrenalin making Bones' efforts at egress nearly impossible. He roared in confusion. His mind and body barely coupled.

Bones struggled to get out of the sleeping bag and at the same time calm Carter. He was failing at both. He shouted to see if Patrick was all right, but got no immediate response. This notched up his anxiety several levels.

≋≋≋

Martha suddenly bolted upright in bed.

She stared across the dimly lit space at a grandfather clock that struck 9:00 A.M.

She felt stricken with a strange, penetrating thought. It was the kind of thought she learned not all women have. It was the kind of thought she, like her coven of special friends, had experienced since childhood.

A sick feeling like black bile poured forth from inside. She realized it was the same kind of thought that came over her that terrible night aboard *Gael na Mara* in the North Atlantic—the night Miread's and Connor's lives were stolen away.

She threw off her covers as if they were woven of snakes and cobwebs. Anxiously, she climbed from the bed. She moved to the dresser, took a cigarette from a pack lying on top and lit it.

Her hands shook visibly. She drew in a long breath, blew the smoke out as if it now burned her lungs, even though she had done it ten thousand times before.

She began to pace worriedly around the great room.

Feeling like the walls were collapsing in, Martha picked up an old sweater that lay draped across a worn antique chair. Placing it around her shoulders, she stepped out the front door of the B&B. There she stood and stared. Anxiety and fright distorted her view of the blue harbor.

She gazed at the boats and the sea beyond. She heard the carved wooden hull model Patrick built swing above her head in the gusty wind. She looked up to see it crazily pulling on its wrought iron hinges.

Before her eyes, with a twisting, wrenching sound, one hinge broke and the hull careened on the other quite out of control. She darted from underneath it. Watching it in horror, it continued to rotate on the remaining hinge, flung about like a wildebeest in a lion's jaw.

Suddenly it broke away, crashing against the clapboard façade before falling to the ground. She stared at it, mangled and ruined, then wrapped the sweater tighter around her shoulders. A wretched fear began strangling her, stealing her breath away.

She gasped and turned back toward the cottage. The three freshly planted fig trees sparkled in the dewy morning sunlight. They moved as if they were alive in the brisk wind. For a moment they looked as if they were struggling to get free of the soil. Martha watched their struggle and knew deep in her soul, as thousands of Marblehead women before her, that something had gone dreadfully wrong for her men at sea.

This realization pierced her body and the good witch could contain herself no longer. She cried out in spasms of uncontrollable anguish. She wailed shamelessly in the Marblehead dawn.

Great cries of despair bellowed coarsely from her lips and she fell to her knees before the three twigs of life. She continued crying in deep gulps and groans. She wrenched at her white flannel robe, holding it to her sobbing eyes, weeping, hunched over and oblivious for what seemed like an eternity.

She saw and heard nothing until she jumped with fright as a powder white hand descended onto her shoulder. Martha turned quickly and looked up to see a demure figure balancing a tray with two coffee cups in one hand. It was the young woman she met at the coffee shop, the one who served her the morning Carter fell ill.

Claire Dubois' hand spoke of consolation, offered without even knowing the problem. Martha reached for it immediately, like a lifebuoy thrown out upon a storm-driven sea.

Claire set the coffee on the ground next to them and offered both hands. She bent down and Martha reached for her. Without speaking, communicating through the touch of her skin, Claire dispelled a portion of the distress and torment that engulfed the frightened matron.

≋≋≋

Aboard *Maxine*, Carter became further unraveled. He worked against Bones unwittingly in his panicked state, the two trapped together in the single sleeping bag like Siamese twins.

Carter's thought process became even more contorted. Racing scenes of disaster coursed across the lobes of his brain. He kept seeing a man he thought was his uncle, a gentleman farmer, crushed and bleeding to death. The victim was trapped beneath a tractor in a ravine on his uncle's farm.

Carter slid down the ravine, careening wildly, dirt and leaves choking him, tree branches slitting his skin as he slid down the steep bank. He heard the farm tractor's engine roar out of control.

A woman screamed in horror from the top of the ravine and Carter looked up. He expected to see his aunt, but it was Martha. She stood on the edge of the ravine above him in her white flannel robe, clutching it, crying into it as she held it to her face.

Carter wondered how the hell she got there. He looked back at the scene of the accident. To his amazement, it was he that struggled to shove the crushing steel from on top his chest. He flailed crazily to push the tractor off, but couldn't; no matter how hard he tried he couldn't break away.

Bones gripped him to his chest and shouted, "Caahtah, Caahtah, stay calm Caahtah. Hold still, be still, I need ya to be still, Caahtah."

Leaning out of the Captain's quarters, Bones shouted, "Pahtrick, we've rammed into somethin', somethin' big, are ya okay?" He looked at his chronometer; it was 9:06 A.M.

≋≋≋

Patrick spoke up, dazed from his fall, slowly regaining his composure. "Holy Christ, Bones, the boat's hit somethin' all right and those blasted pots from the stove hit me." He brushed away steaming hot water from his arms and jacket. Regaining his footing on the angled floor, he quickly checked himself for broken bones and figured, despite the pain in his shoulder, that he was otherwise unhurt.

Strangely, he suddenly recalled the time he was wrong about that; a bullet had grazed his buttock. He didn't find the injury until he dropped his drawers to squat a short time later at his hiding place. His backside seemed cold in the night air. When he reached around to feel it, his hand came back coated with wet, sticky blood. He hadn't noticed it during the confusion. He remembered that the bomb Connor rigged had detonated a full ten minutes early. Flying debris of bricks and mortar and human flesh exploded past them as they raced from the scene. Had their bomb exploded a minute earlier, they, too, would have been blown to bits.

Shaking the memory from his mind, convinced he was intact, he dashed into the captain's quarters. He saw Bones naked, shaken, but otherwise all right. Bones looked at Patrick and Patrick only shrugged. "Hell if I know . . ." was all he said. He turned and raced from the cabin.

An instant later, Patrick leapt up the companionway ladder. It was there, on his way up, clutching the teak hand holds, that he realized the hot water had scalded the back of his hands. Too frantic to worry that instant, it occurred to him he should get ice on the burns as quickly as possible.

≋≋≋

At the top of the companionway his eyes searched the water all around. There was nothing there. He blinked in disbelief. There was nothing, no boat, no rock, nothing in any direction. They were alone.

"What the hell...what did we hit?" he cried aloud.

Stranger was the fact that *Maxine* appeared to be moving in slow motion, her sails drawn tight. The wind still blew as it did before the collision, yet they weren't plunging ahead like before. It dawned upon Patrick suddenly that something gripped her, but what?

Patrick climbed out onto the deck, racing forward while looking in the water along side.

"Holy Mother of God," he cried out and crossed himself as he stared over the port lifelines.

≋≋≋

Bones called up from the base of the companionway where he and Carter had both advanced.

"Patrick, what did we bleedin' hit theah? Patrick?"

There was no reply. Bones continued restraining Carter. The panicky youth tried to crawl past him to get topside. Carter cried out something about getting a "come along" and rope from the barn.

Bones realized Carter was delirious, hallucinating. He wrestled with the youth to keep him below. He held the shivering body tight to his chest and spoke calmly, but firmly.

Carter responded by staying still long enough for Bones to call up to Patrick once more. Still there was no response and Bones became alarmed.

He shouted with a deeper, louder voice.

No reply.

Losing Patrick overboard crossed Bones' mind. He called out again.

"Patrick, ah you theah, what did we hit, man? Give me a report!"

"I'm heah, Bones, I'm heah."

Bones could tell the voice was coming from far forward.

"You ahn't goin' to believe this Bones . . . nevah in my life . . ." Patrick dashed across the deck. "We've rammed a damned containah, Bones. It's a containah! We're jammed into it; we've jammed clear into it!"

Bones, still at the base of the companionway, continued to struggle with Carter.

"It musta fell off a freightah in a storm, like those cars we used to tie on the deck of the *Blackthorn II* yeahs ago."

"Aah we gonna sink? Will we need ta abandon *Maxine*?" Bones shouted.

Hearing these words, Carter reconnected with reality for an instant. He screamed at the top of his lungs, "No, no, not *Maxine*, no!"

"I cahn't tell, Bones, aah ya takin' on watah below?"

Bones looked at the cabin sole fore and aft, tightening his grip on the ghost white captain.

"She's dry Pahtrick, but I'm hearin' watah comin' in somewheah, cahn't say wheah."

Bones was curious, desperate to know what was going on topside—to investigate with his own eyes. It was essential he coax Carter back into his sleeping bag. He gained way by assuring Carter they wouldn't abandon *Maxine*.

Helping Carter back into the bunk, he decided Patrick would have to manage things on deck for the time being and climbed back into the sleeping bag with the freezing lake-captain. Lying in silence, Bones tried to imagine what was happening. He figured they'd struck with such force that *Maxine's* stem breached the container's corrugated metal skin. Apparently, Patrick believed *Maxine* was lodged in the crushed metal. It also meant water was filling the container. The container could sink and bring *Maxine* down with it, depending on how tightly they were lodged inside it.

On the positive side, he considered whether the cargo stowed in the contained was buoyant. It seemed probable and might explain why it hadn't sunk already. It might also explain why they were apparently still attached to it, the buoyancy in the container pushing up while *Maxine* pushed down.

"I'll be damned," he said aloud, "I thought I'd seen it all."

≋≋≋

Bones continued to lie quietly with his warm barrel chest pressed firmly against the body of his young captain. He listened intently for sounds, sounds that would reveal what was going on.

Sounds came into focus. Two made their way into his ancient ears. One was the trickling of water, the other was hissing flames!

Bones suddenly remembered the gimbaled stove in the galley. They hadn't shut off the burners after the collision.

He had no choice; he couldn't just lie there so he climbed once more from the warm sleeping bag. He forced his aching legs to move once again across the companionway to the galley.

Sure enough, flames were burning on the stove with nothing to absorb the heat. Spotting the hot water bottle along the way, he realized its life giving heat could take his place in Carter's bag, at least for a short time. It would free him to help Patrick.

He gathered up the coffee pot and pan that only minutes ago had flung hot water onto Patrick. He patiently refilled them, placed them back on the flames and bellowed up on deck for Patrick.

"Pahtrick, anythin' more you can tell me, Pahtrick?"

"She's bloody well jammed right into the topside of the containah; the force of *Maxine's* tonnage movin' faast broke the damned thin' open. I figger the bent metal haas got a grip on 'er stem like a hound on a rabbit. Whatevah's inside gave way and we're hooked tight to the damned thin'."

Patrick reversed himself at the companionway and backed quickly down the ladder. At the bottom he turned to Bones.

"It sure as hell defies anythin' I've evah seen, but we aah pushing the damn containah forward like a tug pushin' a barge. *Maxine* road up on 'er dead centah. Now the damn thin' is sailin' with us; it's got a grip on us like a Chinese fingah trap!"

"How bad aah we damaged, can ya tell?"

"Cahn't tell exactly, but I'm thinkin' our hull is intact. I'm gonna head to the fo'c'sle and haav a look see. She cut the containah open like buttah, which surprises the hell out o' me. I suppose the damned thin's aah engineered to keep caahgo inside, not fend off deep keel sailboats hittin' it from outside. She must be in deep and I cahn't help believe the containah is goin' to sink when it fills with watah. *Maxine's* buoyancy should pull 'er out as the containah goes down if we're lucky. If 'er stem's breached severely though, we're gonna need help."

With this he stepped close to Bones and whispered in his ear, "and...when the containah breaks away, Bones, we could lose *Maxine*, too!"

Patrick looked into the captain's quarters at the resting youth then turned back to Bones and said again in a whisper, "Look,

Bones, I'm gonna' call fer help then go forward and inspect fer damage. Aftah thaht we can figger out what ta do next."

"Your hands, Pahtrick, the baacks, they're burned."

"Thaht hot water, Bones . . . I'll be all right, 'tis not thaht bahd."

"I'll make ice packs fer 'em." Bones quickly pulled towels and ice from the freezer compartment. Meanwhile, Patrick wasted no time. He turned to the chart table.

≋≋≋

The Irish seaman hastily struck lines on the chart, the back of his hands turning red from the burns. His pencil crossed lines along the rule and he jotted figures rapidly into the log book, adding the time from his chronometer. The task completed, he turned to the navigation station, made adjustments to knobs on the single-sideband radio, picked up the microphone, and began speaking.

His message was brief in case unwanted ears intercepted it. He was cautious on the air. Caution explained why he was still able to do what he was doing after fifty long years. He thought of his not-so-careful brethren, fallen along the way; good men, however reckless in conduct.

Not only was his message brief, it was spoken in a language unknown to any but a few remaining members of his ancient clan, people who lived in the glens of County Antrim. These were people whose ancestors had known the sea from times dating back to the Vikings; seafaring invaders who raided, then mixed with the Gaelic people already inhabiting the region.

The language Patrick spoke was Gaelic with deliberate infusions of ancient dialect that in effect made it a code. It was code none of the Gloucester fisherman who might be cruising near them would understand. Nor would the radio men aboard freighters farther out, and particularly the Harbor Patrol farther in, nor even the *Monarch.* He knew that she cruised these waters regularly.

It was imperative that no unwanted listener understood what he said. He wanted no one to realize he was calling for help to his brothers in arms; men who were bound by oaths and sacred bonds.

Seconds after he released the mic button the recipients of the message responded. A single word of acknowledgment, also spoken in the tongue of the clan, was all Patrick heard in reply. He placed the mic in its clip, paused to contemplate his action, and left the radio on, just in case.

≋≋≋

Within minutes, the engine of *Gael na Mara* roared to life. Her crew let slip her mooring pennant in Manchester Harbor. She moved forward slowly, restrained in the no wake zone. She blasted three times on her air horn, emerged from the harbor then steadily increased her speed.

Soon the North Sea cutter ran full revs toward a pair of hastily broadcast coordinates, coordinates delivered in a language that predated the concept of coordinates.

On the quarterdeck, thick, blue cigar smoke curled around the grimacing face of a rock-hard man. He watched his crew of three young Irishmen, the ones most recently staying at the Purser's Quarter's, raise huge white sails into the cold windy skies above Massachusetts Bay. He estimated he could reach his objective in less than two hours. They lurched ahead into the great blueness.

≋≋≋

By the time Patrick finished transmitting, Bones had filled two towels with crushed ice and wrapped each around hands held out in expectation.

Patrick gripped each towel to force the ice against the backs of his hands. He then went forward to inspect the fo'c'sle while Bones returned to Carter in the sleeping bag.

Patrick pulled open boards of the v-berth and looked for damage. He found none discernable and returned to the galley. He glanced at the hot water on the stove and yelled into the captain's quarters, "Soon, Bones, the watah will be hot soon."

Bending down, Patrick lifted a floor board to inspect the bilge. As he feared, water lapped at the top of the floors. He listened for the battery-powered bilge pump, heard it working, but could see there was no way it was going to stay ahead of the leaks.

Suddenly, he remembered what Carter had shown him the day they launched *Maxine*. His mind leaped with excitement. He shot up the ladder and into *Maxine's* cockpit.

≋≋≋

Bones detected the sea change in Patrick's behavior. He listened carefully to try and figure out what Patrick was doing. Carter had calmed down considerably and was resting quietly in Bones arms. He seemed to receive the infusion of heat more willingly now.

An instant later Bones heard the loud cranking of *Maxine's* diesel as it roared to life. He wasn't sure why Patrick cranked her up, but figured it a good thing. Patiently, he accepted the fact that he couldn't help Patrick right then. He was performing an essential service; he needed to remain with Carter.

As he lay there he wondered how they could have avoided this queer turn of events. He remembered lecturing Patrick and Carter about the men of the *Andrea Gale* being "better at living" and thought for a minute about the hand of fate. How coldly it was often dealt. All things considered, particularly the length of time he had survived on earth, he met the dilemma with great equanimity.

≋≋≋

After the engine began firing steadily, Patrick climbed below. He pulled the companionway ladder off its brass fittings, setting it aside. Flinging open the latch he lifted away the covering board from the forward compartment of the engine. The deafening roar of the engine slammed into his ears. He noticed the water level rising, nearing the engine's oil pan.

Below and in front of the iron-ginny he reached into the water. Shifting his burning hand around, he tried to remember where Carter pointed out the now submersed y-valve on the morning *Maxine* returned to the water. Patrick recalled that Carter had rigged the valve so that in an emergency the engine would draw its intake water from the bilge. Patrick thought the idea clever at the time and was re-thinking it to be brilliant now.

After a couple of seconds he found the valve and switched its position. He could see water instantly shoot up the clear plastic hose leading into the engine's water filter.

Patrick sighed, knowing full well there was still a limited capacity it could pump. If *Maxine* took on water faster than she could pump, they would sink; that remained an indisputable fact. But this would at least buy time. How much time was impossible to calculate.

The engine running would also charge the batteries and that would keep the regular bilge pump operating. It was everything he could do short of pumping manually. The thought of a seventy-eight-year-old with burned hands and a ninety-year-old with bad knees attempting to keep *Maxine* afloat by hand was not promising.

Patrick figured *Gael na Mara* would need a couple hours to reach them. The Coast Guard would have flown a pump out in twenty minutes. He struggled with his decision. He consulted Bones. Bones had decided these matters before and his decisions had cost lives before.

He agreed with Patrick.

CHAPTER 20

ALL THINGS IRISH

The droning of *Maxine's* engine and the heat from Bones' body infused Carter with desperately needed calm. The anxiety and confusion of succumbing to hypothermia changed to exhaustion and he slowly dozed off.

Seeing Carter sleep brought relief to Bones. Reluctant to disturb the passive sailor, he rose to proceed with his plan to fill the hot water bottle and supplant it in his place.

Patrick moved around on deck and Bones assumed he was managing the situation. The simple fact that Patrick hadn't been down to radio further calls for help told Bones that *Maxine*, like her stricken captain, was stable.

≋≋≋

Taking the helm, Patrick kept *Maxine* on course in the direction they were headed when they collided with the container. Unfortunately, this pointed her farther out to sea. He didn't object since the vessel sailed so slowly. The container behaved like a sea anchor, dragging *Maxine* to a barely discernable crawl.

He figured he should not try to break away from the unwanted attachment. Rather, he would keep them together until *Gael na Mara* arrived. If the container did have buoyancy and *Maxine* had ridden up onto it, that explained why she wasn't taking on more water. If they parted and *Maxine* sat back down on her waterline, the lost buoyancy could result in more leakage than the two pumps could expel. Help was on the way with extra hands and equipment, of this he was certain.

≋≋≋

Down below, Bones dressed, filled the hot water bottle, and persuaded the stirring Carter to remain in the sleeping bag. He wrapped the red rubber bottle in a bath towel to aid the slow release of its restorative heat. This would allow time for him to go topside. He would finally be able to check out the strange circumstance they found themselves in.

Before he did, he lifted a section of the cabin sole and examined the bilge. It was nearly full. He was surprised it wasn't worse.

Feeling rested, his legs regaining what strength they had, Bones climbed the companionway ladder. The sunlight blinded him momentarily as he arose from the dim saloon. He greeted Patrick at the helm.

To all outward appearances, *Maxine* and Patrick looked as if they were having a jolly sail on a beautiful spring day. The sun shown bright, the air warmed up, the wind died down a couple knots. All appeared fair and pleasant, that is, had they not rammed into a floating metal island now attached firmly to their keel.

"How's the skippah theah, Bones?"

"He's calmed down a bloody bit, Pahtrick. The watah bottle's not enough to serve 'im propaah, but I cahn't keep below not knowin' what the hell's come of our bleedin' situation. How's yer hands?"

"They feel a wee bit numb, but thaht won't last. I'll feel 'em plenty bahd once they've hahd time to protest. I owe ya fer gettin' the ice in the middle of thaht mess below. T'would be faar worse hahd ya not."

Bones waved away Patrick's thanks.

"I'm goin' forward, Pahtrick; I've got to see what the hell's beneath us."

"Heah, I'll help ya, just let me tie off the helm. She wants to go up into the wind. I think we should keep 'er straight onto the containah. I'm afraid if we turn she'll open a plank or do somethin' we cahn't predict."

Together, with an outward calm of a Sunday club regatta, they worked their way forward. Amidships, looking overboard on the starboard side, Bones could make out the aft edge of the container. Several large black letters stood out in the dim green water. He looked at Patrick and shook his head.

Patrick returned a look of resignation.

There was nothing to say or do. It was a freak accident and that was all there was to it. The means to resolving the crisis was underway, steaming towards them at full revs. All they could do was wait.

Upon returning to the cockpit, Bones sat down to think. He produced his pipe, tamped down a charge of tobacco, and lit it with the scratch of a blue-tipped match. He drew in a long breath and puffed out thick gray smoke that rolled away to leeward.

He assessed their immediate situation. The wind still drew the sails taught. The boat rode high on its waterline. *Maxine* silently pushed the container farther out to sea, albeit very slowly.

The only thing that concerned the old man was the prospect of motion between *Maxine* and the container. If they began working against each other, *Maxine's* planking could open or shear apart. For the time being, however, they seemed locked tightly together and stable in an almost eerie way. Bones acquiesced to the frustration. He waited patiently for *Gael na Mara*.

Patrick went below and peeked into the captain's quarters to see Carter resting. Satisfied, he stepped into the nav station and made an entry into *Maxine's* log. He noted the wind backing to the west and abating a couple knots. He noted the sea lying down, nearly flat in fact. He went on to add several sentences describing their peculiar situation.

The diminishing wind was disappointing. *Gael na Mara* would have to work that much harder to get to them. Despite the apparent reprieve from imminent peril, Patrick was anxious for *Gael na Mara* to arrive. The rescue boat represented more to him than a couple fresh hands and a pump. His life, and those around him, had been reshaped by events that took place aboard her—profound things, including the loss of Miread and Connor. He could never let go of his connection to her, not until he finished *Red Shoes*—at least the way he figured things.

He stopped writing in the log and pulled himself from his memories. He fought an urge to call *Gael na Mara* on the radio to check her progress. But there was no need for another radio broadcast. There was no need to draw attention. It wouldn't take many Gaelic language transmissions before the anomalous activity would stir curiosity in the wrong places.

Patrick had learned that recent threats to U.S. Embassies overseas by Arab terrorists prompted notable increases in listening on the airways. The Arabs and their infernal activities were making the cause of Irish independence harder to advance. As far as he was concerned, they simply hated Jews, and hate for the sake of hate was wrong.

His people, his clan, were fighting oppression in its plainest form. Their land was occupied and they wanted the occupation forces to leave. Had the Arabs, or the Libyans, to be more specific, not been a ready source of weapons, like the shipload of arms O'Hanlon was trying to bring in when the French grabbed him, he believed his people should have nothing to do with them.

≋≋≋

Martha and Claire sat together. They sipped coffee at the white and gray Formica table that graced the kitchen of the B&B. Claire looked around, taking in the white metal cupboards, the old Mixmaster, the round streamlined toaster. They gave the appearance of what might have been a modern kitchen in the year the Formica table was manufactured.

Claire's dark eyes returned to Martha. The matron of the Purser's Quarter's had recovered a great deal of her composure since they left the fig seedlings and came inside.

In her coarse voice, Martha explained her concerns about the sailors off shore. Claire listened intently, the same way she did in the company of her French Canadian *Grand-mere*, the matron of the DuBois family in Milwaukee.

Mamie, whose maiden name was Nicole Anne Dubonnet, lived with Claire's family in that bustling Wisconsin city until 1995, the time of the frail matron's passing. By the time Mamie passed away, Claire had left the nest as did three older brothers before her. Claire's father, Louise Francoise Dubois, Mamie's only living son, was an attorney and professor of law at Marquette University.

The University, founded by French Jesuits in 1881, played a central role in the Dubois family life. Claire's mother, Agnes, whose descendents were German, was a prominent university wife, despite her Lutheran up-bringing, and an admired Milwaukee socialite due to her Lutheran up-bringing. As did her three brothers, the exceptionally bright and studious Claire attended the respected Midwestern University. She graduated with honors and a B.A. in History in 1991.

Moving east, she attended another Jesuit school—Boston College. That is where she resided when Mamie passed away. She recalled the sad return to Wisconsin to attend Mamie's funeral.

Claire, like Carter, was often troubled by the unwelcoming aspect of New Englanders. Student life at the College ameliorated some of her frustration. Coming home, though under sad circumstances, was a pleasant reconnection with family.

Wisconsin folks were as warm and kindly as any she hoped to meet. In fact, among these polite and passive people she was considered more self-assured than most. No one was surprised to discover she received an M.A. from Boston College.

At Mamie's wake, they exhibited puzzled faces as she explained her degree was in Irish Literature and Culture. They wouldn't have been so puzzled if they had known more about New England and Boston College. Nor did it raise eyebrows amongst the University women when Claire went on to explain she was working on a Doctorate degree. They did, once again, puzzle over her dissertation—the comparative development of early language syntax and lexicon of Norman, Gaelic, and Scandinavian immigrants in Great Britain. Martha, the roughly hewn and opinionated matron of the Purser's Quarters, knew little more about her unexpected guest than what she intuitively suspected—a powerful attraction between the pretty woman and the handsome captain of the yacht *Maxine.*

The reason for Claire's arrival mattered not at all to Martha; she was too upset about her ghastly feeling of doom to care about the motivations of the polite and kindly young woman sipping tea at her kitchen table. She was grateful she wasn't alone and chattered about uncertainties and concerns that brought her to the condition Claire discovered her in earlier.

≋≋≋

Bones returned to his station inside the sleeping bag with Carter. The water bottle had served its usefulness, its heat quickly consumed by the recovering youth. Thankfully, it allowed Bones to see their dilemma first hand and talk things over with Patrick.

Carter's condition improved and the danger of shock subsided. Bones checked the time and decided it would probably be an hour or more before *Gael na Mara* arrived from Manchester. He settled in a bit, pleased that Carter was resting. As his body's heat filled the sleeping bag, he, too, became sleepy. He dozed off then awoke when Carter spoke up in a quiet though coherent voice.

"Bones, Bones, are you awake?"

"What? Oh...yes, Caahtah, I'm awake. How aah ya feelin'?"

"I'm not sure Bones; I've never felt like this before. I can't tell what came over me. Is Patrick on deck, is he at the helm?"

"Yes, Caahtah, he's at the tillah and we aah still underway."

"Is *Maxine* okay?"

"Fer the time bein'. Pahtrick has got things undah control, son. You cahn trust Pahtrick, Caahtah, theah's no bettah hahnd on deck thahn thaht bleedin' limey and I'm aaskin' you to trust me, too, my boy. You need ta put the mockers on worryin' and get some bloody rest."

The words pacified Carter and Bones felt a sigh of relief exhale from within the youth's bare back. He could feel it against his own naked chest as he pressed against the lad, filling him with heat, spooning him in a fetal position.

"Bones, I'm feeling like I can think again. For a while there I didn't think I could. I can't figure out what came over me. My thoughts were crazy—I was sure I was dying."

"Caahtah, when you get cold like you did up top theah, boy, things go barmy. 'Tis like the cold shakes out the logic and leaves nothing but a mind absent of heat. Heat is what makes up our thoughts and our ideas. We use it like a pair of eyeglasses through which we see the bloomin' world. If it escapes, and I've seen it 'appen to the best, boy, it's like the lenses 'ave been smashed in their frames. It becomes impossible to see straight through the broken shards o' glass."

Carter lay still a few moments longer, then spoke again.

"Bones, I've meant to ask you, that is, if you don't mind. Why do people call you Bones? Patrick once told me it's because of your real name. What is your real name?"

"Ah, thaht Pahtrick, he's a giddy kipper sometimes. My name is Wilfred, son, Wilfred Albert Matheson. Mates called me Bones aftah I fixed up a few of 'em durin' the war. I nevah got on wif the name Wilfred though. I liked Albert fine, like bleedin' Prince Albert. Didn't think much of Wilfred; didn't give a two bob bit for Willie nor Freddie neithah! I would 'ave been 'appy with Albert, howevah, thaht was not to be, not what my mum wanted, may she rest in peace. My bloomin' sistah called me Albert sometimes, that is, when mum wasn't nearby."

"You have a sister?"

Carter tried to imagine the female likeness of the bushy eye-browed, big-nosed sailorman who looked like a wooden statue found outside seafood restaurants in New England.

"Hahd a sistah, Caahtah, lost 'er cleah baack when I was but a nipper of thirteen. Winifred was 'er name. Mum thought the two names quite propaah, Wilfred and Winifred. I called her Winnie and she'd secretly call me Prince Albert. She was a pip, thaht gul. I loved 'er very much and losing 'er hit hard, Caahtah, the kind of hard that stays wif ya for a lifetime."

"Like Martha still loves Miread," Carter uttered out loud.

He hadn't said it for Bones' benefit; it was merely a thought coming into his mind, finding its way directly out his mouth. For Bones, however, the words jabbed suddenly, like a punch in the belly. Carter couldn't detect his pain, lying away from him. Bones was practiced at keeping his emotions deep within him; for nearly fifty years he'd kept them there.

They both became silent once again. *Maxine's* engine resumed its prominent position in their ears. Their minds fell idle as the droning lulled them both to sleep.

≋≋≋

Patrick stood patiently at *Maxine's* tiller, sailing her as if everything was precisely the way he wanted it to be. If it hadn't been for the unseen parasite attached to her keel, things would be the way he wanted—the way things were going to be aboard *Red Shoes*.

The first indication of change was felt in the palm of Patrick's right hand. It began as a barely discernable feeling of tension. The change set off an alarm in the highly attentive helmsman. He dreaded the prospect of a change in their situation, especially before *Gael na Mara* arrived.

In a fraction of a second, a further sensation transmitted through the carved wooden tiller. This time the feeling was felt in Patrick's shoes as well. The deck beneath his feet rose a couple inches in elevation. It felt like a following wave lifting her from astern, except there was no wave. The sea ran flat.

The second event was too subtle to be detected by the sleeping crew below, but it sent a jolt of adrenalin straight into Patrick's bloodstream.

He looked forward, certain he could detect the bow down on her lines. About three minutes passed and *Maxine* continued sinking on her forward waterline. There was no easy means of detecting how much. Patrick could again sense it in his feet as the stern rose higher in counterbalance.

Several untoward thoughts occurred to him, not the least being a justifiable fear that the container had finally filled with water. It was sinking; sinking with *Maxine* stuck to it like an eel on a shark. If it was going down, so was *Maxine*!

Patrick glanced astern. The dinghy bobbed along behind the yacht, tugging on its painter like a child following its mother on a walk. He expelled a breath of relief, but then suddenly he realized what it all meant—what it would take to get the crew up and on board the dinghy.

Thaht's no easy escape, he thought. *Plenty room fer disaster, with Caahtah sick and Bones half crippled.*

No sooner than the thought cleared his mind another bigger, more detectable change came over *Maxine*. A low rumble rose from below her hull. Patrick wondered if cargo was shifting in the container. *Maxine* dipped and she plowed her stem downward into the deep. Her stern rose at an acute angle, startling the hard-to-impress seaman.

Whoa, theah girl. What aah ya doin', lassie?

He felt out of control of the vessel despite his continued grip on her helm. If she raised more he'd lose control for certain, her rudder rising at too great an angle to cut water.

Keep yer nose up theah, Maxine. Let's not be pitchpolin', old gul.

Patrick looked skyward and considered dropping the sails in a hurry.

That's impossible, he thought. On a broad reach her sails blew into the standing rigging. The main sail would jam in place and refuse to come down. The jib would be impossible to control from on deck.

Just then a voice bellowed up from below.

"Pahtrick, hey up theah, Pahtrick, give us a bleedin' report, what the hell is 'aapenin'?"

"Don't know, Bones, don't like it neithah."

"I'm comin' topside, Pahtrick," yelled Bones. He turned and pleaded with Carter to stay below.

≋≋≋

Carter gained enough clarity of mind to understand that *Maxine* was shifting on her center of gravity. He was going up top. It was his boat, his home, he was the captain and nothing was going to stop him.

He shifted around in his cabin and found a sweatshirt, pulled it over his head and was reaching for pants when he suddenly felt nauseous. He couldn't control the dizziness. He fell angrily back in the bunk and there he lay in hopes of regaining his stomach.

It wasn't going to cooperate. He was sick again. He rolled over on his side and threw up the meager contents of his belly. He wiped his mouth with the towel that was wrapped around the water bottle.

Dropping the towel on the floor to absorb the discharge, the hapless lad rolled back into the middle of the bunk. For the moment he wasn't going anywhere.

≋≋≋

Patrick looked at Bones with frustration and worry.

Another ominous movement pulled *Maxine* deeper at the bow and higher at the stern.

Bones moved aft, stocking-footed in his haste to get on deck, as if he were human ballast. It was instinctive, as if he would have the weight necessary to bring her back in trim. It had no effect.

"Bones, what condition is Caahtah in down theah? Cahn we get him ovahboard and into the dinghy, man?"

"We cahn; I think he's comin' round. But I cahn tell ya right now, things won't go well out theah in thaht damned rubber raft, don't ya know. He was heavin' when I came up top."

"Not much of a life boat—I'll give ya thaht, but it's all we got. Heah, take the helm, if ya please, I'll untie the paintah. When I hand ya the bitter end, draw the blasted thin' along side and make 'er fast."

Bones took the helm and the instant Patrick finished he turned to his mate and spoke.

"Pahtrick, we need to crack on, get Caahtah up heah and seal the bloody companion way hatch. If we shut 'er up tight, she'll haav a fightin' chance of re-surfacing—thaht is, if she breaks away. If she's not holed she might suhvive!"

Patrick agreed, but as he turned to go backwards down the companionway hatch, he queried Bones.

"Should I call the Coast Guard? We got a minute or two. I could get a message off afore we seal 'er up, what do ya think?"

Bones stood silently. He gazed anxiously into the east, far out to sea, as if he could see land on the other side of the great pond. His mind raced. Patrick waited.

≋≋≋

Bones had counseled Patrick and others like him for dozens of years, ever since Samuel Clark and Doc Callahan's passing. His advice, his authority, was legend. His confidants knew his resolve to be absolute, shaped by the wrongs he witnessed and endured, driven by murders perpetrated by Ulstermen and their British conspirators, violence against innocents.

All those past decisions stretched out before him in the great blueness that lay ahead of *Maxine's* sinking bow. Yet, there was one last thing he must complete, the effort he was leading from on shore, the very shore Martha never wanted him to sail away from again. They must return to Marblehead and he didn't trust the Coast Guard.

He imagined Winnie's face as he drew it in the sketch of the "'Figurehead." He avenged her death; he completed that mission. Now he needed to complete this one, this final one, before his life expired.

Bones looked aft to see if *Gael na Mara* was anywhere in sight. There was no vessel, no sail, not a masthead on the horizon. She would be there soon, he was certain, but when?

He recalled the decades he stood on her teak deck; the way she felt under his feet. He pictured Miread's beautiful smile and her lean attractive figure. She loved *Gael Na Mara*, he recalled, and he loved her.

He remained silent a minute longer thinking of his earlier life, and when he could think of it no more he returned to the present. Patrick continued awaiting Bones decision. Although Patrick was Taoiseach, he would follow Bones advice, as he had many times before. Conversely, the youth, the captain of the boat sinking beneath them, would not be consulted.

Finally, Bones stirred.

"Get the boy up top, Pahtrick, and seal 'er up. Maybe she'll snap free; maybe thin's will work out. We need to be cleah o' the bloody area so as not to get caught up in the riggin' if she flails about or springs back up from below. 'Ave yer knife ready to cut away the bloomin' paintah just in case; and Pahtrick, go without me if ya 'ave too . . . do ya undahstand! You explain to Maatha what 'aapened heah, you explain the bloody situation ya heah, Pahtrick?"

Patrick looked at Bones, their eyes meeting in a steely clash. Patrick nodded obediently. There was no point in discussing the point further. He quickly dropped into the saloon and moved directly into the captain's quarters to fetch Carter.

≋≋≋

"I'm sure they will be fine, Martha. They're out doing what they have done a thousand times before, I would think." Claire spoke quizzically. "Isn't that the case, aren't these three men the equivalent of about two centuries of sailing?"

Claire's logic didn't sway Martha who appeared to sink again into an apprehensive state. Claire judged it imprudent to leave.

Finishing their coffee, Martha invited Claire into her great room. They browsed the collection of books and poems Miread had bequeathed her daughter.

Claire sat on the drop-down seat mounted beneath the shelves of Martha's unusual library. She took mental note of the rare and voluminous collection of poems and musings by authors she coincidently studied at Boston College. She thought her professors would be impressed. Many were first editions.

Studying Irish culture hadn't entered Claire's mind when she filled out the admissions application at Boston College. Like most Midwesterners, she really didn't know much about the school. It attracted her attention primarily because Milwaukee was getting small. She figured the Jesuit connection would be a way to leave town without too great a shock to her father and mother.

It wasn't long after arriving at Boston College that its orientation for all things Irish captured her fancy. The campus was beautiful, alive with music, poetry and literature. The mystic nature of the Irish pervaded the campus. It was held out proudly by all who attended the festivals, concerts, poetry readings and gallery exhibitions. Irish pride was everywhere.

In contrast, Claire's own French Canadian and German heritage were thinly nourished back home. No shame was expressed and perhaps a measure of ethnic pride was present, but not like the Irish in Boston—not like Boston College. Claire found no reason to restrain her curiosity. She fell in love with the mystique of the Emerald Island.

≋≋≋

Martha, bearing Irish bloodlines on her father's side, endured more Irish pride than most could imagine, even in New England. Irish pride was all around as she grew up. At times it became overwhelming.

In recent years, Martha veiled her Irish heritage. She didn't join the Irish genealogy club, nor attend Irish celebrations. She still loved Irish poetry and read Irish authors. She did so, however, in the privacy of her great room and not openly at the library. She did so to stay connected with Miread, a connection she feared losing more than anything that could be lost, and Martha was well aware of what could be lost.

Loss caused her to cringe each time she saw a newspaper article about an Irish terrorist, or gunmen or bombings in Northern Ireland. She ached when Carter clipped and shoved them in his shirt pocket, a practice she caught brief glimpses of and wondered why.

She did none of the popular and prevalent Irish things these days, except one. It did not involve harming anyone, at least not in any direct way. She did it for her mother. It brought a level of satisfaction—particular satisfaction that the people responsible for her mother's death would not rest. They would not sleep securely, as did the young Irishmen she hid at the Purser's Quarters.

When she was much younger she did all those other Irish things. However, those times were gone. She could mark their terrible ending to the day—March 22, 1951.

≋≋≋

Gnawing at his cigar and studying *Gael na Mara's* sail trim, the leather-skinned captain estimated thirty minutes before *Maxine* would come hull up on the eastern horizon.

Patrick had briefed him on both the vessel and her captain during his recent stay at Martha's B&B. He thought Patrick was getting too chummy with the young sailor. He couldn't understand why he would take such risks and worse, expose Bones to such danger, to accomplish nothing more than becoming chums with another wooden boat owner. He would have kept them apart or gotten rid of the intruding laker, but he wasn't in the habit of telling a clan chief, his clan's chief, what to do.

The rough-hewn captain of *Gael na Mara* accomplished a simple mission, a straight forward purpose—he transported shadowy men out of Northern Ireland. They were shipped out when British intelligence or Unionist factions gained too clear a picture of who was doing what. The arrangement with Patrick and Martha was simple and effective.

The captain's job was nothing new in the grand scheme of things. Moving fighters through safe houses along the New England coast was practically a vocation. Carried out by fishermen and the Finnian Brotherhood, men like Captain O'Malley and vessels like *Gael na Mara* worked long enough at the task to call it tradition.

None of that need change, thought O'Malley. However, with an outsider in their midst, and Bones and Patrick befriending him, his work was that much harder. He also knew the embedded enemy operative would strike at the first sign of a defect in their security; then he'd have a real disaster on his hands—the ruthless bastard was incorrigible.

In the short run, Patrick's and Bones' safety was the only thing that mattered. If there appeared no immediate threat when he reached *Maxine*, he would let things lie. He wouldn't harm the young captain unless instructed to do so . . . or if Bones and Patrick were lost, leaving him to decide for himself.

He breathed deeply, checked the compass heading, and shouted in the tongue of his clan to a hand on the fore deck. The crewman looked up to see limp telltales on the leading edge of the jib. He raised his hand to his mouth and reported back. Another crewman cranked the handle of a deck wench and the telltales flew straight aft. The captain studied the sails once more, this time satisfied.

≋≋≋

Patrick escorted the pale white captain up onto *Maxine's* deck. Along the way he explained the plan.

Carter looked around, felt nauseated and went white. Patrick held him over the port rail on the opposite side as the dinghy. No point in fouling their life boat. As Carter wrenched dry heaves, a spasmodic rumble sounded from beneath *Maxine*.

Bones called out, "What the bloody hell was thaht?"

Just as Bones spoke his last word, Carter, still heaving over the rail, saw a huge, tumultuous bubble of air rise toward him. It surfaced on both sides of *Maxine*, spreading out in an area fifty feet in diameter. The explosive tumult of water opened on the surface, throwing water into the air and roiling about so violently it threatened to capsize the dinghy.

Just as suddenly, *Maxine*, whose bow was several feet low, sprung upwards. Her stern crashed down and she rocked with such force her mast shook and stays jerked at their turnbuckles.

The crew stood silently gaping at the motion, worried she would de-mast. A few seconds later *Maxine* leveled on her waterline and commenced sailing as if nothing happened.

Bones looking forward, made a course correction, looked at Patrick and Carter and spoke up.

"Cahn you look ovahboard amidships theah, Pahtrick, and confirm the disappearance of thaht bloody containah?"

Patrick quickly stepped forward on the low side and looked into the water. Carter sunk back into the cockpit seat, stomach churning and head spinning.

"It's gone all right, the damn thin' is gone, out of sight... it's gone," he shouted.

"Get Carter back below, Pahtrick, I'll stay at the helm. And throw me my bloody shoes, will ya. I feel ridiculous up heah in stockin' feet!"

Patrick turned to Carter. "Come on theah, skippah,"

Taking Carter by his arm he helped the distraught sailor, still gripping his stomach, toward the companionway.

A couple seconds later they were down the ladder and greeted by a sound they dreaded most; the sound of water spraying between planks. The fact that they could hear it over the droning of the engine shocked them both. *Maxine* could sink in minutes and Patrick realized he needed to get Carter back on deck and commence his plan to abandon the vessel.

"No!" shouted Carter, "I'm not going."

He spoke calmly, but defiantly.

"Not till we're certain she's lost. Not yet."

Patrick wanted to argue, but couldn't. It was what he would say if the tables were turned, if it were *Red Shoes* in peril. Instead he reached into the captain's quarters, fetched Bones' shoes and heaved them up through the companionway hatch. A second later he began ripping up the cabin sole to assess their state of affairs.

≋≋≋

Carter reached into the captain's quarters and grabbed his sleeping bag. He wrapped it around himself and gathered his wits as best he could. Reaching in the storage compartment under the port settee, he brought out a three-foot-long metal bar with a formed rubber handle. He inserted it into a slot in the floor board and down into the large diaphragm pump mounted in the bilge.

He took up position over the pump, gripped the handle and with a deep breath began heaving it back and forth. With this final act of desperation, the last step he could take, Carter joined the ranks of countless Gloucester men, men who did the same during their last minutes on board sinking boats.

Patrick looked up from his inspection to see the pump being worked by the sick, ashen youth. He looked at Carter in amazement and began shouting encouragement, like a wild fan in the soccer match of all time. The captain of *Maxine* showed a faint smile in return.

Patrick turned back to his work, pulling away another section of cabin sole. Ahead of the mast step, near the point where the forefoot met the stem piece, the reason for their imminent peril became woefully clear.

CHAPTER 21

ONLY ONE CAPTAIN

Upon discovery of the main leak, Patrick flew up on deck. In short order the old mates brought *Maxine* about. They headed towards shore. She was sluggish, but at least she sailed for land. If Patrick's estimate was, correct there was scant time remaining. They were going to have to abandon the sinking boat. Regardless, there was no excuse for not making every attempt to bring her back to shore.

Bones stayed on deck and peered into the western horizon for signs of *Gael na Mara*. Patrick went below to monitor the leak and take shifts at the pump. He winced when he looked into the saloon and saw Carter already standing in ankle deep water. Cabin sole planks floated high above the floors. Patrick shoved them out of Carter's way. The young captain pulled interminably at the pump handle.

"Time to take a breathah, skippah. I'll take ovah fer a while theah, laddie."

"I think she's taking on water faster than ever, Patrick. Output is fixed; the pumps are only capable of so much. We've got to slow the intake."

Patrick stretched his arms and shoulders. He touched Carter on the back to signal him to step aside. Carter was unwilling to quit, desperate to save his boat.

"Tis time ta spell ya, laddie," Patrick insisted.

Carter realized he was tired, his feet were submersed and he was cold. He made himself let go and Patrick moved into position.

"What did you see when you were forward?" Carter asked.

"She's leakin' on both sides 'tween planks at the forefoot, skippah. The planks were faast, but the seams were open, probably lost 'er caulkin'."

"Was that the only place she was leaking badly?"

"Cahn't say fer certain, skippah, cahn't see behind the ceilin' boards."

Carter moved through the saloon, lifting cabin sole planks, stacking them on the leeward settee. This revealed the extent of the water flooding in. The distressing sight drove home the worrisome situation.

"Caahtah, I radioed for help, theah's help on the way."

"The Coast Guard?"

"No, skippah, I didn't say I called the Coast Guard. I called friends, laddie, friends more dependable thahn the Coast Guard, don't ya' know."

There was strangeness in Patrick's voice. Carter couldn't discern the nature of it. Patrick never looked up or looked directly at Carter. That alone was unusual; he just kept heaving on the bilge pump handle.

Carter wondered why Patrick hadn't called the Coast Guard. Anyone else would have called the Coast Guard. That's who you call when you are trouble. They have helicopters and spotter planes and high speed patrol boats. They could have a pump out to them in 20 minutes, maybe less.

"I don't understand, Patrick, *Maxine* is sinking! Why didn't you call the Coast Guard?" Carter's frustration and incredulity broke through his plea.

"I got reasons, laddie, you've got to undahstand I got reasons. I know what yer thinkin'. I know yer thinkin' theah cahn be no reason good enough to risk yer ship, skippah. Till now the situation's been undah control, and my mates ah probably neah and they're good lads, men who know how to handle themselves in a bahd situation."

"Patrick, this isn't making sense!" Carter exclaimed. He looked around and saw the water rising. "What do you mean they're good lads? I don't care what they are; can they pump faster than we can? Can they keep *Maxine* from going down? Christ almighty, Patrick, we're sinking!"

"Caahtah, listen to me, listen. *Gael na Mara's* steamin' this way. She'll be heah any moment!"

Gael na Mara!

"The men on board aah capable; they cahn be trusted. There's more heah thahn meets the eye, laddie. Bones explained already, skippah, ya need to trust us, ya haav to trust us. Yer close to knowin' why, laddie; you've kept yer eyes open and you know a few thin's. You've got some questions. I know thaht, Caahtah. We'll talk about answers when we get you and yer boat baack to shoah. But it's best ya don't know everythin' right now; it's best if ya trust us, son."

"*Gael na Mara*?" Carter gasped aloud. He was stunned.

Just then Carter heard Bones bawl out, "Pahtrick, Caahtah, we aah losin' speed and sittin' low, boys. Give me a report,"

Carter crawled over the settees, swiveled on the dinette and sprung for the companionway. He felt sick and thought he would throw up again. He looked behind him just before he climbed on deck. Water was rapidly rising at Patrick's feet.

"She's leaking badly, Bones," Carter reported. "Any sign of *Gael na Mara*?"

"No, not yet and we're losin' way. She's becomin' unstable and it's time to drop sail; how long before the bloody engine swamps, son?"

"Five maybe ten minutes, not long. But I've got an idea."

Gaining strength from the threat of losing everything he owned, Carter moved aft to the lazarette hatch. From the compartment he pulled a canvas sun shade.

≋≋≋

Bones watched as Carter set the sun shade on the cockpit seat. It was twelve feet long by eight feet wide with reinforced bronze eyes on all corners and down each side.

The old sailor suspected he knew what Carter had in mind. More importantly, he knew the operation Carter was putting in motion needed more than a ninety-year-old arthritic, a seventy-eight year-old clan elder, and a barely recovered, seasick, hypothermia victim. They needed help in the form of young healthy bodies. Not only that, they needed it immediately. He stretched his gaze into the west, hoping and praying he would see the tips of *Gael Na Mara's* white sails.

Carter leaned again into the lazarette. This time he practically crawled into the compartment, his feet leaving the deck underneath him. Bones watched and smiled. If the circumstance wasn't what it was, he would have thought the scene comical.

≋≋≋

Carter's feet flailed in the air. A second or two went by and the young captain drug out a half-dozen coiled lengths of braided line. Placing the lines with the canvas, Carter turned to the port cockpit seat, lifted it, and pulled out a large container of axle grease. He had once attempted to use the grease to seal temporary leaks at launching.

From a plastic container full of paint supplies, he grabbed several yellow plastic trowels. On the opposite side of the compartment he snatched a diving mask from a brass hook. Beneath the mask lay a pair of swim fins and he tossed them on deck.

Carter gathered everything he had extracted from the compartment. He then moved quickly to the companionway, reversed direction and shot down the ladder. Patrick hadn't wavered from pumping the bilge. Carter noticed the beet-red color of the back of his burned hands. He reminded himself "...you have to trust them."

The water was thigh deep and Carter wondered how close to losing the engine they were. They needed more time, or they needed help, or both.

He couldn't believe what was happening. He couldn't believe what Patrick said to him; he didn't call the Coast Guard. Also, *Gael na Mara*, of all boats, of all possible rescuers, was steaming toward them; Patrick and Bones were both connected to *Gael na Mara*, and presumably the gun-toting specter that guarded her the night of his visit.

Most of all, Carter couldn't believe there was no time to contemplate the avalanche of strange events cascading down upon him. He had no time to think about how a garden variety shakedown cruise had transformed into a deadly maelstrom.

Shoving these frustrations aside for a moment, Carter moved alongside the aft pipe berth. There he opened a wooden tool chest. He clawed through the box until he laid his hands on a hammer and a carton of long tacks. He pulled them from their home and waded back through the flooded companionway to the main saloon.

Patrick was crouched in rising water, now above his waist. The engine was spitting water everywhere. There was little time remaining. The engine would cease any moment. The only light he saw in the darkness of the disaster was that he could expect the electric bilge pump to keep operating a while longer. The boat's batteries were mounted high in the hull for this reason.

Carter spoke to Patrick, explaining the hammer and tacks. Patrick stopped pumping and together they climbed up top. All hands would be needed for Carter's plan, a variation of an old remedy for leaky ships called fothering.

Carter's plan would go easier if *Maxine* wasn't under way so the crew commenced dropping sails. Within two minutes both great white cloths lay on deck. The jib was tied hastily to the port life lines; the mainsail was rolled up onto itself and quickly tied to the main boom.

Carter paused and looked around; the engine stopped while they lowered the sails. The sickly absence of sound, the bizarre quiet of the scene alarmed the sailor. *Maxine* lay nearly awash, suffering the aspect of a dying whale.

Far aft they heard a miniscule noise emanating from the stern. *Maxine's* electric bilge pump pushed seawater overboard in a piddling stream, a stream that proffered little hope of survival.

≋≋≋

A lean youth cut with chiseled features called down from the upper spreaders of the main mast.

"*Maxine's* hull up on the horizon."

They were close now.

The captain of *Gael na Mara* responded with a nod and continued furtively chewing the stub of his cigar. He fought an urge to radio ahead, hesitating since there would be no point. This rescue needed to occur without interference. He didn't need unwanted assistance. He didn't care to have Good Samaritans arriving in the midst of the rescue. Difficult decisions may be required, decisions not necessarily good for the young captain and his pleasure craft. He was there to save Bones and Patrick. Only if ordered to do so would he go beyond that imperative.

≋≋≋

Bones quickly tied lines on each side of the canvas spread out over the cabin top. A long line was tied at the aft mid-point of the canvas. A relatively shorter one was tied to the fore mid-point. This would enable fore and aft as well as athwart ship control once the canvas was under water and drawn into position beneath the damaged planks.

Patrick and Carter hastily smeared grease over the canvas beginning in the center, then out in all directions. Glances between the two frantic sailors indicated little concern for prettiness. They concentrated on a circle in the center of the rectangle and didn't bother to spread the sealant to the edges.

Carter was cold and shaking again and Patrick spoke up.

"Caahtah, I can't let you go ovahboard to drive those nails. I'll do the duty and no argument, ya heah."

"She's my home ..." Carter began to protest. Suddenly Bones stepped between them and interrupted with a firmness that startled Carter.

"No . . . you will not, Caahtah; and son, there'll be no bloody debate. Pahtrick goes ovahboard when I bleedin' say."

Carter paused. He considered the tone of the words Bones spoke. He stared first at Patrick, and back again at Bones. Something was different, something had changed. Bones just became the final word on board the sailing yacht, *Maxine*. Carter's ownership of the boat, his status as captain, apparently meant nothing.

As Bones looked back at Carter, the younger man recognized a level of resolve and determination he had not seen in the elder before. He looked into the eyes of a man who now decided who would live or die. It was at that moment that Carter suddenly understood he wasn't in control. Decisions affecting both his life and his boat were no longer his.

Bones spoke after a few seconds, calmly explaining in plain and unmistakable terms. "Caahtah, to you boatin' haas been a pleasure. It haas been bloody good fun. Now, this moment, as *Maxine* sinks beneath our feet, those bleedin' truths no longah apply."

Carter cast a glimpse toward Patrick as if to say, "Is this true?" Patrick caught the glimpse and shifted his own eyes towards Bones as if to pledge his absolute allegiance. Without speaking he clearly signaled, "Thaht's right, laddie, now listen to yer captain; he decides if we live or die."

Carter looked once again at Bones. In the place he was now, with the people with whom he stood on deck, the stakes were far different and far greater than he might have imagined. Even his curiosity couldn't have prepared him, or as things turned out, prevented him from being drawn into this drastic place.

In Carter's gut, the sensation was like Dorothy being swept into the tornado, or Alice stepping through the looking glass. He fell ill from hypothermia and lost his rational mind. When he regained it he found himself in a world no longer of his making. It was a radically different place, with different rules—immutable rules.

One of those rules, the one brought down upon him now, was that there could be just one captain on board *Maxine*, and that captain was Wilfred Albert Matheson. Another was that the decisions of this singular captain were absolute. There could be no doubt, no exceptions. From this point forward, Bones would decide what floated, what sank, and who would go down with it.

The appalling assimilation of these new truths came hard. Carter closed his eyes and pushed the flood of thoughts further back in his mind. He hoped to make sense of them. When he re-opened his eyes, he looked again at Bones and saw him as he never had before.

He decided on the spot it was futile to imagine overcoming Bones and his ninety years of age, fortitude and power. More important, beneath the bushy eyebrows and the Greek fisherman's cap, Carter saw benevolence, not evil; he saw strength, not cowardly bravado. He saw in the seaman's dark eyes wisdom, not opportunism.

Carter turned in his place. He assumed a subservient stance. He relinquished command to the older and more experienced. He realized no matter who was in command, everyone on board shared a common purpose, to keep *Maxine* afloat. He stepped rapidly into the cockpit, retrieved the mask and fins and placed them on the starboard deck near the lifeline gate, the point Patrick would enter the water when Bones gave the order.

The early morning wind that chilled the senses out of Carter diminished to 12 knots. The sky was changing to a different blue as the sun rose high on its azimuth. The fineness of the day belied the seriousness of the situation as *Maxine* continued filling with water.

Weather alone no longer posed a threat to their individual lives, that is, if the idea that losing one's boat isn't tantamount to losing one's life. For most people, this might not be true, but for Carter it was. For Bones and Patrick it was, too, which explained, why two men "old as the hills" were racing to finish Patrick's schooner before they died. It became clear to Carter that they desperately worked each day to live in spirit before they died in body. Their restorative was a wooden boat, a boat of their own making.

Then Carter thought another curious thought. In Bones' and Patrick's cases, the compulsion to live again without doubt had something to do with losses they suffered. That might explain the way Patrick behaved the day they met at the movies in Boston. In Bones' case, he suspected loss had to do with the drawing in Patrick's leather wallet: the extraordinary sketch entitled "The Figurehead."

≋≋≋

"Thaht's it, laddies, lower away," Patrick called from amidships. Bones and Carter stood on each side of the bow pulpit lowering the canvas over Maxine's stem. The feat was more difficult than it looked. They gripped all three lines attached to each of their respective sides. Carter also kept hold of the shorter line tied in the center of the forward edge.

Carter watched from the bow as Patrick moved aft. He caught a sickening glimpse of the dinghy riding high alongside his sinking yacht. It occurred to him they would not need the boson's chair to lower Bones onto the dinghy when they abandoned ship. It tortured him that the weather would be fine, the sea flat and they would be forced to abandon her.

CHAPTER 22

ENTIRELY IN THEIR HANDS

Patrick waited amidships as the crew at the bow struggled with the tangle of lines they needed to keep in order. It was essential that the canvas be drawn squarely under the boat.

Once they were roughly in position, they would tie the lines to the lifeline stanchions on each corresponding side of the boat. Carter stepped up to *Maxine's* bow pulpit to secure the fore mid-point line. That's when he spotted an immense white sail on the horizon. He shouted to his mates who abruptly turned to look.

Gael na Mara arose from the blue water like a mythical white swan. Patrick spoke aloud a Gaelic Proverb as he crossed himself. "Furain an t-aoigh a thig, greas an t-aoigh tha falbh!" Then for Carter's benefit, he repeated it in English. "Welcome the coming, speed the parting guest."

As *Gael na Mara* approached, a boat was lowered from her deck. Three young Irishmen, all of whom Carter recognized from the B&B or the boat shop, climbed aboard. The instant the boat touched water they sped towards *Maxine*.

≋≋≋

The cigar man remained on board alone. The sullen-faced, square-jawed captain, glasses tight to his peering eyes, could see *Maxine* lying precariously low on her lines. *She may be lost already*, he thought. His teeth clenched a Cuban. Blue smoke spewed from his lips and rolled aft into the sky beyond the cutter's stern.

He hadn't bothered to tell Bones or Patrick he remembered *Maxine* when she was still *Madrigal,* her original name. He knew her during his early days in the Caribbean charter trade.

The cigar man went on to contemplate the Caribbean and the differences between his charters then and his charters now. He preferred his current command and intended to keep it. The cause was right, compensation good, and it fit his disposition. It fit far better than catering to finicky accountants and their sunburned, bare-breasted wives.

Removing the cigar from his lips he spat overboard and *Gael na Mara* quickly left the spittle behind.

≋≋≋

Carter watched *Gael na Mara's* cloud of white sail grow as she drew close. Filled with trepidation and awe, Carter watched the enigmatic skipper, cigar jutting prominently from his teeth. He cut a raw figure as he attended her wheel, the Irish double ender approaching with confidence and aplomb. *Gael na Mara* possessed an aura, Carter believed, both magnificent and ominous in equal measure. At the very sight of her his mind reeled with bewilderment and commotion.

He couldn't decide whether his situation was going to be better or worse. Already, he was no longer the captain of his own vessel. Already, he realized that the bare truth of these men, and what they did, infected him like a systemic mold. He thought the whole of the situation threatened the core of his being. This development further altered his charted course in severe and unexpected ways.

Carter went on to wonder if this yacht and its dubious crew did save *Maxine*, would strings come attached? Would he be in their servitude? Would his rescuers be like Tar Baby; if he touched them would their black insipid deeds stick to him, too? Would they agree to allow him simply to leave the region, even though he knew things he shouldn't, even if his knowledge was circumstantial?

By this time, it sank in that he knew too much for his own good. His friends were not what they seemed, and their friends were obviously far worse.

What kind of trouble have I got myself into? How the hell did I get here?

Carter's eyes returned to his hapless *Maxine*, the spring in her sheer feebly contrasting the flatness of the sea. She was subsiding into the cold, oily green water. She seemed destined to join the wrecks whose bones scattered the ocean floor from Marblehead to Labrador.

A physically jolting sensation of frustration clambered through him. He wanted to scream. He wanted his life back and he wanted his boat back. He wanted control and he couldn't have it, all because he got sick and *Maxine* hit a damnable container. Why should those things, things that might happen to anyone, strip him of control anyway? Where was the justice in that?

Then again, Carter pondered further, could merely hitting a container bring down his carefully constructed reality? Wasn't it more likely his incessant curiosity caused all this—curiosity combined with naiveté of monumental proportion?

Apparently, my judgment was flawed.

Disgust rose in Carter's gullet. He reprimanded himself for not leaving well enough alone. Why did he row out that night to inspect *Gael na Mara*? Why did he search the Internet for gun-running freighters? Why did he collect articles about people engaged in dangerous, illegal activities? What was he thinking? What was the point?

Regardless of his pleading, he was now locked in a nightmare turned real. He experienced a transformation he couldn't believe possible. He felt like Harvey Cheney in Kipling's *Captains*

Courageous, only he couldn't see how falling overboard, as did the hapless Cheney, was going to lead to anything good. But what choice did he have? Bones and Patrick both implored him to trust them. He knew he needed to trust them.

Carter took a deep breath. His lungs were still sensitive, his stomach off center, but deep breathing helped calm his thoughts. He reminded himself that, in fact, young Harvey Cheney's fall did have a positive outcome. He told himself to hold fast to any glimmer of hope. Unless it became clear his life was directly threatened, it was time to cast away these pointless ruminations and complete his exertions to slow the leaks—to get on with saving *Maxine*. She lived for Carter as a stunning symbol of continuity, a balance between wind and water—an object whose design and existence exemplified peace between contrary forces. The yacht, in all her wooden glory, her beautiful lines, her high purpose of being, represented the sum of his worldly existence, his security. He couldn't imagine life without her. There could be no peace without her.

≋≋≋

The dinghy raced toward *Maxine*. It passed her port side and swept around *Maxine's* stern, coming up on her starboard beam just aft *Maxine's* dinghy turned lifeboat.

Once alongside the crew tied up without speaking. The young Irishman who came to retrieve Patrick at Sewall Point the day they were supposedly off-loading lumber gave Carter a silent nod as he boarded. He strode directly toward Patrick, spoke to him in Gaelic and handed him a two-way radio.

As the others came aboard they kept a respectful distance from Bones. Carter thought the boarders behaved as if they were in the presence of royalty. It was then he realized that Bones' status extended far beyond the decks of *Maxine*. It was obvious, as the situation unfolded, that the bounds of his authority extended to *Gael na Mara* as well.

Bones, though maintaining an air of dignity amidst the rescuers, was finally giving way to over-taxed knees. Patrick shot a glance toward one of the Irishmen who raced to assist Bones with the lines and canvas. Another immediately cleared the way for Bones to return to the cockpit. There he rested, exhausted and gray in color.

Carter and the foredeck hands proceeded with lining up the awning and tying off the lines to the stanchions.

The pace of things picked up and Carter felt in charge again, at least of this operation. This made him feel better despite his apprehension. It appeared as if everyone was working together to save *Maxine* and for this he was grateful.

Once Bones was comfortable, the chief of the boarding party returned forward and opened a bag he threw upon deck from their dinghy. He took from it a wet suit, fins, and mask. He began changing into the wet suit.

Carter joined him and handed him the tacks and hammer. He implored the diver to remember that if dropped, those items would go straight to the bottom. If that happened, *Maxine* would soon follow. He watched with terrible hope as the young Irishman nodded his assurance, moved to the rail and dropped into the water. In an instant, he was out of sight.

Standing upright and turning, Carter saw *Gael na Mara* was nearly upon them. He watched pensively as she sailed ahead on *Maxine's* port side. Once past and tacking into the wind, the lone captain left the wheel, climbed on deck, and lowered the forward jib, then the main.

A few minutes later he brought her about under bare poles. The cutter motored back towards *Maxine.* Carter glimpsed at Patrick and found him speaking quietly into the two-way radio. Carter shook his head in disbelief. He couldn't have imagined this scene.

≋≋≋

Staring in both awe and mistrust at *Gael na Mara,* Carter jumped nervously when he heard the first tapping come from deep below the water line. A few seconds later the diver surfaced for air then dove again.

"Yer plan be a' workin' theah, laddie," said Patrick with a calm voice, holding the two-way radio near his chin. He looked careworn, and Carter could see the hand holding the radio was burned as red as a Maine lobster.

"Perhaaps it's time to fetch yer bumpahs and fendah boards theah, skippah, time to get prepared fer the "Woman of the Sea" to tie up along side."

Patrick cast an outward glance towards *Gael na Mara*.

Carter turned to move aft. The sound of hammering rang through the hull in dull pings that somehow transformed into music.

By Carter's estimation, the canvas should begin to suck directly up against the leaks and wrap neatly around the form of *Maxine's* forefoot. The grease and cloth should be squeezing into the cracks by tons of pressure pushing up from the vast body of water below. The tacks would hold it in place.

All that was needed now was to pump her out, at least enough to get her engine restarted and get underway. This would be the responsibility of the inscrutable "Woman of the Sea."

As Carter worked his way to the stern to retrieve the bumpers and fender boards, he studied *Gael na Mara* And shivered with trepidation. The matriarchal cutter filled the scene, appearing vast and supreme yet mysterious and menacing, too.

The mysterious vessel's captain in turn was studying *Maxine*'s predicament. He gripped *Gael na Mara's* wheel with one hand and held the two-way radio in the other. His teeth were white, his lips pulled tight to hold his cigar. His eyes squinted from the smoke. They met Carter's and swept quickly on, ignoring the young captain's presence, searching only for Patrick and Bones.

Carter recoiled at the glowering intensity of the man. He reminded himself that Bones and Patrick both insisted these were trusted friends.

Friend or enemy, rescuer or slayer, I just don't know.

Finally, without deciding what they were, hoping they weren't the latter, he concluded that whichever the case may be, Patrick and Bones were his friends. They were in this fix with him, not against him. They prevented him from sliding into a coma, or possibly worse, and now they were attempting to save *Maxine*. They did all this at great risk, whatever the legitimacy of that risk. His fate lay entirely in their hands. He owed them his life.

He rigged *Maxine's* fender boards without further inner debate. Once completed, he prepared to catch dock lines from the singular boat whose presence charged him with both curiosity and fear.

Carter looked at his chronometer. It was only 12:30 pm! He looked again in disbelief; he thought it was later. Since dawn he'd nearly died, his yacht was sinking, his world irrevocably changed, and *Gael na Mara* was tying up to his beam. He felt jogged and disoriented.

Carter thought of his log and centered on the necessity of recording what was taking place. He looked down into the cabin to see if it was still dry. To his shock he saw Patrick's fiddle case and his own guitar case bobbing idly in the flooded cabin. Kicking off his shoes and pants he dashed below, wading in the sickening water. He fished them both out and hurriedly carried them on deck. Patrick spotted him.

"Whoa, laddie, quick thinkin' theah, skippah," cried Patrick. "These yachts—they're impahtant, but years o' fierce bahd luck would ha' got us if the fiddle went down."

Patrick's humorous outcry drew a discernable smile from Bones who was resting quietly in the cockpit. Bones re-lit his pipe, acknowledged Patrick's quip with a nod, and kept an eye on the proceedings without speaking.

Claire finally left Martha's at noon. Caught up in the moment, she had agreed to accompany Martha to Gloucester later in the day.

As she walked home through the sunlit town, the breeze still blowing through her jet black hair, she thought about the unusual morning—what happened and why. She was glad she took this Saturday and Sunday off. She needed time away from the irascible roaster, time to take in the events spinning around her. Her sudden interest in Carter and the incident with Martha affected her strangely. She needed time to process.

When she arrived at her apartment, she climbed stairs that worked their way around a tall upright juniper. At the top she stepped onto an outdoor deck. From the deck a sliding glass door opened into the living room of her modest abode.

The deck enjoyed a distinguished view of the harbor. She looked forward to this, her first summer in Marblehead. She planned to enjoy her evening meals outdoors in the fresh sea air, high above the cobblestone lanes of Old Town.

The ancient cottage was owned by an investment banker, who along with his wife and two small children, stayed mostly at a townhouse in Cambridge. The Marblehead house was inherited from his parents, now retired and living in Southwest Harbor, Maine. It was the second of three homes he owned. The third was a salt box on Cape Cod, near Hyannis Port. Come summer, they explained to Claire, who had rented the apartment only two months earlier, she would enjoy the place all to herself. The children preferred the beaches on Cape Cod.

Claire prepared a light lunch, rested a while, and completed some communications. After a couple hours she readied herself for the ride up to Gloucester. Martha said she knew where Claire lived and would pick her up around 4:00 pm.

"Watch for a red Escort, Clayah. Oh, by the way deah, theah's an aart colony on the seaward side of the harbah," Martha explained. Shopping would occupy their time if *Maxine* hadn't docked yet.

Claire was nervous. She was uneasy about showing this much interest in Carter so soon. It ran against her upbringing. Like all proper Midwestern girls, she had been admonished to show restraint.

As a point of fact, however, she could not deny that it was *she* that showed up at the Purser's Quarters that morning. It was *she* that sought contact under the pretense of a neighborly cup of hot coffee.

I'm taking things too far, too fast.

She justified her decision to go to Gloucester, not to see Carter necessarily, but to quell Martha's anxiety. Honor bound, she must complete this obligation she accepted earlier in the day. Honor, her lawyer father said many times, was absolute. His French-Canadian pride and moral passion were deeply infused in his daughter, as they were in his mother, the matriarch of the Dubois family. Martha reminded Claire of Mamie and it pleased her to help Martha, to be even remotely attached to someone who reminded her of Grand-mere.

≋≋≋

Once *Gael na Mara* rafted alongside, Carter stood by and watched Patrick go aboard. Bones remained sitting in the cockpit, the captain of the double-ender glancing his way. Carter saw Bones send back an approving nod, his pipe jutting upward in his teeth.

Patrick and the captain held a brief conference in their native tongue, leaving Carter guessing what they said. After looking his way in the middle of the conversation, they turned back and continued talking. He must trust them, Carter kept repeating to himself.

After a few more words exchanged with Patrick, the captain barked orders to his crew. Patrick proceeded to go below, unescorted. Carter noted Patrick's demeanor was that of one who has been below a thousand times before. His connection to the boat was unmistakable.

The Irish crewmen climbed back aboard, responding to the captain's orders and gear began coming up from her hold.

Using *Gael na Mara's* main boom as a crane, a portable generator and large diaphragm pump were maneuvered on board *Maxine* and immediately set to work. An additional hose, rigged from *Gael na Mara's* onboard pump, crossed the decks and dropped down through *Maxine's* companionway hatch.

Carter peered through the companionway hatch and studied the water level below. He made visual measurements. There was a lot of water inside her; however, there was now reason for hope. The total pumping capacity, including *Maxine's* own electric bilge pump, raised Carter's hopes higher. The loud noise of the generator gave the scene an industrious sound, a sound that for Carter Phillips held great promise.

The diver returned on deck and surprised Carter by addressing him directly. He explained that *Maxine's* planking was scraped badly. The damage missed the butt-joints and her fastenings appeared to be holding; *Maxine* could be towed back in.

His brief report completed, the diver crossed over to *Gael na Mara* and gave the same information to the captain who firmly replied that if they got *Maxine* pumped down he wanted her engine re-started. She needed to motor into Gloucester without *Gael na Mara's* assistance. By evening he wanted to return to Manchester Harbor just as if they had merely gone out for a day sail.

As the captain spoke his orders, Carter noted that he, *Maxine's* owner, wasn't consulted. The orders were given as if they extended to Carter as well. He took a deep breath, acquiesced and concluded he had no problem with the plan. He would be more than happy to continue on his way unaided.

Hearing the report of his vessel's condition and witnessing a drop in the water level, Carter fell back on the cockpit bench next to Bones, relieved and exhausted. The sun fell on his face, warming his skin.

He sat silently for a minute or two then turned to see Bones staring into the southeastern sky. He looked to see what the old man was looking at and spotted two black specks moving slowly above the horizon. He squinted to see what they were. Bones shifted to get a better look.

"Helicopters," Bones said. "Probably from Otis."

"Otis?"

"Otis Air Force base," Bones replied. "Cape Cod."

The black unmarked choppers approached at high altitude. They flew north in a straight line. Carter had seen over-flights the previous summer. He found the unmarked aircraft curious, though he didn't think much of them at the time. He didn't know what to think of them now. He needed rest and his mind reeled in the midst of his calamity.

He closed his eyes and leaned back against the cockpit coaming to allow the sun to play on the back of his eyelids. The special pleasure it induced made him feel like himself again, almost as if none of the strange things happening with his eyes opened were real. For a scant few moments he felt secure and in control.

≋≋≋

While Carter rested, Bones rose on tired legs, taking grim notice of the black helicopters. Gazing across to *Gael na Mara*, he saw her agitated captain reach quickly into the pilot house. The leather skinned man took out binoculars, clawed his cigar out of his mouth and peered at the choppers crossing the sky.

Neither Bones, *Gael na Mara's* captain, nor Patrick had survived this long by ignoring objects that shot bullets, fired missiles or dropped bombs. Certainly, when they worked aboard freighters stuffed to the gunnels with contraband weapons, sighting military aircraft, whatever the reason, struck a solemn chord.

≋≋≋

Carter opened his eyes again and was surprised to see all hands, including the crewman, staring north toward the receding black dots. He looked from man to man as they looked at each other. Carter could see in their eyes they did not consider the helicopters a coincidence. A brooding, apprehensive mood infected the entire group.

The captain of *Gael na Mara* returned the cigar to his mouth, puffed a defiant cloud of blue smoke, and then barked out more orders. This action effectively snapped the crew back to life, back to their duties; not allowing them to linger.

A minute later a tool chest appeared. With the chest in tow, the Irish crewman headed over the rail to *Maxine*. When the water level dropped, assuming it would drop, the crew would restore engine power. The cigar wielding captain watched approvingly.

CHAPTER 23

ALL SAILS ARE DOWN

"Commander Donovan, we've just received a hail from recon helicopters departing Otis, heading north. We'll patch it through."

"Thank you, Mr. Holcomb. I'm standing by."

FBI counterintelligence in Boston made it clear to Commander William F. Donovan of *The Monarch* that this operation was intel only. It was a training mission, designed to accomplish two things: first, improved clandestine monitoring of a terrorist cell within U.S. borders, and second, improved coordination between FBI, CIA, and armed forces intelligence.

Donovan, after three decades of service, knew they were uncontrollably independent agencies and zealously protective of their turfs. This operation represented an effort toward greater cooperation. The idea sprung from international threats against American targets. They were increasing in frequency and ferocity.

Coordinated maneuvers generally met with disappointing results. Rather than cooperate, one agency typically fought another for favorable Congressional funding. That was on a good day. His observation suggested a long history of problems, not the least of which began with MAGIC, the code breaking system devised to spy on the Japanese. Donovan, while searching the Internet on a recent occasion, found records dated 1988 revealing that FDR and military intelligence hid MAGIC from the fledging Office of Coordinator of Information, which, after World War II commenced, became the OSS. Lack of trust and cooperation made Pearl Harbor inevitable according to the pundits, yet most agree the war was inevitable anyway.

Commander Donovan contemplated the problem of secret services filled with ambitious and youthful operatives. These agencies lacked gray hair, people who understood the necessity of restraint, people who understood all was not black or white, good or evil.

In this operation, for example, they were supposed to be watching terrorist cells as they planned and attempted to implement operations. The goal was to observe closely, but not move against those members who in the future would likely be a conduit to more intelligence. The objective was to be able to prevent a terrorist act at the last moment, not a minute before. The intent was to wipe out low-level operatives. Following that was continued monitoring of middle-level decision makers. They, in turn, might reveal the secretive, deeply imbedded leaders, the old guard fighters who were the greatest danger of all.

Donovan heard a squawk erupt from his communications console and responded by donning a head set.

> "Monarch, this is Falcon One, my spotter has located GNM, coordinates to follow, over. Roger that Falcon One, anything further, over. Roger Monarch, the target is rafted to another vessel; all sails are down and they appear to be drifting together, over. Roger that Falcon One, over. Monarch, Falcon Two will make a second pass over to see if we can ID the second vessel. Negative, Falcon One, I repeat, negative. Report to your watch commander at Otis. FYI the FBI identified the

second vessel and its destination already, over."

Donovan flipped a switch on the console. *This is a bullshit assignment.*

He much preferred the drug trade. It was easy to spot the enemy. The insidious effects of drugs were plain and simple to understand. Most of all it didn't mean spying on his own kind, he being Irish and Catholic to boot! Why, his own grandfather was a captain of a fishing boat that participated in questionable activities on behalf of the Finnian Brotherhood, at least as family legend made claim.

Long ago Commander Donovan learned to keep his Irish Catholic heritage contained. It was important to him. However, back when he began his service, it was not an asset.

What really pisses me off is that we're spying on the Irish for no other reason than training. We're really after the Arabs and Palestinians. Makes me feel like a traitor. I wonder if we're selling this intel to the British, and what the hell we're getting in exchange. Wouldn't surprise me.

The captain of the secret listening ship leaned back in his leather chair.

Who am I fooling? I was no less crazy than those chopper pilots in my hey-day. I suppose I was happier when I thought things were black and white, good against evil. Now look at me, spying on my own kind...I've become nothing more than a sneaking spook! It's just as well I can't tell my wife or anyone else what the hell I'm doing out here.

In his 32 years of service, far more than his peers, Commander Donovan never wavered in trust or loyalty, even if he personally found the situation objectionable. As a devout Catholic, he could never have withstood the guilt. He couldn't break a solemn oath of secrecy and his superiors were well aware of that.

With a combination of chagrin and acquiescence, he wheeled his chair around and began completing a duty roster. He paused, looked up, and stared longingly at a photo. It was a 54-foot Hinckley ketch. It awaited him on retirement—two months away. The good skipper smiled a satisfying, even rascally smile.

Another month of sea duty, four weeks in port to de-brief and I'm free!

CHAPTER 24

IF THREE MEN KNOW IT

"Caahtah, everythin' is goin' the direction it ought ta. I'd like ya to come aboard *Gael na Mara* and haav a look 'round," Patrick suggested. I know this haas been a hell of a mornin', laddie, but it's time to correct our misshapen' course, set some thin's straight thaht need ta be set straight. How 'bout it, skippah?"

Carter looked at Patrick. He sensed good intentions. He wondered how it was possible that Patrick could veil his secret life so completely at times like this. How could someone so well found, the picture of fairness and calm, live a double life involving subterfuge, conspiracy, and, presumably, murder. Was his cause that righteous? Was his belief in his cause so enabling? Was his cause, or their cause, for he obviously wasn't acting alone, simply a rationalization for otherwise aberrant, pathological behavior? Did Patrick actually see a difference between his overt and covert lives?

Certainly he must, and apparently he wanted to talk about it. Either way, it was clear to Carter he was in over his head. He needed to make a judgment, now, in response to Patrick's invitation. He needed to decide if going along with his rescuers without resistance was the best thing.

You have to trust them. You have no reason, at this point, not to. They saved your life and they're in the process of saving your boat.

Carter doubted that this was true of the cigar man. *He's following orders, and orders can change.*

Patrick waited for a response while Carter's inner dialogue raced on. Finally, Carter decided and spoke in a voice depicting high regard for the old seaman's authority.

"Permission to come aboard, Skipper?"

"Permission granted theah, laddie."

Carter gripped *Gael na Mara's* life lines and crossed over. As he did he glanced down at *Maxine's* gold embossed cove strip and swore she had risen an inch or two in the water. He took in a huge breath of sea air, looked across the teak deck of the cutter before him, and climbed furtively onto the "Woman of the Sea. "

≋≋≋

"Caahtah Phillips, this is Mr. Ryan O'Malley, captain of *Gael na Mara.*" Carter thought Patrick's voice exuded his richest Irish brogue.

"Caahtah Phillips, Mr. O'Malley, is skippah of the yacht, *Maxine,*" Patrick explained as a matter of seaman-like protocol.

The rust-colored captain of the North Sea cutter sat stiffly upright at his navigation station. He looked up from his log book.

Carter wasn't sure whether one shook hands, embraced roundly or just what gesture was correct when introduced to an apparent Irish terrorist. All things considered, he chose to keep a measured distance.

O'Malley picked up Patrick's unspoken order to welcome the lake sailor on board. He obeyed reluctantly.

"Welcome aboard, Captain Phillips. My crew reports the pumping is going well; the water level in your vessel is dropping."

Carter nodded a form of thanks; however, what struck him was the absence of an Irish accent in Captain O'Malley's voice. Carter knew O'Malley spoke Gaelic; he had heard him.

O'Malley is American, he thought. Yet another mystery he figured he should leave alone, but couldn't. *Even if he is American, why no local accent; surely he's from Boston. With a name like Ryan O'Malley, he wasn't many generations off the Emerald Island.*

"Shall we step into the great-room, gentlemen," the Captain of *Gael na Mara* suggested stiffly. He forced a smile on his tightly contoured face. Carter remained certain O'Malley wasn't all too pleased to have him aboard.

Patrick nodded approvingly. He looked at Carter, lifted the long-billed cap from his head and extended his arm. Carter proceeded in the direction he was being led.

Bones, who had been helped aboard a half-hour earlier, emerged from a forward cabin Carter later learned was the owner's stateroom. He looked refreshed and dressed in a different suit of clothing, making Carter wonder how it was that clothes on board *Gael na Mara* fit him.

Looking entirely at home, in fact behaving almost as if he owned the boat, the sketcher of the "Figurehead" greeted them all. There was an air of authority emanating from Bones, enhanced in fact, by his rested, clean-dressed appearance. Carter watched to see its effect on Captain O'Malley.

"Welcome aboard *Gael na Mara*, Caahtah," said Bones. "I'm certain Captain O'Malley heah wishes fer ya to relax, waarm up, and bloody well rest while the mates work on *Maxine*."

Carter glanced over and the cigar-smoking captain nodded respectfully in Bones' direction.

"She's no bleedin' *Red Shoes*," Bones teased Patrick affectionately, "but she serves the good captain heah suitably fer a vessel 'er age and disposition. She's a few years youngah thahn me and got more bloomin' life in 'er thahn I do, thaht's fer certain!"

A polite though quizzical smile issued from Carter as he began looking around the great-room. He was immediately struck by the extravagant detailing. The saloon was luxurious. The aroma of varnished wood embraced him like an old friend. A tremendous octagonal butterfly hatch allowed sunlight to penetrate the space from above.

The whole of it glowed in teakwood splendor. A soapstone stove with elaborate glazed tiles graced the forward center of the spacious cabin. Brass lamps swung imperceptibly above the settees and the plush leather upholstery was dotted with diamond buttons. *Gael na Mara*'s interior looked like photos of yachts Carter had seen in the smoking room of the East Harbor Yacht Club.

The cost and effort of keeping *Gael na Mara* in this condition immediately entered Carter's mind. He knew what it took to keep *Maxine* in classic form...the bulk of a small inheritance combined with intermittent architectural commissions, and *Maxine* was modest by comparison.

Carter's curiosity began its old tricks as he contrived to devise ways to learn more about her origins. In the instant he stood there, gazing at her fineries, Carter became interested in knowing who provided the money to keep her in this glorious condition. Did tight-lipped merchants and suppliers owe Captain O'Malley favors too, as Marbleheaders apparently owed Patrick?

He paused for a moment and reflected on how widespread Irish pride was in New England. He caught himself wondering which wealthy Irish Catholic families were obviously prideful enough, enamored with boats enough, to find their preservation intriguing. He didn't have to think hard to complete this thought since Hyannis Port was full of them.

Carter then looked for a place to sit; someplace he could witness the entire scene yet exit in a hurry if the need should arise.

In an alcove on the port side of the great-room sat Patrick's fiddle and Carter's guitar, propped against the bulkhead. They were removed from their cases and set out to dry in the warm cabin air. Carter's appreciation was interrupted by the sound of Patrick's voice.

"Captain O'Malley," he said. "Do ya have a fingah or two of Irish whiskey aboard this heah rescue ship?"

A nod issued from O'Malley and a crewman, functioning now as steward, stepped into the galley and reached into an ornately carved compartment. He withdrew a bottle and selected delicate Irish crystal from a cabinet designed specifically to protect it from the motion of a sea-going yacht. Into each of three glasses he poured two ounces of golden liquor.

O'Malley excused himself, stiffly shunning the social formalities, and returned on deck to check the progress of his crew.

Bones, Patrick and Carter, together in one cabin for the first time since *Gael na Mara* arrived, waited patiently as their drinks were served. The steward carried them over on a silver platter, and then disappeared. Handing Carter a glass, Patrick proclaimed, "This'll restore yer heat theah laddie."

Patrick raised his glass, looking first at Bones, then at Carter. Patrick, Carter believed, seemed to be acknowledging that they were all captains; either of men or boats or both. As such, they must uphold a concord of mutual respect, knowledge and trust.

Patrick proposed a toast. Carter saw the old freighter man return, the speechifier he had come to treasure, the man he met at the theatre in Boston. Patrick sounded an ancient Gaelic proverb, spoken first in his native tongue, then again in English.

" Cha sgeul-ruin e 's fios aig triuir air"
It is no secret - if three men know it!

The crystal glasses collided and the threesome swallowed. Carter thought the toast an acknowledgment of sorts, a sign they were all in this predicament together. Bones and Patrick no longer held a great secret from him; rather they held a great secret with him. This being the case, Carter also believed the toast to be a question. Could he keep their secret? Would he keep their secret? Would they allow him the chance, or was he simply too great a risk?

Carter's mind reeled in doubt. He looked around to find a place he could sit alone and ponder his dilemma. Spotting a library of nautical books he moved toward it. As he neared the shelves a feeling of déjà vu grew within him. The library was an elaborate feature in the great room. The shelves were built with fiddles to keep the books inboard when the vessel heeled. It had a small writing table and drop down circular stool. There were drawers and compartments.

Carter suddenly remembered why it seemed familiar. It looked exactly like the library in Martha's great room! Or, the reverse was true; the library at Martha's was a clever reproduction of the library aboard *Gael na Mara. Why would that be?*

Scanning the books Carter reached for Bowditch. He skipped past it when his eye suddenly caught glimpse of a title that surprised him.

He reached up and pulled down a worn, discolored edition of *Riddle of the Sands.* Looking to see if Bones and Patrick were watching, he noticed them speaking to each other while looking over a chart at the nav station. He gripped the sea tale and opened it. The leaves of the pages were brown on the outside edges and dog-eared as if read dozens of times. It was surely an original. Inside the cover, scribbled in fading ink were words that read –

"To Wilfred Albert Matheson, in memory of my blessed father, signed, Erskine Hamilton Childers, President of Eire, October 1974."

A faint pencil note was added, clearly in a different handwriting. "EHC passed from the struggle today, Nov. 17, 1974. He died of natural causes, a rare accomplishment for a statesman in this troubled affair. His greatness was manifest in the fact that he became president of the descendents of the Irish Free State, that portion of the island now called Eire. It is ironic that his constituents are the descendents of the very lot who assassinated his father, my countryman, Robert Erskine Childers! May father and son rest in peace."

The cryptic addendum was signed "B. Matheson." Carter quickly recognized the signature. It was the same as on the pen and ink drawing, "The Figurehead."

Carter gripped the book excitedly, thinking of the story, the ideas and the man who wrote them. He remembered the danger

Caruthers's curiosity got him into. He contemplated the trouble Robert Erskine Childers got himself into.

An Englishman turned Irish sympathizer, Childers married an Irish-American woman. Her father was a Boston physician, a suspected member of the Finnian Brotherhood. Childers, after spurning his own country for their treatment of the Irish, became an Irish citizen. He became the voice of the movement, served as their publicist, and authored a book and papers advocating Irish independence. Ironically, he was shot dead by a firing squad at 52 years of age, leaving a male child who would go on to become the man who signed the brittle edition of his father's book—a child who became President of Eire, 50 years after the death of his father.

Carter continued to hold the book open as his thoughts returned to the immediate situation. He wondered if he was now bound to Bones' and Patrick's secret and perhaps the Irish question itself.

He considered whether his behavior in the next hour or two would be pivotal to his survival. Carter was certain his rescuers, or perhaps captors, possessed the means at hand on board *Gael na Mara* to expunge him from the picture quite effectively if they so chose. No one would miss him. No one would be dedicating a book to him, honoring him for his unwilling, unreported sacrifice to Irish independence.

Carter thought about the outlandish predicament this all presented, not just from his perspective, but from Bones' and Patrick's, too. He tried to place himself in their shoes, assuming for the purpose of debate their cause was right and their histories wholly justified.

Then he reversed the presumption. What if Bones, Patrick, and their thugs were all terrorists? What if they were ruthless and diabolical? Carter wondered if he had been caught up in such an extraordinary existence, by birth or by choice, what he would do. What would be his plan for a cruising sailor who, through no particular ill intent, stumbled onto his carefully constructed deception? Would he invite the interloper to join him, or eliminate him at first opportunity?

Carter looked across the saloon at Bones and Patrick as they continued to speak quietly. If he were one of them, Carter thought, locked in the distressed world of their existence, he would be inclined to maintain the status-quo. There wasn't much doubt that he would eliminate the unwanted intrusion. If his fate were up to Captain O'Malley, Carter speculated as he placed the historic copy of *Riddle* back on the bookshelf, he'd be dead!

Carter believed Bones and Patrick were holding the cigar man at bay. If they weren't around, or for some reason they were lost in this extraordinary calamity, Carter was thoroughly convinced the leathery-skinned captain would act on his own volition and remove the ink spot of his existence from the pages of the unfolding story.

Then he thought – what if Bones were not involved. If it were up to Patrick, he'd still have better than a fifty-fifty chance. Deep beneath the surface, Carter saw in Patrick a passionate and fair man: driven, but committed to his beliefs without a doubt. He hadn't survived these long years while making casual mistakes.

There must be a reason Patrick hadn't acted already to protect the greater cause; to maintain the status quo. Carter suspected his safety was tied to his acceptance into Patrick's inner circle. Patrick's affinity for Carter must be as he concluded several weeks ago—a friend who knows little about you can be a precious friend indeed.

In the end, Carter remained convinced Patrick's devotion to the cause of Irish independence must prevail. Carter knew this imperative was the penultimate framework of the ideologue, and Patrick was obviously an ideologue. It was also the framework of a terrorist and Carter wasn't sure if that meant Patrick was a terrorist, too.

Carter went on to think about Bones. Based on what took place in the last few hours, Carter was convinced his future rested in the hands of the ancient man whose burly chest brought the warmth of life to him only hours earlier. Carter found relief thinking that surely Bones wouldn't order the disappearance of the man he just saved.

Then doubt crept into Carter's mind as he considered the fact that at the time Bones engaged in his rescue, that is, saving Carter from his frightening malady, he may have been acting on instinct alone and hadn't thought through the consequences. Could he, or would he, reverse his direction now that things calmed down?

Carter took another swallow of whiskey. When he lowered his glass the men were looking at him through the streaming light of the teakwood saloon. A chill crept up his spine; he wondered what they were thinking.

He looked to Bones, since he now concluded his fate rested in his hands. He suddenly remembered Bones' telling of his sister. Bones' ruminations of Winifred were almost dream-like now, faint, yet poignant. He hadn't realized it at the time, but now he believed Bones' words were a gift, a talisman of memories that would somehow affect his life in unknown ways.

Now may be one of those times.

Carter considered that of all the men on board these two vessels, only he and Patrick knew of Bones' love for his departed sibling, the girl who called him Prince Albert, the sister he loved and still thought of decades later. The memory Bones shared with Carter while he held his freezing body was singular, more special than all the other secrets Carter had stumbled onto.

With this realization, Carter saw clearly it was right to trust these aged fighters. He needn't adopt or even agree with their cause. In fact, he needn't even discuss it further. He only needed to trust them and make an equal effort at being trustworthy. If he did this, if he simply remained as honorable toward them as they toward him, everything would be all right.

Carter sipped once more from the Irish crystal. As he lowered the faceted glass his eyes caught a glitter. For some inexplicable reason he thought he saw three fig trees. They swayed in the breeze. They were together, growing, safe from harm.

He blinked and the imaginary trees were gone. All that remained was a feeling, a feeling that the unity of the three fig trees was no coincidence; Madame Russalka was no coincidence, Martha the good witch, the innocent glue that held them all together, was no coincidence.

With this image etched deep in his mind's eye, the tension he first experienced going below *Gael na Mara* dissipated. He was safe by his own estimation. He would survive this ordeal and the dangers that followed these dangerous men. All he needed to do was remain stalwart, observant, conscientious, and honorable.

The ominous threat of Captain O'Malley faded, too. The experience of being aboard the classic yacht became pleasant, enhanced by the mellowing effect of the Irish whiskey as its warmth reached down his throat and spread through his chest.

Carter stepped back toward the two old sailors. Emboldened by his conclusions, he picked up the whiskey decanter and raised it boldly to his friends. The bravado of his movements surprised and delighted the old Marbleheaders and they raised their glasses in response. He poured a finger into each and spoke confidently to the men he now stood in league with.

"Captains and friends," he said. "On to Gloucester Harbor."

"Heah, heah," they cheered.

≋≋≋

A report carried down from *Gael na Mara's* pilot house. "*Maxine's* up six inches on 'er waterline, Captain!" The news was everything Carter hoped for.

Maxine was rising from her dreadful cross with fate. If all went well, the mechanics would restart her flooded engine. She would be in Gloucester Harbor by sunset!

CHAPTER 25

THE UNHOLY BUSINESS O' KILLIN'

Carter followed the steward into a stateroom and was shown a locker where clothing hung. He was advised to help himself and make free use of the facilities. The steward departed.

With unexpected serenity, at least partially induced by liquor, Carter stepped into the head and washed his face, arms and hands with steaming hot water. His skin glowed. It felt good. He opened a cabinet and found guest toiletries. He spontaneously splashed Irish cologne on his hands and face. The aroma filled the cabin. Closing his eyes, he breathed the fragrance deeply into his lungs.

A few seconds later he reopened his eyes and stared into the mirror over the sink. The glass was surrounded by beautifully carved teak panels inlaid with black walnut. The image staring back looked tired and pale even though the effects of the whisky brought inner warmth. The reflection transformed slightly as he stared into the steamy mirror. It exhibited a guarded smile.

The aroma of the cologne and the euphoria of the alcohol induced a therapeutic effect and Carter resolved to lie down and rest.

Returning to his stateroom, he discovered as he turned down a blanket, that the crewman had brought aboard the hot water bottle from *Maxine*. It was filled and lay between the covers, warming the bunk.

Surely on Bones' instruction.

On the dresser next to the bed lay a silver tray with hot tea and pilot crackers set out on porcelain china. He delayed crawling into the bunk, consuming the traditional remedy for sea sickness.

Smelling good, feeling clean and convinced the incredible misadventure was nearing its end, Carter slipped from his clothing and crawled into the warm bunk. Like a child embracing a parent he embraced the balmy water bottle, thankful to both Martha and Bones.

In the joy of warmth he contemplated an evening with Claire. As with most things deeply desired, the belief it would finally come true filled his mind with anticipation. His desire was made more intense by the contrast of having believed his life, at least as he knew it only a day ago, was slipping away, sinking into the abyss of the Irish question and the cold of Massachusetts Bay.

Now, as Carter lay in the golden interior of a vessel carved from dreams, the expectation of the pleasures of a woman's voice and the sight of her glistening black hair became very real. Within a few minutes these pleasurable contemplations subsided and Carter succumbed to a cavernous sleep.

≋≋≋

While Carter slept, Patrick and Captain O'Malley crossed over from *Gael na Mara* and stood near the stern of *Maxine*. By O'Malley's estimation she would be back on her waterline in two, perhaps three hours.

O'Malley asked for a word with the clan chief in anticipation of the completion of his rescue mission. He wanted to be far from the guest stateroom on *Gael na Mara*. They neared *Maxine's* stern pulpit and Captain O'Malley explained in plain, unadorned terms what he thought should be done with Carter and *Maxine*. He then voiced his reasons for making such a drastic suggestion.

Patrick stood in the warm afternoon sun and listened. He gave O'Malley his full attention and made no outward indication of the inner turmoil the brazen proposal fomented. O'Malley's arguments regarding the security breach needed to be given a full hearing. Patrick realized O'Malley hadn't been in attendance only a short time earlier while he and Bones sipped whiskey in *Gael na Mara's* saloon and deliberated Carter's future.

Patrick understood O'Malley's commitment to security. He realized the danger to himself and Bones under the circumstances, but suspected, to a certain degree, O'Malley's proposal was self-serving. At first, this frustrated him, but then he reminded himself that self-preservation was to be expected from all soldiers. It's how they survived to fight another day. He thought of suicide bombers springing up in places like Palestine, and couldn't see the logic in it. How were they going to fight another day? He recalled Patton's infamous words, "The object of war is not to die for your country, but rather to make the other bastard die for his." He started to write off the idiotic practice of suicide bombing as either insanity or hysteria, then remembered an observation E.M. Forster made in *A Passage to India*. "Islam...more than a faith, more than a battle cry, more...much more . . ."

Perhaps those words alluded to a suitable justification for the incredible behavior, he wasn't sure. Patrick read that martyrdom was the supreme sacrifice in fundamental Islamic belief with marvelous rewards waiting in Paradise. Then again, he could think of no revolution won by the users of such an abhorrent stratagem.

Patrick, in his role as clan leader, was obligated to listen to O'Malley patiently and to respond without dousing O'Malley's fiery passion for winning. In the final analysis, that was what they were all trying to do—win.

The cause wasn't terror, even though he knew they were responsible for plenty of it. The cause was freedom, self-determination. The road toward achieving it was mined heavily with decisions such as the one O'Malley was asking him and Bones to consider.

The American captain spoke to Patrick in the language of the O'Clery clan and this, too, impressed the clan leader. O'Malley did so for a couple reasons, not the least was to ensure Carter Phillips would not know what he was proposing. The other was to demonstrate his commitment to Patrick, and their clan.

After speaking his mind, O'Malley paused, and Patrick took a few moments to think before he replied. Then he spoke.

"Ryan, in the yeahs you've skippahed fer us we've seen faar worse dangers thahn thaht young man sleepin' 'board *Gael na Mara,*" Patrick replied with firm resolution. "Now don't get me wrong, cousin, no man is above sacrifice fer thaht we've all been fightin' fer. Howevah, this situation is different. Keep in mind thaht theah will not be a time when Bones, me, or you, fer thaht matter, will step out paast the rightness of what we're doin' ta murdah a man fer the sake of our individual preservation. Do ya understand what I'm sayin', man?" Patrick was firm, but didn't want his remarks taken as a rebuke.

"I do understand," Ryan replied, "but you might figure that some would consider the point contradictory. After all, innocent people were killed in the reprisals."

"Thaht's different, don't ya know!" came a snappy reply. "The blahsted British can point fingahs and call us terrorists all they want. Aftah all, they control the press, they control the money, and they control those damned Ulster men and theah murderin' ways.

"Ya realize don't ya, thaht the loyalists target civilians, mostly Catholics. To them it's as much a religious war as anythin' else. To us it's a revolt and we aah goin' aftah the occupying force.

"You tell me how were we ta rise above the oppression? We wanted some control baack, laddie, control o'er our own lives and thaht's all we've evah wanted. We've no desire ta tell the bloody British how to run theah damned island. You've nevah seen an Irish army invade England. We've nevah strung bahbed wire and cordoned off theah neighbahoods. We've nevah captured and tortured theah young, detainin' 'em without trial. Can ya imagine a time when the wearin' o' the green was a capital offense and the judge, jury, and hangman was some lord o' the manor he robbed from our forbearers?

"I'll remind ya once more in case ya'v forgotten, cousin, thaht our clan was pushed from theah threadbare farms and made subservient ta those people—those Protestants who were imported and spread across our land, whose cows grazed our pastures and whose men took our women. Our clansmen's children were deprived o' schoolin' and our men folk deprived of a say in the gov'ment controlled by the culprits who invaded their very soil."

Captain O'Malley believed these points, while likely true, were getting too old to remember, let alone remain motivation for continued fighting. He also realized it was the job of the Patrick O'Clery's of Ireland not to let the young forget; to continue the tradition of hating their oppressors. This was true even in the case of men such as himself, second generation immigrants who never directly suffered oppression as did their kinfolk in Northern Ireland.

O'Malley did not reply nor debate his senior. He was not prone to correct his elders whose direct ties to Ireland apparently knew no statute of limitations for hate, even hate grown moldy with time.

"We've nevah killed innocents like they've killed innocents, eithah, Cousin O'Malley. They kill 'em in body and spirit alike. The north of Ireland's full o' people too dispirited to rise above the oppression and work toward building a nation as a whole, particularly with theah brethren ta the south.

"Besides, how could they with the Protestants bein' the majority amongst them and the Brit's backin' 'em all the while? Do ya' realize, O'Malley, thaht the whole damned island has nevah been unified undah a single leadah, nor fer thaht mattah a constitution, least wise no constitution like these heah United States."

O'Malley Irish heritage ran deep, his father even teaching him the language, but he was an American. He was raised believing the constitution was the center of democratic government. It did strike him as significant that what he always believed to be the normal foundation of government in his country could never be achieved in the land of his ancestors.

"We chose our targets and we planned our attacks as accurately as possible. We went aftah the Brits and Protestant leadahs. But it is a revolt O'Malley; make no mistake o' thaht, and innocent people haav got kilt.

"As faar as we aah concerned, those bastahds cahn prevent the "collateral damage" as the 'mericans liked ta call it, any damn time they want—by getting' the bloody hell off our land! If Bones' current efforts pay off, thaht may be comin' soonah thahn later. Above all else, the killin's got ta stop!"

Patrict's "Irish" was rising. O'Malley smoked his cigar in silent consideration.

After a brief pause, Patrick spoke again. His tone of voice indicating that the clan leader was returning to the topic of O'Malley's original recommendation—the drastic solution he proffered for managing the tear in security. A tear caused by the lake sailor and his sinking yacht.

"Ryan, I'll tell ya only once and I implore ya ta listen with a broad view. Thaht's the only way you'll undahstand. Bones and I haav made a decision regarding Caahtah. He and I both expect it ta be honored. The decision will keep us on the paath towards our goal, don't ya know. Tis a narrow paath, thaht's true. Tis hard ta keep advancin' and not wandah from the paath. Despite the bahd fortune our brothahs haav brought upon us when they wandahed from thaht paath, our clan has nevah killed but fer the exact purpose of our cause.

"We're a clan, Ryan, and you aah a membah; yer blood. You aah expected to obey as I know ya haav many a time. You may be a 'merican, but yer fathah and his fathah and all theah fahthahs afore abided by my fathah and his fathah and his fathah's fathah. I inherited this position tis true, but the weight of it comes heavy and the obligation of administerin' it is divine and absolute. Put plainly,

Ryan, if ya were to disobey, I'd be forced to act, and I'm sick ta the core of this unholy business of killin'."

O'Malley didn't flinch at the threat, nor did he underestimate its veracity. Patrick was fearless, even savage when his status as Taoiseach was threatened. Ryan he had no intention of taking a contrary course to Patrick's authority or Bones' considered judgments. He was simply airing his suggestion.

Ryan, too, had a deep sense of devotion, especially to the memory of his father. Because of that, he listened respectfully to his elder cousin, the clan leader, perhaps the last clan leader, as O'Malley was aware of no off-spring to whom Patrick could hand the responsibility.

"Bones and I haav discussed the mattah at length and with all due respect to yer devotion and yer caution, which by the way we appreciate as much as we appreciate you comin' out heah an savin' our bloody arses, the lad lives and his yacht floats, and I don't haav ta' tell ya our reasoning shan't be questioned."

Patrick regretted the tone of his last remark. He hadn't meant it to be a threat or accusation; he simply meant it to be the final word. O'Malley never crossed any lines in all his years of service, though Patrick sometimes feared he would. Patrick had certainly been around too many who had crossed the line and they were the ones who ended up killing innocent people. This was even true of his half-brother, Connor O'Donnell. The fact this was true was a poison Patrick seemed forced to swallow all the days of his life. It sickened him every time.

"I trust ya, Cousin Ryan; Bones trusts ya, too. Ya realize laddie, thaht in Bones' case he's trustin' ya in a way he haas no othah ta my recollection. Yer the captain of his yacht, laddie; yer sailin' the essence of his being. *Gael na Mara's* not a rich man's toy. Ya must try an' remember, Ryan, she's Bones' connection to his paast, she's his country, his place on earth fer more than half the century he's been alive, longah thahn most of us evah hope to be sailin' the sea o' life.

"It's true he cahn't haav 'er no more, not fer his own pleasure, but so much more is the reason he trusts you. He knows you'll treat 'er right. Take care of 'er. To haav 'er continue to serve the cause and preserve 'er history."

Patrick paused as if he were spent, as if he pleaded enough and needed time to regain his wind. He stood silent for a few moments and when he spoke again he changed directions.

"Ryan, I'm lookin' to pass this double-edged sword of clan leadahship on ta' someone youngah, don't ya know. I was the only child by my fathah's seed afore he was kilt in thaht damnable dispute with one o' our own kind ovah who hated the British most. What a bloody reason ta' die for." Patrick said. He could taste bitter disgust in his mouth.

O'Malley continued to listen though it was clear his solution to the breech in security was no longer under consideration.

"My eldest first cousin, Bruce O'Clery, a priest in Derry, should be next in ascendancy. He's 18 years youngah thahn I and smaart as they come—smaarter thahn me thaht's fer damn sure. He has the mind fer it, but he's paraplegic now. He's bound in a wheelchair thanks to a British bullet fired into a crowd on Bloody Sunday. T'was a civil rights demonstration, for God's sake, inspired by the civil rights marches in this heah country, as a mattah of fact! Nevertheless, it reduced him in body, took away his legs and, laddie, the necessity of speed afoot haas saved my life more times thahn I care to recall.

"I'll say this for Fathah Bruce O'Clery, howevah. His mind races and he and Bones have much in common by way of a gift for thinkin' thin's through.

"Anyway, Ryan, the clan is shy o' men. Faar too many haav been kilt, maimed or just plain soured in this bloody business. Thaht's not to mention the droves who left in mass migrations, like yer fathah, don't ya know—men and women who hahd to leave Ireland since they couldn't suhvive without money or work. Those thaht stayed aah too often lost in a world they cahn't get control of, or fer thaht mattah lack the inspiration to rise above the lunacy and petty squabbling amongst themselves, like thaht which got my Da kilt."

Ryan relit his Cuban and Patrick went on, again in a new direction.

"Ya knew of my half-brothah, eh, Ryan?"

O'Malley drew on the cigar, rolled it around in his mouth, and raised his eyes as if looking for something in his forehead. He nodded his recollection.

"He wouldn't haav been eligible fer taken' ovah the clan propaah anyhow since his Da wasn't clan, but it don't matter since he's been gone since '51, kilt right afore my eyes by a loyalist bullet one night thaht seems like only yesterday.

"T'was right theah on board *Gael na Mara*, don't ya' know. Makes me ill ta think about it, yet somehow the horrible truth of it draws me to thaht boat like a moth to flame. I'm tormented by the memory *Gael na Mara* brings of thaht night, but I cahn't forget the yeahs we sailed 'board 'er so happy and carefree eithah. Theah was plenty o' thaht too, don't ya know.

"The opposin' forces of those memories aah gonna pain me till I die. I'm prayin' the laahnchin' o' *Red Shoes* will set me free, move me on paast the memories of those times, and allow me ta live in peace."

O'Malley glanced up from the water he was staring down at, knocking ash from his cigar. The sea change that came over the old Irishman was clearly discernable.

Patrick winced visibly at the mixture of thoughts and memories, and then continued. "T'was a terrible tragedy to lose 'im, Connah thaht is . . . and I carry the burden of makin' the plan thaht got him kilt. Sure the lad was a fightah. A feral untamed fightah, bravah thahn any I've known since, present company accepted. Howevah, the bloody lad could be reckless. He was one of the kind I mentioned a minute ago. He hahd a terrible time stayin' on the paath of our cause and tended ta get lost in the immediate situation. I could see it in his eyes, once the killin' commenced. He didn't wax philosophical aftah the first round was fired. Then again, I don't suppose anyone does, what with the noise and confusion, the desperate struggle fer survival when yer facin' death in its ugliest form."

Patrick turned to O'Malley. He saw a hard, leathery man not unlike the one he was describing, yet there was a difference. O'Malley was more controlled, more capable of keeping his emotions in check, yet fearless in duty at the same time. Patrick thought it was because O'Malley never directly experienced the horror of mangled bodies strewn across a blood-soaked landscape. He never pried a woman's jaw from the shattered wall of a pub in the aftermath of a Unionist bomb; held it in his hands in mortified shock; a gruesome transfixion that alters one's mind in the worst way. It certainly had Conner's.

"Connah's long gone and I've no child of my own, short o' leavin' off-spring I'm unaware of in some distant port. I've nevah married, though it's not fer want. I cahn nevah ha' the woman I've wanted all these yeahs anyway, I just cahn't. Wouldn't be right, wouldn't be right. Still I'm bound by tradition or some magical force, whatevah the hell ya want ta call it, thaht dictates I name my successor.

"Course I've got Bones ta help me; thaht is, as long as he's around. You'd haav thought he'd be long gone by now, what with his role in this bloody affair. Some men aah just meant ta be. They don't seem ta haav the ability to die. They're the opposite of men like my little half-brothah or those Gloucestah fishermen; those ones lost in the Halloween Gale."

The weather-worn clan leader looked at O'Malley and saw the type of man who is meant to live, particular proof being his survival in Granada, Panama, and most recently, West Africa. Nevertheless, he saw a man given to the black and white of life, not quite ready for the role of clan leader. What O'Malley needed was counsel like Bones, a Merlin, a wizard whose insight and wisdom could serve him as Bones served Patrick. He needed to be rounded out, to be taught the gray areas of life. He needed to gain the balance of a leader who can prevail when contrary forces are pulling in every direction.

Patrick's mind wandered a step further. He resolved to bring Father Bruce O'Clery and Captain O'Malley together in the near future. It wasn't without prospect that together they could be groomed to take over when he and Bones were finally spent, particularly if the Mitchell Commission was successful. He decided to consult Bones, seek his advice on the matter.

On this idea Patrick mused a moment. He realized that in reality, despite his being the leader of his clan, it was *he* who served Bones in the final analysis. It was Bones whose ultimate charisma, intelligence and tact usually prevailed. Sometimes Patrick had difficulty remembering that the O'Clery clan wasn't the only clan benefiting from Bones' wizardry; that Bones served in the highest places of the cause. Still, he was grateful for his intimate connection to the Englishman turned Irish partisan. And while it was true Patrick shared Bones with the greater cause, he was closer to Bones than any man alive. It was a great honor even if the circumstances that created their attachment struck a discordant, sorrowful chord—a chord that rang loud every time the haunting *Gael na Mara* floated into Marblehead Harbor.

Patrick looked out to sea in the direction of the island where the remnants of his clan still resided. He raged internally at being forced to live out his life in exile, even if Marblehead had been good to him. His rage continued as he thought again of the tragically momentous night on the North Atlantic on board *Gael na Mara*. In his mind's eye he saw the figures of a younger Bones and Miread, his beautiful Irish-American wife, a librarian, an intellectual. He shrieked inwardly as he did the night she disappeared into the howling black sea.

The whole affair twisted the survivor's lives for fifty years, and all because of his plan. Who could have predicted the turn of events unfolding as they neared their destination, when a mysterious boat showed up in the wrong place at the wrong time?

Even though Patrick could never place the blame on Bones, Bones was responsible for bringing *Gael na Mara* to the purpose of that voyage. Not only that, he did so with Miread's approval, borne clearly from a compulsion to abide by her Irish-American father's expectations.

It was Daniel Patrick Callahan, Miread's father, a prominent Boston physician and Finnian Brother, who presented Bones and Miread with the magnificent *Gael na Mara* on their wedding day. Bones knew what the doctor had in mind and Doc Callahan was confident Bones was motivated to follow through. The doctor had not imagined his only daughter, his precious Miread, would careen from the deck, never to be seen again, lost in the coldness of an unforgiving North Atlantic on the blackest of black nights.

Patrick continued ruminating in silence.

Perhaps sensing something spinning in Patrick's mind, O'Malley drew mouthfuls from his Cuban then formulated a question designed to get Patrick back on board and out of whatever frame of mind took him away from their conversation.

"Patrick, since you mentioned Bones, I've been meaning to discuss a few thoughts I've had."

Patrick turned abruptly, as if physically shaken from a daydream.

O'Malley continued. "Despite the years I've skippered his yacht, he remains a mystery to me. I've kept my curiosity in check, remained focused on my duties. However, I have questions. I want to ask them. I will abide by any decision not to answer them if you decide I'm getting out of line."

Patrick looked at O'Malley and replied, "Tell you what, cousin...I'll explain what I'm willin' ta explain about Bones, and if what I say answers yer questions, there she'll lay. If it don't, maybe we'll talk more in the future, or maybe not. Perhaps after he's gone, I'll say more. In the meantime, do we have a deal?"

"Deal."

The two sailors, bound by blood and purpose, looked aft at the great pond. In the distance they saw a trawler crossing to the northeast, moving slowly away. They watched till its rigging passed from view.

Patrick began speaking in his native tongue, his words melodious. He chose them with purpose and delivered them with drama. Ryan O'Malley listened as would a student at the feet of Aristotle. He took no notes, he would write down nothing so as never to breach security, yet it would remain indelibly etched in the web of the Irish-American's prodigious mind.

O'Malley's memory was good, the same memory that enabled him to speak a language his father taught him as a boy; the same memory he inherited from his ancestors. It was the memory they used to save the language from extinction when it was banned by invading English overlords hundreds of years before.

CHAPTER 26

A GRAND TOAST TONIGHT

"Portsmouth, Ryan, Portsmouth, England. Thaht t'was wheah Bones got ta be born, don't ya know. More specific, he was raised in a little enclave called Southsea; thaht place wheah Arthah Conan Doyle wrote those Sherlock Holmes stories. As a mattah o' fact, Doyle was a ship's doctah fer a stint.

"Bones ended up bein' the second and last child of Jonathan and Eliz'beth Maatheson. It were 1910 and he was christened Wilfred Albert Maatheson, baptized in the Church of England. Theah small cottage neah the wharves and naval yaahds was visited by people from the neighbahood of boat buildahs and dock workahs. They came round ta wish the shipwright and his pretty wife well since she was a midwife herself.

"Accordin' ta Bones, she hahd delivered a bunch of the local dickens by 'er own hand. T'was 'er turn again, and Jonathan was pleased ta haav a boy ta carry on the Maatheson name.

"His oldah sistah, an outgoin' five yeah old named Winifred, took ta the boy-child immediate like. Bones told me once his sister Winnie, thaht's what he called 'er, Winnie hahd played the paht of a little mothah as guls often do. Fussin' ovah the boy-child, dressin' 'im and takin' care of 'im just like he was 'er baby doll. He hahd a distinct and lovin' memory of young Winnie and I cahn tell ya, Ryan, she hahd a weighty effect on the young lad's upbringin'. Still does, if ya aask me.

"Pa-Pa, as they both called theah Da, was a shipwright caught 'tween the dyin' time of wind-driven wood ships and the birth o' the steamer. He was on and off fer work, but when he did work theah weren't no complaints from the yaahd boss. He worked as hard as any and hahd theah been more work, he'd made more money.

"As it was, the Maatheson's skimped by but Bones nevah complained, least not to me anyhow. He always said they hahd plenty ta go 'round and nevah missed a suppah. By our clan's standards, thaht would have been considered a damn prosperous livin'," Patrick mused.

"Bones also told me that he and his dotin' sistah hahd pretty good educations. Not only thaht, Portsmouth bein' a port city was sort of an international gatherin' place. People were comin' and goin' from all 'round the globe; been theah many a time myself. Inquisitive youngin's like Winnie and Wilfred could pick up quite a broad view o' the world thaht laid out theah beyond the Isle of Wight.

"They was given religious trainin' suitable fer theah station, too, even if it were a Protestant upbringin'. Bones ain't hahd much good ta say 'bout the Protestants since, don't ya' know. Still, when he told me 'bout his upbringin', he didn't harbah any malice toward his teachin's and his mentors; he hahd no reason to, leastwise at the time.

"Bones told me he always figured he hahd a pretty ordinary life as a child in Portsmouth, what with standin' 'round the wharves lookin' up at those great vessels, just like in the fancy pencil drawin' he made, 'The Figurehead.'

"Bones has always been modest 'bout his intellect. You'd nevah know from hearin' him speak, he haas a mind and hahd money been plentiful and his station a bit higher, he'd a been marked amongst the best.

"Ta heah him tell it, t'was his sistah, Winnie, thaht was the real smaarts o' the Maathesons o' Southsea. He used to carry on 'bout how smaart she was and how good she did at her lessons. Bones considered it a terrible shame thaht Winnie couldn't get on ta Oxford, or ta read the lawr. Them was simplah times and the Maathesons, despite bein' good, hard workin' folk, didn't haav money nor connections. Bones was frustrated and perhaps a wee bit ashamed thaht he was given preference bein' the male.

"Baack then, in those days before the First World War, a gul in the south o' England was pretty well destined ta bein' charted a course thaht would 'ave been mightily like 'er mothahs. Winnie, accordin' to Bones, wasn't gonna be treated thaht way. She was too bright, he'd say, too independent ta 'ave 'er tiller steered fer 'er like thaht.

"In fact, if ya heah Bones tell it, she was where he got 'is will ta sail up agin' the tide. Thaht was particularly true if thaht direction was contrary ta wheah one's haart was leadin' 'em. Bold thinkin' at the time, Ryan. Winnie must o' been somethin', all right.

"Well, heah is wheah things got ta goin' a wee bahd fer Winnie and eventually fer Bones, too, don't ya' know. It all began as Eliz'beth staahted seein' 'er friends' and customers' daughtahs growin' up and marryin' the local boys and havin' babies.

"Now havin' babies weren't thought o' poorly as a rule, in fact deliverin' 'em was Eliz'beth's business. Howevah, occasionally some of 'em was caught in a bind, bakin' bread afore theah propah age, don't ya know, and Eliz'beth, bein' the local midwife was consulted fer advice.

"Sure the midwife could plainly see how this was trouble more often thahn not. Worse, it was trouble associated with transient sailahs and rovin' dockworkahs gettin' ta wheah they oughtn't aftah a night at the pub. So, it weren't a terrific leap of logic fer Eliz'beth ta arrive at the conclusion thaht 'er daughtah ought ta be stayin' away from the docks and the pubs.

"Now Bones and Winnie were attached at the hip, and Bones was supposed to be goin' to the docks ta work, even though he was still a boy. They staahted boys out early in those days. T'was when Bones was 'round ten yeahs old and Winnie, fifteen, thaht she would join 'im on walks ta the dock ta bring food or run errands for theah Da.

"As Eliz'beth began to get more concerned about Winnie comin' of age, she staahted to clamp down on the gul's travel round Portsmouth town. Winnie wasn't goin' ta be the type ta take kindly ta bein' controlled, even if it were explained thaht it was fer her own good.

"As Bones tells it, he stahted seein' a rip in the sails t'ween Eliz'beth and Winnie. Bones doesn't know what ta do about it. He loved 'em both. In the end, he made a decision and stuck with his beloved Winnie. He felt his Ma wasn't trustin' Winnie as she ought ta.

"Winnie was smaart in Bones' view; she was strong too, not ta be led 'round or manipulated by a sailah come ashore fer a fling. Aftah all, ya got ta remembah, Portsmouth was famous from times way paast fer its shadowy accommodations fer sailahs taken' shoah leave. It weren't as if 'er mothah's cautions hahd gone unreckoned. Winnie was virtuous. Bones believed 'er ta be the most virtuous person he'd evah known.

"Things weren't helped along at the Maatheson home by the war gettin' so many young men kilt, neithah. The potential mate's fer the ripenin' young women was gettin' smallah all the time. Theah wasn't a family ashore who hadn't lost a young fella ta the terrible goin's on ovah on the continent, what with the bombin' and nerve gas attacks. The only good the war produced fer the Maathesons was steady work fer Jonathan. The British Navy was buildin' ships just a wee bit fastah thahn the Germans were sinkin' em.

"Even Bones, at the early age o' ten, was primin' for battle as he was glued ta the wireless and readin' the papehs. Even worse, or I suppose bettah fer us Irish in the end, he spent a lot a time thinkin' about strategy and tactics, all sorts of thoughts a boy o' ten yeahs shouldn't ha' been thinkin'.

"What he should haav been doin' was carryin' lunch ta his da at the shipyahds and floatin' model sailboats in a pond on the day of our Lord."

Patrick suspended his story when he heard the sound of *Maxine's* engine cranking over below. The iron ginney sputtered then coughed out a white puff from the exhaust port below the stern. She wheezed and choked, then fell silent. He heard a couple muffled exclamations emanate from below deck.

O'Malley was about to turn and go below when the sound of clanking tools resumed, and so did Patrick. O'Malley lit another cigar.

"Well, bein' brightah than most, it didn't take the ripenin' young Winnie long ta figger out thaht theah was a relatively high numbah o' prospective mates comin' and goin' not too faar from the family's cottage. While she was right as fer as numbahs go, the situation was still extremely precarious, what with Mothah Maatheson keepin' 'er on a short leash.

"Now heah is a question fer ya, Captain O'Malley. Let's test yer history education. You tell me wheah the Irish were and what they was thinkin' during WWI?"

O'Malley's reply, conveyed to Patrick's satisfaction, told the story of England making big promises. They were promises England would not keep. Home Rule for Ireland was as sure as sunrise and sunset if everyone queued up to fight the Germans, they claimed.

"My point heah, Mr. O'Malley, the reason fer touchin' on the topic, is the irony thaht this bein' the case, theah were Irish boys, even members of our own clan, amongst the throngs of sailahs touching upon the shores of Portsmouth.

"Coincidently, as I've already pointed out, Winnie Maatheson was comin' into full bloom, don't ya' know. Well, it weren't long afore a truly handsome and glowin' sample of our fine Irish man stock found his way into the aarms of the pretty gul, and I cahn tell ya, O'Malley, fate played strange tricks aftah thaht. But I feah I'm gettin' ahead o' myself.

"Bones wouldn't necessarily boast of it, but heah is wheah I figger he staahted down his own road ta becomin' a strategist. He's helped our island in many ways—even now with the goin's on tween Belfaast, Dublin, and London."

Patrick paused.

"Anyways, Bones took a likin' to the honest face of his sistah's lovah. He weren't jealous, not a bit. He wanted fer ta see his sistah smile; thaht's all. Afore long, it was Bones, a boy turned eleven, who began hatchin' plots fer the two young lovah's meetin' in secret rendezvous. As reward, they'd often let him tag along.

"Now the Irish suitor, a handsome lad of a middlin' fisher family from our clan's region in Northern Ireland, was named Kevin Timothy McCreesh. And I suppose you can figger yerself thaht Miss Winnie Maatheson would fairly soon become Mrs. Kevin Timothy McCreesh.

"Bones says it weren't a straight and easy road fer 'em ta get theah. Neithah Jonathon nor Eliz'beth Maatheson were much interested in haavin' an Irish son-in-lawr, and they put up a mighty fuss thaht tore Bones apart, if ya' heah 'im tell it.

"He loved his parents and so did Winnie, but I don't have to explain how the matin' o' male and female haas got to go on. Bones said it was a happy day when 'is ma and pa finally realized they wasn't gonna lose a daughtah, but gain a hard workin' Irish son.

"Aftah the niceties of a modest weddin', Winnie was whisked off by 'er husband to live in the north o' Ireland in his home village, a tiny town bunched right up against the sea. Things went fine fer the young lovahs, and Bones haas even showed me a couple o' lettahs Winnie wrote him as proof.

"Kevin hahd rejoined the family fishin' business aftah the war. Winnie was takin' into the family, although a bit reluctantly at first. The situation was a wee bit delicate considerin' Winnie was o' the same blood as the source of Northern Ireland's biggest troubles.

"Kevin hahd his way though. His family was not of the mind ta buck the young son who came home after so many hahd left fer good, so many goin' to theah graves from the war. Thaht don't mean some eyebrows weren't raised 'round town, don't ya know. Some people cahn't leave well enough alone."

O'Malley looked inconspicuously toward Patrick and saw the watery eye of an old man who had seen too much. Patrick continued telling his story.

"But fer the most paht, the happy couple commenced directly at makin' a cottage and makin' a baby and makin' fer the local pub as young people do. Bones, back in Southsea, felt sad, kind o' lost I think. He was thirteen now and he loved his oldah sistah. The fact thaht he's kept and showed me those lettahs has got ta mean something, don't ya' know.

"The lettah wheah she swore him to secrecy is the one in which she confides thaht she hahd become pregnant, but hahdn't told Kevin yet. Poor gul was nervous 'bout tellin' 'er husband so she aasked the young Bones' advice. Cahn ya imagine thaht, eh, skippah? Bones givin' strategic advice even as a lad.

"The advice he gave 'er was simple. He told 'er thaht she must square up 'er sails and go straight to Kevin. There'd be no hidin' from the facts and no shame in 'er bein' English and bein' Protestant the young lad told 'er. Playful like he signed the lettah Doctor W. A. Maatheson, surgeon of the sailing ship *HMS Victory*!"

O'Malley wasn't a man given to light humor, but he smiled, knowing the *Victory* was kept at a dock in Portsmouth, England, even at present. The vessel was the command of the venerable Lord Horatio Nelson, the greatest British naval strategist in history, according to everyone except Nelson, who insisted it was Admiral Blake. Nelson parried not when confronting an adversary and the young Bones Matheson apparently advised the same for his worried sister.

O'Malley turned once more and looked at Patrick. This time he saw a distant, hollow man with an aged and contoured face, one that wore a look of helpless anguish.

"A short time later, Winnie's reply came bahck. T'was 'er last lettah in fact, the last lettah ta Bones or anyone else on God's green earth, mind ya. She told Bones a wonderful story, a sorrowful, but wonderful story and Bones thanked God he received it; even if it were too late ta make a reply, ta see or talk or write to his sistah evah again!"

Patrick paused, his voice cracked when he began again.

"Winnie wrote thaht the day's work was done. She had waited till 'er husband returned from the dock. Aftah scrubbin' the fish smell from his body with soap and lemon juice, Kevin had splashed Irish cologne about his handsome face.

"The aroma drew Winnie from workin' in the galley o' theah little cottage. She came to him and turnin' him from the mirror she put 'er arms 'round his sturdy neck and looked straight into his dark shinin' Irish eyes. With all the stren'th o' will the poor lass could mustah, the words of 'er youngah brothah ringin' in 'er ears, she told 'er man she was carryin' his child.

"Kevin's happy smile grew broader and happier than she evah sawr it before. He gripped his bride in a beah hug and spun 'er 'round the baathroom and out into the great room of theah seaside cottage.

"As the jubilation died down a bit, she stopped him once more and explained a few womanly facts about the dates. The realization caused him to pause, but fer only a second. Then, with unbridled love and the bravery of a man willin' ta fish the capricious sea, he picked 'er up again and spun 'er 'round till they were both dizzy and laughin' and collapsed in rhapsody."

Patrick paused. He braced himself and sucked in a quantity of sea air. He exhaled and took another breath before he spoke.

"There'll be a grand toast at the pub tonight . . . Thaht's what the lassie wrote 'er lovin' brothah, Captain O'Malley."

Then the weary seaman paused. He had trouble starting again and O'Malley watched him take in another gulp of air. In a distant tone, a tone that hung like a green mist spread over the peat bogs of his homeland he repeated, "There'll be a grand toast tonight..."

The last word quivered from Patrick's shaking lips.

Captain O'Malley was usually as hard as a rock, but in that moment of uncommon distraction, he absentmindedly loosened his grip and dropped his Cuban over *Maxine's* stern. Its fire sizzled out in the cold green water and caught Patrick's attention. The old sailorman let the enormity of O'Malley's unease go without remark. He had to finish his story; he had to be done with it.

"T'was goin' on 10:00 P.M., accordin' to the police and coroner's report, which Bones has memorized ovah the last seventy-seven yeahs.

"It seems the place was stuffed to the gunnels with locals, who by the way were doin' a fine job o' celebratin' the happy couple's family way. Sure theah was the singin' you always heah, the fiddler backin' the village tenor in a ballad, and theah was a pint at the end fer a reward if the song made a lassie cry. And if you were ta see Winnie sittin' and singin' along with the crowd you'd haav found 'er fittin' right in, even if she were the only Protestant fer miles around.

"Well, it seems theah was anothah Protestant come 'round thaht night, though no one would know it till it came out in the investigation. The police figger he showed up at the height of the festivities, the local lads a wee too drunk with merriment ta take notice. The report stated thaht about 10:15 P.M., theah was a tremendous explosion and a fireball came risin' from the place wheah the town pub hahd stood at 10:14, and was no more! Alarms went off, buildin's nearby caught fire and glass was blown from theah frames fer bettah thahn a quahter mile in all directions.

"When the telegram arrived in Portsmouth two days later, the devastation of the explosion was repeated. The simple and happy lives of the occupants of the Southsea cottage were blown to smithereens!

"Eliz'beth was home alone at the time. She took the brunt of the blahst in a wail thaht stole 'er breath, caused 'er to faint dead away. The young lad who delivered the telegram hahd no idea what was comin' or what the telegram said. Eliz'beth's blood curdlin' scream damn neah knocked him through the doah.

"In a state o' shock, he turned to see Eliz'beth lying dead-like on the cottage floah. Sure the lad didn't know what ta do, but he was able to drag poor Eliz'beth ovah and propped 'er against the divan, and then lit out to find Bones. He knew Bones was workin' down in the Navy yaahds with his Da and ran straight to the whaaf.

"The ghost-white boy found young Bones and gaspin' fer breath told him what haapened the best he could. The shockin' news sent a surge o' adrenalin through Bones which I figger is still floatin' 'round in his blood. Thaht shot of adrenalin may even be what's kept Bones alive fer ninety yeahs. It's pickled his blood fer all I know, pickled it with hate and a desire fer revenge...but I'm losin' track o' my story.

"The messenger boy didn't know thaht Winnie, Kevin and theah tiny seedling deep in 'er womb, hahd been blown ta bits by thaht damned bomb. Eliz'beth never spoke out loud what the telegram said. He did know, howevah, thaht the telegram was from a police headquarters in a town in Ireland. Thaht bit o' information set Bones in flight fer the cottage with instructions to the dazed boy to find his da and tell him the same news.

"Ya might be interested in knowin', Cousin, by a turn o' fate, I met thaht boy, the one who delivered thaht awful news, better 'n twenty yeahs later. He told me of the dreadful calm young Bones Maatheson emanated when he heard the news. He thought Bones was made o' steel, calculatin' and cleah minded. The man told me he saw revenge in Bones' eyes thaht very second. It scared him more thahn seein' Eliz'beth faint!

"Yes suh, Captain O'Malley, the young Bones Maatheson, who hahd been readin' too much about war, listenin' ta wireless reports from the front, declared war hisself thaht day, I'm convinced of it. Bones declared war on his own nation—on England! Only thin' is he didn't know it until yeahs later. Not till he met a particulah membah of our clan; someone thaht hahd important information.

"Ya see, Ryan, a couple yeahs aftah the death of his lovin' sistah, Bones got on board a ship, first as a cabin steward, then mate and so on up the ladder a ways. He was sailin' 'tween Boston and England and doin' ordinary sea time. Thaht's when he met my uncle, Samuel Claark."

O'Malley knew who Clark was, although his name usually surfaced with veiled references to the murky connection between the dubious side of the Boston Irish community and U.S. Intelligence. He kept quiet, as per the rules of the story-telling Patrick laid out., but his face registered surprise.

"Freightahs, as you well know, Captain O'Malley, carry a few pahssengers. Bones met Samuel, who was pretendin' he was a pahssenger on a trip 'cross the pond.

"Samuel approached Bones one day and appeared ta be lookin' fer conversation. They talked and got familiar. Samuel led Bones initially inta believin' he was a businessman, traded in wools and such. He told 'im he made frequent trips between Europe and the United States, usually sailin' out of Bahston.

"Aftah one or two crossin's together, Samuel finally approached Bones with an idea. Bones was first taken aback. Howevah, bein' a man o' superior intellect and havin' a refined mind for piecin' together puzzles of great complexity, Bones suddenly realized theah was somethin' more thahn an idea in what Samuel was sayin'.

"It was obvious ta Bones thaht Samuel knew more about Bones and his lost family thahn he should. He knew of Bones' sistah and how his sistah died. All these thin's came out in conversations ovah a period a time.

"Samuel hahd access ta secrets; he showed Bones documents thaht exposed why Winnie died, who really murdahed 'er. British intelligence was mixed up in the plot. They blew up the pub and coincidently his sistah, 'er husband and 'er unborn child.

"Did I mention, Cousin O'Malley, thaht the bomb killed nine othahs and injured anothah thirty five—all good Catholics, all villagers whose lives and stories weren't much different thahn thaht of the McCreesh's. Aside from Winnie, the only othah Protestant was the bombah, who miscalculated the timin' and was blown to bits—dirty bastahd."

Patrick spat over *Maxine's* stern, as if a black bile sickened him. A couple seconds went by; he spit again to be completely rid of his disgust.

"Bones learned thaht Downing Street was convinced guns were comin' ashore cleah from Belgium inta thaht tiny port town. The docks the McCreesh family owned were the ones suspected of bein' the landin' place.

"Some haartless, cowardly bastahd in London decided the town should be taught a lesson. It was more than a lesson; it was a deplorable act of insanity, a brutal act, a cowardly act by any measure.

"Did they blow up the docks? Hell no! The bastahds blew up innocent people, old men and women, and in this case an unborn child. They went too faar, don't ya know, they went too faar and kilt one of theah own, and worse yet, 'er unborn offspring, a creature who nevah got ta live or breathe, who would ha' been Bones Maatheson's nephew or niece.

"Sure the pain and horror of it all didn't stop at the bordahs of the village, Cousin O'Malley. Bombs don't kill only the ones it rips ta pieces. It kills all theah friends and relatives too, people faar and wide. In Winnie's case, the bomb kilt 'er Ma and Da, hundreds o' miles away. It destroyed the innocent occupants of thaht tiny cottage in Southsea. T'was an outrageous crime!

"I'll tell ya' somethin' else, Ryan, Bones haas nevah let it go. He's nevah recovered from the terror of the bomb thaht drug his family asunder.

"What the dahmnable British nevah realized was all their brutality really accomplished was the creation of a man who would go on to sweah allegiance to the victims and who, fer the next seventy odd yeahs of his life, would commence ta fightin' against his own cruel and conniving countrymen. They made a man they would finally haav to reckon with, as they aah today. Ryan, ovah theah in Stormont."

≋≋≋

O'Malley listened and found the words rousing. He was a member of the clan, same as the people of that tiny village. He took his living on the sea, as did his father and Patrick, and Bones, and even Kevin McCreesh.

Times had changed. He worked on yachts instead of freighters. Still he carried on the traditions. He also knew loss and he knew war, even if the battles of his military days weren't world wars, he knew too well how bullets and bombs killed and maimed.

O'Malley also knew people in battle who had no honor and were nothing more than brutal opportunists. He knew people like the ones who ordered the bombing of that Irish pub so many decades before. Worst of all, he knew they walked among the innocent every day. He knew that if left unchecked they were a threat to everyone's ordinary existence.

The loud cranking of the engine below their feet shook both sailors from their contemplation. This time the engine kept running. The young mechanics called out victory while *Maxine's* engine purred.

The Captain of *Gael na Mara* looked at Patrick who was obviously overjoyed that the engine returned to work. They ended their parley and climbed across *Maxine's* deck and back aboard the "Woman of the Sea."

CHAPTER 27

THE RED-HAIRED BOY

Around 6:00 P.M. the art galleries and curio shops of Rocky Neck began closing their doors. A dark blue evening sky descended upon the art colony. Street lights reflected in the undulating water of Smith Cove. Throughout the late afternoon, Claire and Martha occasionally glanced towards the harbor entrance. Between times, they idly perused watercolors and gifts in colorful shop windows.

Martha eventually suggested they climb back into her red Escort, drive around to East Gloucester, and find something to eat on Rogers Street. Martha recommended a seafood restaurant she occasioned on her rare visits to the ancient fishing port.

A few minutes later, chattering while her bobbing cigarette led the way, Martha pulled up in a parking space outside the Gloucester Fish & Chips Company. The place looked like a Maine fishing cabin. Inside it featured the requisite fluorescent lights and red-checkered tablecloths that symbolized good food to Martha. Together they enjoyed a meal of Martha's favorite sit down dinner, "red snappah."

As their meal came to an end, Claire noticed Martha glancing more frequently out the window and up the fairway of the harbor. A growing look of anxiety appeared in the crinkled corners of the good witch's eyes. Martha lit a cigarette as they stepped from the restaurant.

A light breeze wafted through the harbor and sounds of flapping halyards filled the air. Claire didn't share Martha's anxiety. Conversely, she was inwardly excited, nervous only about encountering Carter this way. So far, they only spoke with a coffee counter between them. Claire shook off her nervousness as the ambling pair, like mother and daughter, walked to Solomon Jacobs Park.

Martha suddenly began tugging vigorously at Claire's arm. She pulled Claire away from her contemplation, having spotted the tall stick of *Maxine* entering the fairway. Her running lights were aglow and the yacht looked beautiful in the blue evening light.

The sloop continued along its way and the Marblehead women went unnoticed by *Maxine's* crew as they motored past the park. They were occupied with making the sleek vessel ready to dock.

Martha sighed deeply. She murmured something Claire could not distinguish and released the young woman's arm as if to signal it was time to go. It was 7:00 P.M. and the two women pondered how to explain their decision to come greet the coastwise cruisers as *Maxine* motored passed the transient mooring field and steamed to the haul-out well at Thomas O'Brady's boatyard.

Claire noticed how intently Martha was watching the boat. She assumed it was simply a matter of being glad to see it arrive. She did not realize the matron of the Purser's Quarters found it curious that *Maxine* was entering a haul-out well instead of picking up a mooring, as would most visiting yachts. Claire didn't understand or comprehend the significance.

A few moments passed and they left Solomon Jacobs Park and began walking toward the O'Brady yard to greet their wayfaring sailormen.

≋≋≋

On board *Maxine* everything was wet. Clothes were soaked, dry provisions ruined, everything coated with a salt film. Wearing dry clothes and carrying provisions supplied by *Gael na Mara*, the crew brought her in as if all were normal. What happened off shore was nobody's business. The sailors were, however, going to have to haul *Maxine* and have a shipwright repair her damage. That part of the story would eventually have to be told.

Bones figured the tale of a coastwise cruiser hitting an unseen object was not uncommon. It should attract no unwanted attention from higher authorities, which was all that really mattered. He wanted no special attention, no distractions, nothing that would impair his communiqués with the Mitchell Commission or attract O'Neil's attention.

Patrick was owed a favor by a man in Marblehead who was owed a favor by a man in Gloucester. Patrick called in the chain of favors on *Maxine's* behalf. If the work was done quickly, it was likely they could avoid the usual scuttlebutt from spreading around town.

Patrick telephoned his friend from off-shore using Carter's cell phone. In a cryptic exchange he arranged for the haul-out well to be ready upon arrival. The work could proceed discreetly and immediately.

Within minutes of arrival, *Maxine* was hoisted from the water. She was out and drying in less time than it took Martha and Claire to walk over to greet them. *Maxine* was quickly draped with a welder's curtain kept on hand to hide the keel of America's Cup boats from competitors' prying eyes. The crew quickly removed the canvas awning tacked under *Maxine's* bow.

≋≋≋

Carter now could see the damage the bizarre collision caused. His heart sank as he ran his hand along the injured planks. Gouges penetrated the wood in deep furrows. They had been lucky, nonetheless. The planks remained in place. Had she been holed, they would have sunk in minutes. One of the remarkable things about wood, Carter reflected, is that it can take such punishment. Metal would have sheered and failed catastrophically.

Regardless of this comparative good fortune, the repair would be extensive and costly. Carter groaned. Planks would need replacing and several ribs, too. Then she'd need to be re-caulked and re-painted and she'd have to soak up again as time on the hard would dry her out.

"Thaht's not so bahd," Patrick assessed.

"She'll be ready to return to service in no time, Caahtah," said Bones.

Their words of consolation fell on deaf ears. Carter was depressed. He didn't have money in excess and repairs would drain his reserves. He would have to go ashore to find design work. He said so aloud, not intending the observation to elicit a response.

"Now don't you be a worryin' about the costs quite yet theah, laddie. Theah's ways to gathah together the funds. Bones and I cahn bring ta beah some favors thaht will carry ya through the worst of it, skippah."

Carter thought about those words for a long moment. Even though he wanted to accept assistance, he realized acceptance would likely ensnare him in a moral dilemma. He doubted he should become more deeply involved in their shadowy world.

Or is it their noble world; their noble cause?

He was certain that was how they viewed it.

Or maybe Bones and Patrick enjoyed financial resources unassociated with their covert lives. After all, it was apparent *Gael na Mara* had once been Bones' personal yacht, though Carter wasn't sure exactly how that might have been or why he didn't currently reveal his ownership of her.

One way or the other, it was possible they enjoyed legitimate wealth. Maybe there was an inheritance. If that were the case, then Carter's dilemma was imagined. His benefactor's gift would be entirely above board—nothing to do with bombings in Northern Ireland, gun running in Libya, or a safe house operated in the sleepy enclave of Marblehead, Massachusetts.

Suddenly, out of the ethereal darkness came a familiar and completely unexpected voice, the crackling coarseness startling the dauntless crew of the yacht *Maxine*.

"What on earth did you boys run *Maxine* into out theah?" Martha exclaimed. There was a trace of reprimand nested plainly in the question.

All three men turned in a jolt, never suspecting their Martha was about to walk up from behind. Not only that, but with Claire Dubois at her arm!

"Ah, Martha . . ." said Patrick, stalling and then fading away, coming up short on words. Carter was wordless, too, though only for a moment. Pulling his wits together, he spoke next.

"Hello, Claire," he interposed, barely able to veil his excitement.

He thought he should say more but nothing further emerged from his lips. He stood silently looking sweetly flummoxed.

After Patrick and Carter fumbled their attempts to answer Martha's perfectly reasonable question, the unflappable Bones finally spoke up.

"Well, Maatha, deah, we cahn't say fer certain." His reply was calm and unruffled.

Maintaining his patriarchal prerogative, the old seaman spotted a stack of timbers used for bunking boats on jack stands. He sat down to relieve his aching knees. Then he took a match from his pocket, scratched it against a concrete block, and lit his pipe in the darkening Gloucester night.

For a moment there was an ill-at-ease silence. Bones weathered it with calm; Carter still couldn't come up with something appropriate to say. Patrick, however, regained his composure and broke back in. When he spoke, sounding a bit playful, he skipped explanations, ignored questions, and announced that since they were enjoying a regular "old home day," McKinney's Pub was serving cold Guinness and he would buy the first round.

The tension floating amongst them dissolved into the salt air. Patrick stepped away and spoke a couple words with the yard manager then turned to the group. Removing his long billed cap with an exaggerated movement, allowing his red-gray ponytail to tumble behind his head, he pointed down the dark wharf toward McKinney's Pub. Following the direction his cap was pointing, the entourage set out in the dark Gloucester night.

≋≋≋

In less than a half an hour, the crew of *Maxine* and their womenfolk were engaged in scuttlebutt in the Gloucester town tradition.

Patrick told stories.

Bones chuckled and nodded, passing his pipe back and forth between his thick, salty lips.

Martha exhibited a satisfied deportment, relieved Bones and Patrick were home safe from the sea. Claire exhibited enticing social graces, glancing frequently toward Carter then courteously back toward the others. Carter, in turn, watched the entire group in quiet amazement.

Irresistibly, as the evening progressed, Carter's eyes fell on Claire more frequently than the others. He listened to her speak, secretly caressing her Midwest accent. To Carter, her voice stood out clearly as she spoke amongst the New Englanders. It kindled a longing for home, almost equal to his now realized longing for her. Together, the table of Marbleheaders and Midwesterners took pleasure in an evening of drink and revelry; the perfect ending of a day of pleasure boating, or so the story was told.

≋≋≋

The back of Patrick's hands argued differently. Martha noticed them, and knew there was more to the story than the men were revealing. She kept silent, even though she was aching to speak; aching to articulate her concern and frustration.

Martha knew that Bones', as well as Patrick's lives depended on her silence. At present, she knew the peace talks conducted by the Mitchell Commission depended on it, too. There were secrets heaped upon secrets that seemed to completely control their lives.

In a childish reaction, arguably to punish or get even with the secretive men, Martha decided she would keep a secret from them. She would not divulge how her special senses revealed the disaster that visited the three sailors that morning and, by some miracle, did not come full term. She would not divulge the wails of anguish she expelled for the love of their ornery souls, the fearful dread she endured at the thought of losing them, as she did her beloved mother so very long ago.

Martha hoped Claire would not expose her secret either, that she would remain discreet. She felt confident Claire would. She believed Claire was intelligent, observant, and capable of the innocent duplicity their gender necessarily employed in the management of men. Ironically, the only thing that actually concerned Martha about Claire was the simple fact that she believed Claire capable of such behavior, and perhaps more. She feared this on Carter's behalf. Martha sensed something peculiar, mysterious about Claire, though she chose not to think beyond the kindness the young woman offered in her time of need.

≋≋≋

By 8:30 P.M. Claire and Carter stepped out onto Rogers Street. They walked quickly toward *Maxine*. The evening was young; Bones had requested Patrick play his fiddle, and asked Carter if he would return to *Maxine* to retrieve it.

"Bring yer guitah, too, son. Let's heah if ya can keep up with a genuine Irish fiddlah."

Carter invited Claire to accompany him. In so doing, he fulfilled the other half of Bones' purpose, without knowing how it was that Bones brought Kevin and Winnie together with a similar plan such a long time ago. Carter fell for the innocent deception.

Together, the young couple slipped into the night to enjoy a private moment, a chance to be together.

≋≋≋

Claire and Carter returned a short time later with the instruments and soon the five visitors to Gloucester Town set about playing and singing.

Patrick drew his fiddle to his chin, his playing filling the rickety tavern with euphoria and jubilation. Carter strummed whimsically on his guitar and together they played Irish jigs and French Canadian contra tunes, filling the raucous house with music.

Time and cares fell by the way as Carter played frenetically to match Patrick's fiddling. Notes emanated flawlessly from the crazed fiddler, eyes afire, nimble body gyrating with the rhythm of his bowing.

Bones and Martha clapped their hands and sang as they did when they were young, when Miread was alive, when they were a whole family. Surely Miread and Winnie both watched from heaven above and Martha considered whether her lost husband, Connor O'Donnell, would be doing the same. She estimated that heaven might not be the point from which he observed the merriment. The good witch mused that it may be Connor, himself, who was helping his step-brother draw the fiery bow across the strings, guided as if by the devil's left hand.

The revelry carried into the night and drink dissolved inhibitions. It became apparent to all that Claire Dubois knew quite a bit about Irish music. Unable to contain herself any longer, she called out a request for "Red-Haired Boy."

Patrick grinned, winked at Bones, nodded to Martha and called out, "The key o' A theah, laddie," to his back-up guitar. Off he raced, sawing vigorously on the popular tune. Carter went chasing him, strumming the back beat in a valiant effort to keep up with Patrick's frenzied playing.

The revelers were further taken aback, and none more than Carter, when Claire, who had been clapping and tapping her feet in time with the music, rose suddenly from the table, pushed aside her chair, dropped her hands straight down at her sides in the traditional stance, and commenced step dancing.

The astounded crowd backed away to give the pretty lass room to maneuver. A superlative smile crossed Claire's face as she saw the crowd's reaction, then she turned toward the fiddler. Patrick, seeing a dancer in his fo'c'sle, rose higher to the occasion and the two revelers put on a show not soon forgotten in Gloucester town.

≋≋≋

For a quick moment, Bones worried about all the attention coming their way. Then he set his strategic mind aside for once and allowed the group to continue in unbridled glee. The risk of a security breach seemed miniscule—who would be spying on them in Gloucester anyway? O'Malley was heading toward south Boston when they departed. Besides, the old counselor wondered if this may be his last opportunity to see Martha and the chief of the O'Clery clan in such high spirits, carefree, and together. For all the things Bones had given in his ninety years, all the choices and sacrifices he made, he clutched this moment for himself. Memories of this night would be his own; memories to supplant all the rest, especially the sad and horrific. With these memories in place, he would eventually, perhaps sooner than later, accept his end.

Bones clapped along as Claire and Patrick performed another Irish dance that took them to and fro, turning round and round, the gleeful crowd roaring with delight. Soon everyone in the rickety building moved in time to the fiddler's bow. The festive rejoinder between fiddler and dancer went on till the "wee hours," as Patrick would have said, had he slowed down enough to say anything.

Claire's was revealing her passion for all things Irish and communicating it freely in music and dance. Carter's passion for

Claire seem to rise like the tide lapping at the pilings outside the pub as he strummed with increasing energy, and his eyes fixed on the black-haired beauty.

≋≋≋

Finally, the late hour pleaded an end to the merrymaking. The weary sailors and their women folk sat around their oaken table and drank nightcaps of Bailey's Irish Crème, courtesy of the proprietor.

It was decided the women should spend the night in tourist rooms Mr. McKinney kept upstairs while the men returned to *Maxine*. Parting was prolonged and excuses were made for one last sip or one last song.

His eyes tired and his mind thick with the day's events, Carter experienced an epiphany. It dawned upon him that until this moment something had eluded him. He suddenly became aware that the three Marbleheaders, together like this for the first time since he met them, were a family. They were a loving, caring family and it amazed him he hadn't figured this out before. As in all families, they had a past, a very colorful one he presumed; a present, which he was participating in at that moment, and something more. This special family enjoyed something profoundly important—a future!

Up until the occurrence of his epiphany, Carter thought Bones, Martha, and Patrick were separate, superfluous old people living alone in their retiring years. He assumed only coincidence brought them in proximity of each other. He believed Martha was a simple, kindly widow, Patrick a free spirit, a rogue. He incorrectly surmised that Bones was merely a tired old man like the cadre of Irregulars populating Tucker's Wharf.

Of course, that was what he was supposed to think, being the victim of their elaborate ruse. All of Marblehead, and possibly the entire world, was supposed to think that; only he, the very clever, the very observant, Carter Paul Phillips, had penetrated their veil of secrecy, only he had seen through their clever disguises.

Or had he? Had he figured all this out, or had the tightly-bound family allowed him to step within their midst; dropping hints, exposing the edges of their ploy, so he could, for reasons all their own, see them for what they really were. Were Bones, his daughter, and her brother-in-law giving him an advantage, treating him special, revealing to him their plight, their exile? Why would they do this? Why would they risk such a breech in security after fifty interminable years?

Suddenly Carter felt an anxious thought creep into his curious mind. The belief that these out-of-the-ordinary friends enjoyed a future was not a given. It was qualified. Unlike ordinary people who had futures by the mere fact they lived and breathed, Bones, Patrick, and Martha had a future only as long as they continued to hide their past. They needed to continue to remain hidden behind false pretenses, as they had for decades. They needed to remain hidden in the illusive serenity of a town where people mostly stayed indoors, where people shunned outsiders, where people were too rich or too busy to care about their neighbors.

Marblehead has been the perfect place to hide, he thought. *And how does Claire Dubois fit in? She probably knows little of what I've learned during the past weeks. Even if this is true, she certainly knows a great deal about the Irish, especially for an employee of a coffee house.*

He recalled the day he first saw Claire, and remembered Patrick whispering in her ear after the encounter with the vitriolic Mr. O'Neil.

Maybe she already knew them; maybe she knew them very well. He couldn't say—he didn't know. *Why not find out?*

≋≋≋

The night ended with Claire asking to sing a song, one last song. The request drew encouragement from all around and, receiving a nod from Bones, Claire turned to Patrick and announced the name of her tune.

Patrick, of course, knew the song well. He turned to look at Martha. Carter immediately recognized the look Patrick wore the night they first met in the theatre in Boston. Carter sat upright in anticipation. The red-haired boy, fiddle still pressed to his chin, leaned toward Carter and whispered in his ear.

"Sure this song, laddie, it haas to be played from the soul, don't ya know. Not the soul as you haav thought o' soul in the past, skippah. Not yer soul or my soul, nor any single one o' the throng heah tonight, laddie. This song must be played from the soul of tens of thousands. From the soul of an entire people forced to leave theah homeland. People staahvin' and dyin' on board the fahmine ships; people comin' to new worlds. Our people, my people, my clan, Caahtah; they aah cast about the whole o' mothah earth and I need ya to follow me with chords thaht speak theah sorrow and theah joy, too, don't ya' know. Aah ya up fer it, laddie?"

Patrick paused while Carter considered the question. The lake sailor understood, but hesitated, unsure if he could deliver. He realized he was an ordinary guy, a plain ordinary Midwesterner. He wasn't Irish and he didn't have an Irish soul. For that matter, he wasn't sure he possessed a soul at all, not in the way Patrick was describing. His life had been devoid of dramatic influences—like the struggles of the Irish, or the Jewish, or the Arabs.

Carter searched his mind for the source of inspiration he needed to meet Patrick's request. Then it dawned on him. He realized his wellspring of inspiration. It was obvious—his passion for sailing. He realized being a sailor was his soul. It was the compulsion driving him out onto the water. It drove him to be pushed before the wind on a wooden boat gliding across distance and time. Carter's soul intermingled with *Maxine*, her stunning lines, her majestic rigging, the smell of her carved teakwood and varnished spars. Along with the recognition of his passion, a feeling of confidence grew. He looked at Patrick and nodded.

Then, as only a true friend would dare, Patrick leaned closer. He came within Carter's personal space—the space around one's self where only the intimate is allowed or expected. He spoke quietly in

Carter's ear. Carter felt the heat of Patrick's breath. The clan leader spoke in a low, mystic voice.

"An' by the way, laddie, Miss Clayah heah, she's more than a pleasin' sight to the eyes, skippah, she's much, much more . . . do ya understand? Well if ya don't right now, laddie, ya will, I'll promise ya... ya will."

Carter was stricken by these unbelievable words. He looked furtively at Claire. She stood ready to sing, confident and intent on ending their evening her special way.

Claire was a mystery, surely not only a coffee shop waitress, not merely a voice who spoke his accent. He wandered again into the perilous curiosity from which he swore he'd stay away. Then the first long resonant note was drawn passionately from the red-haired boy's bow. The entire room fell silent.

Claire placed her white silken hands together as would an opera singer and held them poised at her waist. In a magical gesture, someone dimmed the lights. Carter placed his guitar pick on the table. He would play with his fingers; he would play with his flesh in direct contact with the bronze strings. It was a way of drawing more expression from the instrument. He then joined the bow stroke with a chord that resounded in the quiet room, filling the silent crowd with unbridled anticipation.

Claire began singing, her words flowing mystically into the hushed room.

Kilkelly, Ireland, 1860, my dear and loving son John
Your good friend schoolmaster Pat McNamara's so good
as to write these words down.
Your brothers have all got a fine work in England,
the house is so empty and sad
The crop of potatoes is sorely infected,
a third to a half of them bad.
And your sister Brigid and Patrick O'Donnell
are going to be married in June.
Mother says not to work on the railroad
and be sure to come on home soon.

Kilkelly, Ireland, 1870, my dear and loving son John
Hello to your Mrs. and to your 4 children,
may they grow healthy and strong.
Michael has got in a wee bit of trouble,
I suppose that he never will learn.
Because of the darkness there's no turf to speak of
and now we have nothing to burn.
And Brigid is happy, we named a child for her
and now she's got six of her own.
You say you found work, but you don't say
what kind or when you will be coming home.

Kilkelly, Ireland, 1880, dear Michael and John, my sons
I'm sorry to give you the very sad news
that your dear old mother has gone.
We buried her down at the church in Kilkelly,
your brothers and Brigid were there.
You don't have to worry, she died very quickly,
remember her in your prayers.
And it's so good to hear that Michael's returning,
with money he's sure to buy land
For the crop has been bad and the people
are selling at every price that they can.

Kilkelly, Ireland, 1890, my dear and loving son John
I suppose that I must be close on eighty,
it's thirty years since goodbye.
Because of all of the money you send me,
I'm still living out on my own.
Michael has built himself a fine house
and Brigid's daughters have grown.
Thank you for sending your family picture,
they're lovely young women and men.
You say that you might even come for a visit,
what joy to see you again.

As Claire's lovely voice poured forth the sad refrains there was nary a dry eye in the pub; a place where fishermen and women knew well the sorrows of lives tortured and turned by fate.

Carter, too, was moved by the music. He was thankful to be part of Claire's performance, to make music that was reaching the depths of the audience gathered round, to be part of their lives through music.

Carter looked over at Bones and Martha sitting next to each other a few feet away. They sat obscurely in the dim light. He saw them as he saw yachts on his evening forays onto quiet harbors. He saw only their beautiful lines, their subtle greatness of being. The dim light obscured their flaws and the wrinkles years etched in their skin. They appeared younger, more alive than he ever saw them before.

He also noticed the tiniest glint of reflection come his way. It was a crystalline light cast forth from a miniscule tear. To his amazement it came from Bones. The tear slowly rolled; it rolled down Wilfred Albert Matheson's great leathery cheek. The tear transformed the man who shed it. He wasn't simply Bones anymore, or at least not Bones alone. He was the boy who was Jonathan and Elizabeth's son, he was Winnie's bright and clever young brother, he was Miread's mournful husband and Martha's proud father. He was Carter's friend and confidant, the man who gave him heat.

Carter watched the teardrop fall and his eyes followed the direction the tear descended. There he saw the weathered hand of the ninety-year-old man, traitor to England, counselor to Northern Ireland; the hand of the man who saved his life in the cold of Massachusetts Bay. He continued staring intently and he watched the great hand fold slowly, gently, over the thin delicate fingers of his treasured daughter.

Carter looked back up at Martha who was looking into the eyes of her father. Carter imagined her as the earthly incarnation of Miread Matheson.

His mind reeled with empathy for these extraordinary people. They can't possibly be terrorists a voice inside him pleaded. He looked around; afraid he'd said those words out loud. No one was looking and his denial continued. They can't possibly be part of the killing. They can't be party to events so horrible it was difficult to accept they really had occurred.

Yet they had. Carter knew they had, just as surely as he knew Ryan O'Malley wasn't merely a pleasure boat captain, nor the young Irishmen merely boat hands. He knew it as he knew the black specter aboard *Gael na Mara* would have shot him at the least provocation the night he spied on the boat in Marblehead Harbor.

Carter gripped his guitar as if to physically force the vile thought that they were murderers from his perplexed mind. He focused mightily and continued playing chords both sweet and sorrowful. He looked back at Claire. She sang the song through to its mournful end.

Kilkelly, Ireland, 1892, my dear brother John
I'm sorry I didn't write sooner to tell you,
but father passed on.
He was living with Brigid, she says he was cheerful
and healthy right down to the end.
Ah, you should have seen him play with
the grandchildren of Pat McNamara, your friend.
And we buried him alongside of mother,
down at the Kilkelly churchyard.
He was a strong and a feisty old man,
considering his life was so hard.
And it's funny the way he kept talking about you,
he called for you in the end.
Oh, why don't you think about coming to visit,
we'd all love to see you again.

Carter glimpsed at Patrick and he saw once again the face of the man who moved Carter so compellingly in the dark theatre beneath the streets of Boston. This time, however, Patrick was not staring at a movie screen in an empty theatre. This time the old figure was not searching, reaching around the room for help as Carter remembered that night they first met.

This time Patrick stared directly, unwaveringly at Martha, the woman he surely loved—the woman he longed for more than any earthly object, the woman he desired for more than fifty years but could never have for so much as fifty days.

It was then Carter realized that Patrick harbored a secret love for his half-brother's wife. He was a man torn by desire and allegiance; allegiance sprung from adherence to a code, the law of his clan. The code that made it impossible for a man to have the wife of a brother lost in battle—a code intended to keep every man facing forward in battle, never looking behind him in doubt or jealousy.

Martha Winifred Matheson was married for eternity to Connor Seamus O'Donnell, and Patrick Timothy O'Clery couldn't change that. As leader of his clan, he bore the burden with double weight and only on the rarest occasion, as the curious lake sailor saw that night in the theatre, did the weight take its toll.

Patrick continued staring at Martha as the song faded into applause. Clapping hands and cries for more filled McKinney's pub. Carter looked at Martha, the good witch, the matron of the Purser's Quarters. She turned away from Bones and looked in Patrick's direction. She smiled the faintest smile then returned her attention to her father.

Carter wondered who she was at that moment, which Martha was the real Martha. Was she Martha of her birth, Martha Winifred Matheson? Was she Martha Winifred O'Donnell, widow of a wild young nationalist? Or perhaps she was simply Martha the nursemaid, the matron of the Purser's Quarters, the good witch who drove Carter around in a red Escort, caring for him like the son she never had. Whichever she was didn't matter, he concluded, for she was a dear soul and he—her surrogate son.

CHAPTER 28

SPY SHIP CAPTAINS

The *Monarch*, a medium endurance cutter, was the first in her class to be launched in 1964. She was lightly armed, with 25 mm and 50 mm machine guns. Over the past four years, the *Monarch* was fitted with sensitive electronic listening gear. During normal operations, she steamed in international waters from Greenland, in the north east, down to Cape Cod, and the islands in the south.

The fishermen working the banks spotted her often enough. They knew she was a spy ship, yet to them she meant nothing special. She neither helped nor hindered their catch.

In fact, in many ways, she was no better than they; only bigger—a little over 210 feet on deck. Like the fishermen, she cruised back and forth, catching radio signals in her net and shipping them off to market to be bought and sold by governments and their spies.

The remnants of a nearly dysfunctional Russian submarine fleet cruised the same region and paid closer attention to the *Monarch's* position than the fisherman did. Patrolling silently beneath the surface, they listened for sounds they might detect inside the *Monarch's* steel belly.

The American submarine fleet, in turn, watched the Russians. Every move and every noise the Russians made was charted and analyzed.

Captain Donovan thought no better formula for engendering paranoia could be devised. Everyone was listening to everyone else. What further aggravated Donovan was that he knew damned well that the information he intercepted and delivered higher up was exchanged on a virtually open market. He knew there were games being played by political officers and foreign service officials. He knew the movement of arms, money, and expertise by unscrupulous arms dealers and terrorists knew no geographic or ethical bounds.

The information drew great interest from all major powers, not to mention crime bosses and thugs as well. It really burned Donovan to think his work was being used by criminal organizations. In the battle against terrorism, criminal organizations, unsanctioned governments, despots and fanatics were so intertwined Donovan could barely discern who was who.

The spy ship captain would have been a hell of a lot happier knowing at whom to point his gun so when he pulled the trigger he was shooting an enemy. He reflected longingly on chasing Columbians across the churning crests of the Caribbean Sea.

What grinded Donovan most was discovering that Irish lads, possibly his own relatives, had taken up training Chechen and Palestinian rebels in the god-forsaken art of homemade bombs.

That rankled Donovan's Irish pride. It upset his paradigm of right and wrong. He hadn't joined the Coast Guard to stand around listening as misaligned spooks vacillated back and forth between these two simple ideas. Considering the things he heard on this assignment, Donovan could barely discern right from wrong himself.

To hell with it, I'm just gonna' do my duty.

His frustration was mitigated by the fact that he knew he was right to follow orders. Disobeying them was wrong. Following them was right, something Captain Donovan did without question.

Another thing that wore on Donovan was the rising frequency of chatter among Muslim extremists. These guys were intelligent, deceptive, and funded with generous amounts of cash bled directly off Middle Eastern oil wells. They were running around attempting, perhaps even succeeding, in purchasing biological, chemical, and even nuclear weapon components. They hatched wild, cruel schemes, such as using civil aircraft as weapon delivery systems.

Then again, he thought of how pervasive the problem was.

Legitimate governments are up to the same bullshit!

It would seem everyone was involved in crazy schemes. He recalled the damnable French blowing up Greenpeace's *Rainbow Warrior* in Auckland Harbor back in '85. He chuckled cynically when he thought of the French denying it to the bitter end.

The captain of the *Monarch* rose from his desk and walked to the bridge. He raised his glasses and peered into the eastern horizon. It was a faint gray blue, streaked with pastel yellow and misty orange; the separation between sky and water was barely discernable. Greenland lay far off to the east, Ireland bearing a little south of east.

Soon, he reminded himself, *only two months and I'll be watching the sun rise on board my Hinckley.*

He received word only two days ago that his membership in the East Harbor Yacht Club was approved. He speculated there would be a vast difference in his view of the ocean when seen from aboard his new found freedom.

He continued observing the quickly changing colors rising from the east. His mind continued to wander. *At least the Irish troubles are easy to understand. If only the British got the hell out of Northern Ireland, the trouble would be over. It's that simple; they never should have been there in the first place.*

Then he realized he didn't actually know when the English had arrived in the first place. Who were the indigenous people of Ireland? Could an autonomous society say that it was theirs and theirs alone? Perhaps the Irish question wasn't that easy to understand.

Lowering his glasses he checked his chronometer. It was 08:00 GMT, Sunday, April 5th. He was convinced that the closer he came to retirement, the slower time was clicking by. At its current rate of slowness, the last couple months of active duty were going to equal all the years he already served.

Captain Donovan returned to his thoughts about Ireland.

If the troubles were so simple to end, why hadn't the British packed up and left long ago? Why hadn't a solution taken form before thousands of people were murdered and maimed in the melee?

He didn't know the answer.

At least since Cromwell's time, about the same time his hometown of Lyme, Connecticut, was founded, the British had acted as both governor and protector. This duality was contrary to the image the Brits currently held forth to the world, that is, that they are a peace keeping force, acting on both sides' behalf. Donovan's casual reading on the topic revealed a number of references where the Catholic minority in the North pleaded for British protection. It might be better stated that they were demanding it.

Seeking protection from the leaders of the people who are oppressing you! What a queer situation. Who else could they look to? Who else even cared?

The Spanish, who brought potatoes to Ireland from Peru, gave the Northern Catholics a hand a long time ago, a campaign that ended in disaster. The French, who have been perennially annoyed with Great Britain, took up arms with Wolf Tone in 1798 in a failed rebellion. They haven't been back since.

Considering the list of unfortunate failures, Donovan wondered if the Mitchell Commission, President Clinton's current peace initiative, had a fighting chance of success.

Donovan thought again about Muslim extremists. They were the ones to watch. They were the ones few in the intelligence community understood.

At least the Irish are Catholics and Protestants—Christians in a plain brown wrapper.

Donovan also knew that much of the Irish intrigue was tied closely to Irish-American sympathizers. One didn't need to be the captain of a top secret radio ship to figure that out. Anyone at a public library can go on the Internet and find Web sites of U.S. sympathizers raising money for relief in Northern Ireland.

In fact, links to sites operated by both Nationalist and Loyalist organizations are abundant on the World Wide Web. He had come upon them on a library computer in Lyme, not long ago. At the very moment he pressed the "enter" key, he thought about his own vessel's top secret electronic capabilities. In a rush of what ordinary people might have thought was paranoia, the spy ship captain exited the Internet and immediately wiped the keyboard and mouse with his handkerchief. He promptly left the library with his face covered by his long-billed sailing cap. If he could do what he could do with his shipboard spy gear, he could vividly imagine what land-based computer spooks could accomplish.

Returning to his thoughts about Muslims, Donovan considered that they were a vastly different problem than the Irish. Something about the quickness of their tongues, the foreign sound their languages made as they chattered on the air waves, worried Donovan. He didn't know how to describe his apprehension, but the very timbre of their voices raised his anxiety, filled him with a sense of foreboding.

Not only that, Donovan thought, *intelligence agencies are having an extremely difficult time finding Arab language experts.*

Donovan knew too well that secret, perhaps imminently dangerous messages were making it through the net due to variations in tribal lexicon and regionally influenced elocution. A huge volume of dialogue was bouncing off the ionosphere and spy ship captains such as Commander Donovan had no idea what it meant because there simply weren't enough trained language experts to serve in all the places they were needed.

Donovan mulled over this dilemma. He knew Ivy League schools, especially ones along the eastern seaboard, were the main source of language spies. Universities such as Yale, Boston College, and Dartmouth were frequently recruited by intelligence agencies. Most often the recruits were the scion of wealthy, well placed parents who tolerated their children's indulgent education in arts and languages.

Who would have thought that those liberal arts types would end up as spies?

He recalled reading that Julia Childs the television cooking hostess was once an employee of an intelligence branch many years prior to earning fame as a gourmet chef.

Who would have believed it?

He chuckled.

A voice from an intercom interrupted his humorous thought.

"Captain, we have an incoming message from Granite Station South."

"Send it to my ready room in two minutes," Donovan said.

"Roger, Captain, transfer to begin in 1-2-0 seconds, sir," barked the yeoman. The young crewman checked the position of a second hand on a nearby clock.

> "Begin Message ... Figurehead and Red Haired Boy returning to watch zone. MAX arrival at MH Harbor, ETA 21:00 GMT. Intercepted transmission from MAX to GNM, GNM departing for Montauk, Tillerman to deliver triple expletives, expecting to pick up fresh fruit ... standing by ... End Message."

The message pricked Captain Donovan's curiosity.

When he leaned back again in his over-stuffed chair he did something he rarely did. He wondered about the people, the lives he was spying on. He speculated over who they were, what they looked like, how they talked, what they ate for breakfast.

Perhaps it was his proximity to retirement, that is, the time when he would no longer be required to ignore the humanity of the marks; to put flesh on their bones, see them as people with desire and despair.

Who, he wondered, *are the Figurehead and the Red-Haired Boy? How had they earned such repute? Why were they watched so attentively? Why, when operatives got close, did the feds always pull back? Who was protecting these two—and what about the Tillerman? Who the hell was he? Did he have friends? Did he have a mother? Is he as dangerous as he's made out to be? Is it true they trained him years ago? Is this why they fear him now?*

Donovan pulled back suddenly. *Whoa there Captain Donovan, you aren't out of the service yet. Don't go there. In a few months you can think and do what you want, especially when you're cruising aboard Cassiopeia.*

CHAPTER 29

THE SENATAH FROM MAINE

There exist few words expressive enough to convey the righteous indignation of the Red Shoes Irregulahs. Each day the intrepid sailors were gone the ornery contingent of retired shipwrights and deck hands had queued up to supervise construction. Like clockwork, they would open their lawn chairs, sit and eat donuts, and then, when no work appeared imminent, grumbled and complained uproariously.

"If Pahtrick O'Clery haas made a deliberate design ta build an unlucky ship, he haas come upon no bettah plahn," one of the more articulate Irregulars had warned, wiping glazed sugar from his crusty lips.

The Irregulahs were completely beside themselves when the three wayfaring sailors finally reappeared.

Patrick eased back into his daily regimen showing little concern over the wailing and groaning. Carter crept into the boat shed, hoping to remain unnoticed. He dreaded the moment, knowing he would receive the brunt of the blame for the down time on *Red Shoes*.

Bones, exhibiting the diplomatic skills honed from years of dealing with conflict, hobbled sore-legged over to the group, selected a vacant chair, and sat down with an audible wheeze. As he adjusted himself in his seat, he appeared to Carter to transform back into one of them. He selected his donut, complained about the weather, and pointed out a few of Patrick's mistakes where the clamps crossed the knees.

Initially, the Irregulahs refused to be indulged, demonstrating haughty indignation towards Bones and his efforts at calming the waters of their discontent. Patrick, watching Bones at work, leaned over to Carter and declared in a whisper, "He'll need the good senatah from Maine to negotiate a settlement with thaht motley crew, don't ya know theah, skippah." He laughed at his own joke.

Carter looked at Patrick and smiled. When their eyes met, Carter saw once again the sparkle he presumed came from being back on board his "schoonah abuildin'." Carter glanced from Patrick to Bones and the small group of cranky old men staring dubiously up at him. Carter could see Patrick's point without straining. However, he didn't understand Patrick's joke; he didn't know "the good senatah from Maine."

"Which senator is that?" Carter queried aloud in response to Patrick's assertion. "Edmund Muskie is the only senator I can recall from Maine," Carter said.

"Oh no, laddie! For heaven's sake, skippah, I thought ya read the newspapers, my boy! I'm talkin' about Senatah George Mitchell, don't ya know, the most populah American in all of Ireland, north or south right now, skippah."

Carter admitted to Patrick that politics was not his forte. He went on to defend his reading of newspapers though, reminding Patrick that he occasionally clipped articles of interest and taped them to *Maxine's* log.

Patrick caught his drift.

"Oh, thaht's right, laddie, I was forgettin' you tended to be interested in current events when the news is about things thaht fly, things thaht float, and things thaht come out of the ends of metal tubes then, laddie."

"Well, not always. I'll admit that I'm puzzled over the difficulties people have getting along, like that group down there sitting in those lawn chairs," nodding subtly in the direction of the Irregulars. "I've always abided by a live and let live policy."

Patrick shot a glance his way and replied. "So haav I, skippah, so haav I."

Carter paused, surprised by Patrick's response. He contemplated both the truth and the lie in his old friend's claim. He turned and watched Bones for a few minutes as the elder statesman conducted his mediation, then he added, "I don't think I'd make a good mediator myself. I don't believe I'd know how to go about it, that is, beyond asking everybody to behave and be nice."

"Well then, laddie, you'd do well ta get ta know the workin's of Senatah George Mitchell o' Maine. He and Bones haav things in common, don't ya know."

Carter looked in Patrick's direction to detect if there were secret meanings in his words. Patrick focused on the pad eye he was mounting on *Red Shoes'* deck.

Returning to his own work, Carter managed to bring forth a recollection that President Clinton appointed a retired senator from somewhere out East to lead a peace initiative in Northern Ireland. It dawned upon him the initiative began a couple years ago. He hadn't paid close attention.

Now, however, Carter was living in the center of "all things Irish" in America. Now he had a relationship with Patrick, Bones, and even the mysterious Claire. He no longer considered anything he learned about the Irish to be of casual interest. He decided on the spot that he would take time to search the Internet to satisfy his curiosity.

As tasks progressed aboard *Red Shoes,* Carter observed that Bones remained sitting with the Irregulahs for several hours.

Mediation takes time and trust, he thought.

Carter watched as Bones listened with forbearance to his anxious colleagues. He occasionally doled out the necessary approbations in praise of their knowledge. In time, the disconcerted Irregulahs settled down.

Carter wondered what Bones told them that appeared to satisfy them. From the glowing look in their eyes, Claire's singing and dancing may have been mentioned.

He assumed, considering Bones' edict about secrecy, that no mention was made of the submerged container or the rescue of *Maxine* by the enigmatic *Gael na Mara.* He assumed no word came forth revealing the round-the-clock repair of *Maxine* to her pre-collision glory.

≋≋≋

By mid-afternoon, *Red Shoes'* entire crew, including the pacified Irregulahs, focused on the dozens of jobs needing completion before launching the schooner down the ways. Carter pointed in the direction of the Irregulahs, and spoke quietly to Patrick.

"I don't know what Bones said to those guys, but they've sure changed their colors since we arrived today. One of them actually made a friendly comment to me a minute ago."

"You don't say, laddie?"

"It's true. I asked him to help filter the varnish and he commenced upon the task and even offered suggestions along the way, a couple of tricks I hadn't known. I figured I'd be tarred and feathered for keeping you and Bones away from *Red Shoes* so long!"

"Sure then laddie, now ya know why I've always been given to listenin' to Bones m'self fer so long. He's been makin' things square with contrary factions of ornery men fer decades, just like his mate, the good senatah from Maine," Patrick answered with a grin.

"I see," Carter replied, though he wasn't entirely certain he did. He suspected the remark had deeper meaning. He took the statement to be a continuation of the observation Patrick made earlier in the day about similarities between Bones and "the good senator from Maine."

Carter looked back at Bones, realizing from this point forward he could expect to hear their shared secrets alluded to in subtle ways. Small bits and pieces of information were likely to come forth and they would probably hold greater meaning than he would have thought prior to his awakening to the nature of these secretive men.

For example, what "contrary factions of ornery men" did Patrick refer to? He knew who the IRA and Sinn Fein were, but how many others were involved in the conflict?

He was aware there were both political and armed factions among the Protestants, too. It struck him as odd, though, that none were as famous as the IRA. He had heard or read something about the Orange Order, or Orangemen, or some group whose name had something to do with that color. He knew they were Protestant and that each year they paraded through Catholic neighborhoods of Belfast.

His recollection drew images of riots and calamities as the outcome of these incursions. He also knew that somehow, for the longest time, the British were in the center of the troubles. Aside from the fact that they always appeared in the newspaper as an occupying army, he remained uncertain of how or exactly why.

Furthermore, if Patrick's remark suggested Bones had something to do with negotiating, resolving, or for that matter having any positive effect whatsoever on how things evolved over there, how could he have done so? If what he learned recently was true, then Bones Matheson had lived in apparent exile in this country for the last fifty years. How could he have accomplished anything of the sort while living secretly in Marblehead? A vast ocean separated him from the three main contestants: the Irish Catholics, the Irish Protestants, and the British.

Carter caught his curiosity reaching hazardous levels once again. In his mind, the only solution to this riddle lay in the presumption that Bones and his entourage lived under special protection. Someone looked out for them. Yet, at the same time, they were apparently allowed to operate their safe house.

How could this be?

It appeared as if they received special treatment, exempt from capture and deportation. Perhaps they earned the privilege. Perhaps they provided an essential service at one point or another in the past. This would explain a number of otherwise peculiar aspects of their existence. It might even explain their continued, albeit veiled, connection to *Gael na Mara*. It also occurred to Carter that Bones must have developed powerful links to people in all three places: the U.S., Britain, and Ireland, both north and south of the partition. Carter shuddered a moment at the depth of these conclusions.

Snapping back from his musings, Carter realized he shouldn't be speculating on such things. He tried to remind himself that at one point during his recent awakening, he decided he would never again broach the subject of their secret lives.

But Patrick had made the comment, effectively opening the door for a peek at things that would surely necessitate deeper investigation. He wondered again if accepting the favors and funding necessary to repair *Maxine* would stand in the end as a good idea.

As he pondered this last question, he continued applying varnish to *Red Shoes*' rail. The helpful Irregulah, Carter's volunteer assistant, returned with a donut and stood at the ready like a seasoned mate. He watched Carter's strokes approvingly; no signs of "curtains" or "holidays." The old man seemed to want to help once again.

Carter smiled when he noticed. He could only conclude that people want to do good by nature, even if they frequently can't contain their irascible side. Both sides exist as significant components of their natures. The dichotomy becomes a kind of psychological yin and yang. It seemed analogous to arguing couples who clearly depend upon and even love one another even though they argue incessantly.

Carter paused in this thought and realized at a national level, as in Ireland, this translated into a situation where a vast number of people could become addicted to their conflict. Why wouldn't a thousand years, built largely upon violent conflict, not result in a strong relationship indeed; incredibly, a relationship neither side can live without, despite the fact that it hurts them both in cruel, despicable ways.

≋≋≋

By 3:00 P.M. Carter had moved from his position aboard *Red Shoes* to his position in front of the coffee counter at the Marblehead Roasting Company. The petulant Mr. O'Neil's workstation stood empty. Consequently, the broadest of smiles sprang from the finely formed lips of Claire Dubois. Once again, as it had that night in McKinney's, the air became infused with invisible magnetism.

The winsome couple hadn't seen each other since Gloucester and the anticipation affected a special feeling. The molecules of their bodies vibrated wondrously. The vibration created an invisible resonance somewhere over the counter. The resonance became harmonic, creating a rhapsody that only they could hear.

The door behind Carter slammed and the rhapsody dissipated into thin air. Carter watched Claire's eyes gloss over and her smile invert. He glimpsed into the reflective display case and recognized the roaster in the reflection.

The coffee Nazi paced loudly behind Carter. He moved in the direction of the idle roasting machine. Claire's eyes followed the roaster and then, looking back at Carter, she allowed the tiniest manifestation of her smile to return in subtle protest. She winked silently, turning away from Carter to prepare his Chai tea.

To occupy his time and satisfy his curiosity, Carter turned and glanced towards the roasting machine. He watched inconspicuously as the roaster, grim and intense, removed a replacement part from a shipping box.

The gangly, sullen man opened a toolbox, sifted through it, and clumsily extracted several tools. Appearing as if he had two left hands, he fumbled his attempt to remove the bad part and replace it with the good.

At one point, Carter considered offering assistance. He found the roaster's clumsiness difficult to watch. The increasingly frustrated roaster, unable to muster the full breadth of skills necessary to implement his plan, uttered an expletive not meant for polite company. He threw down his tools, scowled, and departed angrily for the sanctuary of his office.

Turning back toward the counter, Claire met Carter's puzzled look with a subdued, frustrated smile. The look he returned spoke of wonderment.

Why did she work for this person?

Her look in reply spoke of an acceptance of her circumstance. He decided it would be inappropriate to say what he thought. She rewarded his silence by covertly touching his hand, indicating the topic might be broached on another, more private occasion. The cue required little embellishment and Carter whispered a date, time and place across the counter. She smiled and winked again. Their evening aboard *Maxine* was confirmed.

Carter wanted to stay and enjoy more of this covert communication. They were both enjoying their veiled courting ritual. However, considering the proximity of the roaster, Carter determined he could likely re-surface any minute.

With his objective completed, Carter decided to move on. He had agreed to dine with Martha in Beverly at 7:00 P.M. He decided to fill the remaining time by visiting the library. He could quench the thirst of his curiosity about Senator George Mitchell and the Northern Irish peace initiative with water from the Internet.

CHAPTER 30

INVOLUNTARY CONSCRIPTION

Carter once again found comfort in the stable environment of the library. Nothing appeared to change during the week away. Little children zipped around young mothers. Retirees read quietly in the magazine section.

Carter walked over and sat down at a vacant computer. Within a short time, he accessed his e-mail and felt good about reconnecting with the rest of the world. Despite the excitement of his extraordinary situation, he appreciated stepping outside New England via the Internet.

A half-hour quickly transpired as he read and wrote replies to the messages found on screen. His urge to tell someone, anyone, about the things that were happening was nearly overwhelming. Regardless, Carter didn't pass on a word. He admitted to no one that he became dangerously ill on the shakedown cruise. Not a word passed through cyberspace explaining his ambivalent connection to Irish exiles. Nor did he discuss Claire, who occupied a great portion of his mind. He held to the promise of secrecy he made to Bones and Patrick as they tipped Irish whiskey and made solemn oaths on board *Gael na Mara*.

Still, the urge was tremendous. Carter began thinking of friends in Florida who could handle his amazing story. They were people who could keep secrets. The question became, could he? He was tempted; this was the test.

As he sent out various replies, he mustered the will. He told himself it was essential that he match the integrity of the men who saved his life only seven days ago on Massachusetts Bay. They hadn't survived fifty years in exile by talking out of school. He remembered believing strongly, being virtually certain, that the trust Bones and Patrick placed in him contributed in large measure to the restraint demonstrated by the captain of *Gael na Mara*.

Thinking of O'Malley prompted Carter to recall the leather-skinned captain's parting words on the Saturday before. They came in a subdued manner, yet were firm and clear. ..

≋≋≋

"Your crew, Captain Phillips, is valuable. Perhaps more valuable than you can imagine—at least in terms of the intelligence you've gained so far." He said this with a tone of inquiry, pausing as if Carter might admit knowing more than O'Malley already figured.

Carter had remained silent. His mental acuity had returned and with it a justifiable wariness of Captain O'Malley. A few seconds passed and O'Malley continued.

"They are not merely old boatmen, as I believe you initially perceived. I know you know differently now. Their status and importance ranges beyond what I suspect you might believe possible, at least judging by their ordinary appearance."

He paused for emphasis, rotating his cigar between his fingers.

"They have decided you are to be trusted and their trust is a badge of honor. You ought to wear it with pride; however, that's your business. I'm uncertain why they trust you. However, the fact that they do also means you are under their protection."

Carter kept eye contact. He felt apprehension, not fright. In fact, he felt emboldened considering his talks with Bones and Patrick in *Gael na Mara's* great-room. He wanted O'Malley to know he was strong—that his illness had subsided and his strength had returned.

"On the first point, I remain unconvinced. That is, I have no particular reason to trust you. However, who you are, and who I am, are of no particular consequence in the overall scheme of things. On the second point, being under their protection precludes any remedial action, at least at this time, on my part.

"I view your intrusion as unnecessary interference and poorly timed at best. However, Patrick has made it clear that for whatever reason, my conclusion and subsequent recommendation regarding your disposition is to be held in abeyance. He made it clear that you have, in a very short time I would point out, come to mean something important to them, something particularly important."

Carter's posture remained upright and firm. He might not wield a gun, and of that he felt proud. But he did possess a thoughtful, prodigious mind, and he considered it equal to most and better than many. In this he felt equal to O'Malley and so maintained an equal bearing.

O' Malley paused to draw on his cigar.

"Ironically, Captain Phillips, the trust you have earned in the eyes of Bones and Patrick, makes us brothers of a kind, brothers in their trust. This being the case, we are bound to trust each other. We're linked by a connection of circumstance and time and there is no reason we shouldn't embrace it. Our mutual respect, even admiration, for Bones and Patrick is a foundation to build upon. We both sail yachts of historical consequence. I am familiar with *Madrigal*, that is, *Maxine*. I knew her in the Caribbean, and she is a fine yacht with a solid pedigree. However, the most important thing we share is a responsibility for Bones' and Patrick's safety."

Carter looked up. O'Malley's words took him by surprise. He had not thought about things in that way. Of course, he had often considered their safety, for example, in the boat shed, climbing ladders and working on scaffolding. When he asked them to crew on the shakedown, he gave their safety considerable thought, but not in the sense O'Malley spoke of now.

"I, for my part, shall remain vigilant in their protection as I have for more than a decade. By the way, if you haven't figured it out yet Captain Phillips, you too need protection. You are close enough to them on a daily basis that the same protective veil I extend over them encompasses you now as well. You might not believe you need it, or perhaps you are only now, after today's events, realizing the nature of the situation you have come upon. One way or the other, in exchange for your protection, regardless of whether you believe you need it or not, I am requesting your cooperation. I need your cooperation in my efforts to extend to Bones and Patrick the protection of which I speak."

Carter listened intently, anxiously, to the sobering remarks. It struck him as amazing that he faced involuntary conscription into O'Malley's secret service. He suffered the impression it would be most unwise to debate or discuss his apprehension.

Conversely, if he intended to have nothing to do with the proposition, he realized he should speak up and say so now. He also realized that a decision not to cooperate would mean he would have to leave Marblehead and his new friends behind.

Then he thought of Claire's smile. It affected him deeply. He remained silent and listened. O'Malley took Carter's body language to mean he had made a decision in the affirmative.

"Those choppers today, they were flying low. It made us all wonder. Perhaps they want us to believe they were not spying but rather simply out on patrol. I know, in fact, they can fly at 8,000 feet, beyond your ability to see them, and they can read the label on your hat. I've done so myself. In addition, one or another of their squadron is in the air around the clock. You cannot imagine how sensitive their spy gear is."

Carter began wondering. *Did this mean Americans were the main threat? Weren't the British the most compelled to find Bones and Patrick?*

O'Malley hastened his words, giving Carter the impression he wanted to finish with this business.

"There is no harm in you knowing that my father, he too is gone now, was Patrick's cousin. Patrick, in case you have not figured out, is Taoiseach, that is, chief of our clan, our ancestral clan in Ireland..."

≋≋≋

O'Malley's words faded from Carter's mind and his recollection ended. He found them disturbing yet he couldn't run from them. These men saved his life. Things had changed. His paradigm had changed. He wanted to remind all three of them that he had sailed upon this situation coincidently and innocently. His life was that of a sailor and only a sailor. He was merely an observer. He sought enlightenment by riding a gust of wind aboard a classic wooden yacht. None of that included becoming part of a secret plan to protect the covert lives of Irish freedom fighters, if that is what they were. There were obviously those who thought differently, those who believed they were terrorists and deserved summary punishment for their crimes.

These thoughts eventually circled around to the present, reminding him of the reason for his visit to the library computer. He left his ruminations, pushed several keys and moved the mouse.

Within seconds there were ten pages of hits, all describing the multitude of factions engaged in the troubles of Northern Ireland. He called up a published encyclopedia of Northern Ireland's conflict. This shocked him. An encyclopedia devoted solely to the troubles! Opening a file, he retrieved a table of content. He spotted a list of groups involved at some level, past and present, in the fighting, both political and physical. For the first time, Carter truly realized that the conflict had gone on so long that the Irish had institutionalized their own strife.

Carter guessed the list would satisfy questions he had about Patrick's reference to "contrary factions of ornery men." The lengthy columns impressed Carter as a dubious honor roll of groups, parties, and assemblages of every imaginable form. He printed a copy, folded it, and placed it in his shirt pocket for later inclusion into his log.

Carter was about to disconnect from the Internet when he remembered he wanted to do a search on Senator George Mitchell. He entered the senator's name and within seconds a series of hits appeared.

Carter was impressed by the number of references, as well as surprised that a man he hadn't heard of had such a notable history. He had been involved in much more than the recent peace negotiations in Northern Ireland. In addition to serving as a senator from Maine for fifteen years, the last six as Senate Majority Leader, he began his career serving as both U.S. Attorney and U.S. District Judge. Before that, he was an aide to the only senator from Maine Carter could actually remember, Senator Edmund Muskie.

Browsing the hits, Carter learned that President Clinton, upon Mitchell's announcement to retire from the Senate, asked him to lead the White House Conference of Trade and Investment in Northern Ireland. Seven days after his official retirement on January 2, 1995, Senator Mitchell became special advisor to the President and the Secretary of State on economic initiatives in Ireland.

Carter noted that the appointment included *all* of Ireland, not just the North, even though the trade initiative focused on the North. It reminded him how difficult it must be to do something in a country that is fractured by internal strife despite a common heritage and ethnicity.

It appeared to Carter that there had been a significant shift in thinking about the Irish question on both sides of the Atlantic prior to Mitchell's appointment. Somehow, or perhaps someone, and Carter thought of Bones, had convinced both the British and the U.S. diplomatic communities that economic prosperity could more likely result in peace in Northern Ireland than in many previous attempts, dating back beyond any living person's memory.

It seemed to Carter, at a glance anyway, that earlier measures were focused on complete disarmament as a requisite for negotiations. After disarmament, a leadership system could be devised. Carter thought about this. This approach should have produced positive, lasting results. He was no political theorist—but disarmament first, then power-sharing, made common sense.

Ireland proved this approach ineffective according to what he read. To begin with, the contestants were not simply two factions in a McCoy vs. Hatfield style feud. Behind the scenes, bigger hands were at work. The odd mix of the conflicting agendas of superpowers, specifically the U.S. and U.K., were unpredictable and contradictory.

Publicly, the British wanted to be viewed as a peacekeeping force while privately, the Northern Protestant majority depended upon them to maintain their autonomy and domination of the political and economic vitality of the North.

The U.S., while never publicly condoning terrorism and always remaining strongly allied with Britain, was also inextricably tied to Northern Ireland through its own Irish Catholic community, a great number who were powerful political and business figures.

Predominant figures in U.S. history held clear sympathies for the plight of the Catholic minority in Northern Ireland. Officials in the U.S. knew perfectly well the civil rights movement in the South had a great influence on the civil rights movement leading to Bloody Sunday in Northern Ireland in 1972.

Is it possible, Carter wondered, that the "troubles," at least in modern times, evolved into a proxy war between unique segments of each country; the ultraconservative British whose forefathers seeded the north of Ireland for their benefit, and American-born Irish Catholics, whose sympathies for those left behind in Ireland manifested itself in financial and logistic support right up to the present day.

Carter continued reading.

At a gathering in Washington on March 7, 1995, British Secretary of State for Northern Ireland, Sir Patrick Mayhew, summed up the current British position, hoping to achieve three things: a willingness in principle to disarm progressively; a common practical understanding of the modalities, that is to say, what de-commissioning would actually entail; and, in order to test the practical arrangements and to demonstrate good faith, the actual de-commissioning of some arms as tangible confidence-building measures and to signal the start of the process.

These principles became known as the "Washington Three," a number that amused Carter. While remaining a demand to de-commission, the tone of the proposal hinted more of a flexible process rather than an inflexible pre-condition.

Mitchell suspected, if treated as an edict, the Washington Three would become an opposition whipping boy, and all-party negotiations would be doomed before they could begin. The main problem with complete disarmament was an already entrenched pattern of splintering. If one group said okay, we'll disarm, an uncontrollable faction of that group would break off, unilaterally declaring themselves the guardian of the struggle. They would deliberately commit violent acts aimed at disrupting whatever the original group was trying to accomplish. Then, when that splinter gained standing and decided to agree to a peaceful settlement, another more radical and more violent faction would splinter off and continue the violence *ad infinitum*.

The list Carter stuffed in his pocket provided proof of the pattern. The undeniable necessity of the current peace initiative proved that earlier ones never resulted in lasting peace. Mitchell concluded there was no way to accomplish complete de-commissioning prior to commencing negotiations.

This time, according to what Carter read, things would be different. Without overtly disregarding the Washington Three, Mitchell recommended that all parties commit to a set of fundamental principles that would become known as the Mitchell Principles. The Internet page he was viewing listed them verbatim:

A. To democratic and exclusively peaceful means of resolving political issues;

B. To the total disarmament of all paramilitary organizations;

C. To agree that such disarmament must be verifiable to the satisfaction of an independent commission;

D. To renounce for themselves, and to oppose any effort by others, to use force, or threaten to use force, to influence the course or outcome of all-party negotiations;

E. To agree to abide by the terms of any agreement reached in an all-party negotiation and to resort to democratic and exclusively peaceful methods in trying to alter any aspect of that outcome with which they may disagree; and,

F. To urge that "punishment" killings and beatings stop and to take effective steps to prevent such actions.

Reading on, Carter discovered that Mitchell, concerned that all-party negotiations would never get off the ground if the requisite of complete disarmament was required, proposed in a separate section of the principles that the parties consider "parallel de-commissioning."

Mitchell drove home the importance of this flexibility by pointing out what was really needed was a "de-commissioning of mind sets in Northern Ireland." He believed that as trust is built, the necessity for arms diminishes. Until that happened, people, either publicly or secretly, would cling to their weapons. Trying to force disarmament prior to attaining trust simply wasn't going to work.

≋≋≋

Carter paused to stretch. His eyes felt raw from staring at the phosphorus screen. He could see the enormity of the Mitchell Commission's effort. Apparently, Mitchell expected resolution of the three years work in a final agreement by April 10. Only four days away!

If this is what Patrick hinted at earlier, that is, Bones having direct involvement in the peace process, it explained why Captain O'Malley exhibited such concern, even enlisting him in the effort to protect Bones from danger. In four days, the thread of Northern Ireland's momentous conflict may begin to unravel, and with those threads unraveling, the opportunity to weave a lasting peace.

Tired and in need of rest, Carter shut off the computer. He rose from his seat in an introspective daze and walked to the door. He stepped outside into the late afternoon sun, paused to breathe the sea air, hoping to clear his beleaguered mind. He thought about dinner with Martha. He needed a leisurely distraction and could taste the "red snappah."

Adjusting his long-billed cap he walked out onto the sidewalk. Turning, he began treading the cobblestone road that would lead him to the matron of the Purser's Quarters . . . and her waiting red Ford Escort.

CHAPTER 31

LEVEL ORANGE

"Captain, we're receiving digital intel out of Boston," the mechanical voice of the duty officer proclaimed.

"Deliver a hard copy to my ready room, Lieutenant," Captain Donovan barked back with no particular concern. He reviewed volumes of material daily and passed it quickly on per established protocol. He expected nothing peculiar. One way or the other, it didn't concern him. His task did not include interpreting data, just routing it.

Two minutes sped by and a knock at his cabin door jolted him from staring at a nautical chart laid out before him. He still preferred charting his course on paper with mechanical tools, even though there were electronics on board that automatically determined their position within three feet, 5,000 times per second.

"The transmission in hard copy, sir," explained the yeoman. He handed the document to the Captain. A page from an Internet site passed between them, along with a scanned photograph.

The Captain glanced quizzically at the material. A table or list of some kind contained columns of names of organizations or political parties.

He flipped past it and studied a computer enhanced black and white photograph. He looked at it hard. He suddenly realized it was a figure of a man standing in front of a building. It had been taken at a high altitude and enlarged significantly. He peered closer at the figure. He couldn't distinguish his features because he wore a long-billed yachting cap. The subject seemed unaware he was being photographed.

How could he, from two miles up?

He looked at the building from where the mark emerged. He saw letters above the door. He reached for a magnifying glass lying next to the chart table. Studying the photo through the glass, he made out letters. They spelled "Abbot Public Library."

Donovan looked closer at the man. He could make out an emblem on his hat. Try as he might he couldn't distinguish what it said. He called for his youthful yeoman and requested he have a look.

With frustrating ease, the yeoman read back, "Maxine, sir, it says Maxine in fancy type, like a boat name or something . . ."

Captain Donovan dismissed the yeoman and began thinking about what this meant. Looking back and forth between the list and the photo, he confirmed, to his satisfaction who was standing on the library step. He also realized the subject was doing what he was tempted to do a number of times; search the Internet for clues to the mystery of the Irish question—for explanations or reasons for the island's grim, often murderous history.

Captain Donovan took the time to read the entire list attached to the photograph. When he finished scanning the list, he leaned back in his chair and considered if some of his long-lost relatives were represented in this dubious compilation.

Why would he be pulling this off the Internet; why would he be saving it? What would he use it for?

Then Donovan recalled his duty. The spy ship captain took control again. He proceeded to follow orders. There was protocol for this type of event and he put it into motion.

"Yeoman, Level Orange. Get me Graves in New London. Pronto!"

Despite the straightforward process he needed to follow, Captain Donovan had ambiguous feelings about what appeared to be taking place. Perhaps it was because of his own Irish heritage, or perhaps because he was getting old and soft.

The retiring Captain saw things differently these days. He had, for a long time, wondered who the enemy really was in these cases, and now in this case in particular. Why were alliances continually changing? Why did sensitive intel cross over between friend and foe? Why were suspected criminal connections surfacing in shadowy places?

Captain Donovan paused and looked up at the photo of his Hinckley. *Two months, old girl, then we'll be free to roam. We'll be free to ask questions and find answers without duty weighing us down.*

He looked down again at the papers in his hands.

This guy doesn't know what he's getting into. Someone needs to get him off that damn computer. They'll know more about him than he can imagine. He'll never see it coming; he'll never have a fighting chance.

CHAPTER 32

FORCE IS NOT A REMEDY

Amidst the clinking sounds of dishes and swinging kitchen doors, a waitress catapulted forth. Nimbly she balanced two hot plates on a large round tray high above her shoulder.

When she arrived at Martha and Carter's table, she swung the tray down from its lofty perch and placed the white ceramic dishes of baked fish before them.

"Heah ya aah, Maatha, and for you too, Caahtah deah,"

"Thank you, Dahrothy," Martha replied.

Carter looked at the two women, a broad grin creasing his handsome face. *What a couple of characters.*

The scene resembled a stage play in a community theatre back in Michigan, the actors behaving as if they were New Englanders, exaggerating their accents and over-playing their parts. Only these two were the real thing, New Englanders in their native environment—authentic, colorful, and delightfully far-fetched.

Carter reveled in the feeling of being welcome now, a "regulah" as Dorothy had explained to the trainee who seated them upon arrival. Being a "regulah" imparted intrinsic contentment, a feeling of security he hadn't experienced when he first arrived.

The aroma of the baked red snapper distracted him from his thoughts. This time it was he who reached for Tabasco sauce and sliced lemons when "Dahrothy" set his stuffie on the table. His mouth watered as he hammered on the hot sauce and squeezed the lemons. Martha spoke up as he began eating.

Do you like Clayah, Caahtah?" she asked. "I mean to say, do you find Miss Clayah appealin'?"

Carter flushed a shade of red and swallowed the bite of quahog. He took too long to reply, so impatiently, though affectionately, Martha continued.

"Well, I believe I do, Caahtah, and I don't simply mean pretty in the face, even though she certainly is thaht, too; she haas a good soul. Clayah was most kind to me recently durin' a moment of need, that is, while you and your crew were away at sea. Huhr kindness came from a good place, I knew thaht the minute she touched my shouldah. I trust huhr, and in my way of thinkin', trust is the centah of a strong family, now wouldn't you agree, Caahtah?"

Carter helplessly nodded, though he really did agree.

Martha continued to speak freely about him and Claire. He thought her words remarkable. The plain speaking frankness of New Englanders could be just that; however, he was getting used to it, even convinced over time of its merits. She assumed a lot he hadn't even admitted to himself. The discourse had the disquieting aspect of a mother and son talking about the facts of life—a lesson normally falling upon the father to deliver. The matron of the Purser's Quarters was openly bestowing approval on the blossoming relationship.

Carter smiled, but felt awkward and excited at the same time. Finally, he spoke up.

"Well, yes, Martha, I like Claire—I like her very much. In fact, we've made plans. I will be entertaining her aboard *Maxine* very soon."

"I see, Caahtah. Thaht will give you the opportunity to talk to huhr and learn more about huhr, and won't thaht be a very nice thing to do?"

Carter took this to be requisite, not optional advice from his surrogate mother. He wisely nodded. "I'm looking forward to it," he said.

"Well, I know if I were a young woman again, I'd be quite excited about the prospects of an evenin' with a chahming fellow such as you on board a yaaht like *Maxine*."

Carter smiled and gracefully accepted the compliment. He allowed himself to wonder for a moment what Martha would have been like at Claire's age. What she must have looked like, or behaved like. As if reading his mind, she spoke again.

"I was a bit of a romantic at thaht age myself, don't ya know."

Carter sipped the boxed wine that always accompanied the diner's finest cuisine. Martha went on, this time with hesitancy in her voice, as if to make an admission that she felt reluctant, but obligated, to extend.

"I haavn't been entirely forthright with you, Caahtah, thaht is, about my life in the paast; my family, my . . . well, those things in my paast thaht have taken up the lifetime of a woman my age."

Carter's interest, and his brow, rose quizzically. He sensed the thirst of his curiosity about to be quenched with something better than the box wine in his glass. Apparently, Martha intended to confide in him, to trust him like family. In an effort to encourage her to proceed, he spoke.

"I, too, believe trust is the foundation of a relationship," he said. This assured her of what he felt certain she needed to hear in order to proceed. He strongly suspected the time had come for Martha to explain a few things that were partially revealed that night at McKinney's Bar.

She nodded her understanding of his assurance and continued.

"Caahtah, my maternal grandfathah was a man named Daniel Pahtrick Callahan, Doctah Daniel Pahtrick Callahan. Does thaht name mean anythin' to you, son?"

Her tone was as if she just revealed a monumental secret. Perhaps she had. Carter didn't know.

"Well, no, I don't think so, Martha, but I'm not from around here," the latter phrase spoken more to himself than to her.

"You aah now, Caahtah," she mildly reprimanded. "Anyway, Grandfathah was a very influential man in Bahston. I'm guessing you probably ahn't familiah with the Callahan School of Medicine at Harvahd."

She looked up for his reaction as she spoke. Carter encouraged her to continue with his eyes.

"Doctah Callahan became a substantial donah to the University. He was a physician, of course, but also a scientist and inventah. He accumulated a sizable fortune in pahtents for drugs and medical apparatus and the like. Grandfathah's contributions so impressed the president of the university thaht they named the damned school aftah him. He hahd powerful friends. In fact, I later came to discovah he hahd been a membah of the Finnian Brotherhood."

She waited again for a reaction. Carter remained attentive, although he knew little of what she spoke. The Finnian Brotherhood sounded like a secret society. He wondered if they were like the Masons. The sound of its name struck him as ominous.

"Well, none of thaht mattered to me. To me he was simply my grandfathah, and I loved him. From the time I sprang from his daughtah's womb he coddled me and showered me with affection. I loved him baack, as any granddaughtah would, don't ya know. He was a mahvalous, mahvalous man," she said dreamily, as if she could see his face that moment. Carter saw passion in her glistening eyes.

"He and Bones were close, Caahtah, and Bones, thaht is my fathah, as you haav come to know, became more a colleague thahn a son-in-law. They ended up working together on many things, Caahtah—things thaht relate to all this secrecy you haav begun to encountah."

Carter looked up from his emptying plate. Frustrated by her hesitancy to explain things without veiled references, he decided to address the issue directly; he needed to say something and now seemed the time.

"I am aware Martha, of why you have all deceived me, and perhaps that's not the best word to describe it; however, what I mean to say is, from this point forward all secrets, all private goings on, whether old or new, simple or complex, shall not pass my lips.

"I presume Bones explained to you what took place on our shakedown cruise and the agreements we reached in the saloon of *Gael na Mara*. To me, as for them I'm sure, they form a sacred bond—the bond all families enjoy, or can enjoy if they all maintain the level of trust and love I now realize you have for one another."

Martha had winced when Carter used the word deceived. Carter had spoken to her like a son; a wise son, a loyal son. She nearly broke into tears and moved her handkerchief to her eye.

Carter spoke again.

"It's okay, Martha, you needn't cry. You just need to know, I need to explain, I miss my family, too, just as you miss your mother and your husband. We share the pain of deceased loved ones. I see no reason why we can't help each other fill those lonely times and places with red snapper, and trips to museums, anything you want, any time we're able."

Carter paused. He had said a mouthful and he detected a reversal in Martha's demeanor. She would meet his proposition with aplomb. Tears might come another time, but not this day; not this moment. She deserved a family, a son, even if not from her womb. She longed for such a relationship and Carter was making it possible.

Martha sighed, smiled, and leaned forward slowly in her chair. She reached across the table for his hand and, while she held it, she continued speaking.

"Grandfathah met Bones a long time ago through a man I've met, but of whom I haav little knowledge. He remains a mystery to me. Howevah, I don't think he was an evil man. I cahn sense those things. I was neah him when they were all together a numbah of times. Still, I only know thaht the three of them were connected in ways thaht a tiny granddaughtah was not made privy."

The number three caught Carter's attention though he made no gesture or sound.

"They kept Grandmothah and my own deah mothah at a distance while I played freely at theah feet. I remembah them talking, sipping Irish whiskey, and smoking pipes thaht churned out thick blue smoke. I cahn't say I cahn remembah anythin' in particulah durin' those times. Howevah, I sensed a profound seriousness and sometimes knew they shielded theah conversation from me.

"Yes, as I think baack, theah meetings were often very serious. When I add together what I know today, the snippets of information gained ovah these many yeahs, I cahn't help conclude thaht in some peculiar and wonderful way I played a paht, somehow I hahd a purpose in theah meetin's.

"While I know thaht must sound strange, I knew even then, as a tiny child, they were up to somethin' of great consequence. I know now what thaht somethin' was, and I think they believed what they were doin' was for me. They did what they did for me, thaht is, theah children and theah grandchildren. Perhaps my presence amongst them durin' those meetings reminded them of theah purpose, theah sacrifices. I know all thaht sounds faar-fetched, howevah, those aah the feelin's I carry deep down, deep heah inside me, Caahtah."

Martha leaned back and opened a package of cigarettes, shuffled it around, then looked at Carter.

"This habit upsets you, doesn't it, Caahtah," she said.

Carter, caught by surprise, took a deep breath and replied.

"My mother and father both smoked, Martha. If we're sharing histories, you may as well know my parents died from complications relating to life-long habits of smoking. I've dealt with it. I can continue to deal with it. I am not asking you to change who you are. It is apparent, however, that you can somehow pick up both the good and bad feeling in people near you. That being what it is, I don't think I can successfully veil such a strong emotion. Not from someone with special gifts, someone who is *fey*."

Poised as she was to remove a cigarette from the package, she maintained eye contact, did not withdraw the smoke, and continued speaking.

"The mysterious man, an attorney, named Claark, Samuel Claark, was Irish. Very Irish." She paused. "He and Grandfathah sometimes spoke in the old tongue. Not often, don't ya know, since Bones is English and couldn't understand a word they said. I think they did it for sport, to tease Bones a bit. By the way, ya might be interested in knowin', Claark is the Anglicized surname of a very old clan from the North of Ireland, one whose name ought to mean somethin' to ya, Caahtah."

She posed the riddle and waited a moment for Carter to guess the answer. He stirred, but didn't respond, so she went on.

"Samuel, Caahtah, is the Anglicized name for Seamus, and Claark, dear lad, is derived from an ancient clan name, O Cleirigh" she said, and then pretended as if that were of no significance after all. "Yeahs later, they would become the O'Clery's, or the grandson of Clery; the "O" bein' a word all by itself, meaning grandson, don't ya know."

Carters eyes widened in response and Martha smiled at his surprise.

"Exactly how or why they came together I'll probably nevah know. Bones offers little in the way of detail. He haas told me I would be bettah off not knowin'. I haav only been able to recall thaht Mistah Claark and my fathah met first on board a freightah when Bones was a young seaman, a very long time ago—long before Bones met my mothah. I haav always suspected Pahtrick's hand at work. I've always assumed this is how Bones, Grandfathah, and eventually Pahtrick, all came to know one anothah."

As these words came forth, she slowly slid the cigarette back into its package, elusively, like a magician performing a slight-of-hand trick.

"A partnah in Mistah Claark's law firm still manages my grandfathah's considerable estate. The vast majority of it perpetually funds medical research and several chairs at the college. It's all very secretive, but Bones continues as executor.

"It would not be immediately apparent to you, Caahtah, but many, many people consult Bones on mattahs of strategic importance; mattahs I'm rarely made privy to, as if I were still a tiny child." Martha paused to consider her last statement and said, "And thaht is fine with me, Caahtah. I've not the stomach for the Cause any more. I only want to be a family now, like all the families around us—families with children, teenageahs, aahnts and uncles, and Christmas stockings enough for an octopus!"

Carter pondered her confession, her proclamation. He thought about the cigarette package mysteriously disappearing and couldn't help but wonder if their growing closeness might have a positive effect. He thought, or rather hoped, their friendship and the elemental family they were becoming gave her reason not to extinguish herself prematurely. As these musings made their way through his mind, she began speaking again.

"I cahn't tell you more, Caahtah, any more about those three men. I know little more; I know the least about Mistah Claark. Money I believe to be from Grandfather's estate still makes its way to me, though I cahn't use it, thaht is, I cahn't flaunt it. A partnah in Mistah Claark's law firm carries out Bones' instructions regarding the estate and remains deep in the shadows. I am not privy to the particulahs. Bones remains in direct communication through hidden channels. I haav no idea what will happen when Bones is gone. I know he cahn't live forevah. I trust he haas a plan."

Carter looked up to see the sadness in Martha's crinkled eyes. Dorothy stepped jauntily up to their table and placed dessert menus in both their hands. This broke the mood.

Carter and Martha appeared relieved and studied the menus through the confines of large plastic slipcovers. Carter spotted key lime pie, ordered it, and he handed back the menu. The waitress disappeared in a blur of red and white.

≋≋≋

Martha looked over at Carter and carefully considered how much further to go in their discussion. He seemed older, and stronger than when they first met. He seemed capable of holding sensitive issues securely in his grip. She remembered Patrick telling her of the young skipper's determination to save his floating home, to save *Maxine*. "... haalf dead, haalf out of his mind from the chill thaht took 'im and damned neah collapsin' from exhaustion—he pumped. By God, Maatha, he pumped. I practically hahd to pry his hands from the lever ta spell 'im. He measured up, Maatha; like few mates I've ever known."

She pressed ahead.

≋≋≋

"I think you might be interested in knowin', Caahtah, thaht I spent my entire childhood aboard *Gael na Mara*."

Carter quickly turned and leaned forward in his chair. As he did he crossed purposes with the waitress who just then arrived to set his pie on the table amidst the commotion.

"You what?" he cried.

There was silence until the waitress finished her task.

As the waitress stepped away, Martha continued.

"I haav been reluctant all this time to inform you of thaht bit of information, Caahtah. Somehow, I figured it would draw a reaction; particularly now, in relation to your recent experiences with Bones and Patrick, not to mention the dutiful Captain O'Malley. Fact is, I lived aboard huhr throughout my childhood and into my comin' of age. Fact is, Caahtah, I married Connah O'Donnell, Patrick's haalf brother, on board huhr many, many yeahs ago. Not only thaht, Bones, and my deah mothah said *theah* vows aboard huhr only hours aftah she lowered away from a freightah thaht brought huhr heah from Belfaast."

Carter's jaw dropped. He was amazed at what he was hearing yet he could think of no reason to doubt the veracity of her pronouncements. He supposed he should have deduced this long ago. It certainly explained a lot of things.

Martha paused and watched Carter for a couple seconds, giving him time to process this new information. After Carter had regained his composure, she cast an eye about the restaurant and continued.

"Grandfathah hahd her built in Ireland, shipped to Bahston, and commissioned at Flynn's Wharf. He considered hurh a fittin' gift for my parents and so it was thaht the vessel became a membah of our family."

Carter had known from the first time he set eyes on that boat that she held secrets; that she wasn't merely another toy in a great harbor of nautical playthings. Just how special she was continued to astonish him. He could not speak and quickly decided his curiosity would be best served by listening anyway. Martha smiled at the surprised look on his face.

"There's more, Caahtah, if you would like to hear it."

His eyes spoke clearly of his want for more.

"Theah were many memorable yeahs aboard *Gael na Mara*. She remains a fine yacht, as fine as the day Grandfathah gave huhr to the happy couple. Even aftah I came along, Bones and Mothah sailed huhr joyously.

"I was a small gul on my first voyage across the pond, yet I cahn still remembah it. I cahn remembah the cozy nursery they fashioned in huhr fo'c'sle. Bones hahd the crew weave a sort of netting around huhr lifelines to keep me from falling through as I skittered about the deck.

"As I grew up, we sailed huhr in fair weathah and storms. I remembah floatin' in a dead calm in the doldrums on a cruise from Gibraltar to Rio. We hahd a professional crew thaht changed often, though I didn't know why for many yeahs. The trips were carefully planned; I cahn remembah thaht, too. There always seemed to be a purpose in what we did and wheah we traveled. Mostly, we found ourselves in Belfaast or Bahston.

"I lived a golden life on board huhr as a child, Caahtah. I became a teenagah on board huhr; eventually, I discovered the man I would marry on board huhr. I loved huhr all those yeahs the same as you love *Maxine*."

Martha paused, looked quizzically at her young friend and asked, "Caahtah, did you think Bones and Patrick would let *Maxine* sink when you hit thaht containah? They know what she means, thaht she hahd to be saved."

He looked at her in surprise. He didn't think she knew the details of the incident.

"Of course they told me," she answered, somehow reading his mind. "I demanded to know. I haav kept quiet about a lot of things, Caahtah, and in exchange I enjoy certain privileges. I sensed the danger from on shoah and demanded an explanation. You cahn't really expect a fathah to deny a plea from his only daughtah. It hasn't gone furthah thahn thaht, Caahtah, and I reveal this to ya now because you deserve to know how much ya mean to Bones and my unsinkable brother-in-law, Mr. Pahtrick Timothy O'Clery. You've become the remembrance of theah youth, the means to theah salvation, Caahtah. The son and grandson they nevah hahd!"

Carter swallowed these words and followed them with a sip of wine. It hadn't fully occurred to him this might be the case, not in such plain terms anyway. Martha paused to let the words soak in and then continued, hoping she hadn't said too much—hoping Carter understood she considered this good for both her men, and all things considered, good for him, too.

"Only in my later yeahs, while livin' aboard *Gael na Mara,* did I begin to fully realize what was takin' place. Thaht was about the same time I met Connah. Handsome, penetrating eyes thaht saw deep inside me. Pahtrick hahd brought him aboard. Being *Gael na Mara's* first mate, he enjoyed privileges in selecting crew.

"Connah's presence electrified the yacht. He swept aboard, swept me away and only aftah I fell completely in love did I come to undahstand he was fleein' from people who would kill him if they could reach him." She paused a moment, then said quietly, "And not thaht much later they succeeded. They murdered my husband and our hope for a family of our own."

Once again Carter thought he detected a tear, however, Martha maintained her composure.

"Nothing could stop us, though. We continued to sail *Gael na Mara* and the workin's between my grandfathah, Bones, and Mistah Claark remaining covert. Theah activities remained hidden from a world too busy, too lost upon itself to bothah with takin' notice.

"We carried out secret plans to help the Cause. Even though the particulahs of those plans remained hidden from me, the Cause was nevah covered up. Bones, Pahtrick, Mothah, and of course, Grandfathah all spoke plainly about it. They wanted to see the unification of all of Ireland. They wanted the British gone. They wanted the North and the South united. They wanted the bombings, beatings, and the awful strife to end.

"None of those high purposes were veiled from me. I believed in them, too, even though I only evah saw Ireland as a visitor on board *Gael na Mara*. Still, how could I not? Everything and everyone around me in some way served the Cause.

"The exception, at least on a daily basis, was Grandfathah. Outwardly, he maintained his visible and prominent medical practice. He contributed to advances in medicine and education and functioned all the while as a secret general in a secret ahmy. He and all the Finnians took enormous risks, all in the name of the Cause."

Martha took a sip from a cup of murky coffee that arrived via the young trainee. Carter turned down the offering. He dreamed of a latte. Then he dreamed of Claire. Martha's narrative continued.

"It seemed to me, my whole life was absorbed by the Cause. I don't believe Grandfathah ever fully understood the effects all this hahd on mothah, Bones, and especially me. Our entire family, everyone in my immediate circle of relatives, worked for the Cause, and I'll admit, Caahtah, even in my zeal to please my grandfathah, it overwhelmed me at times. Not often perhaps. I was strong baack then, and I hahd been provided an excellent education, both on board *Gael na Mara* and at school.

"Howevah, those times thaht I felt overwhelmed, they were the times I indulged in my own secret—my predilection for thaht which the Irish call *fey*. During those overwhelming times, and I hahd a fair share despite the silver spoon my grandfathah surreptitiously provided, my special senses provided me with a secret place to be. I discovered a way to view the world aside from the Cause and by the by it became my only refuge. It hahd always been special to me, an interestin' and concealable place to be, at least until I met Connah. He was more interestin'. Just like Miss Clayah, Caahtah, just like Miss Clayah."

A knowing eye captured Carter's attention as only a mother's can. The silent look invoked directives like: respect her Carter, love her, protect her, build a family, and never let them go. Don't take risks that might tear them from you, no matter what the cause! Cherish them above causes, make them your cause. Revel in the joy they bring and hold them forth to be shared by all the people around you. The distinct, albeit silent plea ended. Carter seemed mysteriously able to understand everything she said, although her lips hadn't moved.

Martha spoke aloud again.

"Regahdless of the obscure contrivances of our activities and our motivations, Connah and I fell in love, were married, and barely touched the decks as we sailed aboard the goddess of love thaht *Gael na Mara* hahd come to be. Those were halcyon days, Caahtah, and we were oblivious, thaht is, I was oblivious and unprepared for the sea change about to rise and alter our lives."

Carter watched to see if Martha would continue. He felt uneasy hearing all these revelations under the blue green fluorescent lights of the diner. The diner didn't seem the place for such profundity. Then he realized, in fact, it was; it was the perfect place. The sterile environment of the blue green lights, the disconnection to the Cause and its stifling gravitational force upon Martha's life, the diner was the very reason she was able to go on. He listened intently as she continued her story.

"I can only trust you will keep what I tell you now a secret to your grave, Caahtah. This is not for anyone's ears but your own and I tell you thaht because to us, to the three of us, you aah family now, Caahtah. Neither Bones, nor Patrick, nor I haav anyone to carry on our names. You, your yacht, your life and the way you live it, you haav become important to us. If we each hahd a son, Caahtah, you aah the mold from which we would cast him. If this is more thahn you can heah, if it is wrong for me to go on, Caahtah, say so now," she pleaded.

Carter considered most carefully the matron's words. He felt he had already made a similar commitment to Bones and Patrick, and he knew this meant he could never completely disconnect from these people again. He felt nested in their confidence and stood convinced everything would be all right if he maintained the integrity and trustworthiness they showed him. He had already pledged to do so on board *Gael na Mara*.

"I understand, Martha. The importance of never divulging what you tell me is not eluding me."

She began to study him, looking deeply into his eyes. She too had not existed all these years without applying her will to her own survival. Apparently satisfied, she made her decision and continued her tale.

"Caahtah, *Gael na Mara* is a vessel of a different sort. Well, of course, she is a sailboat; the wind blows huhr around and she seems perfectly ordinary in thaht regahd. Thaht said, since she began huhr life on the sea, she haas been a vessel with a particulah purpose.

"People read all the time about guns, ammunition, and bombs making the weapons of war, Caahtah. They also know, as you do too, thaht boats of every kind, ovah time immemorial, haav smuggled guns and ammunition. This is true and incontrovertible. You know this well since you sometimes take note of such occurrences when they reach the newspapeh. I've seen you clip the occasional article yourself."

Martha cast a knowing glance in his direction. He shifted uncomfortably in his seat and cleared his throat.

"All this smugglin' of guns makes grand readin' and gets splashed in our faces on cinema screens all the time. Thaht being the case, Caahtah, I aask, haav you thought much about the lesser dramas of war. Haav you considered covert weapons like psychology, disinformation, or economic warfare?"

With this remark she paused. The pause reminded Carter of Patrick, his way of emphasizing a point. He knew the pause required no reply. Soon she continued.

"Papeh, Caahtah; mere printed papeh. Typed characters on plain white papeh; information, disinformation, weaponry rarely exposed by the scrutiny of the press. These aah weapons of a different kind. They haav chillin' effects when aptly applied.

"Money, too, Caahtah, sometimes real, more often not; I'm talkin' about fortunes and misfortunes thaht move around the world on papeh. Pledges thaht fortunes exist, pledges thaht fortunes don't exist. Papeh thaht proves powah and papeh thaht extinguishes powah. From ancient times until today, enemies haav been doin' battle with both, Caahtah: papeh and powdah."

She paused again.

During these few seconds, Carter considered her points. He reconstructed how often he read of mail packets that moved by mules, trains, and even ships. He thought of how empires stood or fell due to the contents of mere leather pouches carrying "papeh" as Martha's elocution described.

"If you think about it long enough, Caahtah, I'm certain you would agree thaht a relatively small physical space is usually necessary to move papeh to wheah you want it to go; to wheah it is intended to haav its greatest effect. Papeh and money, like guns and bombs, cahn be smuggled across boardahs and one doesn't need a freightah to accomplish it neithah."

Martha spoke slightly quieter, signaling to Carter that her words should not to be overheard nor repeated.

"Well Caahtah, *Gael na Mara* served this obscure, secretive trade since it came down the ways. Hurh buildin', on grandfathah's covert instructions, involved unique outfitting. Nothin' thaht would appear entirely out of the ordinary, except thaht huhr design portended an extraordinary purpose.

"The details of which I speak still exist aboard huhr now, and I don't mean details like the special library Grandfathah built in the saloon for Mothah. I mean secret details, the compartments built inside huhr for transporting contraband. They aah hidden from prying eyes. I'll wager your initial visit aboard huhr revealed none of which I speak. I wager also, thaht a clevah ahchitect such as you would haav figured this out given time. Let's just say, all spaces aboard huhr appear accounted for by overt measurement."

Then the entire aspect of the good witch, his surrogate mother, changed in a foreboding way. The blue-green lights furthered the dramatic shift and she leaned forward once again and reached for his hands.

"Caahtah, we were carrying just such a caahgo when my mothah and husband were lost. I cahn't speak of the details, they haunt me in ways I cahn't bear. My purpose in telling you is not to indulge in misery; howevah, thaht yacht, *Gael na Mara*, is, as you haav suspected all along, no ordinary boat. She haas the lifeblood of Connah O'Donnell soaked into huhr teak decks; t'was ovah huhr mahogany rails mothah fell to huhr terrible death, it's true.

"Pahtrick blames himself for thaht and I don't think he'll evah get ovah it. I don't blame him though, nevah haav. He's stuck with me like glue evah sense. He dotes on me and insists on takin' care of me, yet I could nevah haav blamed him. He hahd a plan, and most of it worked. Mothah's death was a terrible accident, thaht's all theah was to it!"

Martha had wandered a bit in her story, as was Patrick's habit. She refocused and then continued.

"Caahtah, within *Gael na Mara's* holds haav traveled the papeh weapons of war, the tools of peace, the negotiating points, and the intellectual matter thaht hopefully, at this very moment, will lead to changes in the future of Ireland. The product of yeahs of strategic maneuverin' is comin' to fruition.

"Peace is in the making. Bones and a litany of peacemakers aah workin' arduously towards its resolution. Patrick's clansmen aah the facilitators, the first in what they hope will be a long line to step forward and lay down theah arms; to say the killing must end—thaht force is not a remedy. Grandfathah, Bones, and the mysterious Mr. Claark haav strived for decades to bring this mattah to a point wheah all pahties understand what Bones haas preached for a long time: thaht economic prosperity will more likely bring peace to Ireland thahn any othah force—particularly the irrational, horrific force of a damnable bomb.

"*Gael na Mara*," Martha went on quietly, "while only one instrument in the developments occurring in London and Belfast at this moment, haas played a significant role, don't ya know."

Carter absorbed her information like rain on dry ground. He breathed deep and felt fulfilled—felt his curiosity had been justified. He hadn't been paranoid; he wasn't imagining things. These *were* extraordinary people. Their circumstances in life, the agony, the strife, and even the joys, were profound. Not only had they done extraordinary things, they were in the midst of doing them now.

Carter flushed with excitement. He struggled to match the profundity of Martha's words with what he thought she was: a nursemaid, a widow, a Salem witch. Her voice, still coarse, her colloquialisms still colorful, somehow transformed. Her vocabulary changed. She spoke in an articulate, intellectual manner. All through the course of her story she seemed a different person. His astonishment was quite visible on his face.

Martha noticed Carter's reaction and clutched his hands tighter. He felt her assurance in her hands. He felt what she said must be true, the real truth, the truth she and Patrick and Bones previously veiled.

Carter began to understand the reasons for their subterfuge, the rigidity of their covert existence. They had to wait until they believed they could trust him unequivocally before they could speak freely.

"That night in the North Atlantic, Martha, the night Miread and Connor were lost. Did the papers get delivered?"

"Oh, yes, Caahtah. The papehs were delivered. The Cause always did and always will stand above the individual; 'tis the nature of the thin'. We were all in shock, howevah; theah is no doubt about thaht. Certain customs officials conspired to explain our crew losses and thaht ragin' storm provided convincin' covah. There's no doubt thaht deliverin' those papehs was our salvation—the reason we haav maintained our sanity all these many decades."

Martha's countenance was subsiding. The particulars of the event were not what she wanted to convey. The details of the night, the weather, the confrontation—those details were not important to her, nor did she care to relive them. Carter concluded that supper was extraordinarily filling in every other way.

Carter thought again of the number three and how things kept coming in threes: the Washington Three, the three strands of the Mitchell Commission negotiations, and there must be three versions of the tale Martha recounted. He considered how he might persuade Patrick and Bones to tell their stories as well.

≋≋≋

The time came to end their evening in "Bevahly." Carter rose from the table and moved to pull out Martha's chair.

"Martha, how about I drive us home tonight? I believe I can find my way." Carter no longer felt like an outsider. The North Shore felt more like home than he ever imagined possible.

Martha nodded and smiled as she rose from the table.

"Oh—one quick question, Martha, if I may."

She smiled and handed him the keys to her red Escort, automatically assuming the query related to directions back to the Purser's Quarters.

"What year did you graduate from the Callahan School of Medicine?"

Without surprise or inflection, she answered in her coarse, matter of fact style. "The yeah it was named for Grandfathah, my deah boy, 1950." She paused as if to recollect the event, then added. "I don't mean to boast, mind ya, but I skipped a few grades. I enjoyed exceptional tutelage on board *Gael na Mara*, don't ya know? You cahn also deduce why I nevah took the boards."

She paused a couple more seconds.

"All thaht is history now. It cahn't be changed. It will not be in vain, I pray. Not if Bones and the Mitchell Commission succeed. Not if the whole of Ireland and Britain embrace peace."

Carter thought about Martha's story as he drove through the winding streets of Beverly and Salem to Marblehead, the place he now considered home. Forty-five minutes later, Carter and Martha arrived at the ancient cottage. After the usual struggle with the front door, it popped open, Martha stepped in and Carter retreated to his side entrance.

Before opening his door, he gazed up into the breezy blue-black sky. He saw the swaying trees above the cottage and he recognized, once again, the pencil thin outline of the obscure short-wave antenna he spotted before.

All this is real, he thought. *All this is real.*

A shiver ran through him as the cool evening air penetrated his being. He heard the thick, dull fog horn on Marblehead Neck issue its warning. It caught his attention and he wondered, was it an omen? Was it warning him away from a lee shore, of danger he couldn't survive?

He tried to shake off the doubt and succeeded just enough to step inside, climb the stairs and retire to his loft. Tomorrow he would ask Patrick to join him for lunch on Sewall Point.

BOOK III

THE NORTH ATLANTIC

JOSEPH CONRAD
c. 1857-1924

The terrorist and the policeman both come from the same basket. Revolution, legality - countermoves in the same game; forms of idleness at bottom identical.

The Secret Agent – 1907

CHAPTER 33

THE INESCAPABLE WRONGNESS

Patrick stood back from the schooner and stared. Her bright red hull glistened in the sunshine. His arms were sore and his back tired from painting. *Red Shoes*' thirty-eight feet felt like thirty-eight miles once the interminable brushing began. Still, the joy of seeing her painted mitigated the suffering and he smiled contently, despite the pain.

Patrick noticed Carter removing his cap and studying the sprinkles of deep red droplets spattered on the *Maxine* insignia. They looked like blood—fitting in a ritualistic way. Painting the boat felt ritualistic. Shedding blood seemed an appropriate sacrifice. He and Carter were no different from sailors around the world—they all became inexplicably ritualistic at times like this.

Without speaking aloud, Patrick glanced at Carter, and with a wink thanked him for helping paint the object of his redemption. The schooner *Red Shoes* would soon be the boat he and his half-brother Connor would have built together, had Connor lived.

Patrick thought Carter resembled Connor, at least in stature, enough so to prompt an occasional sad or happy memory. Had things only been different, the red-haired brothers would have built *Red Shoes* in Ireland. Also, had things been different, the brothers would have launched her into the gray-green mist perpetually embracing the shores of their homeland. From there, he and Connor would have sailed to places of their dreams. They would have left behind the fighting and strife.

Patrick emerged from thinking about what might have been and reached his arm around Carter and gripped him in a brotherly embrace.

"We got us four months, laddie, four short months till we drop 'er in the pond and see if she floats theah, skippah."

A majority of the Irregulahs boisterously disagreed, that is, with the exception of the old French Canadian named Ernie Rabideau. Ernie was Carter's new assistant. He stepped forward in defiance of the others and asserted his belief that the goal was achievable "...if we work more and complain less!"

Bones, Patrick, and Carter all stared in astonishment, then laughed approvingly and patted their convert on the back.

Carter, for his part, had made a commitment to remain in Marblehead until the launching. Patrick had thanked him profusely, all the while knowing Carter's willingness to remain in Marblehead served another purpose of equal importance.

"We cahn expect our young friend to be a courtin', Miss Clayah," Martha observed approvingly to Patrick the morning after their night at McKinney's.

August 1, Carter's birthday he had learned, would also be the day Patrick's freedom from the bondage of land and history, his voyage of redemption, was scheduled to begin.

≋≋≋

The evening sun descended westerly over the spires and trees of Old Town. *Maxine* floated silently in the still harbor; a wisp of breeze fell lightly from shore. It held aromas snatched from the village. Sweet smells of summer rode the wind and slid across the surface of the water, drying the perspiration that formed on the bottle of white wine. Empty now, the wine bottle stood like a sentry. It guarded the remaining bits of cheese and fruit that adorned the pewter tray Martha loaned Carter especially for the occasion.

The fragrant air twisted and turned through the companionway hatch and found its way to the v-berth in the fo'c'sle. There it momentarily caressed and cooled the warm bodies of Carter and Claire before taking flight out the deck vent, then on toward Marblehead Neck.

As Claire held Carter's back to her chest, spooning him with her slender naked form, Carter couldn't help but marvel over the strange and wondrous world he now inhabited. Only one week earlier, a burly, ancient, Englishman held him this same way, emitting heat as Claire did now.

He smiled inwardly over the differences, which were significant in all the right ways. Carter was thankful for the precious heat each body brought him. One saved his life, the other made life worth living.

His feelings about the events on the waters of Massachusetts Bay seemed overwhelming at the time. They were far less affecting now. He remembered Patrick's words at the pub in Gloucester, "...and by the way, laddie, Miss Clayah heah, she's more than a pleasin' sight to the eyes, skippah, she's much, much more... do ya understand?"

Carter pondered those words. He assumed Patrick wasn't referring to what they just did. He could only imagine where the inference would lead. The delicate creature that embraced him stimulated his curiosity in expansive ways.

"Carter," Claire whispered into his ear. "Did you ever sail *Maxine* to Wisconsin?" Her breath felt warm against Carter's neck.

"No," Carter replied. "I always intended to cruise for a summer in Door County, but never found my way there."

He reached down and drew her silken leg closer to his thigh. "There's no reason not to. I'm planning to cruise the Lakes again."

"My father always dreamed of sailing, but he works continuously, or at least that's the way it seems. He and mother found time to take us to the lakeshore when I was a child. We picnicked and played. My brothers, I have three, devised endless objects from scraps of wood insisting they were boats or surfboards or anything else they could pretend as we played in the waves. They would love *Maxine*, Carter. Perhaps, someday, you can meet them."

The dimming light of evening left the fo'c'sle dark. Their talk of the Lakes made them both homesick and Claire snuggled closer to Carter. She pressed her whole body against his, making as much contact as her slender form allowed.

Carter felt as if they had known each other for a very long time. They spoke like each other, had swam in the Big Lake, and now, by a strange twist of fate, they were together in Marblehead. They shared commonalities far greater than differences. They lived, were educated, and matured to adulthood within close proximity, yet, had been separated by a great body of fresh water. They were together now in the way of the world, the way the world was meant to be—the way it kept turning, kept producing its wonders.

"Claire, are you of Irish descent?" Carter quietly asked then quickly added, "I mean, obviously Dubois is French, but do you have Irish blood on your mother's side?"

"French Canadian," she corrected. ". . . and I have not a drop of Irish blood . . . that I am aware of anyway."

Carter remained silent for several moments. Claire, too, remained silent and then offered more information.

"I'm German on my mother's side, however, I would venture to say you are wondering why I pursued academics in New England and became so enamored with the Irish?"

"Well, yes, even though it's none of my business, and if you would rather talk about something else . . ."

"No, I'm pleased that you have extended your thoughts into my mind as well as my . . ." she coyly truncated her remark. She made her point quite clear by way of a pinch in a vulnerable locale.

Carter was embarrassed.

He lay still, hoping she couldn't detect his modest humility. The last thing on earth he wanted was for Claire to think of him as a womanizer. He wanted to turn around and embrace her, convince her that her voice alone, her words without accents, the song she sang with such spirit in Gloucester, those uncomplicated things meant as much to him as her gender. Her mind, her history, her perfection of being drew him to her. He wanted her to know he felt at home with her—the home he left years ago after his parents passed away. He wanted to tell her about Pyramid Point and Leland Harbor and Grand Traverse Bay. He wanted to know why she came east, why she studied at Boston College, why her interest in all things Irish reached proportions quite unusual in the ordinary lives of Midwesterners.

Perhaps in time he could learn what she intended to do with her expansive knowledge of the Irish people, their language and their art—a people with whom she shared no kinship by blood, only passion. Carter's mind raced with thoughts he wanted to speak but couldn't.

Claire continued to lie silently against him. After a while he sensed in the rhythm of her warm breathing that she had fallen asleep. It dawned upon him what time in the morning she must be at work. He realized his time with her must end. He also thought of the coffee roaster, the despicable object he was, his untenable behavior. He wondered again why she worked for such a creature.

All things considered, like her warmth against his body and the momentary merging of their souls in passion, he decided he would do well to check his thoughts about her employer. He was unworthy of deep consideration. Still, the inescapable wrongness of such behavior couldn't be entirely ignored, and again he remembered Patrick confronting O'Neil that first morning in Marblehead. Patrick would have none of it. He stood against O'Neil instantly, prepared to confront the belligerent without hesitation. Carter wondered if Patrick's way was right. The question of rightness or wrongness sped through his mind. Which should it be, passive, or aggressive? Is belligerence a condition that ought to be crushed, tolerated, or negotiated into something else?

Claire moved slightly and her touch brought him back to the present. He thought of the late hour and rolled over, embracing Claire once again, whispering his plan to ferry her to Tucker's Wharf.

A sound of disappointed acquiescence issued quietly from the mysterious Claire. Carter withdrew from her arms and stepped onto *Maxine's* cabin sole, the cold reality of the ordinary rising up to meet him. He moved through *Maxine's* darkened saloon to find his clothes.

Carter thought again of asking Claire why she put up with the irascible roaster. He found it difficult, under the circumstances, to resist blurting this question out loud.

≋≋≋

After a brisk dinghy ride across the inky water of Marblehead Harbor, they walked along the lamp-lit streets of Old Town. Carter's curiosity stole his discretion and he imitated Bones at his diplomatic best.

"Claire, is there something special you are planning career wise? Is there particular work you are intending to do where your educational achievements play a role?"

Carter winced when he realized he sounded like a high school guidance counselor. Claire turned to look at him in the white paleness of a street lamp.

"Carter, has no one told you there are circles within circles?" Her dark eyes gleamed with delight and a clever smile turned the edges of her lips upward. She repeated her proverb, "There are circles within circles."

Carter returned her smile with a baffled look that further delighted the mysterious coffee maiden from Milwaukee, and he shrugged innocently.

"That is why I work at the Marblehead Roasting Company. That is why I get up at 4:00 A.M., and put up with the ornery Mr. O'Neil. That addresses your real question, am I correct?" She reached for his hand and smiled. "Those things I learned in college, the art and science of language and music, those things aren't likely to keep me afloat, as you sailormen say. I have to be patient, clever, and better than all the rest and that takes time and sacrifice. You're an architect; you know the complexity of fine design. It can't be hurried."

She paused and looked directly into his eyes.

He in turn acknowledged the trueness of her remark with a kiss she willingly accepted.

"In the meantime, I have to earn money, Carter. I have to have a day job, at least for a while. I enjoyed the privilege of university parents who financed my education. There comes a time, however, when the ideal has to face the practical."

Carter nodded in agreement, acknowledging the logic of her explanation combined with his own need to go ashore from time to time and work as an architect.

"There are circles within circles . . ." she teased, tugging him along. They behaved like children on the beach on Lake Michigan—tagging each other, laughing giddily, filling the quiet properness of Marblehead with the capricious sounds of newfound affection.

Suddenly, Claire broke away and ran ahead and Carter sprang forward in pursuit. Together they ran through the night as if to catch their dreams amid the cottages and cobblestones of their new and mysterious home.

CHAPTER 34

BENEATH THE GOLD DOME

"Well then, laddie, Bones kept *Gael na Mara* floated in a berth in Bahston long side a fleet o' fishin' vessels in the early yeahs. Thaht's wheah she floated 'tween 'er laahnchin in '32 and the time we fled, well, moved, to Maahblehead in 1966.

"I was 'er first mate, don't ya know. Thaht's how the plan fer thaht particulah trip in 1951 began; thaht's wheah this whole dahmn thing began I suppose. Hahd I known then what I know now, I might haav been able to..."

Patrick paused.

He found it difficult to keep speaking. He had never actually expelled the words or admitted aloud the anguish he suffered for doing what he did; for being responsible for the deaths of two people he should never have allowed to die. The realization struck hard and Patrick's throat tightened. Over the decades, the only people he might have considered telling had been there! Certainly no clan member, let alone an outsider, warranted an explanation. It wasn't proper for the Taoiseach to go around explaining himself.

Then again, if redemption was his purpose, if he expected calm seas aboard *Red Shoes*, the story must be told. The time had finally come and Carter Phillips was the person to hear his confession. He realized this their first night together at the diner, after that movie that seemed to take him back in time. If the thought hadn't verged on blasphemy, for Patrick in his way was a religious man, Carter's mysterious arrival was like the coming of the Savior..

The young lake captain, the son he never bore, the confessor he desperately needed, sat silently on the bench at Sewall Point looking at him, waiting for him to speak. Patrick swallowed hard and continued.

"Sure, then laddie, I don't suppose ya would haav figured ya might evah see me pressed fer words, don't ya know. But there's no shame in tellin' ya I've not told anyone what haapened thaht night, not exactly. I've kept it heah inside fer so long, I cahn't say fer sure I can get it out, skippah."

"Patrick, I don't mean to intrude, I'm just interested, curious, that's all."

"Well son, the thing's ya been seein' and the thing's ya been hearin', I couldn't hold ya ta blame if ya picked me up, held me top side down and shook it out o' me. I expect it's time ya know a few thin's. I may as well get to it, I ain't gettin' no youngah and too much of it's leakin' out my seams to go on pretendin'.

"Caahtah, I'm hopin' ya got an open mind. The story I'm gonna tell ya, skippah, might swallow haard if ya cahn't keep an open mind. I've nevah told it afore fer thaht, and a few othah reasons. I've nevah figgered people outside the Cause would undahstand. Ta grasp what I'm tellin' ya, it might help ta realize some of us got ta accept harsh realities faar beyond the happier place of pleasure yachts and coffee houses, don't ya know."

Carter winced, then dropped his eyes as if he were being scolded.

Patrick sensed Carter's frustration, realizing he inadvertently sounded accusatorial. He quickly interjected.

"Now don't get me wrong theah, Caahtah. I wish everyone could live in a world like Maahblehead, with its fine yaaht clubs and libraries and thin's; in fact, thaht's the point. Everyone should haav thaht right. All people should haav the right ta choose theah future, or at least participate equally in its gov'ment. It's plain ta see thaht wealth cahn't be hahd by simply wishin' it, but fairness cahn. Fairness is a state o' mind. People should sit down together and agree ta be fair. Thaht haasn't happened in Northern Ireland in better thahn 800 yeahs.

"What I got ta tell ya, thaht is, ta tell my story complete, is some thin's I'm not too proud of as I look baack on 'em. They seemed right at the time... I pray ta God they was right. It seemed thaht way when I was a' standin' in the middle of a war, a fight for my clan's say in theah future. Ya got ta remembah, Caahtah, I came from a land invaded and occupied by people who hahd no business bein' theah."

≋≋≋

Carter nodded in acknowledgment, although he still harbored countless questions about the veracity of Patrick's assertion. It was as if he might be right and wrong at the same time; that viewpoint and context were as significant as records and realities.

The ideas of viewpoint and context made him think of the Amish in Northern Indiana, not far from where he grew up. They effectively convinced themselves that modern technology, such as cars and computers, were unacceptable. Yet an arbitrary position along the continuum of history that included technology such as wheels and plows was embraced, even sanctified.

Viewpoint and context; perhaps these two concepts are the starting points of understanding and we tend to forget them.

Carter listened as Patrick continued.

"Guns and bombs are all people heah about in the bloody newspapehs. Theah is intrigue aplenty in the exchange of aarms, and the movin' of 'em round in ships, don't ya' know. I'll wager thaht's what ya been figgerin' we been up to, leastwise based on those articles I found taped in *Maxine's* logbook."

Patrick wore an apologetic look, but continued without delay.

"Well, I ain't gonna' sit heah and deny thaht at one time or anothah I've bought or sold a fireaarm. Howevah, I don't think thaht tells the story yer most interested in hearin', skippah.

"Ya see, Caahtah, money cahn be used fer a hell o' a lot more effect thahn ordinary trade. It cahn change people's minds, change theah behavior; it cahn cause 'em to look away at the right moment, or be where ya want 'em at the right time. Hell, theah's no end to the possibilities money cahn bring to the undahside of war; ta thaht secret side o' fightin' thaht sees no daylight nor the scrutiny o' newspapeh reporters."

Patrick looked over at Carter.

The young sailor didn't admit his apprehension at hearing Patrick's story; he was already committed, his decision to learn more was firm. What it would mean to him in the future he could not precisely predict. Was this all going too far? He was no longer absolutely certain. Carter kept thinking of the peace process, the Mitchell Commission. He was anxious and curious of its outcome. The information he read on the internet indicated that even if resolution was achieved by the deadline laid down by the Mitchell Commission, just two days away, there would still need to be an island-wide referendum to adopt the plan.

Would people from across the entire island overcome anxiety and fear and vote to commit to a long-term process of de-commissioning weapons and peaceful coexistence? Could they be fair, as Patrick believed they could?

"Now, what I'm tellin' ya, laddie, thaht is, about money and such, is about the same thin' I was told a long time ago by my fathah's next youngah brothah, thaht would be my Uncle Seamus.

"Theah was six brothers altogethah, four of 'em died fer the Cause. The second oldest, he arrived in this country at an early age, hahd found hisself in trouble, 'round '21, just aftah the Easter

Uprisin'. He and Da hahd a boat, a sailboat, come about the size o' *Gael na Mara*, similah lines, too, though not at all fancy and sparklin' like the 'Woman of the Sea.'"

Carter saw Patrick look up into his brow to recollect her image.

"They named 'er *Asgard*, ya' know, the home o' them Norwegian Gods, and the two o' 'em was makin' trips ta Belgium and baack, weighin' several tons heavier on the return theah, skippah, if ya get my meanin'. My Uncle hahd a mind like Bones; smaart in business, smaart in fightin', and smaart with money."

Patrick paused and looked at Carter directly.

"Do ya' know what Taoiseach means, Caahtah?"

He could see from Carter's quizzical look he did not.

"Thaht's a title, Caahtah, tis Celtic fer chief and it's spelled strange, like most Celtic words, leastwise compared with English. Even though it's pronounced T-shuck, with emphasis on the T, it's spelled..." and Patrick wandered from his story long enough to remove a pencil from his cap and wrote out the spelling on the brown paper sack in which Martha packed their lunches.

Carter read the word, divined that Patrick's father was Taoiseach, chief of the O'Clery clan, and that meant Patrick was, too. Carter carefully tore the spelling from the bag and slipped it in his pocket.

Patrick smiled at the predictability of the young captain's habits and continued with his story.

"By August of '21, theah enterprisin' ways hahd landed them on a hit list and by October '21, Uncle Seamus planted Da in the bloody ground, victim of a squabble over who hated the British most, kilt by a splinter group of his own kind. Baack stabbin' bastards! The damnable island is infested with distrust and ill will. Hard enough ta fight a foreign enemy, don't ya know. Ta haav to watch yer backside ta keep from gettin' kilt by ones who were yer allies the week before is lunacy.

"The punishment beatin's and revenge killin's haas been out a control fer as long as I cahn remembah. And funerals; my god, laddie, the funerals baack home, they aah all I remembah from my boyhood. Haahdly a day, let alone a week would go by thaht black wasn't worn and let me tell ya, skippah, black is no fittin' color to be worn in an already gray-green land."

Carter imagined a dreary landscape, wet with fog and mist, filled with people pale from the shock of death, dressed in the black of mourning.

"Well then, I suppose ya could say the blackness o' the place drove Uncle Seamus away. He hahd to run, truth be told, or he'd be in the next casket paraded through town.

"I'll say this fer Uncle Seamus, he hahd a plan. He put thaht plan in motion as soon as he realized his gun runnin' days was ovah. Turns out thaht he placed substantial portions of his and Da's proceeds in the form of gold in a Belgian bank. He did this on the advice of a shrewd and mysterious character Uncle Seamus would never identify; took the man's identity ta the grave, too. I've always suspected the man was a criminal, though it wouldn't be hard fer someone ta say the same 'bout Uncle Seamus!

"Now then, laddie, Uncle Seamus, got hisself to 'merica, changed his name to Samuel, thaht is Samuel Claark, and bein' smart like he was and havin' money the likes of which most Irishmen nevah know, he hid hisself deep. He didn't run straight ta' New Yaahk or Bahston, wheah everybody and theah brothah would haav known him or chased aftah him fer his money. Instead, Samuel went to Chicago and hid hisself amongst Polish, Hungarians, and Greeks. He was a young lad still and made connections with the Catholic Church and the Democratic Party. They quietly took him in. Sure it weren't long, son, thaht Samuel Claark was attendin' yer alma mattah."

Carter turned abruptly toward Patrick.

"You're joking, Notre Dame? Your uncle attended Notre Dame?"

"Well fer Christ sake Caahtah, the place is full o' Irish, don't ya know? T'was the perfect hidin' place weren't it? Out in the middle o' nowhere, surrounded by Indiana farmland; a stone's throw from Chicago, reclusive and cloaked in religious piety. Good plahn, ya haav ta agree, eh, skippah?"

Carter was taken aback. *Notre Dame*, he thought. He never fully realized its connection to Ireland or, for that matter, the Irish question. When he studied there he was absorbed in architecture; he ignored any Irish aspect of the place.

"Well, Samuel, yer alumni brothah, he went on to become a successful attorney. I'm told he donated sizable amounts to your alma mattah, this place wheah you and he learn't yer fancy aarts."

Patrick paused to sip his coffee from the white styrafoam cup Martha packed for each of them in their lunch bags. Carter avoided his as inconspicuously as possible.

"You would haav liked knowin' my uncle and he would haav taken ta you as well, I figur. He liked a man who was willin' ta open his eyes and see the wonders thaht surrounded 'im. He respected the man willin' ta take a risk.

"I suppose, an' fergive me if I sound like I'm boastin', but this put Connah and me in his good graces, too, even from across the pond. O' course, the plain fact thaht I inherited my fathah's title hahd somethin' ta do with it. Samuel felt a certain allegiance we all felt, still feel, when it comes to the clan."

Two seagulls swooped nearby. Their arrival drew the attention of both sailors, though neither was willing to share their lunches.

"When Samuel Claark left Chicago he moved to Cleveland, Ohio. Theah he began practicin' the lawr. Amongst his many clients was the Great Lakes steel shippin' giants Cleveland/Conrad Ltd."

Carter immediately recognized the name. He had seen it hundreds of times on freighters working the Lakes, painted in giant white letters down the box-like sides of the gigantic vessels.

"Samuel partnahed up with a couple Jewish lads, from farther east, upstate New Yaahk, I believe. The firm hahd the unlikely name of Robinowitz, Rosenberg and Claark. He rose quickly in the firm. His work placed him in the centah of Great Lakes Maritime lawr. The minin' and shippin' industries throughout the region used him regulah ta fight theah battles.

"T'wasn't long afore he and his partnahs were inchin' into New Yaahk City, and the 'cross Atlantic lines. Weren't long aftah thaht afore ties to Bahston were made and the eventual establishment of connections ta the Bahston Irish community. Samuel's Irish sympathies had been hidden from view, but haahdly forgotten, don't ya know.

"'Tween him and his Jew partnahs, they hahd some things goin' on and not all theah clients was o' the charactah considered yer most upright and law abidin'...thaht's the strangest paht o' bein' a lawyer I suppose. The confidentiality we depend on ta keep our legitimate secrets intact is only an unscheduled meetin' or an off-shoah transaction away from bein' a bloody crime."

Patrick paused and Carter nervously wondered if he was about to head in a different direction. He waited patiently and Patrick looked down, shook his head slightly and looked back up, as if he resolved a point of wonderment in his mind.

"I suppose, come ta think of it, thaht in the business o' fightin' a revolution as it were, ya got ta expect thaht yer gonna commit a crime soonah or later. Whether ya believe it, admit it, or just plain deny it, it haapens and only time and the stories we make up will prove ya right or prove ya wrong."

Carter sensed that not enough time had transpired for Patrick's history to be judged, that he was still fighting his fight. He was likely still committing crimes, at least by somebody's measure. One way or the other, Carter could see his friend's extraordinary history had become a noose around his neck that he desperately wanted to remove. He needed redemption, and while confession was the first step, he ultimately needed vindication. Someone needed to pass judgment, and either kill him or free him from the terrible burden. It was apparent he was looking to Carter for the latter.

Both sailors finished their lobster rolls and chowder and leaned against the picnic table to take in the view of the harbor. They fell silent for a few minutes. Patrick finally stirred.

"Samuel got hold of information 'bout Bones' oldah sistah's death. Haas Bones told ya 'bout his sistah Winnie, Caahtah?"

"Briefly, when we were together on board; though I wasn't completely mindful of what he told me," Carter replied.

"She was murdered in a bombin' along with 'er husband and their unborn child. Pahdon me fer bein' plain spoken with ya' Caahtah, but bombin' and killin's central ta my story from this point forward. I cahn't mince words and get this out. Aah ya okay with thaht, skippah?"

Carter glanced at Patrick and nodded, apprehensive, yet prepared for the worst. After all, he knew the ending, Miread and Connor both died. How bad could it be in the middle?

"Bones and Samuel became friends, or I should say they began to exchange information and ideas. Thaht, made fer a lethal combination, don't ya know. When Bones discovered, through documents Samuel purloined from U.S. Army Intelligence, thaht his own sistah's blood was spilled at the hands of British agents workin' in collusion with the Loyalists, he went berserk! He couldn't fathom his own countrymen playin' a role in the murderin' of his sistah, not ta mention the ruination of his ma and da in theah agony and despair ovah 'er loss.

"It turns out certain Irish sympathizers in the U.S. Army hahd stole the files from the Brits just in case they needed 'em. How do ya like thaht, eh? The U.S. stealin' from the Brits. Tis a strange world, I tell ya Caahtah, a very strange world."

Carter glanced toward Patrick once again, trying not to look surprised.

"Ya realize, Caahtah, thaht William Donovan, 'Wild Bill' we called 'im, the first directah of the CIA, was both Irish American and an attorney. He hahd a great sympathy fer the Cause. Tis rumored his grandfathah worked at doin' the same thin' fer the Finnian Brotherhood as Captain O'Malley does fer us, don't ya know."

Carter tried hard not to appear naïve or insignificant.

"Not much later, Samuel Claark brought Miread's fathah, Doc Callahan, and Bones together, too. I suppose ya could say in doing so they formed a particulahly useful and extremely covert capability theah, skippah. By the time I got involved, I haav to admit, we was all mighty dahmned high on ourselves. Too dahmned high."

The old sailorman swore before spitting and continuing.

"Fer Bones' part, laddie, he decided then, and I suspect he's nevah thought diff'rent since, thaht he would help any Catholic Irishman thaht wanted ta kill a British soldier.

"Jesus, those was bahd yeahs. Ya haav ta wondah—did they haav to happen to get wheah we aah now, with the good Senatah from Maine acting as our go between, tryin' like hell ta make peace, Bones feedin' the whole bunch what they need ta know ta try and bring it ta an end.

"Doc is gone; Samuel is gone, only Bones remains. He's desperate ta see it finished afore he dies and cahn ya blame 'im, son, cahn ya blame 'im?"

"Bones works for the Mitchell Commission—is that what you are saying?" Carter queried.

"Not exactly, Caahtah, 'tis not thaht simple. What I'm sayin' is this: Bones Maatheson staahted out to avenge his sistah's murdah. Ovah these dozens of yeahs, revenge motivated him ta make connections, gather intelligence, and counsel interveners. He stirred thin's up. It's been a long battle, some bahd thin's haav happened and now he's done with the plainness of revenge. Bones knows revenge cahn't bring Winnie and 'er little seedlin' baack ta life.

"Now, at this moment, he's tryin' ta facilitate peace with the wisdom he's mustered ovah time. He's brought ta the table the even-handedness thaht cahn only come with time. And no one, not on eithah side of the negotiatin' table of politicians, faction leaders and heads of state ovah theah in Stormont, cahn match Bones' experience and wisdom. They all need 'im and they all know it. He's the centah; he's the Figurehead."

"What about you, Patrick, what are you in all this?"

Patrick clicked his tongue and shook his head. "I'm Taoiseach of the O'Clery clan, Caahtah, thaht's all." He paused a moment to breath as he sat upright, turning to look at his young protégé. "Sure and soon I'll be handin' down thaht dubious title ta the next bearer. It won't be long now. I've made my decision as ta who thaht shall be, or perhaps *they* shall be is a bettah way a puttin' it.

"In the meantime, I've made anothah even more important decision. Bones has carried it forward to the Mitchell Commission, quietly of course, but it will be known ta everyone soon.

"I've made a decision to lay down our arms, laddie. I'm surrenderin' our cache o' weapons. I've ordered 'em to be delivered into the hands of an International Commission, headed by a Canadian general with whom Bones haas contact. It's ovah fer the O'Clery's; we aah done with the killin', once and fer all. We'll not lay to waste anothah human life in the name of the Cause. Thaht's not to say we've changed colors mind ya, and they cahn kill every last one of us if they must. It simply means peace haas to begin sometime, somehow, and we aah makin' thaht time now, Caahtah! We hope, we expect, othahs ta follow; but somebody hahd to be first."

Several questions sprang to mind, as Carter's curiosity once again started taking control. This would necessitate a trip to the library. He thought of another question to ask Patrick presently and spoke up.

"If the O'Clery clan is disarming, why is Captain O'Malley so quick to brandish a weapon?"

"Captain O'Malley will be held to my edict soon enough, laddie. Fer the time bein', he is instructed, in conjunction with othah associates ya best know nothin' about, ta keep Bones alive and in one piece fer as long as it takes ta get thin's settled in Stormont.

"Stormont?" Carter queried.

"Stormont is wheah Senatah Mitchell, General de Chastelain, the Canadian I mentioned, and thaht Finlandah, Harrie Holkeri, aah scurryin' about. It's wheah the seat o' gov'ment haas been in Northern Ireland. To be more correct, it is wheah the seat o' gov'ment haas been when the bloody British haav pretended to allow a token measure of self gov'ment."

"I see," Carter said while wondering how to get Patrick back to the story about the night Miread and Conner were lost. So Patrick, a while ago you were explaining how your plan for the crossing on *Gael na Mara* went bad. I don't mean to pry, I'm just curious."

"Yes, thaht's right, laddie, I was, and I will before we aah finished heah. First, skippah, ya got to think about yer history." He sipped again from the coffee cup in his hand. "In the world o' shippin', thin's were changing durin' those yeahs aftah World War II. Belfaast ship buildahs and British-controlled shippin' companies were facin' somethin' they hahdn't faced fer a long time.

"Ya see, although the great shipyahds in Belfaast appeared ta be Irish owned, the fact o' the mattah was thaht any business is undah the control of its biggest customahs. Thaht meant thaht the largest employah in Northern Ireland was kissin' the arse o' the British shippin' and passenger liner companies and hahd been fer a dahmn long time. Don't think thaht didn't haav somethin' ta do with our troubles, don't ya know," Patrick proclaimed, casting a wary eye toward his young confidant.

"The largest dry-dock in the world is in Belfaast. At the time *Titanic* was built at Harland & Wolff's, theah were fifteen thousand employees earnin' about two pounds a week. Despite the fact thaht Ireland remained neutral durin' the war, she built tons o' British warships. Thaht cost her dearly when the Germans bombed two thirds o' the yaahds into oblivion, but ya already know how thaht conflict ended.

"My point heah is thaht the dancin' couple, Belfaast ship buildahs and theah British customahs, were thinkin' hard 'bout the industry's future aftah the war. Britain didn't want to lose a relatively well-trained and inexpensive labor force and the Protestant -controlled majority in Northern Ireland didn't want ta lose theah best customahs.

"The question became critical when a couple o' changes began occurrin' 'bout five yeahs aftah the war. The world of shippin' woke up ta the fact thaht oil transport was gonna be the main commodity ta be moved by ships. This was because airlines hahd begun movin' a lot o' other products. They snatched up markets in faar corners o' the globe. Bulk transport of oil, obviously springin' from the Middle East, was not goin' anywheah in jets. Ships were gonna move oil and ships of enormous size were gonna be needed!

"The British, laddie, even though Bones and I got no love fer 'em, aren't stupid. They were, and intended to remain, the main economic engine in Europe.

"Howevah, the vanquished Germans and the revivin' French were poised to grow. The U.S. was given 'em a lot o' help, too. Not only thaht, the othah vanquished nation emergin' durin' those post war yeahs was Japan, don't ya know.

"We know now thaht they was the most formidable. Samuel, Doc, and Bones figgered as much baack then." Patrick paused for dramatic effect.

"Samuel and his partnahs was workin' deep inside both the shippin' industry and U.S. intelligence, that is, the post war CIA, which, of course, was run by an Irish brothah who gave them audience whenevah they aasked. Therein was the beginnin's of the plan fer thaht damnable trip across the pond you was just askin' about.

"Some o' the fine points of what we set out ta do on thaht trip I'm layin' aside heah, Caahtah. The question o' whethah or not we hahd enough horsepowah to accomplish everythin' we planned is hard ta answah. Certain aspects o' the operation got undermined by shiftin' loyalties and the traitorous nature o' people the plan depended on.

"On the othah hand, Samuel, Doc, and Bones were certainly correct in the grandah scheme o' thin's. I sometimes think thaht only my paht o' the plan failed thaht night . . ."

There was a deepening sound of despair in Patrick's voice.

"We hahd loaded *Gael na Mara* with counterfeit money, an' don't aask who printed it or how we got our hands on it. We was mixed up with seedy characters and we nigh came to regret it.

"Along with the money were forged documents. The documents hahd been carefully prepared by Samuel in collaboration with his lawr partnahs. The documents were intended ta haav an effect on contractual agreements relatin' to ship buildin' in Belfaast. Just how those documents were ta do theah job I nevah knew. Suffice it ta say thaht ships intended ta be built in Belfaast would end up bein' built by Nippon Heavy Industries!"

≋≋≋

"T'was about this time o' the yeah, baack in '51, thaht we shoved off, laddie. T'was early in the season, too early really, but we was brave and confident. The weathah posed no particulah concern as we was used ta some rough stuff out theah. *Gael na Mara* cahn take about anythin' ya cahn throw at 'er; you cahn see thaht in 'er, eh, skippah?"

Carter nodded, but didn't speak, not wanting to stall Patrick's tale or see it head some other direction.

"Sure then, off we went, lightly aarmed with powdah, heavily aarmed with papeh, and lookin' like a cruisin' family out fer an adventure at sea.

"Theah was the five o' us: Bones and Miread, Martha and Connah and, of course, m'self. Though Bones was captain and m'self first mate, I was really the plannah o' the trip and laid out the course and timin' and such. We established a watch rotation as we hahd done so many times. Soon we slipped into thaht state o' mind thaht comes when the blue water o' the North Atlantic fills the horizon in every direction.

"When yer playin' with fire like we was though, ya cahn't expect thaht everythin' is goin' ta be like a damned holiday. O' course, we knew the risks, we knew we could get burned; howevah, the precautions we took were substantial.

"Still, unbeknownst to us, certain bastahds we should haav nevah trusted to keep theah mouths shut leaked information; they delivered our estimated arrival time. Ya see, Caahtah, I thought everyone ovah heah would behave like I expected o' my clan. I thought if ya fought fer one side, thaht would be the side you'd be on when the battle ended, when the smoke cleared.

"Turns out different, don't ya know. In the bloody counterfeit business ya get linked up with people who aah workin' both sides and don't give a dahmn who wins or loses. I suppose the way they looked at it, once they started committin' crimes, it really didn't mattah on whose behalf they were committin' 'em fer. In the end, they was workin' fer the money . . . period.

"Later, well aftah our incident thaht night, Samuel and Bones, through secret connections, were able to figger out thaht the counterfeiters was stuffin' portions o' profits into offshore accounts in the Grand Caymans. Of course, they hahd planned on not bein' around when we come lookin' aftah 'em. What they hahdn't figgered is thaht theah aah few places on earth the Irish didn't get to in those famine ships of old!"

Patrick wore steely eyes as he recounted this part of his story. Apparently, he believed the counterfiters were the ones most directly responsible for Miread and Connor's deaths. Carter assumed this meant that the likes of Captain O'Malley were sent to find and kill them. Carter remained silent, careful not to exhibit an accusatorial posture.

"We ran into a few bits o' weathah ovah the days o' the crossin', but nothing too bahd till we neared our destination. Then, wouldn't ya know it theah, laddie, the luck o' the Irish couldn't keep the pond from risen' up against us.

"Theah was nothin' we could do, 'specially turn around. So we battened down hatches and shortened sail fer the final hours. We hahd ta keep *Gael na Mara* movin'. Samuel hahd made it clear afore we shoved off thaht the documents were time sensitive. They needed ta be wheah they was goin' if they was ta do theah work, don't ya know. We pressed on."

CHAPTER 35

VIEWPOINT AND CONTEXT

"Well, laddie, the cold spring wind blows thick. It pushes boats hard, but I suppose I'm not tellin' ya somethin' ya don't know theah, skippah.

"Solid walls o' wind was shovin' us about on top the slippery pond. Ta make things worse, we was nearin' the northwest coast o' the island and seas were runnin' high. As we neared shallowah ground, the seas got more confused, dancin' 'round on top a goodly swell.

"Connah and Martha was on watch and Bones kept a nervous eye on them in turn. Miread and I was hunkered down below. Sure I was sleepin' in the pipe berth aft, and despite the ragin' weathah was restin' good.

"Miread was supposed ta be restin', too, but she was feelin' nervous I suppose, what with 'er only daughtah on deck in the drivin' rain, in the black o' night. At one point, I think it t'was 'round 2:00 A.M., I heard 'er in the galley makin' hot soup and tea fer 'er daughtah and son-in-law. I hahd said to myself, she ought to be in the sack gettin' as much rest as she cahn, cause our watch was next. But in case ya don't know, son, yer not gonna tell a mamma not ta fret ovah 'er daughtah; no way in hell, I don't care if the whole dahmn universe were collapsin'."

Carter saw his point.

"Course, in my opinion, Maatha didn't need no frettin' ovah. She hahd been ta sea since she was a wee lassie. Besides, Maatha and Connah were so full o' life t'was like they was immortal.

"Thaht's the way of the young, eh, laddie? When they was together there seemed to be an aura engulfin' 'em, followin' 'em 'round. Kind o' made 'em look buoyant, I thought, like they was floatin' up above the decks all the time.

"Sure they was a joy ta watch, filled the whole crew with a feelin' like we was all immortal. The whole of *Gael na Mara* was lit up by theah passion and when ya add thaht to the natural beauty o' thaht splendid vessel, ya got yer'self quite a lucky ship theah, skippah.

"Well, perhaps thaht was our problem. Perhaps we took too much fer granted. We pushed fate a bit to faar 'cause later thaht night thin's went straight ta hell.

"By the time I crawled out of my berth ta go on watch, I was greeted by a glass thaht hahd dropped even farthah. With a terrible bahd feelin' startin' to brew, I stumbled onto Miread gettin' dressed in oil skins to join me. I don't think she evah did get rest like she was supposed ta. I could see a bit o' fatigue in 'er thaht normally wouldn't haav been theah."

Patrick paused again, as if to imagine her image that night. When he continued his voice seemed soft and distant.

"She was a pretty woman, Caahtah, statuesque ya' might even say. Weren't hard ta see why Bones fell fer 'er. She talked nice, too. I used ta admire her even tempah and focused mind. She was devoted like 'er fathah ta the Cause, though I always thought it was from a book-learned point o' view, if ya know what I mean."

Carter recollected the photos of Miread in the B&B. He recalled the sparkling eyes of a young mother as she held her baby girl for the camera.

"You know as well as any, laddie, the incredible motion of a boat flung about in raging seas, spun on top of tremendous swells, the wind blowin' the rain horizontal and every line taught as a fiddle string waitin' ta pop. Now double thaht and it's what ya got wheah the North Atlantic meets up with the rocky shores of my homeland, skippah. The northwest coast o' Ireland is rugged and dangerous in fine weathah let alone in a blow like we was gettin' thaht night. We hahd our hands full, but was still figurin' on makin' landfall 'round the northern tip ovah ta Rathlin Island.

"I hahd made arrangements ta rendezvous and exchange the documents, seein' as how they needed delivery faast. The counterfeit money we shipped would be dispensed ovah the next month or two as we cruised into the Irish Sea down ta Dublin and ovah ta Manchestah and Livahpool."

"You sailed into English ports? Wasn't that dangerous?"

"Sure we sailed to England, whenevah we wanted, laddie. I already explained how the workin's o' money could cause people ta change theah minds and look away at just the right moments. We knew a lot o' people in the right places and Bones is an Englishman, don't ferget."

Patrick returned a smile in the direction of the flummoxed youth then returned to his story.

"I hahd arranged ta be met by a fishin' boat run by a clan membah. He hahd takin' up livin' in one o' the little cottages thaht occupied Rathlin Island a couple yeahs earlier. His name was Nolan O'Clery and he was a kind o' a lonah who fished around and kept mostly to hisself. A more trustworthy soldier couldn't be found.

"Nolan worked a small trawlah, though thaht would haav been a big word fer it. He called 'er *Taisie*, aftah the princess of Rathlin Island. Anyway, she'd be fine fer the job, a near plumb bow, double planked up forward ta take a heavy sea. She hahd a little cuddy and short mast fer a storm sail. Even in the rottin' conditions we was facin', I saw no worry in bein' met and sure enough in the end, loyal as 'er mastah, the *Taisie* come ta greet us.

"Ended up, Nolan's arrival was momentous in ways even he couldn't haav guessed. Sure he was as surprised as we were at the situation we steamed into thaht night. The three o' us is alive today cause o' him, but I'm getting' ahead o' myself."

Carter took note of the number three while staring back in anticipation.

"He's gone now, too, old Nolan. I used ta send him money so he could buy anothah boat. My people baack home tells me Nolan was nevah right aftah thaht night."

Patrick shook his head as if he didn't want to accept that simple fact that there existed yet another thing he had caused to happen in his zeal to further the Cause. Carter could see Patrick's mind working. He knew he was reminiscing. He could only guess at the profundity of the memories passing through the old man's mind.

"Christ, I'm gettin' old, don't ya' know. Haavn't got much time left neithah, I suppose. We ought ta get baack to work on *Red Shoes* . . ."

Patrick stood suddenly as if to leave and looked at Carter as if expecting him to rise too. Carter remained seated, his eyes fixed and anxious, clearly wanting to hear the remainder of the story.

Patrick sat back down, though hesitatingly, and Carter saw once again the look from the theatre. The dazed, sad look of a man on the edge of a decision he didn't want to make; the face of a man with just enough strength to persevere if someone stepped up and lent a hand, just as Carter did in the dark cavern of the movie house, and did again now.

"Ernie, the Irregular who's my new friend, he told me this morning he was going to get that bunch to pitch in and lend a hand. He was going to get them started on varnishing after lunch. He's a good man, a mate that's there when you need him—trustworthy to the end. I think you'll be surprised to see how much work gets done today.

"You know, Patrick, they are all good men, the Irregulars. I suppose one has to be willing to tolerate their ornery façade. I think they needed a leader, someone like Ernie, one of their own. It may sound odd, but we're both outsidahs to them, don't ya know."

Patrick looked at Carter and beneath his red-gray mustache his lips turned up in a grateful smile. After a deep breath and an equally deep sigh he continued.

"We was beatin' with a double reef in the main and a storm jib set as tight as a bodhran drum when Miread and I reported on deck. We relieved the standin' watch and they went below.

"I told Connah to make sure Bones got some rest. His propaah turn in the rotation would come 'round soon enough. He hahd a tendency ta try and keep watch continually when the weathah came up. Aftah all, he was Captain. He carried on his baack the weight o' the whole ship and the dangerous stratagem he, Samuel, and Doc Callahan hahd devised.

"I looked at Connah and he acknowledged my request. My God, Caahtah, the lad was full o' energy, even aftah a full watch in thaht ragged black storm. I suspect the idea o' crawlin' into his berth with his young wife kept 'im charged up plenty. How could ya blame 'im neithah? Martha was a darlin' in 'er youth. I haav ta admit I still see 'er thaht way m'self...tis funny how thaht works." He paused as his imagination formulated a pleasant memory.

"We hahdn't taken a star sight fer 24 hours. We trusted our ded-reckoning, t'was all we hahd. I figured we'd hold course till dawn. Thaht would haav roughly set us on our rendezvous coordinates.

"T'was black out and the only light on board was a glow in *Gael na Mara's* binnacle. We hahd been in communication by short wave radio with Nolan earlier thaht night. Our transmissions hahd been brief, so as not ta raise suspicions. He was prepared to shove off at the designated time, but othahwise remained on his moorin', waitin' patiently.

"All of a sudden, like the crack o' thundah, the jib blew out and the sheet fell limp. T'was so dark, Miread and I could see nothin' forward o' the main. The remaining portion of the sheet flailin' raised a hell of a racket and sent a rush o' adrenalin through us both.

"Ya look baack in hindsight, Caahtah, and ya say ta yerself, why did I send 'er forward? What made me do it? Why did I figger thaht sail hahd ta come down? Why couldn't it just flail away out theah in the dark until dawn broke or the wind laid down? Dahmn thaht blahsted rag! I should haav just let it blown ta shreds."

After a moment, Patrick's regret subsided enough to continue.

"Sure ya know, Caahtah, no captain would haav done different. Yer out theah ta sail propaah and lettin' a damned sail flail in the wind is no good; yet, was it worth a life?

"Then there's the question o' why I didn't go forward myself. Son of a bitch, I've aasked myself thaht a thousand times ovah. But Caahtah, when yer assigned the forward deck you aah expected to do yer job and do it without complaint, and despite 'er appearance on land, thaht of a well-mannered librarian, Miread Maatheson carried 'er weight on board a boat.

"No foremast jack could out pace 'er and the damned woman, may she rest in peace, was forward in the blink of an eye. T'was 'er job and she was intent on doin' it."

Carter heard Patrick's voice crack and turned to see the old man bend forward slightly, looking at the ground. He rocked back and forth, like he was on board a sea-going vessel right then. This movement went on for a long moment.

"Miread shot up onto the cabin trunk and untied the jib halyard from the main mast. Then she stepped forward into the darkness and thaht's the last I saw of 'er. Seconds aftah she disappeared, a rogue wave picked *Gael na Mara* up at the bows, twisted 'er sideways like a dahmn child's toy and thaht jib just kept flappin' and shreddin' in the blackness. It weren't comin' down like I expected.

"The commotion and my hollerin' brought Bones and Connah up on deck with Maatha trailin' aftah 'em. I yelled above the howl o' the wind ta help Miread, and the three of 'em clawed theah way forward. To my horror the next sound ta came aft was the high pitch screamin' of Maatha callin' out Mothah, Mothah, oh God!

Mothah! Then I heard the othahs callin' out 'er name as well. It t'was then I fully realized she hahd gone ovahboard!"

Patrick was rocking violently now. Carter reached for him automatically to calm him down. The old man gasped. He exuded a guttural cry of agony.

"Miread, deah Miread, I'm sorry, gul, I'm sorry!"

The old man convulsed in sorrow and regret. His long red-gray hair fell around his face and hung there as if to cover his agony and shame. He couldn't hold back the pain, the belief that he'd killed an innocent woman. His hands went to his face, his red-gray hair crumpled in his fingers, and the old Irishman wept.

"I should haav gone forward," he groaned. "I should haav done it myself. It was blowin' bahd, she was tired, I knew it was bahd. I should haav . . ." His shoulders convulsed again.

Carter didn't know what to do. He placed his hand on Patrick's shoulder and felt the heat of Patrick's being in his palm. A few minutes passed while Patrick regained his composure.

"I'm being foolish, Caahtah, I cahn't seem ta control my feelin's. I'm cryin' like a wee babe. It ain't propaah; maybe I bettah stop. I thought this tale needed ta be told, but by God, I'm not sure I cahn do it." He paused again for breath.

Carter waited. A sea change came over Patrick. It reminded Carter of a squall brewing on the big lake.

"Well, dahmn it ta hell, laddie! I'm gettin' this story out if it kills me. It's got to be done, skippah. By God, if Nolan hahd been this cowardly thaht sickening night, none of us would be heah ta tell the tale. If Miread hahdn't leapt to 'er duty, sure then none o' us would leap to our duty. I gotta stop quiverin' like a child and get on with it," he said resolutely. He took a deep, even breath and continued.

"Maatha ran aft. She was white as a dahmn ghost. I remembah the look on 'er tortured face as she cried out 'Mothah's ovahboard, she's gone!' A jolt of dread shot through me. Those words mean death about ta haapen. There's nothin' worse ta hear—not in a black storm.

"I hollered above the wind and told 'er ta reach in the pilot house fer the searchlight hanging on the stahboard side. I immediately spun *Gael na Mara's* wheel and brought 'er into the wind. Connah suddenly hollered aft thaht he saw 'er. 'Ovah theah, two points off the port beam,' he cried.

"I yelled at him to keep his eyes on 'er, not ta look away fer any reason. Bones threw a buoy, but it looked real small out theah on thaht violent, churning sea.

"Maatha drew the search light out and aimed it in the direction Connah was pointin'. Connah moved aft and took the light. He pointed it toward wheah he was lookin' and I heard Maatha suddenly shriek, 'Theah she is, I see huhr, I see huhr!' I looked, but nevah saw 'er. I nevah saw 'er again. I couldn't keep my eye on 'er as I hahd ta keep lookin' forward. I hahd ta bring the vessel into the wind, ta stop 'er from sailin' into the night.

"Bones leapt on ta the cabin trunk without delay, took up the topping lift and dropped the main while I cranked ovah the iron ginny. Connah joined him aftah he handed back the search light to Maatha, assuring his wife we'd get 'er ma baack on board.

"I watched silently as Bones and Connah furled the reefed main. They moved quickly in the darkness and lowered the shredded jib whose sheets were flailing 'round, threat'nin' ta knock anothah of us ovah board. I hollered at Maatha fer a report. She cried out somethin' I couldn't distinguish. It sounded like 'A light, ovah theah, a light.'

"The instant the sails were secure I swung the wheel baack in the direction Miread went ovahboard and *Gael na Mara* responded sluggish in the confused seas. I turned toward Maatha ta see the direction she was pointin' out the light. Then I turned baack again ta check the riggin' as we came about. I saw Connah standin' on the cabin trunk, where he hahd just moments ago been securin' the main sail. I blinked and rubbed my eyes. He was lit up by a bright light. I thought 'what the hell,' and looked baack to Maatha wonderin' why she was pointin' the dahmn search light in Connah's direction. I feared she hahd fallin' er somethin', but she hahdn't. She was still pointin' our light at Miread. She hahdn't left 'er station though the decks was rollin' so wildly I haavn't a clue as ta whethah she still hahd poor Miread in 'er sights.

"I looked forward again and saw Connah wavin' his hands and leapin' up and down like he was tryin' ta get attention, tryin' ta wave somebody down. He was lit up like he was on a stage.

"I followed the source of the illumination and turned into the night ta see it comin' from anothah search light off in the distance. Thank God, I thought. *Taisie* hahd arrived and just in time! God bless Nolan, God bless the lad!

"A surge of relief ran through me. I turned baack ta holler at Maatha, ta tell 'er help hahd just arrived. Then suddenly, I heard a crack, a sharp report thaht caused me ta jump. I looked forward. I thought *Gael na Mara's* side shroud hahd pahted. Thaht was the last thing we needed. I hahd nightmare visions of de-mastin'.

"Then from up forward Bones yelled baack to me, 'He's hit, he's hit.' Hit, I thought, hit by the shroud? Hit by a turnbuckle come loose? I squeezed the rain out o' my eyes and looked forward, but now the light was gone.

"It was dark and I could barely make out two figures, one lyin' sprawled across the deck and the othah hunched ovah 'im. Son of bitch I cried! There we was, Maatha pointin' the search light toward Miread, Bones standin' ovah Connah lyin prone on the cabin trunk, and me with my hands frozen ta the dahmn wheel, grippin' it ta save our souls.

"Then it seemed like time stopped; it seemed like the storm went silent. I looked all around into the blackness. It was all movin' in slow motion. I looked ta find thaht othah light and it weren't theah. Why would Nolan turn his light out—what haapened ta Connah?

"It seemed like a long time went by, but it must haav been only a few seconds. Then I heard Bones shout out, 'He's shot, the bastahds shot 'im!' His words were distorted, unreal soundin' as they blew baack with the wind. I remembah thinkin', what the hell is he talkin' about? Why on earth would Nolan shoot Connah? What was goin' on?

"Maatha also heard Bones shout those terrible words. She heard loud and cleah and God fergive 'er, she instantly turned around and pointed the light at Connah. She wouldn't realize till later thaht this instinctive movement sealed 'er mothah's doom. Anyone would haav done the same.

"When she spun baack around and Miread was no wheah ta be found, she realized the two most horrible things in the world just haapened. When she turned to see 'er dyin' husband she lost sight of 'er dyin' mothah! The only hope we hahd o' findin' Miread was lost thaht instant."

Carter listened in horror.

Patrick caught his breath and continued.

"'Ow bahd is he?' I cried. Bones looked up in the cold darkness. 'Bahd, Patrick, real bahd.' Maatha way trying ta doctah him. I looked 'round, tryin' to figger out what the hell hahd haapened and wheah the othah damned boat went.

"I couldn't see nothin' out theah. I was blinded by our own spotlight. Bones was holdin' it on Connah while Maatha struggled ta' save 'im! I looked into the black night and called out fer Miread, but I got no reply. I didn't know what ta do. I took *Gael na Mara* out o' gear fer fear we'd run ovah 'er and kill 'er with the dahmn prop. Fer the time bein', theah really weren't much more to do. We were bein' attacked and the black bastahds were hidin' out in the dark.

"I ducked into the pilot house and drew out an M1 Carbine and a Colt .45 and climbed up on deck. I handed Bones the automatic pistol, and no sooner thahn I did, anothah loud crack broke the silence and a splintah of wood from the cabin top broke away neah me and disappeared.

"'Maatha, Maatha,' I hollered, 'we got ta turn off thaht light.' Bones looked at me then at his strugglin' daughtah. 'No,' she cried, 'I've got ta stop the bleedin'.

"No soonah thahn those words were spoken, anothah shot rang out and a second piece of the cabin trunk splintered away.

Bones decided he hahd to act. He bent ovah and placed his ear ta Connah's mouth. He reached fer my brothah's wrist and checked fer pulse. Maatha gripped Bones and shrieked. She anticipated what he was about ta do. Bones' mind was made up. With absolute resolve, he clicked off the search light. Fer Maatha, I guess thaht dull click sounded the end o' 'er marriage, 'cause she wailed, oh lord, she wailed!

"I pained as well, Caahtah, I pained real deep fer I just lost a brothah. But ya know as well as I, Caahtah, theah can only be one captain on a boat and he's the one thaht decides who lives and who dies. 'Tis true I'm Taoiseach and the dyin' man was my blood, my clan; but Bones was the captain o' the ship. I was sailin' undah his command and it was his decision, same as it was a week ago out theah in Massachusetts Bay."

Carter listened and understood. This caused him to think, however, that this made Bones primarily responsible for Miread and Connor's death, not Patrick. He uttered this fact and Patrick responded.

"Sure thaht would seem ta be the truth of it, Caahtah, and Bones haas insisted so hisself. But it was me thaht sent Miread forward to bring down thaht dahmn jib. It was me thaht arranged fer the rendezvous. It was me thaht hooked us up with those bastahds with the printin' press! T'was me thaht got 'em both kilt. I'm responsible! Bones only did what hahd to be done once the circumstances unfolded. Of course we hahd to shut off the dahmn light! If we hahdn't theah would haav been five dead. Whoevah it was shootin' at us out theah in the dark was shootin' ta kill, not ta apprehend."

Carter saw the wound cut deep, the guilt was overwhelming. He decided not to debate the point. Patrick believed he was responsible and perhaps he was. Maybe he was right, maybe he was wrong. Thinking for another moment, Carter remembered his conclusion about the rightness or wrongness of the Amish.

Viewpoint and context…

He repeated this eloquent mantra and considered whether it might assuage Patrick's guilt. He was about to speak when Patrick continued.

CHAPTER 36

IN NO FERGIVIN' MOOD

"With our light turned off, the table was turned a wee bit. We drifted in the dark, gnashed about in the ragin' seas. T'was pitch black, and if they turned theah light on again we'd blast 'em.

"First, though, we hahd to get Maatha below fer she couldn't hold 'er silence; but who could blame 'er. I reached fer a second carbine havin' already passed mine on ta Bones as I helped Maatha down the companionway.

"She didn't want ta go; she wanted to resume searchin' fer Miread. I lied to 'er, Caahtah, I told 'er we'd find 'er the minute we was free from the blasted trap we was in. Maatha knew it would be too late, but she accepted my lie and moved ta the gun locker. She was ready ta fight, don't ya know.

"I told her ta stay below and pass up ammo. If we were injured she was our only chance fer gettin' doctored up. She reluctantly accepted this argument aftah I begged 'er again ta stay below. I hahd no authority ovah 'er. I couldn't make 'er. I shot baack up on deck and she remained behind. I breathed a sigh o' relief. I couldn't haav beared ta see 'er shot too.

"The storm was in no mood ta quit right yet and we couldn't see a dahmn thin' in any direction. But neithah could our enemy! I looked at my chronometer and decided ta remain in place fer twenty minutes. Thaht was the time I gave Miread in the watah. I figgered she was in fer ten already, though I couldn't say as everythin' seemed to be speedin' up and slowin' down in the madness that engulfed us.

"I proposed this plahn ta Bones who, once again, hahd ta decide who would live or who would die. This time though, thin's were different. This time he would haav ta decide 'bout his own wife's life. God help a mahn faced with thaht decision.

"We both knew Miread couldn't last long in the cold watah. She was strong and brave, but she was a wisp o' a woman. She didn't haav no fat fer insulation and ya know all 'bout losin' yer heat theah, laddie.

"You cahn undahstand now why Bones and I was so determined not ta let ya succumb ta the cold last Saturday. You cahn see now why Bones stripped naked hisself and held on ta ya until ya came baack 'round ta the livin' theah, skippah. He wasn't gonna let thaht haapen to anothah person on his watch and I suppose I weren't neithah."

Carter felt a pulse of anxiety rush through him. He now realized that to these dauntless men, his situation offshore the previous week was a continuation of that awful night aboard *Gael na Mara*—a continuation of the battle they previously lost. But this time they had succeeded. They saved his life. He hadn't imagined any of this to be the case at the time.

"The motion of the waves hahdn't subsided. Connah's body was slidin' 'round on the cabin trunk and I hahd ta do somethin' to secure the poor lad. He deserved a propaah burial. He hahd fallin' fer the Cause like so many of our clan.

"I told Bones ta covah me and I crawled forward ta lash Connah ta the deck till we could get underway. He nodded and stayed at the helm. I kept my carbine with me. When I reached Connah, ta my utter horror I heard him call Maatha's name! He was still alive! 'Maatha, he whispered...Maatha'—and I spoke up, tellin' 'im she was nearby.

"I thought hard 'bout what ta do. I looked toward the forward hatch and thought 'bout whethah I could lower 'im down. It didn't look possible. I thought perhaps I could lash 'im ta a harness and drag him baack down the deck ta the pilot house.

"This seemed reasonable so I moved ta untangle the jib sheet thaht lay on deck. I realized it was still attached to the winch at the cockpit. I hollered baack ta Bones ta haul the winch on my word and I heard a muffled 'Aye.' I don't believe he undahstood the lad was still alive and I didn't bothah ta explain.

"I hahd just finished lashin' Connah ta the jib sheet when suddenly a light appeared from less thahn twenty yaahds off the port bow. It struck me like a fountain o' flame. I remained crouched ovah Connah. I heard the report of a small caliber weapon in the distance.

"A spilt second later, I heard the peculiar sound of a bullet whizzin' by my head. It smashed into the cabin trunk just inches away. I felt a sharp pain in my back. I couldn't reach the place thaht hurt. I knew I was hit, but I couldn't say if it were a bullet or a splintah—turned out ta be the lattah.

"A split second later the crack of a carbine shot out from the cockpit. Bones let go several rounds. I dropped ta the deck and the light went baack off. It were pitch black again.

"Bones cried, 'Pahtrick, you all right', and I shouted a quick report. I figgered Bones hahd taken out the search light but I couldn't be sure. I couldn't say fer certain the light went out the instant Bones fired the round. The only good thin' I could surmise was thaht the bastahds only hahd small arms on board and thaht probably meant it weren't a navy patrol boat. I figgered the Brits hahd an agent on board a boat manned by loyalist hoodlums. It's nevah hard ta find a crook disguised as a patriot in Northern Ireland, on eithah side, I'm sorry ta say. It seemed likely they were promised the money and hahd big plans fer it.

"The rain increased and began pourin' down in a deluge. I looked 'round fer Miread, but could only see a foot or two beyond the boat. I realized the wind hahd laid down some and thaht was why the rain came down straight.

"I figgered it was good cover and I whispered ta Connah ta hold on, ta stay alive. He coughed up blood. It was so dark, the blood looked like black bile spewin' from his mouth. I turned away and retched. I couldn't keep control o' myself. The rain poured down and washed away my weakness. I crawled aft ta the winch.

"Sure then I began crankin' the handle and could feel the jib sheet go taut as it took up the weight o' my dyin' brothah. I worked the winch fer a minute or two. Suddenly the rain-filled sky flashed bright as the bastahds turned on theah search light. They hahd maneuvered around toward our stern, the light then comin' from a different angle. At the same instant small arms fire rang from both vessels with Bones firin' away and the same true of the loyalists.

"Theah was no way o' knowin' if Bones' shots did any good. He was firin' blind, mostly tryin' to hit the light or a muzzle flash if he could spot one. The light washed across *Gael na Mara* and moved aft toward me. I laid out flat just undah the protection of the gunnels. I heard the crack of a shot in the distance behind me and the glass of the pilot house window smashed. From below I heard Maatha cry up, 'Aah you all right Bones, is Patrick all right?' and Bones made a quick reply, telling her to stay below, away from the pilot house.

"Even though we was gettin' rounds off and forcin' 'em to keep turnin' theah light on, it started feelin' like we was a sittin' duck. They was a powah vessel and we a sailboat. Eventually, they would out maneuver us unless Bones got in some lucky shots. Even then, we couldn't say how many they hahd on board. It were obvious they tasted blood and hahd thaht money on theah minds.

"I got Connah all the way aft and Bones crept forward enough ta help me drag 'im into the cockpit. I told him he was still alive and Connah made an audible groan. We looked at each other and wondered if we should try and get him below so Maatha could work on 'im.

"Bones checked his pulse again, shook his head ta tell me theah was less thahn no hope and decided not to carry out thaht plan. He didn't want to send a dyin' man down below fer Maatha ta stare at, helpless and alone like she was. I couldn't argue the point. At least Connah was in the cockpit so we could take care o' his body. T'was like his presence gave us reason ta fight. The loyalist bastahds and theah British puppetmastah bloody-well murdered him with a lucky shot. Thaht alone kept our blood hot out in thaht cold pourin' rain.

"A few more minutes passed and I didn't like the way the weathah was changin'. *Gael na Mara* is a fine boat in a heavy sea and I figgered thaht was to our advantage. There ain't a power boat built thaht sits as well in the watah in a blow. As long as the weathah stayed up, we was bettah off. Problem was, thaht weren't the direction thin's was goin'. Of all times fer a storm to blow through, this wasn't one of 'em. Yet thaht was goin' ta be the luck o' the Irish thaht night. The sea was layin' down.

"Afore we knew it, the dirty bastahds hahd come 'round the opposite side, flipped on theah dahmnable light and the shootin' commenced again. We was beginnin' ta feel like a wagon train with Indians circlin' us just like yer old time movies with Gary Coopah. The similarities weren't funny at the time, I cahn tell ya. I couldn't see how this was gonna end in anythin' good."

Carter listened intensely and agreed without speaking. The only good he could see was that somehow Patrick survived to tell the tale.

"Well then, laddie, fer what felt like an hour, they kept probin' around, firin' off rounds and tryin' ta find our weak points. We kept low in the cockpit, both of us returnin' fire and not haavin' a clue as ta whethah we was gettin' any where.

"This sparrin' must haav been gettin' on theah nerves too, cause they started cuttin' in closer. I believe they was thinkin' hard about rammin' us and as the wind laid down and the seas calmed a bit, I could see wheah they might be thinkin' this would work. They kept probin' our stern. This was smaart cause *Gael na Mara* could haav takin' a pretty good smashin' up forward. Not so at the stern. They knew our weak spot, all right. But they also knew we was firin' from the stern and thaht was keepin' 'em off, makin' 'em think twice anyways!

"Trouble was, we was gettin' a wee bit tired. There's a particulah kind o' fatigue comes ovah ya aftah thaht initial adrenalin rush fades away, even in battle. We was already worn down from the storm, we needed food and watah. Maatha set ta work ta try and get us some. In the meantime, it was clear our loyalist adversaries were gettin' tired and impatient too, in the worst sort of way. They was gettin' boldah and were staahtin' to run up our stern.

"It was still so dark ya could barely see yer hand in front o' ya face. The rain poured out o' the sky, muffling the sound of theah engine. They was on top o' us afore we heard 'em or made out their ominous black outline. Each time theah roared toward us they was gettin' braver. I figgered they was about ta do somethin' bold or stupid; somethin' ta break the impasse. I also figgered what they were doin' was likely ta get the whole lot of us killed. If both vessels went down, there would be no hope of anyone survivin'.

"Bones and I hunkered down in the cockpit. Maatha slipped us a couple pilot crackers and mugs o' hot tea. She spotted Connah's body in the cockpit and gasped fer breath. I took 'er in my arms and held on to 'er. She convulsed deep down, silent like. Tore me apart to heah 'er chokin' baack 'er tears. A woman haas a right ta cry, Caahtah. They've earned the right ta cry, what with the burden o' sharin' this heah planet with duplicitous men. Even the good 'uns like Connah. He was like you, son, strong, proud, in love with his 'merican wife."

The remark surprised Carter. He couldn't imagine he was like Connor. He wondered if Patrick was making reference to Claire.

"Connah just hahd the history followin' on him like a shadow. He couldn't shake it off. He carried the genes of centuries o' fightin' and they took ovah from time ta time. He lost control. You laddie . . ." and he turned and looked directly at Carter, "yer free . . . you live yer life and stay the hell away from poisoned men, criminals, and opportunists. You hold on ta thaht young Clayah and ya keep 'er away from poisonous men, too."

Carter kept quiet and listened. This was a time to pay attention and recognize wisdom being imparted. But he was curious. Did Patrick mean something more, something he wasn't grasping? Why was he so concerned about Claire when he spoke of poisonous men? Was he talking about the cretin she worked for? What did Patrick know about her that he hadn't picked up on. Or was Patrick simply transferring to Carter and Claire his experience with Conner and Martha? Maybe he needed to redeem himself by offering advice he should have given his half-brother long ago.

Pausing a moment for his words to sink in, Patrick slowly returned to his story.

"I checked my chronometer and it was time ta depart, ta make our move to escape, least if we was goin' to follow my plan. I was about ta aask Maatha ta go below and stay out o' harms way. Up until then, we hahd maintained radio silence, seein' as how we weren't sure who was tryin' ta kill us. I told 'er thaht if we was kilt, she should take 'er chances and call fer help. In the dark, I could barely make out 'er reaction. I couldn't be sure what she'd do.

"I was about ta turn ta Bones ta confirm our intentions. She pulled angrily at me and in thaht deep guttural voice shouted baack, 'They've killed my mothah! They've killed my husband! They've destroyed my life!' I interrupted 'er by grabbin' holt and pullin' 'er ta my chest. She cried and cried, but what upset me most was 'er words; in 'er angry proclamations was the history o' my clan.

"What the black bastard's hahd done made me angry, too, but moreovah 'er words, they made me ill. 'Maatha,' I pleaded, 'don't go wheah yer headed, lassie, don't let 'em turn ya ta hate and killin'. We'll get out o' this dahmn mess. I'm sorry lass, we'll get out o' this mess.' T'was little consolation fer what the poor thing was in the midst o' sufferin', but it were all I could think ta say.

"No soonah thahn I spoke those words, which I hahd scant faith in accomplishin', the muffled roar of an engine growled in the night. With a smashin' explosion, I turned to see the enormous black specter rise up ovah our stern. The idiotic bastahds were rammin' us!

"Bones fired off a couple rounds from his carbine. The muzzle flash lit the night. But fer the sound it was like a flash of an old time camera. Theah she was, our attackers bow, crashin' into us just one point off the stern post. Theah was a cacophony o' smashin' wood and grindin' metal. The flash o' the carbine burnt the bizarre image onto the back of my eyes. I cahn see it now as I haav a thousand times. We all fell ta the cockpit floor. I was afraid our own weapons might misfire and shoot one o' us as we tumbled about. It was ovah quick like.

"I felt blinded and couldn't get my bearin's fer a couple seconds. They meant ta hit us square on the stern, ta get our rudder.

"I reached around, feelin' in the daark fer Maatha and felt a limp body next to me. I gasped and reached fer it and it didn't move. T'was dead weight and suddenly I realized I was grippin' Connah's corpse. Son of a bitch, I was mistakin' it fer Maatha! The instant thaht realization came upon me, I heard her groan a few feet away. She was callin' Connah's name.

"Turn's out she banged 'er head against the binnacle when she fell. I think maybe she was out cold fer a couple seconds. I reached in the direction o' the sound and called 'er name. Thaht same moment I heard Bones stir. I turned to check on him and she grabbed holt o' me and wouldn't let loose. I called out ta Bones and he said he was okay."

Carter unconsciously gripped the wood of the seat where they sat. He shifted nervously, but remained silent as Patrick continued.

"'How much damage, Bones?' I aasked, then realized he probably couldn't see any bettah thahn me. 'Judgin' from the sound, I think we took a bahd hit, Patrick,' he said. I turned again to Maatha and aasked 'er ta go below fer a torch and ta listen in the aft cabin fer watah.

"Maatha pulled away without speakin', but I felt 'er anger. She weren't cryin' or fearful any more, don't ya know. I was afraid at thaht very moment she hahd become truly Irish, one whose hatred fer theah enemy hahd poisoned the blood, like the immortal poison of a vampire. I dreaded thaht thought and pushed it from my mind. No good could come of it. I turned ta figger what ta do next when all of a sudden an engine sounded again, roarin' above the storm.

"The wooden leviathan crashed onto our starboard quahter like Melville's white whale. I didn't know 'bout Bones, but I wasn't expectin' 'em baack so soon and hahdn't even got holt o' my carbine. Bones hahd though, and I heard the report. I saw the flash of six rounds fired in rapid succession, as faast as he could pump cartridges into the rifle's breech.

"Again theah was the horrible sound of breakin' wood and twistin' metal, and fer an instant, the loyalist boat hung on *Gael na Mara's* rail, tauntin' us, darin' us ta fight. I reached fer a winch handle. I was ready ta board the bloody thin'.

"Suddenly, I felt the monster begin to slide away. The second she was off, I crouched down to feel the damage and a dim light came on. It was Maatha with the torch. I turned ta take it from 'er and pointed the light at the damage.

"What I saw sent a wave o' dread ovah me. *Gael na Mara* was smashed bahd! The gunnels was crushed, the deck was stove in and, worst of all, I could make out sprung planks though they was above the watah line.

"I quickly leapt to the port rail to look at the damage from the first strike. It were just as bahd. Son of bitch, I remember thinkin', those bastahds are gonna do it! They aah goin' ta sink us!

"As I moved the light around ta inspect the damage, it crossed Bones' face. I saw in his eyes the same conclusion. We both realized if theah was anothah strike, it would be all ovah but fer the cryin'.

"I told Bones we should crank up the engine and try to meet the bastahds on the bow; *Gael na Mara* could take a beatin' on the bow. He nodded in acknowledgement. I realized he agreed more cause theah was nothin' else ta do than it bein' a good idear.

Eventually, the powah boat would out maneuvah the old girl anyway, especially if the sea went flat.

"I turned ta reach fer the engine start button, and no soonah thahn I touched the dahmn thin', the low life bastahds struck us again! Somehow, they must haav got on more way 'cause this time the whole of *Gael na Mara* shuddered from the impact. I couldn't believe the force, and thought fer sure thaht this time we was finished. I figgered we was dead men floatin' and it were only a mattah o' time afore all was lost. I kept thinkin' o' what ta do fer Maatha; some scheme ta save 'er life!

"When I regained control aftah the impact, I pressed the engine staaht button again and she cranked ta life. T'was just like we was out fer a Sunday sail. My spirit 'rose a notch. I was willin' ta accept any form o' victory about thaht time, even if it barely made any diff'rence.

"I reached fer the gear lever. About the instant I touched it, I felt a strange, muffled impact pound through *Gael na Mara* and my heart went ta my throat. I thought somethin hahd gone wrong when I engaged the engine; maybe the prop shaft hahd been bent or somethin'. Thaht same instant I realized our unwanted guest hahd lunged forward. She was bein' shoved anothah foot or so into us. It was thaht moment that it dawned upon me somethin else was goin' on.

"I turned to Bones and he looked at me. We both turned to see our enemy's hull as it began to draw slowly back down from its perch on our gunnels. It appeared to be down at the stern, much furthah down than it oughta. This made no sense. If she hahd holed herself crashin' against *Gael na Mara*, she would haav been down at the bows.

"'What the hell is goin' on?' Bones said. Then we heard the muffled roar of anothah engine. It came from faar off—behind our attacker. Then we heard a distant smashin' sound. T'was then we heard the sound of rifle fire, but it weren't comin' our way. A second later, the high bows of the loyalist boat crashed back into *Gael na Mara*, only not with nearly the force as before. 'She's bein' pushed!'

cried Bones. He hahd pieced together what was goin' on. 'It's Nolan,' he shouted, 'it's Nolan!'

"Sure I couldn't figger out what the hell he meant, laddie, me bein' quite a bit slower thahn Bones, don't ya know. 'It's Nolan, Pahtrick, he's rammin' the bastahds from astern,' he shouted in glee! 'I'll be damned,' I cried.

"Then theah was more rifle fire. 'Bones, theah shootin' aftah him. They're gonna kill 'im! We gotta do somethin', I hollered. We both aimed our carbines, but theah weren't anythin fer us ta shoot at. The bow o' the attacker's vessel was high on our gunnels and we was low in the cockpit.

"I climbed up on our port deck and crawled quickly along the cabin trunk. Once I was forward o' the main I could see thin's bettah. The light was now very dim, a deep charcoal gray. The rain was slowin' way down and the smell o' gun powdah and engine exhaust wafted through the air. I called baack fer Bones who was hollerin' ta Maatha ta fetch more rounds; to hand 'em up through the forward hatch.

"The faint light o' dawn began ta reveal what was goin' on. Better yet, because the attackahs was distracted, we were free again ta move about. From *Gael na Mara's* foredeck we were at a bettah angle and stood much higher thahn in the cockpit—enough so thaht our rifle fire could finally staaht ta do real damage. We began spittin' steady rounds into the powah boat's cabin house. We could see movement through the portholes.

"I realized I hahd left *Gael na Mara* in gear and when I looked baack I could see we was pullin' away from the attackers' vessel. They ignored us, or so it seemed. They was seriously preoccupied with Cousin Nolan's attack on theah stern, and they dahmn well should haav been. They were way down at the stern. Nolan, God bless 'im, must haav cracked 'er open with *Taisie's* hardened bow.

"Fer a couple minutes I got scared and worried fer Nolan 'cause the bastahds were firin' a lot o' rounds in his direction. We laid in a steady stream o' lead in an effort to draw theah attention. The forward hatch opened at our feet and Maatha started shovin' ammunition boxes on deck. I told 'er to go aft, take the wheel and spin us 'round ta starboard and tie 'er off, then stand by and stay out o' the line o' fire. We heard anothah crash. Nolan hahd struck again; what a lad!

"We looked ta see if we could see 'im and realized the loyalists hahd shot out the windows o' *Taisie's* bridge. Theah didn't appear ta be anyone at the helm. Fer a minute I thought they hahd kilt 'im. Sure then we saw his head pop up fer an instant and baack down again. He was stayin' low, the crafty buggah.

"*Taisie's* plumb bow was strong and the double plankin' did theah work, but I couldn't see how this was goin' ta last. She couldn't keep this up much longah. *Gael na Mara*, bein' free to move, turned ta starboard and set us broadside to the sparrin' vessels.

"I hollered fer Maatha to pull us out o' gear. Then Bones and I took covah behind the cabin trunk and fired our best broadsides ovah and ovah into the cowards' crippled vessel. *Taisie*, by this time, was clearly takin' on watah. In the faint light, we sawr 'er goin' down by the bows.

"I looked baack at the attackahs' vessel and the stern rail was in the watah, but it was hard ta say how long she could float like thaht. We must haav hit a couple o' the bastahds in the exchange o' gun fire 'cause their return fire slowed way down. Eithah thaht or they was busy tryin' ta figger a way ta save their miserable arses. Then somethin' happened I wasn't figgerin on!"

"*Taisie* lined up and charged again. She plowed through the thick gray watah real slow, like a tired old tug. We could see she didn't haav much way on, but she plowed ahead anyway. We wondered what Nolan was doin'. At thaht speed, rammin' the bastahds wouldn't o' hahd much effect.

"The next thin' ya know, we see a flame-like glint on board, inside *Taisie's* cuddy. I thought, son of a bitch, she's on fire! I motioned ta Bones who was layin' a steady stream of lead into the bastahds' vessel. He nodded grimly when he saw what I pointed at. We watched as the brightness of the flame grew in the gray dawn.

"As *Taisie* advanced on 'er objective, we then realized the flame was movin' 'round. It wasn't a dahmn fire on board aftah all. Nolan hahd holt o' a petrol bomb and was carryin' the dahmn thin' out on deck. A piece o' rag stuck out the top o' the bottle and was burnin' bright. We 'bout shat our pants.

"Within seconds, Nolan began crawlin' out onto *Taisie's* forward deck. She was lolled forward somethin' terrible, way down at the bows. We didn't think he could remain standin'. The bastahds on board the loyalist boat must haav realized what was goin' on and staahted firin' at him.

"We laid in rounds ta draw 'em off. This forced 'em back inside theah cabin ta take covah. Bones and I watched in horror as Nolan crawled belly down out toward his bow pulpit. He hahd the dahmn flamin' bottle in one hand. We thought fer sure he was goin to get himself burnt and theah would be nothin' we could do. In fact, worse was in the makin'. It became cleah thaht my battle-crazed cousin was going to ride *Taisie* straight into theah stern and lob the bottle o' flame onto the bastahds deck!

"But fer the fact we couldn't see a good end fer Nolan in this maneuver, we got the distinct impression this was definitely goin' to be the end fer the dirty cowards. We were even more convinced o' this outcome when, from across the short distance between our vessels, we suddenly smelt the deadly odor of petrol comin' up from the watah. It wafted through the morning air, horrifying and glorious at the same time. Nolan hahd bashed in theah fuel tanks and she was leakin' petrol all 'round us.

"Bones and me watched in utter shock as *Taisie*, my cousin riding 'er bow like Neptune on a Nautilus, drove straight up the bastahds' arses. Nary hahd a second passed and the tiny bottle of flames in Nolan's hand shot forward through the dawn sky. Afore even hittin the deck, the flame lit the petrol vapors floatin' above 'er. Theah was a tremendous whooshing sound thaht came as a ball o' flames roared skyward.

"The explosion was so bright and violent thaht Bones and I swung our arms up to covah our eyes. An instant later Maatha was on deck ta see what haapened. She turned in time ta see the hellish ball of orange and black flame rising above the stricken crafts. She screamed in unbridled horror, and this time theah was no stoppin' 'er. Bones rushed quickly aft to embrace his mortified daughtah, ta bring what comfort a fathah could.

"I went aft and untied the tiller. The two boats were completely engulfed in flames only a dozen yards off our starboard beam. I moved us away in case ammunition exploded on board. I searched the watah fer signs o' suhvivers. I sawr someone in the watah flailin' about and shouted ta Bones ta get me the glasses. I peered into the dull mornin' gray and found the hapless swimmer. It weren't Nolan and it weren't Miread so I left 'im ta drown. I kept movin' on. God save me, but I was in no fergivin' mood.

"I kept searchin' fer Nolan. Maybe I could retrieve his body or maybe I'd run onto Miread. With the lattah thought in mind I aasked Maatha if she would be willin' ta go below and prepare us a hot meal. I didn't want fer 'er ta see 'er dead mothah in the watah if I did come on to 'er. Everythin' would be okay I assured her. She went below and I moved *Gael na Mara* forward with the intent of commencin' a search pattern 'round the burnin' vessels.

"Not long afore I got 'round ta the other side of 'em I spotted a yellow life buoy. My heart suddenly raced. I realized it was *Gael na Mara's* buoy, the one Bones hahd cast off fer Miread! I reached fer the glasses. I screwed my eyes ta the lenses and found the speck of yellow. It was small in the watah. I could make out the shape of an arm clingin' ta it.

"I didn't know whethah or not it might be Miread! I prayed it would be. I couldn't be sure so I kept silent. I motored *Gael na Mara* in the direction o' the buoy. As I got neah my hopes raised. I thought I saw movement. If it was Miread, she was alive! I called fer Bones.

"I motioned out ahead and he stepped forward and up onta the cabin trunk. When he pieced together what was goin' on he quickly untied a boathook from *Gael na Mara's* starboard shroud. Just as quickly, I left the tiller and pulled a rope laddah from the lazarette and swung it ovah the rail. Seconds later, we were comin' along side. I slowed, then kilt the engine. We coasted forward, still unsure o' who we was seein' in the buoy.

"Just then, Maatha showed up on deck and she quickly figgered out what was goin' on. I cahn't say fer sure if she realized Bones and I thought perhaps the body in the ring was Miread. At thaht point it didn't mattah.

"Within a couple minutes we hauled Nolan on board *Gael na Mara* He was singed from stem ta stern, but still alive and breathin'. Sure we was glad to find the lad. I was relieved ta see Maatha leave 'er sorrows the instant she began doctorin' up our rescuer. Thaht don't mean any o' us were particulah happy, don't ya know. We hahd, howevah, lived ta fight anothah day and thaht is all a good soldier should expect."

Carter patiently listened as his friend finished his story. He relaxed in his seat, his anxiety subsiding.

"Fifty years later, the war may finally end, Caahtah, at least the war as I haav known it. What with Bones advisin' the Mitchell Commission and the British showin' more willin'ness to end the troubles, maybe it haasn't all been in vain."

Patrick exhaled a sigh that seemed to rid him of decades of pain. Carter sat watching. The old sailor took a turn looking out across Marblehead Harbor. It was framed with trees filled with spring flowers. Boats moved about like water bugs and a clear blue sky shown down upon the inlet.

Carter studied Patrick as a fluid calm visibly transformed his friend. He, too, felt a tremendous sense of relief as he gathered together their lunch bags. "Let's check on Ernie and his crew."

Patrick looked over at Carter, breaking his gaze across the harbor. He had expelled his story and his words seemed to waft across the great harbor and out to an uncaring sea. His face looked younger, his eyes clearer, his brow as smooth as a newborn's belly. Rising from their bench, the two sailors headed back to Old Town.

CHAPTER 37

AN ENDLESS CONTINUUM

Carter thought Patrick Timothy O'Clery never looked better. His step was high, his freckled face bright in the Marblehead sun.

Leaving Sewall Point astern, Carter and Patrick strode jauntily past Crocker Park. A mild spring breeze brushed their faces as they paced quickly along the cobblestone street. The temperature neared seventy-five degrees and the air was bone dry. Both sailormen were thinking "perfect varnish weather."

Arriving at the boat shed and passing through the wooden gate into the backyard, they greeted *Red Shoes* glistening cadmium red. Carter noticed the long row of *empty* lawn chairs and donut boxes half full of crullers and scones! Instead of sitting like an ornery men's choir, the Irregulars were crawling over *Red Shoes* like ants at a picnic.

Ernie skittered about them; foreman, leader and inspiration. Carter turned to Patrick. A grand smile spread broadly across the Taoiseach's suddenly youthful face. For the Irregulars, as well as Patrick, life would never be better. They worked together toward a single goal.

Carter watched the scene in silent wonder. He thought of the Mitchell Commission and the peace negotiations across the Atlantic. There too, in a place he could only imagine, droves of people strove toward a common goal. Like Patrick, they, too, were building, building something that would transform them, redeem them. They were building the prospect of peace.

This thought prompted him to get back on-line and check the progress of the talks. It was Tuesday, and Thursday was the deadline. Time was running out, just as it was for these old men. He wondered if, as were the Irregulars, Mitchell and the others were making their last moments count.

Carter turned to speak to Bones, but he was gone! He looked quickly in Patrick's direction, worried by the sudden disappearance and Patrick acknowledged his alarm.

"Well theah, laddie, he hahd to take a long distance call, don't ya know. Things aah heatin' up across the pond; he'll be baack theah, skippah!"

A clever smile crossed the old Irishman's face. Ernie barked out a call for more varnish and Patrick, the obedient yard hand now, turned to fetch it in the confines of his boat shed.

≋≋≋

While the crew worked tirelessly on *Red Shoes,* Carter walked around Old Town picking up equipment and hardware from various suppliers and chandleries. As he moved around the town, he detected a spark of interest regarding *Red Shoes'* progress.

The word leaked out that August 1 would see her down the ways. Carter gave a brief update on her progress to each merchant or supplier he visited.

"I'll settle up with Pahtrick later, son," would come the familiar reply when he tried to settle a tab.

"In faact, you cahn tell the old boy this will even the score fer the time bein'," more than one merchant explained, treating Carter like an old friend, issuing secretive, knowing smiles. The note of familiarity in their voices made Carter feel his acceptance, cementing his future in the tightly knit community.

Carter could barely contain his anticipation. He couldn't wait for his birthday to arrive. It would be more than a birthday; it would be the day *Red Shoes*' crew, his colorful New England family, returned to a world of ordinary existence. The day that normalcy, snatched from them fifty long years ago, would be theirs once again.

However, for *Red Shoes* to be a truly lucky ship, for Bones, Patrick and Martha to be truly free, he figured matters in Stormont needed to be resolved. His friends would only ever be as free as the collective people of Northern Ireland. If Nationalists and Unionists, Protestants and Catholics all succeeded in moving toward peace, then *Red Shoes* would be the luckiest ship on the water. He decided he would visit the computer station at the library the following morning.

≋≋≋

Carter was exhausted when he finally arrived at the B&B that evening. He intended to arrange a coincidental encounter with Claire, but the entire afternoon and evening flew by without a break. Arriving at the top of the steps of his loft, the ancient floor timbers creaked under his tired weight. Carter turned on the lamp next to his armchair. As gold light filled the room, he was surprised to see a small, portable, laptop computer sitting on the night stand.

Martha! She's at it again. How could she have known I have been searching the Internet?

Carter recalled once again her special gift. A broad smile stretched across his face. He opened the laptop computer and pressed the start button. The cold, silent box whirred to life and a bluish image appeared on the flat, iridescent screen.

Carter sat and drew the little computer onto his lap, realizing a telephone line had been attached. He was already rigged to surf the net. He no longer needed to be concerned about a computer being available at the crowded library. It was then he discovered his second surprise: an e-mail from Claire!

"You are welcome!" it said, in big colorful letters. When he moved the cursor butterflies and fairies trailed behind it. "I dropped this off for you to enjoy. A little birdie told me you like electronic toys. I hope you find it useful," her message read.

Carter moved the cursor again and smiled inwardly at the feminine colors and images. He continued reading.

"When I brought this by, Martha invited me to stay and enjoy tea with several interesting, unusual friends she was entertaining in her great-room. She graciously introduced me to each of them. They appeared to be gathered around a mysterious looking woman, Madame Russalka, they called her. She was a kindly *babushka* that reminded me so much of Mamie. I nearly cried when she spoke to me in broken English.

"They were all so very nice. I think Martha might have told them about you and me. We seemed to be the center of conversation. They were busy making blessings and imparting wisdom for our benefit, particularly Madame Russalka.

"At one point the old woman took my hand and held it very firmly, longer than one would have expected, longer than I was comfortable with. She studied my palm and I looked about the room and realized the entire group was somehow connected to her. They all seemed to be infusing their thoughts through her. It was strange; I guess you would have to be there to appreciate it. When the ancient woman finally released my hand, she wore a broad smile and bright sparkling eyes. It was extraordinary."

The message ended with an invitation: "I'll see you soon, Carter, and you can see me, too, up close, very close. Perhaps this weekend? Your detractor will be away. He frequently goes someplace on the South Shore and cavorts with his nasty friends.

"I hope you enjoy your computer, and, I suggest you not leave the unit connected to the Internet while you're away. We wouldn't want unwanted guests finding their way to you . . ."

Carter paused wondering what she may have meant by the remark, ". . . viruses and bugs and all that," her note went on to say.

Carter then replied with an immediate acceptance along with profuse gratitude for the excellent gift. As Claire had been correctly informed, he loved electronic gadgets. He wondered again who would have told her so. He could only think Martha must have been at work. She was the little bird, and he would thank her at breakfast.

≋≋≋

The following morning, Wednesday, April 8, Carter awoke bright and emboldened with the prospects of the day. It was 4:45 A.M. He looked forward to breakfast with Martha, coffee with Claire, then being on the water to check *Maxine*. Until breakfast was served, he sat in the dimly lit loft and worked at his new computer. It seemed the perfect time to search the Web.

He typed in RTE, Radio Telefis Eireann, the national broadcasting service of the Republic of Ireland. He placed it in his favorites. He repeated the same steps with the BBC and CNN. This would provide a rounded view of the peace negotiations, he concluded. To complete his inquiries, he would monitor English speaking short wave radio newscasts from other nations. Having a short wave on board *Maxine* made it easy.

As the laptop whirred while the system loaded, Carter thought about Bones and his role in the Mitchell Commission negotiations. He was hesitant to ask questions directly. He was afraid of being rebuffed, yet wanted to know how deeply Bones was involved. Was he in the middle or on the edge; did everyone seek his advice, or did he serve only one faction? Was he being protected by the U.S.; had Clinton ordered his protection? Had Senator Mitchell been told to seek his advice or had Bones engineered Mitchell's assignment to the Commission?

Exactly where did Bones stand in the labyrinth of secrecy and stratagems? The ancient Englishman hadn't mentioned any of this to Carter and there was a certain separation Bones maintained about some things. Aloofness was common in captains. The responsibility for critical decisions, often life or death, was theirs and theirs alone. They decided the ship's course, who would engage in battle, who would live or who would die. The ship's crew, no matter how trusted or loyal, decided nothing unless there was a particular need.

Although Carter hadn't been able to breech the subject of the peace talks, he didn't feel the same reticence in his desire to learn the full story behind the deaths of Miread and Conner. The turn of fate that resulted in his surrogate family's secret life in Marblehead seemed open for him to explore. When an opportunity availed itself, he would ask Bones to tell his story; then he would have three versions. The magic number would satisfy his curiosity and end his speculation.

≋≋≋

There are five hours difference between Northern Ireland and New England, and that meant it was already mid-morning at the negotiations. Talks would be moving ahead at full speed. The deadline for the end of the talks set by Senator Mitchell was tomorrow, Thursday, April 9.

On their Web site, CNN reported that Strand Two, the relationship between North and South Institutions, wasn't going well. The Irish and British governments were assigned to draft this strand, and their work went slowly.

The issues were complex. The Nationalists wanted strong North - South institutions; in fact, they would prefer to reunite with the South. The Unionists, however, feared this relationship and expected the British, and specifically, Prime Minister Tony Blair, to keep it from happening.

If North - South ties were strengthened, then Unionist factions believed they would lose privileges they now enjoyed as a majority. It would also denigrate the historical and, to them, essential relationship they maintained with England. They considered themselves British, not Irish. Strong ties to the South meant nothing to them.

According to CNN, when the position paper, drafted by Irish Taoiseach Bernie Ahern and Prime Minister Blair, was handed to the delegates, the Unionists declared, unequivocally, Strand Two was nothing but a "Nationalist wish list."

According to Ulster Unionist Party leader David Trimble, his party would walk out if Strand Two was not renegotiated. According to RTE, Trimble convinced Mitchell he wasn't bluffing and the BBC added that Mitchell asked Blair and Ahern to re-negotiate Strand Two.

According to the information Carter read on the screen of the glowing lap top, tension was high. Ahern effectively pitched Strand Two to the Nationalist delegates and he could have simply told Blair to go back and do a better job convincing the Unionists.

Conversely, Blair was in the peculiar position of being criticized for having been too accommodating. Blair realized the tight grip England historically held needed to be loosened. However, he was also a realist, and welcomed the opportunity to renegotiate in an effort to keep the Unionists in the peace talks.

Already a large segment of the pro-British community was outside the talks due to the withdrawal of Ian Paisley's Democratic Union Party. The DUP represents the most conservative faction of those who do not want to surrender their grip on Northern Ireland.

RTE reported that even though Blair was prepared to renegotiate, Ahern was in an incredibly delicate position. Renegotiation definitely meant the Nationalists would have to give something up if the Unionists were to maintain their position. This view tended to obscure the real issue: the gradual and sustainable evolution in both sides' belief systems. Mind sets, as Mitchell had pointed out a number of times, would need to change. This would take time, and necessitate, at least in some measure, the need to agree to disagree and continue moving ahead.

Carter moved the cursor to the "shut down" position and tapped the mouse pad twice. The machine whirred a few seconds longer, clicked, and then fell silent. He sat motionless for a moment, contemplating the coalescing paradigm he entered into that night in Boston when he accepted a kindly, but mysterious, Irishman's invitation to see *a schoonah abuildin'*.

Witches, terrorists, secret societies, peace negotiations—it was all too incredible. And Claire, how could he have ever dreamed of Claire?

How can all this be...how will it end?

It was after he thought those last words that he became suddenly aware of their absurdity.

Things don't simply end. Peace doesn't simply start or stop. Love isn't present then absent. All things lie in place on a continuum; his life, his yacht, his time amongst these strange and wonderful people—all were points along the way. His architecture, his designs, they all lie somewhere along an endless continuum. These secret people and their secret lives had opened his eyes to places and ideas he had previously never given a thought.

Martha's guttural voice rose from the base of the stairs and penetrated his contemplation. She called him to breakfast. He blinked away his wonderings and sat up quickly, lifting the computer from his lap and called down the steps, "I'll be right down Martha—coming right down."

CHAPTER 37

BETWEEN RED SHOES & MAXINE

The order to steam south and lie off Marblehead came as no surprise to Captain Donovan. He already pieced together what was taking place and who it involved. This time, instead of only receiving data from the vast ether of space, he sent his own message. He was compelled to act.

It's the Irish in me.

They were close to an agreement in Stormont and the Figurehead could use all the help he could get. Running interference, even modest in scope, seemed the least he could do, particularly from his unique position.

His personal transmission, or rather his truncated series of transmissions, each sent in different electronic medium, would be extremely difficult for his superiors, or anyone else, to discern. He learned a trick or two over the years.

The message itself was innocuous. He ordered a gift, a laptop computer; that was all. His frequent communication with people in Marblehead to arrange his membership at the East Harbor Yacht Club made shore-side communications appear commonplace. Soon, in less than six weeks, his Hinckley would be tied up on her new mooring just off the dock at the EHYC. Then he would be free to cruise and contemplate all the questions building in his mind. Once free of the service, he could make direct contact. He could actually observe on the ground, or on the water as it were, the people he had become so curious to know.

He was well aware of *Red Shoes*' launching date. The spy ship captain even knew her assigned mooring in Marblehead Harbor. *Cassiopeia's* newly acquired mooring was purposely positioned near the coasting schooner. In fact, he arranged for *Cassiopeia* to swing on a can right between *Red Shoes* and *Maxine*.

It was strange, he thought, that he had become so interested in the welfare of the young lake captain. It was even stranger he had gone so far as to arrange for the laptop computer to be gifted to him, all in an effort to keep him out of the public library. Donovan suspected the curious, even naïve, young man would fare poorly amongst the insidious circle of people associated with what was taking place in and around Marblehead, South Boston, and Belfast. Particularly in such close proximity to O'Neil.

That bastard is blight on the Irish name. What were they thinking when they enlisted his help?

He felt good that he took a small step to buffer the innocent lad from the rising threat. He'd take a bigger one if he could. He was certain of the inevitable misconduct of some of those with whom the young man inadvertently became close.

Further, Donovan could hardly believe his own government formed alliances with the likes of the untrustworthy bastards from the South Shore. He suffered an exceedingly bad feeling about the whole affair. This kind of subterfuge would end roughly and he saw no reason for the lake captain to become a victim. Donovan saw in the young man his lost youth. He saw a free spirit, an adventurer pursuing his course in life. It appeared to Donovan, at least for the time he tracked the lake sailor's activities, that up until now Carter Phillips was as free as the wind that filled *Maxine's* sails.

Donovan was frustrated that he had spent his life serving under someone higher than he—someone always telling him what to do, when to do it, or how to do it. By contrast, the lake sailor seemed gloriously liberated as he, too, would soon be, for the first time in his life—only a few weeks away.

CHAPTER 39

THE OFFSPRING OF LORD NELSON

Bones Matheson bit the stem of his pipe and shifted in the wheel-mounted chair as Carter spoke his request. Bones smiled inwardly. Martha and Patrick both had sought his advice prior to telling Carter their versions of the story.

Bones gave the matter considerable thought and told them an explanation was due the young captain. Carter exhibited an uncanny curiosity. Bones was aware of the Internet searches, the questions around town, even intelligence reports he was shown by colleagues. All these things suggested the lad was capable of piecing information together on his own.

Bones figured that if he wanted to keep Carter out of trouble, particularly until an agreement was reached, parceling out a limited amount of information would be prudent. This would satiate his curiosity for a short time, at least. Threats of violent reprisals were pervasive; they were all, including Carter, at risk to some degree. The danger increased in probability the closer the goal was reached in Stormont. Despite island-wide support, attributable in great part to Bones' secret efforts, incorrigible splinter groups conducted the business of terrorism as usual.

Fortunately, Bones noted in Carter a remarkable propensity for loyalty and trust. Bones knew the arms dealer who befriended Carter in Florida—M . J. Maxfield. He was an individual Bones knew he could rely on for information. He had corresponded with Maxfield immediately after Patrick mentioned Carter's surprising reference to his old compatriot, one day at Sewall Point. He knew the level of caution Maxfield fastidiously practiced. He was well aware of the dealer's penchant for recognizing trouble at its earliest juncture. If Maxfield trusted Carter, that alone spoke volumes.

However, as with most good things, Carter came with a price. The young architect was compulsively curious. It was only a matter of time, Bones figured, before the lake captain would come to him for his version of what occurred that black night off the Northwest coast of Ireland.

≋≋≋

"Caahtah," the old seaman began, "I cahn see you 'ave hahd somethin' ta do with the Irregulahs comin' 'round actin' useful instead of cryin' on all the time. Ernie's a bleedin' good mate. He's been squirmin' around in 'is lawn chair for months.

"If ya think baack, though ya 'ave only been with us a short while, the bloody chap nevah did most the complainin'. It was the othahs thaht tended to sod about, not Ernie. If I hahdn't been so pre-occupied with things lately, I should 'ave nudged him ta crack on myself."

Bones turned toward Carter.

"But I didn't son—you did! Ya kept your eyes open; ya took hold of the situation. Ya changed the situation and made it bettah. Ya did it naturally, without connivin' and manipulatin'. Ya might think nothin' of it, my boy, but I 'aapen ta know thaht changin' things for the bettah requires awareness, undahstandin' and a measure of diplomacy I'll wager ya didn't realize ya even hahd!"

Carter looked up as they sat by the boat shed's coffee pot. He deftly avoided the muddy stimulant. He looked at Bones in acceptance of the compliment, surprised his elder had taken notice.

"When ya detect compassion in the bleedin' air, son, it is time ta put the mockers on and ease the tiller. It is time ta fall off a point or two and allow some of it ta fill your jibs'l. The wind o' compassion cahn save a lost sailah, my boy, it can lift ya from the doldrums, of thaht I cahn attest." Then under his breath Bones muttered, "Particularly since it is so dahmn easy ta lose—ta lose what compassion ya might 'ave been born wif."

Bones rolled his wheel-mounted chair closer to Carter. "It cahn be stolen from ya, son. It cahn be swept away on a cold wind, like thaht unpleasant episode you experienced last week aboard *Maxine*.

"However, like last week, the heat of compassion cahn be infused baack into ya. Like last week, it's often necessary for someone else to put it baack inside ya. Sometimes, like the heat ya lost ta thaht cold March mornin', anothah body haas to be theah ta save ya. It cahn be regained, it's not an impossibility, though some people, like thaht coffee roaster thaht employs your pretty maiden, appear lost without the hope of redemption—wandering daft in the cold abyss of prejudice and discontent."

Carter agreed entirely with the elder statesman's observation. He was surprised, however, by the reference to the irascible roaster. He hadn't made a connection between Bones and the ornery malcontent. He had no recollection of Bones patronizing the Marblehead Roasting Company. He wondered how or why he knew the hostile Mr. O'Neil. Then he contemplated how long the old counselor lived in this seemingly innocuous enclave. It was apparent, Bones knew just about everyone.

"How does what I'm babblin' about explain the night things went so bloody bahd out theah on the north Atlantic? Well, son, I'm gettin' to thaht. Howevah, to undahstand the context, ta understand the outcome, ya 'ave to undahstand what P.G. Woodhouse once said—'theah aah circles within circles, my boy . . . theah aah circles within bloody circles."

Carter sat upright in his chair when he heard those words.

Claire used that same analogy!

His surprise attracted Bones' attention. Carter realized how noticeable his reaction had been and he attempted to hide it by leaning over and drawing a cup of coffee. When the coffee reached the brim of his cup he set the pot down and leaned back into his chair. In the few seconds that passed he convinced himself this had been no coincidence. He never heard that humorous analogy before; why would both Bones and Claire use it in such close proximity in time and place? Perhaps it was merely a local colloquialism.

Put it aside; don't disrupt Bones with spurious inquiries.

Still, he made a mental note to return to the coincidence later; perhaps ask Claire a few questions.

"I suppose what I'm tellin' ya, son, is thaht a human bein' can lose compassion when things they cahn't control overwhelm 'em. A giddy kipper cahn be gettin' along in life, growin' up with family, and mates, fit as a butcher's dog, then suddenly, without warnin', 'ave his bleedin' tranquility blown ta bloody pieces—destroyed forevah.

"A bleedin' bomb, fer example, a bleedin' bomb cahn tear a person from the sanctuary of normal life and transform them into a cold shell of theah previous self. It's a horrible thin', what a bloody bomb does to those left standin', Caahtah."

Bones looked up into his brow, then looked down and air wheezed from him like steam exhausting from a tired locomotive.

"Blown ta bloody pieces," the ancient mariner repeated.

The lake sailor winced at the pain in Bones' throaty words. Bones rolled his chair over to the coffee pot and refilled his brown-stained cup. He looked back at Carter and changed directions in his story. It reminded Carter of Patrick. He wondered who picked up the habit from whom.

"When ya was a little nipper baack in Michigan, son, did your daad evah show ya how ta build a crystal radio?"

Carter smiled and nodded. He remembered his dad showing him a torn-out page of an electronics magazine that listed all the parts needed to build a simple listening device. His father then reached into his pocket and handed him a small yellow envelope that contained a crystal he acquired from a friend who was a ham radio operator. Carter's recollection was interrupted as Bones spoke again.

"Me too, son. It was a fascinatin' thing, and with it I could bloody well hear radio broadcasts cleah from across the English Channel. In faact, with thaht little radio, I began listenin' to the war ragin' on the continent. World War I. I listened and I learned; and what I learned was the details of makin' war. I learned about strategy and maneuvers; about bombin' and mustard gas. Things no little buggah should 'ave been concerned with.

"It was at thaht time I also learned, the hard way, the worst way, thaht horrible things cahn happen to the innocent, to the unsuspectin' and fate will 'ave its way, Caahtah. Fate will 'ave its way."

Carter saw a dark glaze envelope the old man's eyes; the skin around his salt and pepper beard appeared sullen and gray.

"Very burdensome, son, troublesome fragments of knowledge as I think baack on them," Bones said with a somber voice. "I cahn attest, I cahn signify, theah aah terrible effects from a bomb thaht extends faar beyond the blast. Those secondary effects cahn twist a growin' child's life into somethin' awful, somethin' uncontrollable, somethin' ta fear; and in a short time thaht is what I became. Thaht is what the bloody bomb thaht killed sweet Winnie did to me."

There was a long silence as Carter tried to imagine Bones as dangerous and fearsome. The Bones Carter knew was rich in wisdom and benevolence, not belligerence and foreboding. Nonetheless, Carter imagined a man of ninety years most likely had been many men and done many things.

"I am aware, Caahtah, thaht you 'ave made a study of the numbah three. You aah quite right ta do so. Tis a magical numbah, indeed. I value the numbah highly myself. In faact, I nevah let anythin' happen more thahn three times, good or bahd, without doin' somethin' about it," the ancient seaman explained with a wink and nod.

"Three times I've experienced circumstances thaht came entirely by surprise. Three times, like tidal waves tryin' to swamp me, I've hahd to confront treachery so malevolent thaht I cahn't believe I survived to tell about it, and I normally don't tell. Seein' how curious you aah, Caahtah, I'm gonna make an exception."

Carter tried to look appreciative, but remained silent.

"While the buggery of fate played merry hell with the ones I loved, I was nevah directly afflicted. I 'ave nevah been bombed, nevah shot, nevah fallen overboard; yet I 'ave witnessed all those things 'aapen to my people, the people I loved.

"I've been the last bugger standin', been left behind, dashed in spirit, yet physically unharmed. I've been doomed to crack on, live the next day and the day aftah thaht, even when I bloody dahmn well didn't want to—even when I'd 'ave preferred to 'ave been dead. It seems like an eternity thaht I've bore the weight of those incredible occurrences. The thin's I've done in response . . . well, they were the manifestation of revenge, and now those thin's, too, 'ave become a heavy burden of which I alone bear.

"In hindsight, 'tis plain ta see I went too bloody faar, the same as the otherwise good people of Northern Ireland. I was the cause of a great amount of my troubles, just as they aah of theahs. I realize, looking baack, thaht when I learned of Winnie and Kevin's murdah I went barmy, something snapped in my adolescent mind. All of a sudden, my mind was consumed with a black bile, thoughts no adolescent should evah think.

"From thaht point on, my imagination poured forth with ways to avenge my sistah's murdah. The more I contemplated the poor gul, my own flesh and blood bein' blow apart with huhr little seed growin' inside, the deeper and more concentrated became my hatred. Thaht's when the lessons gained through thaht crystal radio solidified. I began hatchin' plots and schemes. In time, Caahtah, I put them inta motion. In time, revenge became a bloody obsession."

Bones shifted uncomfortably in his wheel-mounted chair. Carter thought for a moment he wouldn't continue and would roll back to the masts where Ernie's crew laid on another coat of varnish.

"You may be interested in knowin', Caahtah, thaht despite infamous deeds in this insidious endeavor, revenge as an emollient is as crooked as a nine-bob note. I know today, though I didn't baack then, thaht it accomplishes nothin'. It did not obviate my anguish. If anythin', it carried me furthah away from a reasoned perspective. In retrospect, I cahn see thaht the only thing revenge accomplished was delayin' the time it would take me to regain a propaah state of mind."

Bones paused to re-light his pipe.

"Thaht bomb, Caahtah, thaht bloody chuffin' bomb, did more thahn kill those innocent families in thaht pub. It destroyed the home and hearth of those left behind.

"Mum and Da nevah was able to comprehend what 'aapened. They weren't young; they weren't able to find shelter in the devisin' of plots and seekin' revenge. They stood naked in theah sorrow and, eventually, the cold rains of despair sickened them. Theah very thoughts became a disease thaht killed 'em, same as if they were blown to shreds by thaht bloody explosion thaht killed theah only daughtah."

Bones drew the pipe from his lips and knocked white ash into an ashtray lying next to the coffee pot. Reaching around behind him he withdrew a folded bag of shag tobacco from his trouser pocket. He tamped in a fresh charge while continuing his oration.

"It was a numbah of years later thaht the second tidal wave struck. It too, like Winnie's death, nearly sunk the ship of my existence. I was workin' as a merchant marine ta stay alive. There was no inheritance, no eatin' from a silver spoon. I was alone in the world and hahd ta work ta earn my keep.

"I didn't mind workin' though; in fact, I believe work has been the iron thaht's kept my blood red. But bein' pressed into a lonely existence by a bomber I nevah knew, for a cause I hahd no part of, was dauntin'. I wanted answers, I wanted to know why, why me?

What hahd I evah done to deserve such a bloody fate? What good would evah come of it?

"Eventually, those questions took me ta sea. In a young man's mind grows the idear thaht somewheah out theah on the watah the answer to all questions cahn be found. Somewhere across the vast oceans is the progenitor of universal knowledge, and, Caahtah, you of all people, bein' a sailor, a captain of thaht fine yacht, you know well of what I speak.

"I found somethin' out theah on the watah all right, son. I made an incredible discovery, or perhaps it might be bettah stated thaht it found me. Through extraordinary chance events, I learned my own countrymen, Englishmen, thaht is, hahd plotted the murderin' of my sistah and 'er family. My own people, Caahtah, Mothah England; the offspring of Lord Nelson, for God's sake! The bloody descendents of the authors of the Magna Carta! What on earth hahd come ovah 'em? What the hell were they thinkin'?"

The great barrel chest of the old seaman collapsed in a thick breath of exasperation. Carter watched his elder intently. Bones recovered, unwilling to give in to his frustration, exhibiting the fortitude of his ninety years. He hesitated only long enough to regain his comportment.

"Before I became acquainted with Patrick's uncle, Samuel Clark, the man who blew the gaff, I hahd no cleah idear who it was I needed ta kill to avenge my lost family. All I knew was thaht someone was responsible. I also knew thaht the individual, the physical instrument of theah death, was already dead. Like Joseph Conrad's secret agent, he too was blown ta pieces. The bomber thaht killed my sistah took 'er and many othah innocents wif him, the barmy bastahd! This played merry hell on me. Who would suffah my wrath? Who would pay the fiddlah?

"T'was Samuel Claark discovered theah was more to the deaths thahn met the eye. There hahd been a conspiracy. Plenty othahs hahd been involved in the plannin' and killin'. I learned somethin' else, too, somethin' thaht caused me great vexation. I learned it was true thaht the McCreesh docks hahd been used ta land contraband weapons!

"This fact was a terrible blow to my righteous indignation—to my belief thaht they were all innocent. I suppose if I was pressed to declare the one thing I know about Northern Ireland, it is thaht no one is entirely innocent. No one is entirely without blood on theah hands . . ."

Carter found Bones' words difficult to accept. He never believed entire societies could be bad; misled by bad leadership, perhaps, but not bad as Bones was suggesting. Bones must have seen the doubt in his young protégés eyes.

"Well, maybe I'm reaching to make a point, son. Whatevah the case, I'll admit thaht learnin' thaht the McCreesh's ran guns took some time ta work through. Even if the local mates hahd been off loadin' guns, I believed then and still do. Targeting innocents for murder is criminal—fiendishly criminal. Murderin' innocents to induce terror is wrong, regardless of who does it.

"There was a lot going on ovah theah durin' those times. There haas been much confusion and presumption on all sides for a very long time, longer than any livin' bein' can recount, bejesus! Eventually, howevah, with Samuel's help, I bloody-well pieced together the enormity of the conspiracy.

"By the time all aspects of the disastah were revealed, I hahd to accept thaht theah would be scant opportunity to reach my goal of biblical revenge; an eye for an eye and all thaht. It would be hard, if not impossible, to find, punish, and then walk away from the dozens of people involved. Patrick and Martha haav told me they both talked to you about Samuel Claark."

Carter nodded.

"Then you aah already aware thaht he was a man of enormous stature and intellect. His mind nevah ceased its workin's. Despite the fact thaht no one cahn be right all the time, no one cahn predict the confluence of events occurring in space or change the gravitational pull of complex interactions, he came bloody close.

"As I've explained, it was Samuel who discovered what happened to Winnie and it was Samuel who ultimately contrived a plan to open the doors I thought I needed to open to achieve my single goal. He figured it out. He pieced it together as papeh crossed his desk. Then, as he intended, that is, according to his plan, I became his associate. I am also 'appy to say, even proud to say, thaht I also became his friend.

"You see, Caahtah, Samuel Claark did not reveal what he hahd discovered to simply open a pathway for me to gain revenge, although thaht is initially how I responded. Samuel hahd a much different reason in mind. It was Samuel who introduced me to a faar more complex form of battle thahn my self-schoolin' in the arts of strategy hahd previously devised. My personal lust for revenge was base by comparison. What he hahd in mind was faar more sophisticated. It required creative thinkin', mathematical calculation, and deduced reckonin'. What he intended was brilliant and momentous, and did not require torturin' and killin' people as our enemy remained so willin' ta do.

"As I learned of his intent and his plans, I came to accept thaht my original goal, the pursuit of plain revenge, was merely a sign of immaturity, not determination, and certainly not honor. I immediately recognized the value of what Samuel was contrivin', that is, social change through political and economic means. He stood as the first person I encountered durin' those times who openly distained the misguided, malevolent practice of killin' as a means for achievin' political power. He hahd thought paast such folly. I thank God thaht fate brought us together when it did. I would 'ave eithah given way to madness or I would surely 'ave died tryin'. I'm alive today because this noble man intervened when he did."

Carter was paying strict attention now.

"In a brief time, I became aware thaht Samuel Claark hahd significant political and financial support—support from high levels. People with money and influence also saw what I saw. Important names, figures in this country's hidden power structure, were bloody-well intrigued by the strikin' charactah of the man—his clarity of mind, the indisputable logic of his proposals. As fate would 'ave it, one of these prosperous and influential men would be the one who fathered the nipper I would later fall in love with and marry. He was Miread's sire, Doctor Daniel Patrick Callahan.

"Callahan was an extremely wealthy Bostonian, a physician and a scholar. When I finally met Doc Callahan, I realized the likelihood of achievin' a higher purpose in life. It was miraculously within my grasp. Thaht was when the false idol of gross revenge lost its deceivin' attraction."

Carter was beginning to understand the transition this meant for Bones. He could see the transformation from avenger to counselor had been profound.

"Unfortunately, despite the richly rewarding relationship thaht emerged between Samuel, Doc, and me, the implementation of thaht which we all conspired to achieve still manifested itself in extraordinarily dangerous maneuvers.

"You see Caahtah, the opposition still recklessly wielded guns. Thaht's wheah the Red-Haired Boy and his half brother, Connah, come baack into the picture I'm tryin' ta draw for ya."

Carter had never heard Patrick referred to by this descriptive moniker, the Red-Haired Boy.

Bones smiled. "Pahtrick and his half-brother were fearless men. Pahtrick still is. I would not advise confusing his spells of passion as signs of weakness."

Bones accompanied this observation with a look of thoughtful warning as Carter recalled the encounter between Patrick and the coffee roaster that first morning they met at the Marblehead Roasting Company.

"It was Pahtrick and Connah thaht became the physical arm of our threesome's campaign. Of the two, it was Connah, as you may 'ave surmised, who was given to revisit his innate malevolence once provoked. It was no surprise thaht the butcher's bill for this sad deficiency was paid early on. He was a good mate, nevertheless, and a colorful, exciting young man. I felt proud when he married my daughtah, Maatha, as you haav learned.

"The third treacherous tidal wave washed ovah me when I lost Myriad and Connah, both in one fatal night, on board *Gael na Mara*. Thaht vessel reminds me of 'em each time I cast my eyes upon 'er. I cahn't be aboard 'er without goin' barmy, yet I cahn't be without 'er. It's a hell of a dilemma and therein lies the importance of Captain Ryan O'Malley. He keeps 'er afloat. He sails 'er in my absence; he keeps Miread and Connah on the water, alive in the wind and in my memory."

"Today, Pahtrick haas charted a different course, he haas decided to forsake brute violence, and more important, to end his clan's part in it. Perhaps it was the loss of 'is brothah thaht did it. It's hard ta say. People like Pahtrick aren't quick ta forget.

"Perhaps ovah time, Caahtah, our mutual friend haas simply become braver and smaarter thahn the rest. Cowardly and afraid? No suh, thaht shall not be the epithet of the Taoiseach of the ancient O'Clery clan. It is a fearless, wiser man thaht sets down his bleedin' arms at the strategic moment."

Bones turned and leaned forward toward Carter, rolling his wheeled chair within Carter's personal space, the space only a friend or perhaps a grandfather can occupy.

"I shall be long gone, Caahtah. I will not be heah to see thaht epithet engraved on Pahtrick O'Clery's gravestone. The task will 'ave to fall on someone youngah, someone like you, son. Someone who undahstands what haas 'aapened heah; someone who knows the magnitude of Pahtrick's selfless act and what it will mean to those innocents who won't be blown to pieces, not like poor Winnie. Do ya undahstand what I'm aaskin', Caahtah? Do ya undahstand yer bloody importance?

"What Pahtrick is doin', de-commissionin' the secret paramilitary thaht became his clans' legacy, is why we aah at the negotiatin' table in Stormont. It is why theah is a spaark of hope. The issues aah complex, exceedingly complex; howevah, de-commissionin' is the single most significant reason an agreement will be reached in Stormont. Without it, we get nowhere. Without it peace talks will be only thaht: interminable, ineffectual talk. Won't mattah if an agreement is signed or not. Complete de-commissionin', even if it takes time, is the ultimate truth of our success. Pahtrick Timothy O'Clery and the O'Clery clan are the wellspring from which the watah of success shall soon be drawn!"

CHAPTER 40

CAPTAIN OF THE AFTERGUARD

"Anger is an irrational state of bein', Caahtah. We all know it, but thaht doesn't stop us from sufferin' it. As adults, we learn to control it, but when we're young, bejesus, thaht's anothah mattah altogethah," Bones continued. When Winnie was murdered, I felt anger as if it were the only feelin' possible. I was too young and faar too angry ta be left alone with my thoughts. My parents, without meanin' any haahm, offered little support, and in time, my agitated mind grew worse.

"My anger rose in those early years and my hatred malformed into a mountin' lust for revenge. I became focused upon a singular goal and the rightness or wrongness of thaht goal was nevah corrected by an adult. I nevah talked to anyone about it; parent, teacher, nor vicar. No one stepped forward and told me plainly thaht thaht kind of thinkin' was wrong, thaht revenge is a like the sirens of old, drawin' sailahs toward inevitable doom.

"I needed guidance; someone needed to take my helm; someone needed to lead me through the labyrinth of anger and despair. Someone needed to guide and inspire, to teach a young nipper the futility of unbridled anger. It nevah 'aapened when I was young, but eventually thaht was the role my friend and mentor, Samuel Claark, assumed."

Bones paused as if thinking a spurious thought. When it seemed to gel in his mind, he looked at Carter and spoke.

"I would point out, son, thaht much of the story I just told is allegorically true of Northern Ireland as well. Thaht place and its people haas been blown apart by relentless explosions—bombin's, murdahs, and beatin's. The sufferers of thaht horror aah angry beyond the comprehension of ordinary folks.

"Like myself in the days of Southsea, they 'ave no parents eithah, so to speak, no adult ta guide them through theah anger. Due to the fractious bleedin' history of the place, it haas become an island devoid of a unifyin' leadership. As Pahtrick haas pointed out, the place haas nevah enjoyed a constitution, a single guidin' point of inspiration. No individual haas evah risen to the dauntin' task of capturin' all theah loyalty, all theah allegiance."

Carter understood his point, and nodded.

"In time, my anger was diffused and guided in a productive direction, but not till I realized the similarities between my life and those hapless people of thaht bloody island. I came to undahstand thaht my personal and their collective experiences were analogous. They wanted, as I did, for a process, a way of bein' thaht will deliver them from their nightmare. Thaht, my son, is comin' close to takin' place in Stormont."

As Bones paused to draw air through his pipe, Carter waited, thinking to himself. It dawned on him he was expecting a story from Bones similar to Pahtrick's—guns blazing, heroes ramming an evil enemy's boat. It appeared instead that they were each telling a different story; the one each held inside them, each unique.

For Bones, that black night resulted in more than the death of his American wife and a narrow escape for him and his daughter. For Bones, it was the commencement of a profound change in thinking, a defining moment. It changed his role in the conflict from avenger to counselor. He could thank Samuel Clark for this change and Doc Callahan for the financial resources to support it. His new work would be resolving conflict, not perpetuating it.

In doing so, and particularly after Clark and Callahan's passing, Bones became the captain of the afterguard from whom presidents and prime ministers sought guidance. He stood on the quarterdeck of a vessel racing toward peace, guiding the helmsman as he steered the craft onward. He watched over the shoulder of the navigator and infused confidence and fortitude into the captain, all the while remaining hidden in the background.

Bones moved to work his pipe. The motion jolted Carter back from his thoughts. After a couple of seconds of drawing air over white ash, Bones lifted the pipe from his thick crusty lips and continued.

"People in Northern Ireland live next to each othah in theah physical bodies, yet do so in separate states of mind. They aah a disconsolately polarized society; bloody angry with each othah and in many ways they dahmn well haav a right to be—both sides, Caahtah, the Protestants and the Catholics."

Bones' unabashed observation surprised Carter. He expected no sympathy for the Protestant loyalists who were at the center of the destruction of Bones' family in England.

"I would point out, son, thaht it's easy to find sympathy for the minority, the oppressed. Speakin' first hand, it feels good ta crack on and fight for the rights of the subjugated. But contemplate the problem from the othah point of view. Think of it from theah perspective. Separate the history and the rhetoric and picture yourself in the position of a bleedin' Brit tryin' to stay alive and raise a family in thaht partitioned land they insist on callin' theah home. These aah the scions of empire buildahs. They ahn't ashamed of occupying a foreign land, they aah proud of it. They believe they 'ave brought prosperity and innovation to a god-forsaken place thaht hahd none. They believe theah ancestors hahd a right to expand theah borders and bring with thaht expansion freedom, opportunity and wealth.

"These heah United States aah a splendid example of the very point of which I speak, bejesus! Look how things 'ave worked out heah. I've witnessed first hand the remnants of the Indian reservations. It's a faar worse record of oppression and dominance thahn anythin' you cahn point to by the Protestants in Northern Ireland."

Bones paused to allow his words to be absorbed.

"Ovah the yeahs of my life, I've found and continue to find the special truth of Northern Ireland. I accomplish this by 'aavin' gained an objective viewpoint. I found high terrain thaht later became the soil from which grew a broader undahstandin' of the troubles.

"'Tis like those fig trees Madame Rusalka and Maatha persuaded ya to plant in front of the B&B. Life cahn coexist undah extraordinarily contradictory conditions. Theah aah ways for the most divergent, most unlikely species to find common ground and prospah in what might initially be considahed impossible conditions.

"You, my young friend, ya come by this ability to see into thin's naturally. Perhaps it was thaht ahchitectural training, I d'know. More likely it's thaht incessant curiosity thaht bleeds from your bein' like the blood from the hands of thaht statue in Mexico.

"When Madame Russalka posed 'er clevah riddle, t'was you thaht proceeded unfettered to define the solution. Ya laid out a plan to enable fig trees to grow in Marblehead! Thaht was good son, bloody good. I cahn't help but think thaht feat cahn be attributed to your willin'ness ta listen ta othahs when they speak, ta learn from othahs when they impart knowledge. Then ya cracked on and applied what ya'd learned to circumstances as contradictory as Madame Russalka's amusing conundrum."

Carter modestly passed over the compliment. He remained silent and continued to listen.

"Thaht bein' the case, if we apply thaht same logic to Northern Ireland, I think ya too cahn see what I began ta see undah Samuel Claark's tutelage—thaht once dozens of generations o' families 'ave been born and live on foreign soil, the place transforms.

It changes in expansive ways, and changes of thaht magnitude simply cahn't be wished away. They cahn't be ignored, and most of all, they cahn't be undone or controlled by walls and barriers.

"The people who consider themselves loyal ta thaht bloody island next to 'em, my homeland, deserve the right ta live in the midst of the altered place we call Northern Ireland. The remaining challenge, the only rational thin' ta do in thaht case, is to devise a process thaht will become, as it evolves, a more peaceful, productive coexistence."

Bones leaned back once again. He touched his pipe as if that alone would keep it lit. Carter appeared convinced that peaceful coexistence was the only realistic outcome of the troubles in Northern Ireland. Bones continued.

"Ah but son, now comes the English, Lord Muck, the greatest and the worst of modern societies. They 'aavn't bloody helped mattahs ovah theah despite theah own love and hate for the place. In faact, it is arguable thaht their ambivalence haas been a considerable factor in the island's tortured history. Why did they evah occupy it in the first place; 'ave you evah aasked yourself thaht question?

"The island is romanticized today; song, dance, art and all thaht taken at face value is true. But ya might remembah the bloomin' place is a bog, a barren, windswept land; still they hahd to 'ave it. Once they took it, they needed to maintain control or the peoples of the north would continue southward as the Vikings hahd done in times paast. The island was doomed to become part of the imperial expansion thaht Great Britain perpetrated on lands as faar as Captain Cook could plant a flag. Cleah ta the Maldives for Christ's sake, cleah ta the Maldives!"

The old counselor shook his head as he gripped the pipe in his thick leathery hand.

"In time, the place became devoted to Catholicism. While I maintain no ties to organized religion, I cahn't ignore both the good and bahd it renders upon society. In theah zeal to sanctify life, the good people of theah persuasion 'ave nevah gained a cleah undahstandin' between birth control and ovah population. It's incredible if ya think about it. The outcome haas been a barren rock, overcrowded with people faar greatah in numbers thahn sustainable by any logical measure.

"Some argue thaht overpopulation was the fertile ground from which the great famine grew! It was not a mere crop failure. Gross overpopulation, thaht is, no attempt whatsoever at controllin' birth, bloody well hahd somethin' ta do with it.

"But theah were othah reasons as well, and here again is wheah British complacency, perhaps culpability, is bound ta be discovered. Were you aware, Caahtah, thaht tons o' food was exported from Ireland durin' the great famine? The bloody fools conducted export trade as if nothin' was takin' place.

"A lack of understandin' and timely response by British overlords contributed as significantly as the bloomin' fungus thaht wiped out the potato crops. By the time the British finally responded, they did too little too late."

Carter listened intently, although he had previously picked up fragments of this information on the Internet. He wondered at the time about the veracity of the blame attributed to the British. He realized the Web, as powerful and accessible as it was, enjoyed no peer review.

He wasn't entirely certain Bones was correct either. He obviously wielded an axe to grind with England. Carter felt an atavistic attachment to England, perhaps even a diffuse loyalty. He wondered if Bones was aware thaht he had been raised Protestant. Carter recollected how his Protestant upbringing was subtly detected by the Catholics at the University of Notre Dame as a graduate student.

Lost in these thoughts, Carter suddenly noticed Bones reaching for his ear while cocking his head in a strange manner. The movement was unnatural. At first he worried something life threatening might be happening to Bones, that he might be having a stroke or seizure. A jolt of adrenalin spurt into his blood. He checked his anxiety after a couple seconds as he realized Bones was merely adjusting a hearing aid.

Bones was listening to something, his mind totally occupied and his eyes pointed off into space. He gazed blankly for a moment and then noticed Carter quizzically watching him. While pressing the object into his ear with his right hand the old sailor raised his left with his first finger in a gesture indicating he wanted Carter to hold on for a minute. Seconds continued to pass and a somber look clouded Bones eyes. He was no longer in the boat shed, no longer in the middle of a story about times past. Something urgent was taking him away.

It must be the negotiations!

As he waited, Carter reprimanded himself for missing the peculiar fact that Bones had a small receiver stuffed into one ear.

Bones continued listening. He was intently monitoring a transmission. Carter could only guess who was sending it. Bones was wired for sound, linked intimately to the proceedings in Stormont in ways Carter hadn't guessed.

The young lake sailor would learn later that Bones was listening to a last minute press conference called by Dr. Ian Paisley, a staunch anti-agreement loyalist. Paisley previously refused to participate in the negotiations and now, at the eleventh hour, had arrived at the gates at Stormont. After being refused entry, Paisley and supporters pushed past guards and staged a protest at a monument dedicated to the legendary Unionist, Edward Carson. Paisley claimed that if given the right to hold a press conference, the crowd would disperse immediately thereafter. Under those terms, Dr. Paisley was allowed to deliver his protest speech. Bones would need to respond and advise immediately. It was 9:00 P.M. in Belfast, and the Mitchell Commission deadline was only three hours away.

A few seconds later, without speaking a word, Bones lowered his hands. He looked up at Carter as if nothing had happened; nevertheless, Bones' story was over.

Carter, realizing something of consequence was occurring though not knowing what, set upon shifting his attention in the direction of Claire's small apartment in the center of Old Town. Seeing Claire would do him good in ways unrelated to peace talks, secret transmissions, or political chicanery. With Claire, he could simply be relaxed. He could close his eyes and touch her powdery skin. He could feel like he was home; no accents, no secrets. Thankfully, she was unconnected to the intrigue swirling around Marblehead, the political and dangerous maelstrom with its epicenter arising from his new friends.

CHAPTER 41

EVERYDAY LIVES

Ryan O'Malley felt extremely uncomfortable. Carrying a gun through the arrival gate at Logan International Airport could lead to problems he didn't need.

Father Bruce O'Clery was being followed. That much had been confirmed in both Belfast International and London Heathrow airports. There remained uncertainty over who sent the pursuers. Patrick feared an attempt on Father O'Clery's life.

Loyalist factions were becoming extremely agitated as the hours sped by in Stormont. If they became aware of the O'Clery clan's plan to decommission, they would attempt a counter move, something bloody, something to goad the clan into keeping their arms, daring them to kill again. Murdering Father O'Clery would do nicely and O'Malley felt the pressure.

Patrick had summoned the paraplegic Irish priest to join him and Ryan in Marblehead. The clan's announcement to completely disarm would require a public face. New faces, a team perhaps, a compassionate and stalwartly team.

Linking Father O'Clery, a benevolent and brilliant man, with Ryan O'Malley, a no-nonsense realist, was ideal, and on this weighty pronouncement, Bones had concurred. Patrick would simultaneously step down. There would no longer be a Taoiseach, a single chief. Besides, Patrick would soon launch *Red Shoes*, and when he did, his worldly paradigm would irreversibly change.

O'Malley held a crumpled copy of the *Boston Globe* as if he were reading it. He checked his chronometer intermittently; it read 8:00 P.M. The arrival time came and went. His anxiety rose despite the normalcy of delays that pocked the airways.

Ten yards off, standing at a telephone kiosk, and acting like a businessman with briefcase at his feet, was Dennis Mahoney. He also felt the weight of the arrival of Father O'Clery. A gun pressed snugly to his ribs, he decided to monitor Father O'Clery's arrival personally after Patrick explained O'Malley's purpose in being there.

At first, Mahoney, chief of Logan security, insisted O'Malley not carry a firearm. After assurances from Patrick, who spoke with grave concern, he acquiesced. He owed Patrick a couple favors and decided to personally back up the secretive escort.

No one else in security was informed; Patrick had insisted. Logan security leaked like a sieve. Patrick knew it and Mahoney knew it. Mahoney could do little about it. Higher ups did the hiring and firing. He felt bad about it—very bad.

Mahoney refocused his attention as passengers began arriving at the gate. He watched a skycap emerge pushing Father O'Clery through the door into the lounge area. O'Malley greeted his charge.

≋≋≋

Carte crossed the cobblestone street just below Claire's apartment in Old Town and glanced up to see her sitting on the deck, awaiting his arrival. Music carried down to the street, causing his smile to broaden as they made eye contact. He anticipated their meal together, which he carried from the deli, and their lovemaking sure to follow

Stepping inside the apartment, Carter found a small television tuned to CNN. Claire explained she had been watching for news of the Northern Ireland peace negotiations. Carter was disappointed. He wanted a few hours away from "all things Irish." Then he realized given Claire's educational and personal interests, he should have known she would be paying close attention to the negotiations. A second look into his feelings added the realization that he was jealous, plain and simple. He wanted her full attention.

As if she could read his mind, Claire took the food from his hands, placed it in the refrigerator, then drew him back onto the deck. The evening sky shown indigo blue and the view of the harbor over the trees and houses drew Carter's thoughts away from petty jealousy.

Claire stepped between him and the harbor lights and looked into his dark eyes. She reached around his neck with delicate hands. Drawing him close she kissed him lightly, then more intensely as he reciprocated affectionately. Within a few moments the cool air of the ending day impelled them into the apartment and even further, into the bedroom.

≋≋≋

An hour later the couple was satisfied and famished in equally contrasting measure. Food from the refrigerator spilled out onto Claire's dining table.

She asked Carter if he would turn on the television for a few minutes. He kneeled down, turned it on and turned up the volume. Nothing of immediate consequence was being reported, so he turned down the volume, but left the television on.

Together they lingered over their repast, talking of plans Carter proposed for sailing *Maxine* to Newport, Rhode Island, after launching *Red Shoes*. When Claire heard he was intent on her joining him, she admitted she was nervous about sailing. She was excited about the prospect, but apprehensive about her lack of experience. She said she felt overwhelmed by the apparent complexity of a sailing yacht like *Maxine*.

Carter was about to assure her she could relax and he would do the sailing when suddenly he noticed subtitles with the words

"Northern Ireland" cross the television screen. He stepped quickly to the set, turned up the volume and together they watched and listened.

Tired men in gray suits loosened their ties and shuffled through the doors of an office building. They were pursued frenetically by cameras and mic booms. A correspondent spoke while holding a microphone to his lips and a headset tight to his ear. He explained that the deadline of midnight April 9 passed hours ago and no agreement had been signed. Claire's hand cupped her mouth and anxiety crossed her face. Carter looked intently at the screen.

The correspondent went on to say negotiators were focused, nonetheless, on completing their work. Tony Blair, Bernie Ahern, George Mitchell, and the dozen stake holders were pressing on into the early morning hours to complete what they were determined to accomplish.

A jostling, hand held television camera caught the attention of a tired and haggard Mitchell. Obvious fatigue bore on the senator's face, yet a glint of hope pushed through the weary eyes. He portended a man unwilling to give up.

"We're are on the verge of reaching consensus. It doesn't matter if it happens on the deadline precisely, the deadline will not preclude an agreement. Peace is not a function of deadlines; peace is going to come as an outcome of an entire shift in thinking by a society of compassionate, intrinsically good people.

"The other day, two women approached me on the street, thanking me profusely for my efforts. Thanking me not only for their sakes, but their children's and grandchildren's as well. It was standing there with those women when I suddenly realized it was they, these two grandmothers, who were the true peacemakers; everyday people who could no longer abide the disruptions of their everyday lives.

"Sometimes," the senator from Maine explained, "everyday people lose sight of the forest when so many trees grow in the way, especially trees that have grown for 800 years!"

The correspondent signed off. Claire and Carter looked at each other, both apprehensive, both wondering why this meant so much to the other.

A tearful Claire embraced her Lakeland lover. Each held their respective thoughts inside; each knowing things the other didn't about this remarkable event, sharing its moment together, yet separated by secret oaths they had made for vastly different purposes.

≋≋≋

Standing high above the other mountains of New England, the topographic vastness called Mt. Washington occasionally snatches the jet stream and drags it earthward. The lonely weather station at its peak holds the record for the highest wind speed ever recorded on the surface of the earth—231 miles per hour!

Carter was thinking of Mt. Washington. A wind storm was brewing while Claire slept peacefully in his arms. Gusts blew ominously outside her apartment, clamoring about in the way no sailor could possibly ignore.

If it increased so much as a knot he would have to rise in the Marblehead night, go to the harbor, and check *Maxine*. He probed the soundscape for an indicator. Something he could monitor as he listened to the coming gale; something that would cue him when to go.

A new sound emerged, a vibrating sound. It chattered and clicked at a high rate of speed. As a gust threw itself against the building, the chattering would increase then decrease as the wind passed on toward the harbor. After a couple minutes, he detected the predictability of the sound and chose it as his barometer. If it continued to increase, he would have no choice but to rise and tend *Maxine*.

As the night crept by, the wind continued to make sounds only a landsman could sleep through. He looked across the bed at the clock sitting on the night stand. Tiny red lights showed 2:35 A.M.

7:35 A.M. in Belfast, he calculated.

He realized Claire needed more sleep. She apparently remained oblivious to the gale. She would need to rise at 4:00 A.M. to begin making coffee. She had reminded him earlier in the evening that the irascible roaster had gone to South Boston for several days. She would need to cover extra duties. He marveled at her diligence in the face of an employer as annoying as O'Neil. There must be something about the job that kept her working so faithfully.

The chattering sound, which Carter decided was a wire, probably a television antenna, changed pitch in direct response to a powerful gust that enveloped the old cottage. In his many years living aboard, Carter considered himself to be an expert on chattering wires. He had risen countless times in the night to tie off his or his neighbor's halyard so he could go back to sleep. He finally gave in and decided enough was enough; he must go down to the water.

Without disturbing Claire, Carter rose, dressed quickly, and dashed off a brief note in the shadowy light cast by a streetlight shining through a window. As he slid open the glass door to the deck, he was greeted by a thin, but distinctly horizontal, sheet of rain as it rode the blowing wind. He realized it was going to be a dreadful trip out to his yacht.

He was about to bolt for the stairs when his attention was suddenly drawn to the chattering wire. He took note of its increased volume, now more a clattering sound than when he heard it from inside the apartment. Something about it struck him as odd. His ears automatically traced its location in the dark night. It sounded as if it were coming from somewhere near the wood railing surrounding the outdoor patio.

This made him curious. Why would that be? He was expecting the wire to be a television antenna, probably mounted on a chimney or TV tower.

A nearby street lamp cast a blue-gray light over the deck and Carter turned to follow the source of the sound, his curiosity overcoming the driving rain. He passed by deck chairs and moved toward the railing. The sound increased as he neared its origin. As he approached, he realized the wire was banging against the cap board.

The sound was very distinct, even in the competing wind and rain. Carter reached for the wire with his wet hands. It was bare, probably copper; it was too dark to see. He could only speculate because of the feel and the way it bent to his touch. It had apparently been stapled to the underside of the cap rail. The vibration of the wind must have loosened one or two of its fastenings.

He touched the wire and followed it along the rail. Carter's mind raced to figure out why a wire was there at all. What purpose did it serve? Was it meant to keep gulls off the rail; was it something a builder left behind? Neither those nor any other reason he could think of made sense.

A tremendous gust bellowed through the trees and a branch broke overhead dragging his mind back to his original purpose; to get out on the water and secure *Maxine*. His curiosity erupted and he convinced himself *Maxine* would be okay a few minutes longer. He followed the wire in one of its directions then retraced it in the opposite direction. It followed along the rail, then down under a trim board where the landing met the deck. On the opposite side of the landing he picked it up again. It went to the corner of Claire's apartment and disappeared into a tiny drill hole.

He rose from where he was crouched only to be clobbered by another blast of rain and wind.

This is an antenna, a short wave radio antenna...what else could it be? It sure as hell isn't a clothes line!

Carter stood in the blowing rain, curious and confused. It was a short wave radio antenna, he was certain and his conclusion raised the question, why did it lead into Claire's apartment? Where was the radio? Did the wire go downstairs through the wall framing and serve the usually absent landlord? Perhaps he was a short wave listener, a hobbyist?

The only other thing that might make sense, and it didn't make sense at all, was that it belonged to Claire; it was *her* shortwave antenna, attached to *her* short wave radio.

What an absurd thing. Why would Claire have a short wave radio?

The question rang in his ears as he descended the slippery steps of the deck. He kept rolling possible explanations through his head and none were suitable. All raised questions; suspicions he would have to unravel later. *Maxine* beckoned.

≋≋≋

The horizontal rain continued pelting Carter's face, soaking his clothes. He raced his dinghy across the churning harbor, bouncing over slippery black wavelets as he came nearer his floating home. He suffered a moment of confusion. A panicky feeling shot through him as he peered through the darkness. He couldn't spot *Maxine*.

She's missing, she's slipped her mooring!

Then, just as abruptly, he realized he was confused by the appearance of another boat where there hadn't been one before. The vessel must have arrived during the afternoon. It put him off his position. He had seen the empty mooring lying to the southeast and thought it was *Maxine's*. Now he realized the empty mooring was the one reserved for *Red Shoes*. Patrick had pulled strings with the Harbor Master so he could swing next to *Maxine* when he launched his "schoonah."

As Carter raced toward *Maxine*, he studied the mysterious boat, the one that confused him. It was a Hinckley 54, ketch rigged. She was beautifully fitted out; dark blue, perhaps black, it was too dark to tell. Her new sail covers held tight, even in the blow.

Carter made out the name on her stern as he swept by. *Cassiopeia*. He liked that name.

He arrived a moment later and nosed the bow of the dinghy gently against *Maxine's* starboard beam. He secured the painter to a deck cleat and then stood precariously in the inflatable and unsnapped her lifelines at the gate. Finally, he hoisted a foot aboard the swaying vessel, heaved himself to her deck and moved aft.

Carter quickly unlocked and slid the companionway hatch open. He reached inside and drew a flashlight from a holder mounted on the bulkhead. With light in hand, he strode forward on deck and completed his inspection within minutes. Everything looked good, the chafing gear still in place.

This worry settled, he stepped onto her cabin top and secured a slapping halyard. Halyards throughout the harbor clanged against masts in a cacophony of sound that surely prevented sleep.

He looked over at *Cassiopeia*. She sported internal halyards and stood silent and stately in the blow. He admired the lines of the Hinckley. She was shippy and new, and as he studied her in the dim light, he saw no imperfections, only the sleekness of her designer's original lines.

A short time later, drier and warmer, Carter lay in the captain's quarters listening to the halyards of Marblehead Harbor. They sounded incessantly in the strengthening gale. *Maxine* swayed and tugged at her mooring.

Carter couldn't sleep and he knew he wouldn't, but it wasn't the halyards that kept him awake; it was the wire—the vibrating sound of the wire pierced his mind as it had pierced through the wall of Claire's apartment. He tried vainly to think of a reason, an explanation, anything that would make clear the presence of a short wave antenna in so close a proximity to his new-found love.

After a lengthy time, he convinced himself the light of dawn would provide the plain, simple answer. He pushed back his ubiquitous doubt. Then, surrendering to a sickening feeling not unlike the first moment one realizes they have contracted the flu, Carter curled under the covers. The unavoidable truth was that not everything in Marblehead was as it appeared. Not his friends, not their histories, not their deeds; nothing seemed innocent and easily explained anymore.

For the first time in a long while, Carter felt lonely. He thought of his father and mother. He longed for afternoons on Pyramid Point. He remembered friends left behind in Florida. He felt agonizingly alone with only the companionship of his wooden boat, the only safe refuge in a place where nothing was quite the way it ought to be.

Trying stolidly not to succumb to self pity or suspicion, Carter brought the peace negotiations back to mind. He checked his chronometer. It was 3:30 A.M.

8:30 A.M. in Stormont.

Although Carter had no way of knowing, President Clinton wrung off ten minutes earlier after speaking at length with Bones Matheson, the captain of the afterguard. They discussed last minute details and back up strategies. Bones carried forth the wisdom of his mentor, Samuel Clark, and the good intentions of his father-in-law, Doctor Daniel Callahan. The ancient counselor lectured on the importance of viewpoint and context, bolstering Clinton's perseverance and encouraging to him lead, to assert the strengths the United States brought to the process.

≋≋≋

At 3:45 A.M., President Clinton dialed Senator George Mitchell on a secure telephone line between the White House and Mitchell's office in Stormont.

Like Carter, but for different reasons, Clinton couldn't sleep either. He told Mitchell he wanted to do something; he wanted to help. He conveyed Bones' advice and Mitchell acknowledged that he had also been communicating with the ancient Englishman.

Clinton offered to call Blair, Ahern, Trimble, or Adams. He concurred with Bones, that the hour of greatest exertion had finally arrived. Everyone should press on and come to an agreement—complete what so many in Northern Ireland wanted and worked so hard to achieve: to move forward, to change forever the tide of violence and discontent that washed relentlessly upon the shores of their everyday lives.

CHAPTER 42

A MARVELOUS COINCIDENCE

The orange-clad flight crew of the Coast Guard recovery helicopter crawled through the paper thin doors of the silent chopper. In an instant, the bright red machine was powered and blades began whirling in the blustery winds of the mounting gale.

The pilot barked out the pre-flight checklist while the co-pilot replied in staccato affirmation. Taking into account the severity of the weather, the crew began communicating with the air station control tower. A few seconds later they made contact with the watch commander on the *Monarch*.

Seas were rising, however the swells hadn't built to the point that landing on the flight deck of the *Monarch* would be particularly dangerous; not yet anyway. The one-hour-and-twenty minute flight could change that.

They could airlift Commander Donovan with the rescue cable if the situation prevented landing. They would not be able to re-fuel if they couldn't land on her deck. That possibility left little room for error; the safe flight time, depending on wind direction and speed, was approximately three hours.

A few seconds after receiving tower clearance they were in the air, the vertiginous blades tilted eastward over the churning maelstrom in the Gulf of Maine.

≋≋≋

Commander Donovan insisted he deliver the intel to the ground operative in Marblehead personally. He saw no reason to buffer himself from dangerous assignments in the final weeks of his commission. In fact, he believed the opposite; the more action the better. Time would fly by.

Cassiopeia had already been delivered to her mooring. The Hinckley Company arranged for a delivery captain to sail the vessel from Southwest Harbor to Marblehead.

She arrived at 3:00 P.M., Thursday. It was now 1:00 A.M. Friday. He should be in Marblehead before dawn. She hadn't been on her mooring eight hours before the gale began to build. He wondered how she was doing. Delivery captains were notoriously bold; however, they tended to come up short on simple matters like securing a vessel on a mooring. The delivery captain may, or may not, have anticipated the gale. In about four hours, as Donovan set his full plan into motion, he would be able to check her himself.

≋≋≋

The hour was late, but lights were on at the B&B.

Martha prepared tea and sandwiches and welcomed her new guest. The side door entrance, the one used by the young Irishmen, had been hastily modified to accommodate a wheelchair.

Only hours before, Patrick's cousin, Father O'Clery, landed at Logan Airport. Martha had met Father O'Clery only once before, and even in that brief encounter, she found him charming and intelligent. He read voraciously and this she liked most of all. She promised access to her library as soon as the young Irishmen finished the wheelchair ramp at her front door.

Earlier in the evening, hours before Father O'Clery's arrival, Bones rang up Martha on the telephone. He had nothing particular to say; he apparently just wanted to talk. The matron of the Purser's Quarters found this hugely suspicious. It was she who usually pursued the old sailor, feigning reasons for checking his well being. That Bones would call only to chat worried her greatly.

Throughout the day, her intuitive mind detected a negative influence permeating the ether of Marblehead. She felt the rising tension brought about by the conclusion of the peace talks. The tension felt like invisible hands clutching her throat, making it hard to breathe. She detected worry in her father's voice, but wouldn't have dared ask why. She figured if they spoke long enough, her special sense would innately unravel the mystery.

She nearly wept as they ended their conversation. Something was awry, but she hid her feelings; she didn't want her father to think her weak, though she no longer knew why. Martha concluded her father was in danger and probably Patrick, too. By offering to house the Irish priest, she figured she would be able to monitor their activities. She would watch out for them as best she could.

≋≋≋

Claire Dubois did not know Commander Donovan even though he frequently intercepted and relayed her radio transmissions. However, it was Commander Donovan, through the handler in Boston, who arranged for Claire to deliver Carter a laptop computer to keep him off the Abbot Library Internet system.

As a rule, Claire didn't know the recipients of her reports beyond the voice of her handler. She, like language spies stationed around the world, had a singular, innocuous purpose. They were positioned to listen and listen only. They were injected into inconspicuous places like businesses, universities, even churches. The "nests" were usually linked to people with obscure military or Foreign Service backgrounds. They were not supposed to make contact or become directly involved with the people to whom they were listening. Above all, they were not to draw any conclusions or attempt to intervene.

Claire was cognizant of the fact that she had been drawn closer to her marks than normally allowed. Oddly, Boston approved and encouraged the exception. She figured it was somehow related to the imminence of the peace negotiations.

Becoming attracted to Carter was entirely her own doing. She saw no particular danger in allowing her feelings for him to grow. She figured he was unaware of the relationship of the others to the peace negotiations, although she could not explain why she was to give him the laptop computer. She believed whatever he was doing on the Internet at the Abbot Library concerned someone, somewhere.

The note Claire found when she woke at 4:00 A.M. explained Carter's absence. She made herself ready for work and completed her morning report to Boston. It was still dark outside, but the wind was diminishing.

She hurriedly departed the apartment through the sliding glass door, stepping out onto the deck. She noticed her short wave antenna wire hanging loosely beneath the cap board of the railing. There were people to manage that sort of problem. She would transmit a request to the Agency from the radio at work, that is, if the inept roaster hadn't done something to screw it up like he managed to screw up the coffee roasting machine.

For a second she wondered if Carter might have noticed the wire. She figured it had been dark when he left and only an obsessively curious person would bother to notice. She hoped Carter was too concerned about *Maxine's* safety, as his note explained.

She thought about Carter as she walked to work. She reminded herself she was not in Marblehead to fall in love, but rather to monitor three marks; the Red-Haired Boy, who spoke an obscure Gaelic dialect few could interpret; the Figurehead, though he presented no language problem; and the Tillerman, the Red-Haired

Boy's nephew, who also spoke the dialect fluently although he was American.

Boston considered the Tillerman the most critical mark since it had become known he was considered for ascension to clan leadership, the position currently held by the Red-Haired Boy. The potential shift in power made Boston curious.

Claire was not informed of the clan's leadership role in decommissioning, nor how that feat would impact the peace agreements. Since Claire's recruitment into the National Security Agency, her work met Boston's needs poignantly. The surprising opportunity unveiled itself while the bright Midwesterner was still a post-graduate student at Boston College.

Unbeknownst to Claire at the time, Frank Dubois, her professorial father, who provided similar services nested inside Marquette University, was told by the agency how Claire's exceptional academic achievements coincidently fit a specific need. Listening for intelligence agencies was a family legacy, one Claire's Mamie specifically approved of after French separatists in Quebec caused Mamie's husband, a government official, such grief despite the noble purpose they sought to achieve.

The fruition of the peace negotiations proffered an honorable assignment and Frank discussed the situation with the grand matriarch. Upon her approval, he cautiously introduced Claire to the family secret.

Although Mamie never spoke directly to Claire about this unusual family tradition, she took satisfaction in her granddaughter carrying on this important role. She died soon after, and Claire would learn of Mamie's involvement in her secret career path, as well as the family involvement in the French separatist movement, at Mamie's wake several years later. During a private moment, Frank explained a few things about the family that first surprised Claire, but then made sense of things she felt akin to without really knowing why.

Carter Phillips, on the other hand, was a marvelous coincidence. His arrival, though entirely random, brought her even closer to the marks and closer to her own feelings about her life in this strange and interesting place. The only down side in all this seemed to be the bad fortune of working undercover in a coffee shop. She was warned during training she might endure some discomfort on assignment, but O'Neil was too much to bear. Still, it was obvious his past involvement with so many factions associated with the Irish question made his establishment the perfect base for operation.

She was also warned about O'Neil's volatility – as far as she was concerned, the more often he was away from Marblehead the better.

≋≋≋

Commander Donovan suited up. He placed the essential documents detailing the threat in a waterproof pouch. He zipped the pouch inside a pocket of the orange flight suit.

The watch commander sent a yeoman to his ready room to inform him the chopper was on the radar. It had been a couple decades since he operated on either end of the basket.

Better choppers, better training, same horrendous wind and rain!

Only ten minutes earlier he stood on the bridge looking aft, confirming the necessity that he be air-lifted off the crazily rolling cutter. He had watched the inclinometer swaying wildly like a conductor's baton as a philharmonic orchestra hammered out the 1812 Overture. The powerful beams of the deck lights didn't even reach the landing pad; the air was filled with precipitation, the wind swirling chaotically around the superstructure of the brawny, but shrinking cutter.

Donovan despised the sea when the *Monarch* shrunk beneath his feet. He was thankful it didn't happen often. In three decades on the Atlantic, in all its glory and all its rage, it happened less than a half dozen times. One of those was the night of the Halloween Gale, the so-called Perfect Storm.

The spy ship captain never reached a point where he didn't feel humbled by the North Atlantic's incomprehensible power. Remaining humble kept him cautious. The same went for his crew.

Even the yeoman standing before him now, an otherwise fearless young lad, exhibited extreme caution. He couldn't believe Commander Donovan was taking on a mission himself. The yeoman watched apprehensively as his Commander strapped on the hood of his flight suit. It gave the determined captain the distinctive look of an astronaut about to be flung into space.

The airlift took more time than planned, the additional minutes worrying Donovan. His mind kept recalling the night a chopper under his command was forced to ditch during the height of the Perfect Storm. It was on his watch. The hapless crew ran out of fuel and plunged mercilessly into the raging sea.

Four crew survived—the fifth was lost.

Afterward, Commander Donovan personally donned his dress uniform, traveled to the crewman's home in Vermont, and delivered the dreadful news to his parents.

It was a more heartrending duty than imagined. He could still feel the pain he witnessed in the parent's eyes. He felt responsible; it was on his watch. The inescapable feeling that he let that young man die now played a part in his insistence to execute this mission himself. He was determined to fly in this storm and deliver his secrets to Marblehead, secrets that couldn't be transmitted by radio because foes were listening, too. Worse, friends who mysteriously became foes, depending on the direction of political winds, were listening as well. It was a treacherous business and Donovan knew this well.

After take-off, they flew westerly into a headwind as dense as molasses. It exacerbated his alarm over adequate fuel. Donovan pushed the memories and doubts from his mind as the red machine fought against the coming gale. This mission couldn't fail; they couldn't drop into the sea short of their goal. The president had authorized the operation the instant the Brits determined that Father O'Clery wasn't the target, but rather, Bones Matheson, the Figurehead—one of their own countrymen.

The assassination of the Figurehead, if successful, would throw the peace negotiations into chaos. Blair, Ahern, and Mitchell were all in agreement on this point and they secretly appealed to the president to contravene.

President Clinton had shared something Bones told him once as they talked politics on board Ted Kennedy's yacht on Martha's Vineyard. "There are circles within circles, old son..." Apparently, Clinton remained convinced the old counselor was in the center of all of them.

Donovan realized this was not the time for the Figurehead's counsel to be lost; Clinton believed he deserved every conceivable measure of protection. Only a few more hours were needed to complete the agreement, Mitchell assured Clinton. Good Friday, April 10, 1998 would be a day, both historic and symbolic, for all the peacemakers and their constituents.

The irony, Donovan thought, of the British being the source of confidential documents outlining the murderous plot, was overwhelming. The British were always considered the greatest perpetrators of the troubles in Northern Ireland, and now they were stepping out of their typecast place to assure the peace process moved ahead. He could only guess the Prime Minister and his colleagues were the precipitant influence and his respect for Tony Blair burgeoned.

≋≋≋

Dawn arrived in Marblehead to a windless sunny sky. Daylight shown in the porthole and Carter awoke reaching for his chronometer.

Good grief, it's 9:20 A.M.!

He had slept soundly for hours after the gale blew through.

Maxine floated idly on her mooring, the air cool and fresh. Sea gulls could be heard arguing above, and below the strange sounds of yacht club launches whined oddly in Carter's ear, eerily magnified by *Maxine's* hull.

Crawling out of his bunk, he slipped into a robe and stepped into the galley to turn on the stove. He placed a pot of water over the warming flame and set out a china cup and Portuguese sweet bread he carried on board the day before.

Reaching into the head, he grabbed a wash cloth. When the water in the pot began to whistle he poured some onto the cloth and energetically wiped his weary eyes and face.

Turning to the nav station, he reached for his log book and sat down at the dinette. He recollected his disturbing discovery of the wire in the middle of the night and jotted down an entry.

The pot on the stove began to whistle again and he climbed from the dinette and returned to the galley. As he reached for a tea bag from a compartment above the stove, he noticed through the porthole the black hull of *Cassiopeia.* She lay motionless in the sunlight.

She was, as he suspected, brand new. Her white braided sheets looked unused, as if they just rolled off the spool at the chandlery. The deck and cabin sides were unmarred by footmarks and inevitable bruises of hard sea time. Her main boom hung from the topping lift at a slight angle upward and the sail covers looked to Carter as if they had just been steam pressed like a military dress uniform.

Suddenly he caught a glimpse of someone moving.

The lack of a dinghy tied to her beam had made him think no one was aboard. Then he realized someone could have been brought aboard by a yacht club launch. It dawned upon him the owner might have even been there all night. When his tea was ready, he donned khaki pants and a polo shirt. He slid open *Maxine's* companionway hatch and climbed up into the cockpit holding the steaming cup with one hand.

The cool morning air greeted him, the smell of salt water mixing with the aroma of his tea. He breathed deep and his chest expanded, filling with New England air. He felt better, a lot better, restored from the feelings of loneliness and suspicion he suffered in the dark hours at the height of the gale.

Gazing along *Maxine's* teak deck and up her rigging he decided to make a thorough inspection to determine if anything blew loose. He strode forward checking shrouds and running rigging, sneaking occasional glances at the Hinckley. He saw no further sign of life, no movement that might initiate an introduction, a chance to meet his new neighbor.

He whiled lazily at his inspection and after a few minutes his stomach reminded him there was sweet bread waiting down below. He decided to abandon his curiosity and his effort at neighborliness in favor of sustenance and returned to *Maxine's* dinette.

Once again he climbed below. As he passed the nav station he looked at his chronometer.

2:45 P.M. in Stormont.

He flipped a switch on his short wave radio then pressed a pre-set button. A British accent spoke aloud, confirming he was tuned to BBC world news.

≋≋≋

Less than ten yards away, unbeknownst to Carter, Bones Matheson sucked air into his pipe without lighting it. He had the good sense to restrain from stinking up the cabin of his host's luxurious stateroom. The Hinckley was new and he could show some respect, he thought. She seemed to be a lucky ship and that he liked.

He enjoyed little sleep during the gale, no proper sailor could. Now he felt awkward, hidden away in the belly of *Cassiopeia*. Commander Donovan, whom he had never met but whose introduction was made directly by President Clinton, insisted he take the captain's quarters. He had implored Bones to try and get some rest.

The Coast Guard Commander had seemed frustrated about not knowing his new boat. He clambered about the galley, yet was damned happy to be aboard. Eventually, he was able to prepare a meager breakfast. There hadn't been time to provision between the hour he was air-lifted off *Monarch* and the time he arrived in Marblehead.

It had been 3:45 A.M. when the Commander informed Patrick and Bones that Bones should accompany him aboard *Cassiopeia*.

Patrick had embraced his ancient friend as if it might be for the last time. As Bones and Donovan departed with the Irish lads as guards, the Red-Haired Boy spoke out in an ancient Gaelic dialect only the guards understood.

"Is fhearr teicheadh math na droch fhuireach."

Then he translated it into Bones' native tongue.

"Bettah a good retreat thahn a bahd stand, old friend. Stay hidden, thaht bastahd O'Neil haas disappeared. Nothin' but trouble gonna come from thaht one, don't ya know. We should haav figured the gobshite would try somethin' stupid. O'Malley's fit to be tied. Nothin' we cahn do now but wait. It's all in the hands of the lads in Stormont. Nothin' much more ta do but listen ta thaht wee bug in yer ear and learn how it comes out."

The two somber friends embraced once more. Bones realized things could go badly, thinking of Lord Mountbatten and the explosion aboard his fishing boat that killed the statesman without warning or provacation. His bushy eyebrows formed a sad look over his glassy eyes.

Bones didn't think his last telephone call was a proper good-bye. He should have held her once more, he should have told her he loved her, that he was grateful for all her care and companionship. But their time was up; he had to go with the spy ship captain.

He had put a slip of paper with the name and telephone number of Samuel Clark's law partner into the freckled hand of the fiddler. He spoke quietly so the rest gathered around couldn't hear.

"Take bloody care of 'er, Pahtrick, take care of my little guhl."

≋≋≋

Once the goodbyes had been said, the young Irishmen hurriedly ferried Bones and Donovan out onto the harbor in the midst of the gale. When they arrived at *Cassiopeia*, Bones noticed Carter's dinghy tied up to *Maxine*.

He feared Carter would hear them clambering aboard during the early hour, particularly with the special effort required to hoist Bones onto the deck. It was important that no one saw him being spirited away. The plan was for him to stay hidden until the agreement was reached, whenever that might be. While confidence was high it would be within hours, Bones Matheson lived long enough to know that anything could happen right up to the moment the signatures dried on the paper.

If things didn't go well, Donovan would sail *Cassiopeia* offshore; they'd rendezvous with the *Monarch* and Bones would be brought aboard until the danger subsided.

O'Malley had argued earlier that Bones should be aboard *Gael na Mara*, not *Cassiopeia*. Commander Donovan prevailed and O'Malley decided he would stand guard nearby. He'd float close to *Cassiopeia* and serve as a distraction, perhaps lure O'Neil away if he showed up. Perhaps eliminate the threat altogether if he could grab a chance. O'Malley's oath to Patrick to disarm began on the signing of the agreement, not before.

≋≋≋

As Bones observed the morning sun through a deck light overhead, he thought again of the plot to kill him. He considered the paradox of both his pursuers and his rescuers. He thought of Robert Erskine Childers and the strange circumstance of being killed by the islanders he hoped to unite.

Would this be his end, too? Would O'Neil and his estranged faction succeed with their scheme to end the talks?

In hindsight, he reasoned that O'Neil should have never been released after his questioning back in '79. He should have informed the Brits of the role the traitorous O'Neil played in Lord Mountbatten's murder. The problem back then was whether they would have believed him. They still considered Bones a traitor.

O'Neil, conversely, was on everybody's payroll at one time or another. He had no soul.

Bones thought again of the similarities between his life and Childers'. They were both English. They both devoted their lives to Irish unity. They both married American wives and each bore a single child. The unfortunate Childers only lived to age fifty-two, while his son, seventeen at the time of his execution, went on to become the President of Eire in 1973.

Bones, on the other hand, was amazed by his own longevity. He frequently wondered why he was left standing after so many conflagrations. This might be his last, however, since he was poignantly aware that O'Neil was good at only one thing, and that was killing.

He thought again of Childers' early demise and was thankful for so many years with Martha and Patrick. The three of them lived this long as a family, no ordinary family perhaps, but a family—his family.

He sighed deeply and shifted his position on the thickly cushioned chair. He contemplated his 90-year-old body. It was a living vessel filled with a potage of British blood and genes. Of all the things that happened over the long course of his life, he realized once again, after three quarters of a century of denial, he was an Englishman. While it was true he had been wronged horribly by his own kind, his blood lines were unalterable.

Bones smiled inwardly at the irony of the current scheme to protect him, to hide him away aboard *Cassiopeia*. He was aware of Tony Blair's hand in his protection. He would consider it an apology by his countrymen, as it were, though piteously late in coming.

Still, it indeed arrived, an auspicious gesture of reconciliation by his long-lost countrymen; men whose fathers, he suspected, would have shot him on sight. Through either the vagaries of fate or his own Herculean effort to mediate the dispute, the British now conspired to keep him alive inside the yacht of a Coast Guard commander he only suspected existed prior to their meeting.

Bones studied his chronometer and pondered the workings of his long time friend, George Mitchell. He could try and contact him, try even harder to participate in the final negotiations, or offer some final advice.

Then he realized it was over for him. The others would have to lead now and that was how it should be. He taught them what he knew: the importance of viewpoint and context. Moreover, he taught them to think objectively, yet infuse objectivity with compassion and understanding.

The ancient counselor's thoughts of himself and his situation began to fade and he began thinking about Winnie. He thought of her pretty face, imagined her voice as they played in the alleys and streets of Southsea. He wept a tear for her lost soul and considered what his life would have been had she lived. Then he thought of the futility of such thinking. He couldn't change what happened; there was no going back and undoing history.

Rather than pity himself, he made an oath to remember Winnie as the wonderful sister she had been. He then went even further; in his mind he forgave the men who killed her. At the same time, he thanked those who now redeemed the appalling act; for they likely were saving his life, and more importantly, enabling a peace agreement.

≋≋≋

By 10:30 A.M. Carter was satisfied that he was not going to be meeting the owner of the Hinckley this day. Whoever was below seemed to be in no hurry to climb out on deck. He thought that odd.

After one last look around *Maxine* to ensure her well being, he prepared to board his dinghy and head to shore. He figured there was plenty to do aboard *Red Shoes* and plenty of days ahead in which to do them. He was starved for good coffee. The antenna issue raced through his mind once again.

That posed a problem. He didn't want to confront Claire in the coffee shop. He was upset about it though, so much so that he wasn't sure he wanted to see Claire right then.

This thought hurt him and he struggled, trying to remain reasonable and open-minded. He thought instead he should talk to Patrick. Patrick hinted in Gloucester that Claire "was more than a pleasin' sight to the eyes . . .." What that might have meant he couldn't be sure, however now seemed the time to ask. The antenna justified his asking.

Carter boarded his dinghy, checked his oars, released the painter, and floated away from *Maxine*. He pulled the starting chord on the engine and it roared to life, blue smoke shooting from its backside. He caught a glimpse of movement at the companionway hatch of *Cassiopeia* the instant he pulled the gear lever forward.

By the time he was clear of both boats' bows, he watched a white haired man, handsomely groomed and youthful in appearance, step out into the late morning sun. The rugged, square jawed man sported stylish sunglasses, was dressed in yachting khaki's and held a coffee cup to his lips. Carter sensed the man's pleasure, the obvious joy of being aboard his yacht.

Carter watched as the skipper of *Cassiopeia* looked out over the harbor in the direction of Marblehead Neck. He turned and leaned gently against the lifelines, looking across at *Maxine* floating silently on the next mooring over. He studied her longer than Carter would have expected.

Carter thought about motoring back and introducing himself. He paused, took the gear lever out of forward and coasted a few seconds.

He changed his mind.

He didn't want to appear too anxious, or too friendly in that Midwestern way that garnered no respect in New England. Instead, he pushed the gear lever back into forward. He'd meet his new mooring mate soon enough. They'd be next to each other all summer; there would be ample opportunity.

He turned the dinghy toward Tucker's Wharf and twisted the tiller handle to give it gas. The salt air flooded his nostrils and he tugged the long-billed cap tighter to his head. After a minute, he turned once again toward *Maxine* and *Cassiopeia*. His eyes widened.

He decelerated and quickly spun the dinghy around on its keel. He sat rocking in place, looking back toward where he had come and stared at *Gael na Mara*. She glided stealthily toward the two yachts. At the stern was O'Malley, up forward two young Irishmen. They were preparing to pick up the empty mooring next to *Maxine*, *Red Shoes'* mooring!

This is interesting, he thought, reaching for his field glasses. Lifting them to his eyes, he watched the crew of *Gael na Mara* as they prepared to pick up the mooring pennant. He swung one point to port and glimpsed the handsome white-haired man. Carter could see he, too, had taken notice of the Irish cutter.

For a second, Carter thought the white-haired man was going to try and help *Gael na Mara*, even though there was nothing one could do to assist another yacht picking up a mooring.

Carter returned to *Gael na Mara*. He saw O'Malley, wearing the perpetual grin of cigar smokers, turn her great, wooden wheel as he reversed her engine. Seconds later, the foredeck crew secured her to *Red Shoes* empty can.

Carter was about to end his vigil and head to shore when he suddenly noticed *Cassiopeia's* owner gesture over to O'Malley. Puzzled, Carter couldn't figure out why. He didn't think O'Malley would do more than make a cursory greeting in return. Instead, to Carter's surprise, the two men began a lengthy conversation. When the discourse ended, *Cassiopeia's* owner stepped back into his cockpit, pushed open the companion way hatch, and disappeared below.

Carter swung the glasses back to *Gael na Mara*. O'Malley and the crew were not on deck. He figured they must have gone below. He remained in position another minute.

Nothing changed and he decided he should go find Patrick and Bones. Perhaps they could tell Carter what was going on. He looked at his chronometer; it was 11:10 A.M.

4:10 P.M. in Stormont.

He became curious to hear more news. Within a couple seconds he was speeding toward Tucker's Wharf.

≋≋≋

Ernie greeted Carter with a pensive look. The Irregulars were scattered about *Red Shoes*, some on deck, some on scaffolding, all working at various tasks. They all turned toward Carter, quizzical contortions splayed across their olden faces.

"We thought Pahtrick was with you, Caahtah. None of us haas seen Bones yet today eithah!" Ernie exclaimed. He nodded toward the empty wheel-mounted chair.

"I haven't seen them, Ernie, I was expecting them to be here," Carter replied. He tried to veil his anxiety at the surprising news. "There was no note, nothing that explained where they went?"

"No, Caahtah, not a thin', and we aah low on vahnish, don't ya know!"

Carter remained anxious. He assumed Ernie would know if something were wrong. He couldn't tell if the lack of supplies was all that Ernie was upset about. Rather than wonder, Carter asked the old-timer straight away.

"Has Bones ever simply not shown up to work on *Red Shoes*?" he asked.

"Well, Caahtah, let me think . . ." and the old man held a varnished finger to his stubbly cheek contemplating the question.

"Up until ya took 'im off ta Gloucestah heah a couple weeks ago, I would figur it would haav been three, maybe four yeahs. Just aftah we staahted this little ship. I cahn recall he felt puny one day and stayed away."

Carter didn't like the sound of the innocent reply one bit. He realized Bones' disappearance could easily have something to do with the peace talks and that could be either good or bad. He thought of Martha and speculated it would frighten her terribly if he ran up to the B&B to find out what was going on. He continued his questioning.

"What about Patrick, Ernie? Where do you figure he might be?"

"Not sure 'bout Pahtrick eithah, skippah. Bones always knows; thaht's how we usually find out wheah Pahtrick haas wondered off ta."

Where were they? Why hadn't they left Ernie some notice of where they went?

He thought of O'Malley showing up with *Gael na Mara* and decided that they must be okay or O'Malley wouldn't be hanging around on board the cutter. This deduction calmed him.

Carter excused himself, turned around and headed back to Tucker's Wharf. He was intent on collaring O'Malley and finding out what the hell was going on.

CHAPTER 43

THE ANNOUNCEMENT

Carter sprinted back to Tucker's Wharf, leaped into his dinghy and raced out into Marblehead Harbor, steering directly toward *Gael na Mara*. The disappearance of Patrick and Bones was unnerving, but Carter found partial relief as he motored around *Gael na Mara* and noticed Patrick's Whitehall tied to her starboard beam.

This explained Patrick's whereabouts; however, it was unlikely he had ferried Bones out in the sleek rowing boat. Perhaps Bones was with Martha. Carter wished he'd checked the B&B first, but if Patrick was aboard *Gael Na Mara*, it surely meant Bones was all right.

Carter glanced over toward *Cassiopeia* hoping to see the white-haired captain moving about. The boat swung quietly on her mooring. It looked as if there was no one on deck.

Maxine swung peacefully on her pennant next to the Hinckley. *Gael na Mara*, the largest and most majestic of the fleet, towered over them. She gave Carter the impression she was guarding little sisters.

The threesome of yachts created a beautiful composition, Carter thought. The number three struck him, as it always did, as the center of something magical. Together they floated in a way that caused Carter to realize *Cassiopeia's* appearance in the fleet was meant to be; her appearance could not be a coincidence—this was not a chance meeting.

Carter remained still, sitting in his dinghy for a couple of moments, lost in the vision of the three yachts. He snapped out of his wonderment the instant Patrick and Ryan O'Malley strode out of *Gael na Mara's* pilot house and onto her quarterdeck.

They hadn't noticed him. They peered first at *Cassiopeia,* studying her for a few moments. Then they both glanced obviously toward *Maxine.* It was as if they were making an inspection, checking to see if all was well with the fleet. Carter smiled inwardly. He thought they looked like a commodore and admiral of old.

Patrick and Ryan turned to head back inside *Gael na Mara*'s pilot house when Patrick spotted Carter floating idly in his dinghy a dozen yards away. He motioned to O'Malley who nodded to Carter, but then stepped back inside, disappearing from view. Patrick waved the lake sailor to come aboard.

Carter noticed he didn't call out or make a noisy welcome, which is what Carter would have expected from Patrick. Instead, he seemed subdued, perhaps even apprehensive. Carter waved and smiled, reprimanding himself for jumping to conclusions.

Surely everything is all right...

≋≋≋

"Aye, laddie, welcome aboard theah, skippah."

Carter began pulling himself up from his dinghy and onto the deck of the Irish cutter. He greeted Patrick with questions in his eyes, questions Patrick already anticipated.

"Sure, everythin's fine, laddie. Bones and Maatha aah both safe, don't ya know." He reached for Carter's arm and helped him the rest of the way on board.

"Ya see, laddie, Captain O'Malley and I aah standin' watch. Theah's a raptor on the loose and we aah lettin' it be known it haas to take us first afore it cahn reach its prey. We scoot out on deck from time ta time ta make sure the scoundrel knows we aah heah."

Carter looked puzzled. Something dangerous was going on and Patrick was making light of it.

"Shouldn't nothin' haapin' out heah in broad daylight, laddie. Then again, some people aah just plain crazy… just plain crazy," he repeated under his breath. "Best we step inside and I'll fill ya in on the mysterious fun we aah haavin' heah. Theah's been a threat Cahtah, a threat on Bones' life, don't ya know."

Carter knew it, his intuitive feeling *was* right. Something dangerous was going on. His heart rate jumped although he worked hard not to show it.

"Theah aah lowly people in lowly places thaht would like to see the peace process fail, skippah. Ears ta the ground haav picked up a rumble thaht Bones ought not be offerin' more assistance. Those same ears thaht's been listenin' on our behalf haav been talkin' to higher ups who want the process ta produce results. They've made arrangements to hide ole' Bones away from trouble fer a while."

Carter's desire to know where must have shown clearly because Patrick quickly added. "Close, Cahtah, close enough fer me and Captain O'Malley to intervene if we haav to."

"You mean he's on board—he's in his stateroom?"

"Not quite, laddie," smiled Patrick, "but close, skippah, very close."

Carter wasn't in a mood for games, but detected a tone in Patrick's voice suggesting he would only provide information on a need-to-know basis. Carter backed off, stifling his curiosity.

Patrick and Carter stepped below and into the great room of the exquisite yacht. O'Malley joined them from the nav station. All three sat at the gimbaled dining table. Patrick attempted to lighten the atmosphere with conversation, but the mood of the three sailormen remained gloomy, like Gloucester men after a bad day fishing.

The steward he met previously carried out a tray of pilot crackers, cheese, and smoked fish. Setting it down quietly amongst the solemn, anxious men he departed without a word. A minute later he returned with a pot of coffee.

Simultaneously, in a gesture of nervous preoccupation, they all checked their chronometers. If the scene hadn't been so moribund it would have been humorous. Checking their timepieces seemed to be the only thing the three could do. It didn't change their situation, however, and it didn't speed things up. If anything, it caused time to appear to move slower. Carter got bold and finally spoke up.

"I'm curious about news from Stormont; can we tune in the BBC, better yet, RTE?"

It was as if he spoke an epiphany. Patrick and O'Malley had been so concerned about the threat to Bones they practically forgot the threat itself would end the moment an agreement was attained.

O'Malley glanced toward the steward who immediately departed. Within a few seconds, through speakers mounted in the teak bulkhead over the fireplace, news came from across the pond.

≋≋≋

Tea was being served at the same instant in the great room of the Purser's Quarters. As Martha calculated, providing a place for the paraplegic priest kept her comfortably aware of the goings on.

The three Irish lads completed the ramp into her great room by 11:00 A.M. and Father O'Clery smiled broadly as he wheeled himself up to Martha's library around noon.

Martha turned off her constant companion, the television, for the occasion; Father O'Clery was a special guest. She doted over her visitor.

While she prepared lunch and chatted with the priest, Martha noticed the three Irish lads still mingling about outside. They passed around the house, appearing through one window then the next. They smoked and talked as if nothing were afoot. However, she knew very well what they were doing and why they were there. She prayed the same protection was being proffered her father, wherever he was at this moment. Seeing the young sentries in place outside her home, Martha was reassured O'Malley's protective hand was everywhere at once.

Carrying a pewter tray into her great-room, Martha seated herself and served her guest. Father O'Clery graced their repast and they began eating. After a few bites and pleasant conversation, she felt her intuitive feeling rising within her. She felt certain the end of the negotiations were near. She was hopeful they would be positive. If they were, the outcome would change their lives. They could be like normal people again, a real family.

Her optimism was met with a measure of caution. Intuition was one thing; but she also knew the actuality of the agreement itself was another. A complex document still needed to be drafted, typed, copied, and ultimately signed by people with a long history of disagreeing. This made her nervous. She restrained the urge for a cigarette and proposed to Father O'Clery, currently preoccupied with the gilded volume of Hans Christian Anderson, that they turn on the television set to see if there was any news from Stormont.

Commander Donovan and Bones, his special guest, were sitting in the main saloon. The modern styling of the yacht had caught Bones' attention and he had expressed his admiration of its construction openly. Donovan then dialed in the BBC at Bones' specific request.

Donovan thought about the gravity of the situation. This was a fitting commission, he said to himself, protecting the Figurehead, an action of high intrigue; it was damn near as good as chasing drug dealers! His Irish grandfather would be proud.

He flipped a switch and speakers mounted in teakwood adorning his saloon spoke aloud. He stepped from his nav station to join his honored guest.

The coffee shop was quiet. A young person Claire took to be a student worked on a laptop computer. An older gentleman, a frequent customer, sat quietly reading the New York Times.

Claire looked at the clock on the wall near the roasting machine. It read 1:00 P.M.; the post lunch calm had begun. She calculated the time in Ireland, and realized it was 6:00 P.M., the close of their business day.

Anxiety over the agreement ran high and Claire decided to turn on the news. She turned first for the short wave radio in the back, but decided against leaving the front untended. She was hoping Carter would drop in. It seemed strange he hadn't. She hoped it wasn't something she said or did the night before. She concluded that perhaps something was wrong on *Maxine*, perhaps the wind damaged her and he needed to attend to the repair. She reached for the small stereo behind the counter and switched on WGBH, Boston.

The door of the café opened and the noise drew her attention from the radio just as an announcement broke in. A man walked in dressed in a crumpled, ill fitting suit, looking conspicuously like an employee of an undercover agency.

Claire recognized him at once, though they had been together only a couple times six months earlier. Exhibiting no recognition, she continued wiping the counter as if he were no one in particular. It was her handler, the voice she simply called Boston, and she knew that something was terribly wrong, something related to the disappearance of the petulant O'Neil.

The weary-looking man approached the counter. He looked around the café, said "I'll have a regular," and slipped a tiny piece of paper across the counter when no one was looking.

Claire glanced down and read "We need to talk—right away."

Pretending to take his order she jotted down a quick reply on a pad – "After the announcement."

He looked puzzled and she could see he must not have been listening to a radio. Out loud she said "And that will be one dollar and twenty five cents."

While he reached in his pocket to get money she turned up the radio.

≋≋≋

The listeners aboard their yachts in the harbor, in the great room of the Purser's Quarters, and in the Marblehead Roasting Company paid close attention. Anticipation leaked adrenalin into their blood as if they were all attached to an IV in a hospital ward. The newscaster's voice crackled, then ceased.

The voice of Senator George Mitchell, chairman of the Mitchell Commission, the leader of a two-year campaign toward peace, began speaking with restrained excitement:

> "I'm pleased to announce that the two governments, and the political parties of Northern Ireland, have reached agreement. The agreement proposed changes in the Irish Constitution and in British constitutional law to enshrine the principle that it is the people of Northern Ireland who will decide, democratically, their own future. The agreement creates new institutions: a Northern Ireland Assembly, to restore to the people the fundamental democratic right to govern themselves; and a North/South Council, to encourage cooperation and joint action for mutual benefit. It deals fairly with such sensitive issues as prisoners, policing, and de-commissioning.
>
> This agreement is good for the people of Ireland, North and South. It was made possible by the leadership, commitment, and in these last few days, the personal negotiating skill of Prime Minister Tony Blair and the Taoiseach, Bernie Ahern.

Their commitment has been evident by their presence here for days, their hands-on style, their all-night effort, and we're honored by their presence.

If the agreement is approved in referendums North and South, it offers the chance for a better future. But to secure that future it will take the good-faith efforts of the leaders gathered here, and the commitment of all the people of Northern Ireland. Making the Assembly work and making the North/South Council effective, will test these leaders as much as did getting this agreement. The people of Northern Ireland will make the difference.

This agreement proves that democracy works, and in its wake we can say to the men of violence, to those who distain democracy, whose tools are bombs and bullets: Your way is not the right way. You will never solve the problems of Northern Ireland by violence. You will only make them worse.

It doesn't take courage to shoot a policeman in the back of the head, or to murder an unarmed taxi driver. What takes courage is to compete in the arena of democracy, where the tools are persuasion, fairness, and common decency. You should help build this society instead of tearing it apart. You can learn something from some of the lives you've destroyed, like those of Damian Trainor or Philip Allen. They were two young men, best friends, who saw each other as human beings, not as a Protestant and a Catholic. Philip was to be married with Damian as his best man. Instead they lie buried, near each other, sharing death as they shared life, victims last month of a brutal and senseless murder. Their deaths showed what Northern Ireland has to endure. Their lives showed what Northern Ireland can be.

This agreement points the way. For that, credit must go to many people, especially those here today. We will shortly hear from each of the political leaders of Northern Ireland. Let me first speak of them collectively. They have negotiated tirelessly for two years. They've constantly had to strike a balance between their obligations to their constituents and the needs of the larger society. That's hard to do in any democracy; it's especially difficult in this divided society. Through it all they kept their sense of purpose. And they delivered an agreement that's fair and balanced and offers hope to the people of Northern Ireland. For that they deserve the gratitude of their people and the just verdict of history.

≋≋≋

"And thaht moves us ahead on a very long paath Commandah Donovan. We've taken up a new position on the great continuum," the ancient seaman added cryptically, mouthing the stem of his unlit pipe.

Commander Donovan tipped his teacup, and smiled.

"Now, Commandah, you bloody well must haav plans for this bleedin' craft, is theah a place in particulah you'll be headin'?"

Within seconds, charts were produced and spread across the saloon. "The Indian Ocean," observed Bones thoughtfully. He carefully studied the charts. He also studied the owner of the lucky ship . . . the Maldives, he thought again.

≋≋≋

Patrick rose suddenly setting the gimbaled table in motion. A wide grin crossed his colorful face.

"Caahtah Phillips, my boy, allow me ta introduce ya to my replacement, Mistah Ryan O'Malley. A little later, I shall haav ya meet his colleague in peace, the good Fathah Bruce O'Clery. Together they haav an announcement o' theah own ta make. In the meantime, a toast—a toast ta *Red Shoes*, laddies!"

Cut Irish crystal once again emerged from the carved wooden cabinet. The steward smiled and poured fingers of gold Irish whiskey into the glasses.

The relief was palpable, as though the group had just made landfall after a rough passage. But as sailors, they realized it would be temporary, the joy of landing. It always was. They were sailors and their lives intermingled with the water, regardless if it be salt or fresh. The one thing they knew with certainty was that every landfall offered the joy of returning to the water. Soon they would once again hoist great white cloth and sail upon the sun-spawned wind.

Patrick was the most joyous of all, for his return to sailing would be aboard the vessel of his redemption, the wooden boat crafted with his hands and mind—*Red Shoes*.

≋≋≋

"Ah, tis a fine thing, child," said Father O'Clery as he offered Martha his kerchief. "A tear o' joy fer us all, a tear o' joy fer us all."

What the good priest couldn't have possibly known, for his insight was limited compared to the good witch Martha, was that she wept not for Ireland, even though what happened brought plenty of joy. Rather, Martha O'Donnell wept for Carter Phillips.

A strange feeling came upon her moments after they turned on the television. It was a feeling of great contradiction. On one hand, she somehow knew there would be an agreement, on the other, she knew Carter was in trouble. Now, in the seconds following the announcement, her joy passed quickly and she wept for the coming pain she realized her adopted son must soon endure.

The kindly priest handed the matron of the Purser's Quarters his handkerchief.

She took it and wiped her eyes. She nodded pleasantly, concealing her anguish as she had done time and again these past fifty years. There would have been no point in revealing them; for what she felt, what she knew was going to happen to Carter, was far beyond anyone's control—even the kind and passionate Father Bruce O'Clery.

≋≋≋

"I've been sent to get you out of here. They can't locate O'Neil. You need to close the doors, we've got to leave—now," Boston whispered across the counter, the coffee cup hiding his lips.

The urgency in his voice robbed Claire of the much anticipated pleasure of hearing the announcement, the exuberance of a job well done, the joy of final resolution.

No matter, she thought, as she brushed aside her disappointment. She could see he meant business, and he meant now. Her father drilled into her the importance of the essential trust between listener and handler. She obeyed without reply.

Turning to the back wall and opening a cupboard door, Claire flipped open an electric panel and threw the main fuse switch; everything shut down, the radio, the lights, the great coffee roasting machine, everything. Seconds later she scooted the customers, with no explanation, out the front door and locked it.

Boston headed out the rear, checking to see if the way was clear, his hand in his jacket, gripping his service revolver. Claire followed on his heels.

With less than a nod in passing, two men dressed in ill fitting repairmen coveralls strode quickly back into the building Claire and Boston had hastily departed. The men would retrieve the short wave radio and secure the interior.

≋≋≋

Claire sat quietly next to Boston as their aircraft lifted off the Logan runway. Despite her training, despite her satisfaction that she had contributed to the peace process, her inner being roared in anguish. When the aircraft reached altitude, the listening spy excused herself and walked forward to the restroom. There she pulled tissues from a dispenser, buried her head and cried until she could cry no more.

Four hours later, Claire Dubois unceremoniously landed in Tucson, Arizona. There she was driven thirty-five miles southeast and lodged at a Sonora Desert Inn. She would remain in the desert for an indefinite period of time, hidden among the ubiquitous saguaro cactus. When that time ended, she would be unceremoniously assigned her next listening post.

Boston, after helping her to her suite, opened the door of the dusty black SUV. As he stepped inside, preparing to leave, Claire asked if it would be possible to speak with her father. Boston, without committing one way or the other said he'd get back to her soon. He closed the door and drove quietly into the searing desert night.

Claire watched morosely until the red tail lamps faded into the dusty night air.

CHAPTER 44

GREAT MYSTERIOUS QUESTIONS

"Well, skippah," Patrick said with a high degree of frustration, "when O'Neil went missin', thin's got hard ta predict. Amidst all else thaht was goin' on, thaht slippery bastahd stole away. Sure ya know, laddie, when one thin' goes akimbo on a dahmn yaaht then two er three moah's got ta haapen in short ordah. The next thin' ya know, Clayah's gone, too!"

Carter listened politely though he was deeply distraught. He wished powerfully for Patrick not to wander in his explanation. He desperately wanted to know what was going on, to understand why Claire disappeared. He wanted to know who she really was. It was obvious that despite their intimacy, she lied to him and hid things from him. This angered him until he thought about the fact that he, too, had been keeping secrets: what happened off shore of Gloucester, his adopted family's bizarre lives, to name a few.

But his secrets were small, he told himself, only partially convinced. They were unimportant—at least as they related to his and Claire's relationship. He hadn't thought his omissions would hurt anyone, not like her secrets were hurting him now. In his case, he simply needed to honor his adopted family's peculiar circumstance. They would have been at risk if he revealed what he knew. He had no way of knowing the same was true of Claire. Whatever the reasons, Claire's disappearance was tearing him apart. He was aching in his heart and in his mind and it was apparent to all three of his friends.

Despite the sympathetic kindness Martha extended and the contemplative gaze of Bones, who seemed otherwise preoccupied with something of great concern, Carter needed solace and he sought it from Patrick. Carter was certain Patrick knew more about Claire than he wanted to admit. It was time for the old fiddler to speak up. The mossy table at Sewall Point, where they sat together now, provided the perfect place to narrow Patrick's attention.

Patrick continued speaking.

"O'Neil is a good example of the indescribable bahdness thaht comes from an ageless legacy of hate and violence. He's the embodiment of spoilage and whenevah theah's a mold growin' as long as our troubles, someone like O'Neil is gonna rise from it, don't ya know."

Carter did not have great difficulty relating to what Patrick was saying. He certainly saw the roaster's reviling nature for what it was. He continued to listen, praying for Patrick to remain focused on his most burning questions—where was Claire, who was Claire, why did she flee?

"Sure thaht O'Neil carries some o' the same genes as Connah. Tis as if O'Neil, just like Connah, cahn't contain the history thaht haas growed up inside him. Yet thaht explains only the worst half of Connah, whereas it explains all of O'Neil. My half-brother hahd an entirely different half—a good half thaht always seemed to rise above the bahd. O'Neil, laddie, haas no good half, only a bahd half and a useless half; that's all theah is to it.

"Despite Bones' and my warnin's to the contrary, membahs of yer gov'ment's secret societies set O'Neil up in thaht little roastin' company. They set him up as a front for theah operations, then the stubborn buggahs turned 'round and nested yer pretty maiden inside. She was ta keep an ear open fer Bones and me and Captain O'Malley.

She was ta listen fer trouble 'cause she could understand our native language. This was ta go on till the endin' of the talks."

Carter's attention rose.

"Of course, we was grateful fer the lattah. Though ya probably ouht ta know thaht Miss Clayah nevah knew thaht we knew what she was doin', thaht is, Bones and m'self. Maatha was nevah informed one way or the othah. Neither Bones nor I saw any particulah benefit in thaht. Hahd ya not come along and got ta be such good friends with Maatha, our Miss Clayah and Maatha would haav nevah met, least by the way Bones and I figgered it."

"But Patrick, why didn't you tell me what was going on? You hinted that night in Gloucester. And now I need to know what's happened, are you going to tell me?"

Carter was disturbed with the way he made his plea, he didn't want to sound weak or desperate, even if that was how he felt. "What I mean to say, Patrick, is that I wish to know what you can tell me about Claire. I understand that you may not be comfortable telling me all you know, or perhaps you know less than I think. Either way, I need to understand what's happening here. Is she safe, will she return, am I going to be able to talk with her?"

Ending his supplication Carter anxiously awaited a reply.

≋≋≋

Patrick, frustrated and wishing Bones was nearby for consultation, looked to the harbor as if it would inspire him, provide him with answers to the perfectly understandable questions Carter posed. He saw the trio of boats, *Cassiopeia*, *Maxine* and the watchful *Gael na Mara*. He thought of *Red Shoes* and his desire to be finished once and for all with the Irish question—to become Patrick O'Clery, schooner man and no longer Patrick O'Clery, Taoiseach.

It was at this moment Patrick Timothy O'Clery enjoyed a personal revelation. A feeling overcame him unlike any he experienced before, unlike any he expected to feel in his remaining years.

It suddenly occurred to Patrick that in the last month he became something more important than a schooner man or Taoiseach. It occurred to him he became a father to the amiable young lake sailor; a surrogate father as such, not merely a mate or co-captain, not merely a brother in boat building, but a father, like his own Da was to him.

The red-haired fiddler turned toward Carter and placed his freckled hand on the distraught youth's shoulder. In the kind voice of a story teller, as he spoke the night they met in Boston, he explained to Carter everything he knew, not only about Claire Dubois, but about the inimical Mr. O'Neil, about a man he simply called Boston, and, for good measure, he revealed the truth about *Maxine's* mooring mate, Commander Donovan.

By the time Patrick finished, he also detailed the island-wide referendum due to follow the announcement of the signed peace agreement. He discussed Father O'Clery and Captain O'Malley's joint declaration of a complete de-commissioning of clan weapons, and how they hoped this action would cement the peace agreement in place.

De-commissioning by a leading clan would be the foundation for more paramilitaries on both sides of the conflict to step forward and follow suit. The mere signing of the peace accord was not the end of the peace process, he explained, but rather the beginning.

"And theah ya haav it, laddie, patience and perseverance. If Bones Maatheson haas been able ta manage it fer ninety yeahs, sure a fine strappin' lad like yerself cahn manage it fer ninety days. But, skippah," the father figure cautioned with a benevolent smile, "thaht curiosity o' yers, ya got ta keep it in check, don't ya know!"

Carter smiled back in earnest. "I'll do my best," he assured Patrick. "I'll do my best." He repeated the promise as a mantra, like a Vedic hymn to be sung for eternity.

The two sailors rose from the moss-covered bench and walked toward the boat shed. *Red Shoes* and her crew of Irregulars, tirelessly working toward her launching, would be waiting.

Patrick knew that the woes of the young and heartsick were easy to overcome in the greater scheme of things. Carter Phillips had a long life ahead. While he sympathized with Carter's immediate predicament, it wasn't in his mind to mislead him into believing that all life is as easy as a broad reach on a calm sea. It certainly hadn't been for Martha, Bones and himself, nor the families from which they sprang; nor would it be for Northern Ireland, even with a newly signed peace agreement in hand.

CHAPTER 45

NINE-TENTHS SATISFIED

Breakfast with Martha changed after the arrival of Father O'Clery. Carter observed that Martha's decorum subtlety adjusted for her frocked guest. He found the adjustment humorous and interesting. The matron of the Purser's Quarters still spoke in her guttural voice, though she softened her social commentary. Carter noticed she had removed several choice adjectives from her frequent exclamations. Even though Martha never smoked at the dining table, Carter noticed there was no longer a cigarette to be found in the crotchety old house.

Carter also found Father O'Clery to be good company at the breakfast table. He was an intelligent, well read and a widely experienced man, reminding Carter a great deal of his professor at Notre Dame.

Father O'Clery and Captain O'Malley's recent pronouncement, their declaration of complete de-commissioning, was received world-wide with praise and solicitude. The timing was critical, just as Bones foretold. Carter felt a deep sense of gratitude for the opportunity to be in proximity of such noble events. He felt privileged to be associated with daring individuals such as the priest sitting across the breakfast table from him. They were the progenitors of peace.

What Carter did not overtly realize was that these same people were conspiring again and he was the subject of their conspiracy. They were all of the belief Carter should be kept busy. It would distract him from frustrations over Claire.

Each day the good witch and the good priest would encourage the lake sailor to proceed directly to Patrick's boat shop. Work was steaming ahead at a frenetic pace. A full month raced by with Carter barely coming up for air—barely taking a few moments for *Maxine* whom he worried would feel neglected.

Still Carter embraced the opportunity to work steadily on the schooner to avoid thinking about the thing most missing from his life. He was determined to follow the increasingly obvious program prescribed by the ones who seemed to love him most, the ones who hadn't abandoned him.

The care and support of his surrogate family filled his life with physical things to do and they filled his mind with unspoken assurances of eventual recovery. The medicine was working. Only occasionally did he find he needed to gulp down his curiosity or resist a powerful urge to try and find Claire.

≋≋≋

With the *Red Shoes* Irregulars hard at work instead of continually criticizing, production aboard the ruby-red schooner moved faster than Patrick had hoped. The August 1 launching remained set in his mind, but now, with the extra hands, he was able to complete the interior.

To this task, his surrogate son brought a level of design and refinement Patrick could only dream possible. Had Patrick been left to his own devices, *Red Shoes* interior would have looked more like a freighter cabin than the venerable work of nautical art Carter was handily fashioning.

When Patrick expressed surprise and gratitude, Carter jokingly stated, "I studied design for seven years, not seven days, laddie."

The young lake sailor laughed at his own joke and drew smiles from Patrick and Bones. They delighted at his apparent recovery from the depressing loss of the elusive Claire. Not only that, they could see Carter's focus and resilience infused the whole shop and all its workers with a positive charge of energy.

Even the good witch Martha, in her corduroy robe, in the great-room of the Purser's Quarters, felt his energy. It permeated the ether of Marblehead. Martha smiled broadly as her family's work progressed. She measured it her own way as the three fig trees grew in her tiny garden. She tended them lovingly each morning after breakfast.

Father O'Clery sat nearby, sharing the sunshine that bathed them all—even on the foggiest of Marblehead mornings. The Irish priest was amazed at the miracle of the figs and thanked his Lord for all the miracles unfolding in the lives of this new and unusual parish. These thanks he mixed profusely, dutifully, with his prayers of hope for the island-wide referendum. It was scheduled to occur on May 22, the coming Friday.

≋≋≋

The island-wide referendum originated with Bones and his colleagues. It would serve as proof of the commitment to peace by all the people of the island. Bones worked daily toward its success. He told Carter a couple of weeks prior that a poll taken on May 8 indicated 59 percent in favor, 29 percent against, and 12 percent undecided.

As the referendum neared, more often than not, Bones reached for his ear to listen to the tiny radio receiver disguised as a hearing aid. Moments later, he would return to his interminable task of monitoring Ernie's progress on the mast. The mast was coming along fine; however, Bones was only nine tenths satisfied with the prospects of the referendum. Despite polls reporting island-wide support, there were still the deeply entrenched Loyalists. Somehow they always seemed bigger than their numbers actually depicted. Their vociferous and dogged insistence that the agreements were a sham hurt; it couldn't be ignored.

Even worse, Bones believed, the hard line Loyalists appeared to be pinching themselves off into a precarious position. They were so far out they were beginning to be ostracized by everyone. Further, there were indications they were becoming an embarrassment to the Blair government. This was a shame, Bones thought, for clearly throughout the agreements Blair never abandoned the Unionists and, in fact, in terms of plain numbers, the majority of Unionists were supportive; reluctant perhaps, but supportive all the same.

The main thing worrying Bones now was the lack of consensus amongst the Unionists as a whole. The bitter and vitriolic Dr. Paisley, despite the rightness or wrongness of his beliefs, enjoyed that peculiar political state known as a plurality, that is, of the total number of Loyalists, his Democratic Unionist Party enjoyed the greatest membership.

Bones knew well there is intrinsic power in a plurality and a clever holder of that power can wreak havoc on the true majority because the true majority is, in most instances, a fragile coalition of weaker minorities bound together only in opposition of the holder of the plurality; otherwise, they agree on little else.

From the outset of the peace negotiations two years earlier, Bones tried everything in his diplomatic medical bag to bandage together a broad consensus amongst Loyalists. This was particularly hard for Bones considering his personal history and his family's tragic mistreatment at the hands of the government to which the Loyalists were so anxious to cling. Through it all, the old counselor was unable to move Dr. Paisley, the master of the plurality, in a cooperative direction.

"No surrender," was Paisley's ubiquitous catchphrase, and it was always followed quickly by his overstated justification that, "We won't negotiate with murderers." In those sanctimonious, holier-than-thou proclamations, the Moderator of the Free Presbyterian

Church, Dr. Paisley's title, believed unequivocally that he held the high moral ground.

Bones agonized over the contradiction of his protagonist's recurrent statements. He wondered endlessly how Dr. Paisley could be so right and so wrong at the same time!

Evidence clearly demonstrated that violence against Northern Ireland's Catholic civilians was significantly higher than violence inflicted on Protestants by the Catholic dominated Republican paramilitaries. In fact, Bones knew that even though no Loyalist paramilitary was a household word like the Irish Republican Army, they were ubiquitous and extremely dangerous, frequently brutal.

Overall, however, Loyalist violence against Republicans tended to be hidden in Protestant violence against Catholics. It was considered sectarian violence and carried religious connotations.

Conversely, the IRA, PIRA, real IRA and all the other fractious IRA's were fighting for unification of the Island, an objective they shared in common despite their divergent approaches. Theirs was a political, more than religious, war.

Bones remained deathly fearful the plurality of disenfranchised Loyalists, armed with a vociferous spokesman and ample backing from their secret paramilitaries, would do something dramatic to foul the referendum.

Much to his surprise, although a man of ninety years is essentially beyond surprise, the Loyalist Volunteer Forces or LVF, declared a cease fire on May 15 while at the same time urging a NO vote on the referendum. It was a clever maneuver, he had to admit.

≋≋≋

Carter, in the meantime, shied away from closely monitoring the referendum. "All things Irish," at least for the time being, caused a pain in his heart.

Building cabinetry for *Red Shoes* galley did not, so that is where he focused his attention. He did, however, notice the *Globe* as he sat in an uncomfortable chair at the Crab Claw's Grind, his new and disappointing coffee retreat.

The cover photo showed U2, the popular Irish rock band, holding a concert to promote the referendum—to get people out to vote. Joining U2 on stage was John Hume and David Trimble.

Carter smiled slightly for he had learned from Patrick that Bones had advanced their names to the selection committee in Oslo for nomination to receive the Nobel Peace prize. Patrick explained to Carter that Bones' only regret was that he couldn't, in good conscience, add Dr. Ian Paisley to the nominees; after all, the often acerbic reverend received the largest number of votes of any Northern Ireland politician. It would have been the crowning achievement in Dr. Paisley's long career to receive the Nobel Peace prize. However, that would not be. Carter had recently seen Dr. Paisley on Internet news casts. Though not feeling inordinately qualified in his opinion, Carter agreed with Bones that to hear him speak, to see the rancor in his eyes, it was clear that he was not a man of peace.

≋≋≋

In the end, when the votes were counted, the majority of the people of the emerald island took the next step forward. The All Island Referendum passed in the North and in the South with an overall 85 percent YES vote.

Bones realized, as the voting tallies came in, it had been the first all-island polling since 1918. He also took grave note that an exit poll reported that 94 percent of Catholics favored the agreement while only 55 percent of Protestants approved.

He suspected this disparity would mean the Belfast Agreement, while significant in tremendous ways, had not received the broad Unionist consensus for which he hoped.

Still, the ancient counselor smiled at the outcome. He felt pride in what he and the others accomplished, and of Tony Blair's accomplishments in particular. Though he made no mention of his admiration for Blair to any member of his Marblehead family, he felt once again the warmth that comes from being part of a bigger family, of being British. The brewing storm of the Paisley plurality would be the next challenge to meet, but not his. He sailed down the continuum of peace-making as far as he intended to go.

≋≋≋

By the fourth of July, *Red Shoes*' interior was completely framed in. Water tanks arrived from a metal shop in Revere; plumbing and electrical fixtures were mounted and then the fine joinery.

Patrick watched in silent wonder as Carter labored diligently alongside his boatbuilding mates. The soon to be schooner-man mused at the simple beauty of Carter's thought process, the way he paused, studied and sketched his alternatives.

Occasionally the architect would construct a scale model and study it at various angles, scrunching close, considering different aspects. The old sailor's excitement rose as he joined Carter in the examination of the model; their faces only inches apart, their breaths passing through the model as they spoke their observations.

Patrick never before knew, let alone thought about, how an architect worked, only that they existed. He wondered now at the creative well-spring that must exist in the mind of his surrogate son, overjoyed that the water of such a spring was sprinkled over his yacht of redemption; a baptism of beauty in form.

≋≋≋

When nightfall arrived and dinner was taken up by Martha, Carter would studiously walk to Tucker's Wharf, climb aboard his dinghy and motor out onto the water to explore the bustling harbor. With summer vacation in full swing, Marblehead became a dreamland of lights, colors, boats, and sailors. More than a thousand yachts surrounded *Maxine* and *Cassiopeia* as they swayed together on their moorings.

Dance bands played at the yacht clubs and expensive motor cars delivered wealthy vacationers to their "cottages" on the Neck. Carter would frequently land his dinghy at a yacht club float. From there he would walk the cobblestone streets of the quiet and exclusive Neck. He studied the mansions these people called summer homes and wondered, as he often did among boats in the harbor, who occupied these magnificent places.

Despite the excitement of summer vacation, there remained in Carter a subdued but discernable, melancholy. It wasn't outright sadness nor was it overt depression. Still, in his idle moments, like these evenings on the water, his thoughts kept slipping back to Claire.

When he played his guitar, sitting in the dark of *Maxine's* cockpit, he could sometimes hear her voice. He imagined her singing the sad lament that glorious night in Gloucester. If he struck a minor chord he could see her porcelain face framed by jet black hair. If he played fast he saw her step dancing, arms straight down in the traditional pose.

In an increasingly vain attempt to control his feelings, Carter moved about his yacht in overt attempts to reconnect with *Maxine* before she became infused with Claire's spirit. A trip to the engine room to check filters and fluids worked well, but then he'd go to the fo'c'sle for some reason and the most painful of all memories would be laid bare. He would recall how they made love, warm in each others arms, their bodies intertwined in passion.

Finally, something inside snapped. It was during an otherwise innocuous trip to the fo'c'sle. His desperate need to find Claire wasn't going away. All the good intentions of his surrogate family, keeping him busy and caring for him as they were, weren't changing the intransigent feeling the lake sailor felt for his mysterious coffee maiden.

Carter's oath to keep curiosity in check was well intended, but he became convinced it was strangling the essence of his life. Curiosity was the wellspring of his creativity, the source of the uniqueness separating him from the dull and ordinary. It was, he thought, why Claire shared her being with him, loved him, in fact, equal to the way he had fallen in love with her.

There must be a way to reconcile the feelings overwhelming him each time he entered the fo'c'sle. He couldn't disavow the fact he loved a mysterious and missing woman. To pretend he didn't was a fraud of his own peculiar making, a condition he could no longer tolerate.

He resolved to undo the emptiness enveloping him and set upon the challenge of figuring out the right thing to do. This line of thought brought him quickly to the captain of the afterguard. He sought the counsel of the man who garnered within him the fullest of life's experiences – he spoke to Bones.

≋≋≋

"Bloody well sit down, old son. This is gonna take a bleedin' bit o' time. In fact, why don't ya make us a couple of those fancy coffee drinks on thaht chrome contraption thaht haas mysteriously shown up ovah theah?"

Bones pointed with his pipe stem toward the boat shed's coffee station. Patrick had asked Martha to find an espresso machine and Bones' volunteered to pay for it.

Taking his cue, Carter strode up to the machine. It stood large and modern next to the boat shed's antiquated brown-ringed coffee pot.

Bones smiled as the lake sailor carefully ground fresh beans. They watched as coffee filtered through two spouts into a small stainless steel cup. An enticing aroma filled the air. Patrick had become a customer, too, and from time to time Ernie joined them. The other Irregulars never came around. They liked their coffee "regulah," New England style, cream and two sugars. No espresso, no foam.

Carter turned back to Bones. "There must be a way to get a message to Claire. I can't be certain of course, but I think she cares for me as much as I do for her." He paused to swallow a sip then continued. "Perhaps there is a way to make contact with her father or brothers. She told me about her brothers. She said I'd like them and they'd like me. I can't believe any of her men folk wouldn't be concerned about her happiness."

Bones sipped his latte. Despite the desperateness of his feelings, Carter nearly laughed out loud at the sight of foam covering the whiskers above Bones' thick lips.

"I haav no doubt they do, Caahtah. Huhr fathah is very protective as I've been known to be m'self," Bones said.

Carter thought of Martha.

Bones wiped his mouth and discovered the reason for Carter's earlier smile. He smiled too and then asked Carter if the foam was gone from his whiskers.

"The difference heah, Caahtah, is thaht theah aah good reasons to be protective, thaht is, beyond the normal anxiety a bleedin' fathah haas for his only daughtah." The old counselor's demeanor suddenly turned stolid and darkness came over his previously jovial face. "Seven days ago O'Neil was spotted in Libya, then five days ago in Palestine. The wily buggah haas slipped out of sight once more. This time, howevah, Israeli intelligence is aftah him and they'll play merry hell wif 'im if they find 'im. His life won't be worth a two-bob bit, and thaht's not ta say I approve of theah methods. I'm simply pointin' out the severity of the bleedin' situation."

The old sailor sipped again from his steaming drink. His demeanor appeared to be lightening up and he returned his pipe stem to his lips.

"Clayah won't be reassigned till thaht barmy bastahd is eliminated. Her fathah, whom I've known for a long time, will see ta thaht. I cahn make a call on your behalf, but Caahtah, old son, heah is wheah you aah goin' to haav to hold still; you need to be patient. This will take time."

Carter looked at the Figurehead and realized that "taking time" might mean much longer in Bones' paradigm than his own.

"Keep on your current regimen. We aah bein' watched as much as we aah watchin' baack, do ya undahstand? You aah safest, and so is Miss Clayah, if theah appears to be no furthah connection between the two of you. It's best if it appears thaht the love of the young and restless dissipates, as if you two haav moved on."

Bones shifted in his chair, began to wheel it toward the mast, and Carter followed alongside.

"It was in old England wheah the phrase red herrin' was first coined, Caahtah. Did ya know thaht bleedin' fact, eh?"

Carter suspected a Patrick-like tale in the making. Patrick obviously learned some of his storytelling style from the old seaman.

"It came about durin' the old times when Bobbies began usin' dogs to track criminals. Eventually, the bloody thugs got smaart and would toss rottin' herrin' on the trail behind 'em. The hounds would be distracted by the powerful odor and couldn't regain theah prey.

"Well, Caahtah, I'm talkin' about the same thin' now. The busyness you aah engaged in wif Pahtrick and the crew haas several purposes, not the least of which is exactly as I just described. Workin' dawn till dusk, stayin off the Internet, keepin' ta yourself aftah dark, all those things will throw O'Neil off the trail thaht would lead to Clayah, and you, too, fer thaht mattah.

"He nevah did like you, old son. He thought you'd be gettin' in the way, even if by accident, and thaht didn't sit well wif 'im, the barmy bastahd.

"You see, Caahtah, your lovely Clayah was a bleedin' good listener. She did what they hired huhr ta do real well. She ovahheard O'Neil and his disreputable associates from the south o' Boston, and when she heard what they were plannin', she wasn't shy about passin' the information on ta huhr handler.

"Boston in turn placed into motion countermeasures thaht interrupted the blighter's ability ta follow through with certain moves against the O'Clery clan—moves thaht would haav hahd a profoundly negative effect upon the clan and the outcome o' the bloody peace agreement.

"Although none of us aah absolutely certain thaht O'Neil haas figured out who leaked 'is secrets, no chances haav been taken with Miss Clayah; as by now you haav figured out. By the nature of how spyin' works, and just as often doesn't work, theah is great danger until O'Neil is found, hence Clayah's complete removal from the scene."

Carter readily understood the imperative of Bones' words, but was stunned by the profundity of his remarks. Carter realized he, too, remained under the protective veil of his atypical family of Bones and Patrick. He had incorrectly figured that after the referendum passed all the excitement was over. He thought they were free from the intrigue surrounding the agreement and free to live out their remaining lives like normal people. Now Carter realized that was not entirely the case, and furthermore, may never be.

Bones watched silently as this realization overcame his young protégé. He could see it blow over Carter like a gray wind foretelling yet another gale. Bones felt confident over time, as all good sailors must, that Carter would weather the storm and be wiser and stronger for having done so.

August 1, 1998. 14:05 GMT
Wind West, North West – 4 knots
Sky Hazy, Humid
Temp., 84 degrees F.
Red Shoes joined the fleet.

Patrick's ignominious first entry into his log belied the red-haired boy's unfathomable excitement. He closed the gilded gift from Martha and Carter. They had acquired the leather-bound logbook in Beverly at the nautical gift shop next door to Martha's favorite seafood restaurant.

Patrick's sparse entry barely told the tale of the day of *Red Shoes* launching, a day that brought out so many townspeople, Carter couldn't believe his eyes.

The lake sailor gazed at the crowded wharf. He recognized dozens of people from whom he purchased supplies and equipment during the previous five months; they in turn brought their wives and children who skittered wildly about in the throng. Several of the young Irishmen from the other side of the B&B milled around the wharf, smoking cigarettes and talking to each other quietly in their foreign tongue, displaying a joviality Carter rarely noticed before.

The captain of *Gael na Mara* was on the hard as well; his vessel having moved in close, as if to serve as midwife at the birth of Patrick O'Clery's lifelong dream. Standing next to Captain O'Malley was Commander Donovan, now captain of the pleasure yacht, *Cassiopeia*.

Donovan's dream also lay on her mooring, the one between *Maxine* and *Red Shoes*. His dream would soon carry him across the seas, and to this end charts of the Indian Ocean and the Maldivian atolls were still spread out on his nav station.

Bones, who recently made frequent trips aboard the sleek yacht, had made copious notes and course headings on the charts. The Figurehead had sailed to the Maldives when he was a young merchant mariner, back when it was still a British protectorate.

Patrick skittered about, nervous with anticipation. Watching the product of years of work floating above the ground, hanging from the crane, elicited the same response in him as it did Carter each season he launched *Maxine*. Carter smiled at the thought that his surrogate father was made of the same fears and passions as he. All the years Carter worried at launch time seemed okay now, affirmed since it was true of Patrick O'Clery, as well.

Looking again into the crowd, Carter found Martha. He half expected to see her dressed in her flowing corduroy night gown. The gown would have been a fine uniform of the day, he thought. Instead, she dressed in an aqua blue dress that might have been worn by Lauren Bacall at the launching of Humphrey Bogart's yacht. It might have even been worn by Martha on her wedding day.

Martha's hair was set high and lipstick painted her lips as red as the red schooner swinging above the wharf. She wore the pearl necklace that always adorned her neck when she and Carter dined in Beverly. In her frail but steady hands, Martha clutched a champagne bottle. It looked bigger than it really was, exaggerated by her diminutive stature. A broad smile seemed permanently fixed on brightly-colored lips.

Trailing around the good witch like handmaidens to a queen was her gaggle of sister witches, all from Salem, all chattering in excited tones and exhibiting exaggerated gestures and waves.

Nearby, to Carter's surprise, sitting with Bones as if she were the belle of an imaginary ball, sat the inimical Madame Russalka. The elder witch looked as though she had just stepped from a gypsy peddler's wagon. She leaned forward on a crooked cane, smiling without an overt smile, casting a magic spell upon the proceedings, granting Patrick's most present wish: that *Red Shoes* would be a lucky ship.

Bones, sitting next to the gypsy queen, gripped his pipe stem between his thick, crusty, seaman's lips. Carter noted that the pipe pointed at the proudest, highest possible angle. It looked perhaps as if Madame Russalka's magic must have thrust it there. Then Carter contemplated whether it was the magic of Bones seeing his family together, out in the public, out from behind the veil of their previously covert lives that caused the pipe to rise.

Patrick's loyal subjects, the entire contingent of *Red Shoes* Irregulars, had set their lawn chairs on the wharf the night before to secure the finest view. Lined up as they were at Bones' side, and he next to the gypsy queen, caused the whole lot of them to look like they were auditioning for a fantasy film.

Ernie, the proud and regaling yard boss, titular leader of the Irregulars, gazed at his crew who in turn gazed in awe as the vessel was lowered to a point where the proud, smiling Martha smashed the green and gold bottle while calling out the red schooner's name to the cheering crowd. A more proud and dignified crew of boat builders hadn't graced Tucker's Wharf for many decades, perhaps since the war, the big one, the one in which Ireland remained neutral.

≋≋≋

Despite his curious gaze as he studied the vast crowd, Carter was entirely unaware that he too was being watched. Standing silently behind a window on the third floor of an ancient sail loft looming above Tucker's Wharf were two specially invited guests.

As per Bones' invitation, they arrived, traveling incognito from the Sonoran desert. They were spirited into Marblehead late the previous night. The visitors stayed in secret rooms hidden high in the abandoned sail loft. A third man, an armed escort dressed in a crumpled blue suit and looking perpetually weary, stood several paces behind the father and daughter from Wisconsin.

Standing a couple steps back from the window so they couldn't be seen, the youngest of the trio, her jet black hair brushed behind a beautifully sun tanned cheek, pointed out Carter Phillips to her father.

The professor-lawyer-spy drew field glasses to his eyes.

A second later, with one arm wrapped gently around his daughter, Louis Francoise Dubois indicated that he did indeed see the man to whom she pointed. With a smile and a hug, Claire's loving father acknowledged his daughters joy, her unrestrained elation to once again be in proximity of the man she loved.

JOHN BRIGHT
c. 1811-1889

Force is not a remedy.

Speech at Birmingham, England – November 16, 1880

EPILOGUE

DECEMBER 2004

An ancient fishing dhoni sailed cautiously toward a single mast rising above the wasted atoll. The son of the Maldivian captain peered through a tarnished brass telescope, shouting down from his perch at the masthead. He spoke in his native Dhivehi.

"Papa . . . it's a sailboat, just as the old man said."

The boy skittered higher up the rig. He watched as *Maxine's* hull broke the horizon. The crew gazed across their vessel's bow, hoping to see the stranded vessel.

The creaking dhoni tacked closer to the crescent reef, then hove to in deep water. The brown-skinned boy continued peering through the spyglass, reporting each detail with the ebullience of a youth on his first rescue mission.

≋≋≋

The wiry, sun-leathered gang of fishermen launched Patrick's vadhu dhoni. The old Irishman climbed aboard and raised the dhoni's lateen sail into a growing noontime breeze. Within minutes, the dhoni skimmed into the crescent shoal of the atoll.

Maxine sat upright in the center of the atoll, stranded on a small circle of land, her keel sunk deep in the mud. At first glance, the scene reminded Patrick of the mythical ark on Mount Ararat.

A dog's bark made Patrick jerk to attention. He immediately recognized the bark as that of Sir Tom, the only sign of life on the devastated atoll. Patrick groaned with anxiety and apprehension. It wasn't the lost resort that raised his anxiety—that could re-built. It was Carter, or more specifically, the fear of losing Carter that caused his heart to move upward toward his throat.

Steering his vessel toward *Maxine*, Patrick prayed to a Catholic God on a Muslim sea. He prayed his surrogate son would suddenly appear on *Maxine*'s deck, affirming that he had survived the tsunami. Tacking in closer, it became apparent that Sir Tom was standing on an object lodged in the sprawling arms of a denuded tree. The hapless creature and the tree stood about twenty-five yards ahead of the stranded sloop. There was no sign of Carter on board *Maxine*. Patrick sensed the pall of death and spotted several corpses lying in the sand on the beach ahead.

He sailed closer, dreading what he might see, thinking he would at least retrieve Sir Tom. It was then he suddenly realized what the three-legged dog was perched upon. A broad smile creased the freckled leather face of the Red-Haired Boy.

≋≋≋

Carter Phillips was jarred from his hazy world of recollections by the sudden, shrill bark of his canine sentinel. His first cognizant thought was that of dread, recalling his fractured arm and the door crashing into his head.

A further round of yelps jolted him from his morbid state. He cocked his head forward. A spasm of pain accompanied the movement, filling him with nausea he fought to keep down. In a few seconds, he was able to look in the direction Sir Tom pointed. There on the horizon, he saw two boats: a large fishing vessel and a small vadhu dhoni. He lay back again and breathed a tremendous breath of relief.

It's Patrick, Sir Tom; it's got to be Patrick!

The three-legged dog affirmed his conjecture with another round of yelps broadcast emphatically in the direction of the swiftly approaching dhoni.

≋≋≋

"Sure then, laddie, all this time you was laid up in this heah tree you nevah knew yer great wooden lassie was right behind you, eh, skippah." Patrick O'Clery spoke calmly, chuckling in his kindly way.

Carter wanted to respond with a clever quip. However, each movement Patrick made to untangle him resulted in a painful tremor. He whispered a brief thanks between sips of water from a goat-leather pouch the fishermen sent ashore with Patrick. Swallowing a rejuvenating mouthful, Carter inquired how it was that Patrick survived the tsunami.

"Well then, laddie, I cahn't say theah was much to it; it all haapened in an instant. Ya know, skippah, or perhaps ya don't, thaht a tsunami cahn travel over 500 miles per hour undah watah. The damn thin' slipped under me and was gone in seconds. It weren't till the blasted thin' hit the shallows of the atoll thaht it gained height and started trippin' o'er itself."

This was all Carter needed to know, at least for the moment. The next question's answer was one he truly dreaded. After deliberately blocking all contemplation of the possibilities throughout his time in the tree, he finally blurted out—"Has there been word from Male? Was it struck, too?"

"Too soon ta say, Cahtah. Theah's no way ta know . . ."

"I feel as if I've been in this tree for days."

"It's only been two hours since the wave hit, son. The fishermen aah anxious to get ta Lhaviyani atoll and see ta theah own affairs. They'll drop us in Male.

To Be Continued

In the next Carter Phillips Adventure

GLOSSARY OF SAILING TERMS

Abaft – The area of a boat behind the midpoint or a designated point.

Abeam – The area next to the middle side of a boat.

Astern – Behind the boat.

Athwart Ship – Across the vessel, rather than in line with the vessel.

Backing to the west – In reference to the wind changing direction from east to west, often an indicator of improving conditions or increasing barometric pressure.

Beam – The measurement across the widest point of the hull. The word is sometimes used to refer to the approximate middle side of the hull since that is where the measurement is taken.

Beating – Sailing to windward. Pointing into the direction of the wind. The same as close hauling and usually a rough ride.

Beauford Scale – An accepted scale for expressing the force of the wind.

Benthic Organisms – Creatures found in the depths of salt water.

Bilge – An open area below the flooring where water accumulates.

Bitter End – The end of an anchor line that lays behind the bitts it is attached too. It also means the end of the line not attached to or working on something.

Bollard – a large steel post for tying off ships.

Boom – The spar that secures the bottom (foot) of the sail. It is attached at the base of the mast and extends aft where it is controlled by the main sheet.

Boot Stripe – A painted stripe just above the water line of a boat. It is usually about 4-6 inches wide. Generally considered decorative, but also indicates the boat's design waterline.

Boson's Chair – A canvas chair to hoist crew up the mast for repairs.

Bowsprit – The timber spar that extends past the bow of the vessel to which a fore stay is usually attached.

Bumpers – Large rubber bumpers/fenders for protecting a yacht tied up to a dock.

Bring Up Fast – To secure, or tie down, usually objects together.

Cabin Sole – The floor that is walked upon in a boat.

Clamp – A longitudinal structural member on wooden boats that ties the tops of ribs together and becomes a plate upon which the deck beams rest.

Carvel Planking – A shaped plank that is designed to receive caulking.

Cleating Off – To tie to a cleat, a deck fitting for securing rope.

Ceiling Boards – The inner wood paneling of a yacht. Not necessarily the ceiling as commonly referred to in a house; a house merely being a poorly built boat.

Cockpit Coaming – The raised boards that frame and surround the vessel's cockpit.

Come About – To tack a boat into the direction the wind is coming from.

Cove Stripe – A very thin, carved line that defines the sheer line of the boat. It is commonly filled with gold leaf as a decorative feature.

Cuddy – A small cabin on a boat.

Curtains and Holidays – Descriptions of varnishing mistakes. If a spot is missed it's called a holiday; if too much is applied and the varnish slumps or drips it is called a curtain.

Ded Reckoning – This is short for deduced reckoning. A means of charting a course by merely keeping track of time, speed and direction. It is the only alternative when sun, moon, stars or modern electronics are unavailable.

Design Waterline – That point where the boat should sit in the water as predicted by the naval architect.

Double Ender – A vessel whose stern comes to a point, somewhat like her bow. This design is also sometimes called a canoe stern.

Down the Ways – Wood rails upon which a cradle holding a newly constructed boat slides down into the water. Launching a boat.

Fender Boards – Wooden planks that lay outboard of bumpers or fenders. They are usually about 6 to 8 feet in length and protect the boat while tying up to pilings or other boats.

Fid – A piece of wood that forms a railing to keep things from rolling off tables or shelves when a boat heels.

Flemish Coil – To coil a line by laying it flat and circling around itself.

Fluky Wind – Wind that changes direction and intensity unpredictably.

Forecastle, Fo'c'sle – The space below the forward deck. Usually the lower ranking crews quarters on large vessels. Pronounced *Fo'csal.*

Forefoot – The large section of wood that lies below the stem piece and before the keel on a wooden boat.

Foremast – The forward mast on any multiple-masted vessel.

Foremast Jack – A reference to low-ranking crew that lived in quarters forward the foremast (the least comfortable place on a boat).

Gear Box – The equivalent of a transmission in an automobile.

Gimbaled – Hinged so it (i.e. table, stove, lamp) remains level as the boat moves.

Halyard – A rope that raises a sail.

Hanking On – Clipping a sail on to a stay.

Hard, On the – Referring to a boat being out of the water for repair or storage.

Heeling – The tilted angle of a sailboat underway.

Helm – The device that turns the rudder, either a wheel or tiller.

Hove To – (heave to) To hold the vessel into the wind.

Hull Speed – The theoretical limit of the speed a displacement hull vessel can attain. In fact, under certain conditions displacement hulls can exceed hull speed but not by a great amount.

Hull Up – The point where a look-out can see the hull of an approaching vessel.

In Irons – A point where the boat has come up into the wind and sails can't be made to draw, resulting in no forward movement.

Inter-Coastal Waterway – A series of connected channels, rivers and bays that form a protected passage from southern New England to the Florida Keys, protected from the open waters of the Atlantic.

Iron Ginny – A slang reference to the engine of a sailboat.

Jib Sail, Jibs'l – A sail flown before the mast, from a forward stay.

Jibe – To tack a boat away from the direction the wind is coming from. A dangerous maneuver in anything but light wind.

Keelson – The lowest member of a wooden boat's framework.

Knees – Structural members on wooden boats that add support between the ribs and deck. Knees form a structural triangle that adds rigidity.

Lazarette – A small compartment or locker located aft the cockpit. It is typically a place for storing docking lines and other hardware used in the cockpit area.

List of Particulars – A list of equipment and specifications of a yacht.

Line – The proper term for rope used to control sails.

Lines – A term meaning the shape of the boat, as the designer drew lines to define its shape. Sometimes it is used in reference to the vessel's designed water line, that is, where it should float when sitting in the water.

Loll – Instability, as in the case of a vessel whose center of gravity is too high, or caused by taking on too much water.

Marlin Spike – A metal spike around 5 inches long often used for prying apart strands of line for splicing and other chores on deck.

Mooring Pennant – The line attached at the mooring buoy going up to the bow cleat or Samson post of the vessel. It often has a second small line with a buoy and flag attached to it. The flag staff can then be reached by someone on deck to make it easy to bring aboard.

NOAA – The National Oceanic and Atmospheric Administration.

On Station – The position of warships in a blockade.

Pad Eye – A stainless steel or bronze deck plate with a molded loop through which deck hardware (like blocks) are attached.

Painter – The line that comes off the bow of a dinghy used to tie it to the mother vessel.

Pitching – Rocking fore and aft.

Pitchpoling – When a vessel rocks fore and aft so much it topples over on itself. An exceedingly dangerous event.

Point – A point is 11.25 degrees on the compass rose, making 32 points total.

Port – The left side of the vessel when standing aft looking forward.

Quarter Deck - A term usually applied to large vessels describing the most aft and sometimes raised deck. The position the captain normally takes to watch over the entire vessel operation.

Running Back Stay – An additional stay used to hold the mast up. The are two, one on each side, and are only rigged while on one tack or the other.

Sawn Oak Floors – Large solid sections of wood upon which the cabin sole rests. It is not the floor that is walked upon, that would be the cabin sole. Floors in this context would be analogous to floor joists in a house.

Set – The direction a tide or current pushes a boat.

Sheer Line – The primary line that defines the curve of the topsides of a boat. It commonly has "spring" which means it comes upward on both ends. Or it might be reverse, meaning it droops downward on each end. Or, it may be flat, like modern speed boats. *Maxine* and *Gael na Mara* each have "spring" on their sheer lines.

Sheet – A rope that controls a sail.

Sheeting In – To bring a sail under control, or improving its performance, by pulling on the rope (called a sheet) that controls it.

Shrouds – The wires and/or ropes that hold a mast up on each side.

Spars – Masts and booms when referred to collectively.

Spline Weights – Also known as "Ducks" – Lead weight with a bent rod protruding that holds a plastic spline in position to draw curved lines on a boat plan.

Spreaders – Struts that hold the side shrouds away from the mast, thereby creating a structural triangle that holds the mast upright under sideway forces (wind in the sails).

Sou'wester – A New England fishing hat with a short bill and a long backside to keep water from going down the back collar.

Standing Rigging – The shrouds and stays that hold a mast in place.

Starboard – The right side of the vessel when standing aft looking forward.

Stays – The wires and/or ropes that hold a mast up fore or aft.

Stem to Stern – The front to the back of a boat.

Stem Piece – A large, shaped, solid section of wood that forms the forward-most shape of a wooden point. It is where the forward plank ends are fastened. It is essentially the bow.

Tack – To change the direction of the boat into the wind.

Telltales – Short strands of lightweight material taped to the leading edge of both sides of forward sails. Used primarily for performance sail trim. If both telltales blow directly aft then the wind is even on both sides of the sail (optimal performance).

Tiller – A long bar of wood used to control a rudder.

Topmast – The upper mast attached atop the main mast on square riggers.

Topping Lift – A line or wire that extends down from the top of the mast to the most aft point on the boom. It holds the boom off the deck when no sail is hoisted.

Well Found – A vessel shone to be in good condition upon completion of a marine survey.

Yawing – Moving with a wobbling motion, particularly while sailing down wind with following seas.

HISTORIC TIMELINE

Ireland has never enjoyed a long-term or widely-accepted central government. It continues today to evolve in both leadership and political paradigm. For this and other reasons it is exceedingly difficult to create a clear and definitive timeline of Irish political history.

Following is an abbreviated history of Northern Ireland and its relationship with Great Britain, specifically England.

References to Robert Erskine Childers, Erskine Hamilton Childers and his son Erskine Childers III, all prominent figures in modern Irish history, are shown in bold type.

The author recommends readers interested in Irish history make an independent study using this timeline as an initial guide. There are numerous resources available and the Internet is a good place to begin. Even though the Internet is an un-juried resource, most sites offer references for verification and further research. Several universities in the United States and Northern Ireland maintain essential, accessible databases for research purposes.

6,000 BC
First human settlements, believed to have migrated from Britain.

2000 – 300 BC
Celtic peoples known as Gaels invaded Ireland (a.k.a. Hibernia).

432 AD
Christian missionaries arrived, most notably, St. Patrick.

600 – 900 AD
Ireland's Golden Age took place during the European Dark Ages.

795 AD
The first of two waves of Viking incursions began, primarily Norwegians.

910 AD
The second of two waves of Viking incursions began, including competing Danes. Over time, the Irish quelled incursions and the Vikings settled into Irish life, becoming merchants and seamen. Eventually, alliances were formed and the Vikings became involved with Ireland's own internal struggles.

1014 AD
The Irish defeated Norwegian & Danish forces at Clontarf (near Dublin). A period of kings and clans followed, competing for power, none rising to unify the island under a single authority.

1169 AD
Norman settlers (Vikings who settled in Normandy, then to England and Wales) began arriving, many as refugees banished by the English king Edward the Confessor.

1200 AD
King Henry II and his son John infused greater English influence by installing foreign-born lords and earls into Ireland giving rise to Anglo-Norman clans. Eventually, every native ruler was legally the tenant of an English earl, baron, or the English king directly.

1400 – 1500 AD

Irish lordships gained prominence and English influence waned. However, rivalries prevented unification.

1500 – 1550 AD

Henry VII and Henry VIII reasserted English control over Ireland. Henry VIII succeeded at having the Irish Parliament declare him king of Ireland. Henry broke with the Catholic Church and commenced a gradual transplanting of English and Scottish Protestant settlers.

1550 – 1600 AD

Henry VIII's daughter Elizabeth became Queen and previous and unsuccessful rebellions caused her to implement more stringent measures to stabilize English domination of the Island. The Irish, with aid from the Spanish, conducted the Nine Years War, ending in an English victory.

1600 – 1650 AD

James I came to power, succeeding Queen Elizabeth in 1603. He encouraged English and Scottish settlers, particularly in the areas of the uprising. Meanwhile, Irish nobles fled and historians believe this to be the real end of Gael civilization in terms of political dominance in Ireland.

1650 – 1750 AD

England, through the hand of Oliver Cromwell, completely subjugated the island. James II, an overt Catholic, was ousted by William of Orange and Protestant ascendancy was secured. By the year 1665, only 20 percent of the land was controlled by Catholics. By 1695, penal legislation was enacted against Irish Catholics and dissenters. Acts were passed prohibiting them from practicing their faith, stripping them of their wealth, restricting their education, and preventing them from buying land, holding office or voting.

1750 – 1800 AD

Rebellions in the 1790s failed and ongoing immigrations began dispersing Irish people around the globe, particularly to America. Reportedly, one-third to one-half of American Revolutionary forces were Irish born or direct descendents. In response to the rebellious Irish Catholics, the Protestant based Orange Boys organized in 1795. They evolved into the Orange Order, so named for William of Orange, victor of the Battle of the Boyne in 1690 (the ousting of James II). Wolf Tone formed the United Irishmen and with assistance of the French attempted a failed rebellion in 1798.

1800 – 1801 AD

The British passed the Act of Union in 1800 and abolished the Irish Parliament. A United Kingdom of Great Britain and Ireland became official in 1801.

1823 – 1829 AD

Daniel O'Connell organized the Catholic Association resulting in the ability of Catholics to hold office in Parliament by 1829.

1830 – 1840 AD

237,000 Irish immigrants entered the United States.

1840 – 1850 AD

The Great Famine hit Ireland. An extreme dependency on a single crop, a potato brought to Ireland by the Spanish from Peru, played a significant role in the famine. There were a series of crop failures. Additionally, there were failures by landowners and government to address the problem. Ireland still exported food during those years, while their own population suffered malnutrition and starvation. For many, emigration was the only hope for relief and the Passenger Act of 1847 was passed. The act granted eligible emigrants 10 cubic feet and a supply of food and water on board what would become known as "coffin" or "famine" ships. An estimated 20 - 40 percent of the passengers died en route or shortly after arrival at their destination. Approximately 800,000 Irish immigrants entered the United States during this period alone. Although historians agree that Britain was not solely responsible for the terrible event, the issue has remained highly sensitive and a left a bitter legacy in Anglo-Irish relations. It was too little too late to quell the misery.

1860 – 1880 AD
American Irish descendents form the Fenian Brotherhood and clearly state their purpose: to form an independent Ireland. By 1870, a new movement calling for home rule for Ireland began and a Home Rule bill was introduced in 1886 but failed. A second was introduced shortly thereafter and also failed to be enacted, but did serve to focus the debate.

Robert Erskine Childers, an Englishman who became an advocate of Irish Home Rule was born in 1870. He authored papers advocating Irish home rule and wrote a fiction novel titled *Riddle of the Sands*. He was eventually shot by an Irish Free State firing squad. His son Erskine Hamilton Childers would become President of Ireland (Eire) in 1973. In turn, the President's son Erskine Childers III would become a prominent United Nations diplomat.

1880 – 1915 AD
The Gaelic League was formed to promote the Irish language and culture. Sinn Fein was organized in 1905. The Irish Republican Brotherhood believed the British wouldn't release control unless forced to by violence. Another version of the Home Rule bill was introduced and passed in 1912 but suspended when England was drawn into WWI. Promises were made that if Ireland helped England in the war, Home Rule would be a certainty.

Erskine Hamilton Childers was born November 11, 1905, the son of Robert Erskine Childers and Mary Alden (Osgood) Childers. He would become President of Eire in 1973.

Robert Erskine Childers and his American Bostonian wife, Mollie Osgood, used their yacht, *Asgard*, a gift from his wife's father, to run guns from Belgium to Northern Ireland in 1914 for the Ulster Volunteers (a nationalist organization) in advance of the Easter Uprising of 1916.

1916 AD
The Easter Uprising of 1916 was another in the series of failed attempts at securing Irish independence. Eamon DeValera, one of the leaders of the Easter Uprising (the only surviving one), would later become a prominent Irish Free State leader.

1919 AD
WWI ended, however, frustration mounted over the failure of Britain to enact Home Rule and tensions rose leading to the Irish War of Independence. For several years Northern Irish forces, which were now known as the Irish Republican Army, fought British armies. Unorthodox guerrilla tactics by the Irish resulted in an Irish advantage, but the war wearied people on both sides. The British offered to meet and treaty talks began in December 1921.

Robert Erskine Childers moved to Ireland, became an Irish citizen, and was made Director of Publicity for the First Dail. Childers published several papers including "Military Rule in Ireland" and "Is Ireland a Danger to England"?

1921 – 1922 AD
Michael Collins, leader of the Irish Republican Army, agreed to British terms of peace which included partitioning Northern Ireland from the 26 county Irish Free State to the south. The Irish Free State was granted dominion status. The northern counties would remain under British control to pacify Unionist Protestants.

1922 – 1923 AD

Disagreement over these terms resulted in the Irish Civil War and former allies fought against each other. It came to an end in 1923 when the Irish Free State wore down its opposition known both as the Irregulars and the IRA.

Robert Erskine Childers sided with Northern Ireland and the Republican (nationalist) cause and was eventually hunted down and arrested by Irish Free State soldiers. He was charged with possessing a handgun, found guilty by a secret court marshal, and shot by a firing squad on November 24, 1922, while awaiting an appeal.

Irish Republican sympathizers in various forms continued to resist British rule over the following decades.

1929 AD

Erskine Childers III - was born. He was the son of Erskine Hamilton Childers and grandson of Robert Erskine Childers.

1937 AD

Eamon De Valera gained prominence in the Irish Free State and replaced the 1922 Constitution of Michael Collins with one of his preference and renamed the Irish Free State, *Eire* (Gaelic for Ireland).

1940 – 1950 AD

Ireland struggled with issues surrounding WWII with many believing England was still the enemy. Unable to condone Nazi Germany however, the island remained neutral during the war while allowing Allied forces to visit Irish ports and airstrips as necessary.

1948 AD

The Republic of Ireland Act established the lower 26 counties a free country, independent of Britain. In effect, this country was, or had been known as the Irish Free State, Eire, and the Republic of Ireland.

This did not include Northern Ireland, which was part of the United Kingdom, situated on the island of Ireland.

1960 – 1965 AD

By the 1960's the civil rights of the Catholics had become blatantly abused with gerrymandering intended to secure Protestant dominance. Northern Ireland unionists, supported and protected by Britain, and nationalists, backed by the IRA, became more polarized.

1967 AD

The Northern Ireland Civil Rights Association was formed in January 1967 in direct response to callous abuses of Catholic civil rights.

1968 AD

The first of numerous civil rights marches, fashioned loosely after the civil rights marches in the American South, began taking place. The national Irish television station RTE captured Royal Ulster Constabulary beating marchers and public officials which eroded confidence in the RUC.

1969 AD

The looming crises deepened and in August the British sent troops in to quell the rioting. On August 14, 1969, five Catholics and one Protestant were killed. The Provisional IRA was formed in response to criticism that the IRA wasn't doing enough to protect Catholics.

1970 – 1971 AD

The Unionist government, with British backing, used internment without trial in an attempt to control the riots but the maneuver backfired and raised widespread animosity towards its enforcers. Internment was critically objected to by the international community as inhuman and degrading. Many of the people detained suffered beatings and alleged torture. Later the European Commission for Human Rights found Britain guilty of torture; however, the European Court of Human Rights ruled the practice was inhumane but did not constitute torture. The practice of internment galvanized support for the Northern Irish in places like the U.S. where financial and technical support increased.

1972 AD
Bloody Sunday occurred on January 30, 1972, a riot that ended with 13 men dead and 14 others seriously wounded. The British army opened fire on rioters, claiming later that the rioters fired first.

The Unionist (Protestant controlled) parliament at Stormont was disbanded by Prime Minister Edward Heath who felt they weren't able to control the civil war. Direct rule was returned to Westminster. The Catholics welcomed the fall of Protestant government but were unhappy that control returned to the English. The IRA stepped up its bombing campaign.

By July 21, 1972, bombing and fighting reached another pinnacle in what would become known as Bloody Friday. Nine deaths were caused by 21 bombs. Civilians were killed and the IRA blamed the authorities for failing to pass on warnings in time.

Secretary of State William Whitelaw granted special status to all prisoners convicted of terrorist related crimes. The prisoners used this status to claim political prisoner privileges and eventually authorities argued the practice undermined discipline.

1973 AD
Erskine Hamilton Childers, the son of **Robert Erskine Childers,** became President of Ireland (Eire). He was considered vibrant and hard working, but died suddenly on Nov. 17, 1974, during a speech in Dublin of a heart attack. His funeral was attended by world leaders including Lord Mountbatten, who would later be killed by Irish terrorists.

1975 – 1985 AD

On March 1, 1976, Secretary of State Merlyn Rees, Whitelaw's successor, phased out the special status. Kiernan Nugent, the next prisoner to arrive at Maze prison, was ordered to wear a prison uniform. He promptly refused and wore a blanket from his bed instead, giving rise to a six year long "blanket protest."

Lord Mountbatten along with several family members was killed on August 27, 1979, aboard his fishing boat in Donegal Bay, Ireland, by Provisional IRA bomber Tom McMahon. McMahon, who has since renounced his affiliation with the IRA, was convicted and sentenced to life imprisonment.

The next level of protest at Maze prison began with a hunger strike. After 53 days, the strike was called off with prisoners believing their demands would be met, but in fact were not. Bobby Sands, then ranking member of the Provisional IRA at Maze prison, began a second strike. Sands died 66 days later. One hundred thousand people attended his funeral. His death provoked riots and street protests in cities around the world.

By the end of hunger strikes on October 3, 1981, ten men had starved themselves to death. Outside the gates of Maze prison 61 people were killed in continuing violence.

1987 AD

The Provincial IRA set off a bomb at an annual Remembrance Day memorial gathering in Enniskillen killing 11 people and injuring 63. The event shocked the world and further eroded support for the Provisional IRA.

1988 – 1993 AD

Patrick Mayhew and Peter Brooke, consecutive Secretaries of State, held a series of talks that helped focus issues into three strands: relationships within Northern Ireland, relationships between

Northern Ireland and The Republic of Ireland and relationships between Ireland and Britain. The talks failed, however context for future peace processes was created.

John Humes, SDLP Leader and Gerry Adams, President of Sinn Fein, went on to conduct talks and debates resulting in a joint statement in April 1993 stating that everyone had a duty to move away from armed conflict. Many believe the dialogue laid the foundation for the road to the Good Friday Agreement years later.

By October 23, ten people were killed when an IRA bomb exploded prematurely in a shop in Belfast. With the exception of the bomber, who also died, the victims were all Protestant civilians.

On October 30, the Ulster Freedom Fighters, a Protestant loyalist faction, killed 6 Catholics and 1 Protestant in the Rising Sun bar in Greysteel, County Derry.

1994 AD
In January, President Bill Clinton arranged for Gerry Adams to attend a peace conference in the United States. Lasting peace in Ireland would become a Clinton Administration priority. By August, the IRA vowed a complete cessation of military activities. However, the IRA was not the only militant entity.

British Prime Minister John Major, believing the IRA ceased military activities, agreed to open exploratory talks with Sinn Fein.

1995 AD
On January 9, President Clinton asks retiring Senator George Mitchell of Maine to become a special advisor to the president and secretary of state on economic initiatives in Ireland.

British Secretary of State for Northern Ireland, Patrick Mayhew, sums up current British position on decommissioning paramilitary arms with three points—A willingness to disarm progressively; a common understanding of how de-commissioning would actually take place; and, commencing with some disarmament immediately as a show of good faith. These points, delivered at a gathering in Washington, became known as the "Washington Three."

A White House decision to invite Gerry Adams to the president's St. Patrick's Day reception is strongly criticized by Britain.

Britain begins to warm to the prospect of internationalization of peace negotiations. The Irish particularly wanted American involvement, which the British initially resisted. This warming by the British demarcates <u>the first pivotal step</u> towards the eventual "Good Friday Agreement."

Widespread effort to decommission paramilitaries on all sides continued in hopes the commitment would lead to serious talks.
On May 24, A Northern Ireland Trade Conference is held in Washington.

On November 28, John Major announced a "twin track" system for conducting peace negotiations. It called for decommissioning guerilla arms and proposed setting a date for all-party negotiations sometime in February 1996.

President Bill Clinton becomes the first sitting American President to visit Northern Ireland.

A newspaper report claimed Libya had provided Britain with information disclosing that over 130 tons of arms had been shipped from Tripoli and twenty PIRA activists were trained in Libya.

1996 AD

President Clinton asks George Mitchell to continue service after the trade conference and lead proposed Northern Ireland peace talks.

On January 24, the Mitchell Commission releases the "Mitchell Report" also known as the "Mitchell Principles," which called for adherence to principles of democracy and non-violence. In a separate section of the report, the concept of parallel disarmament was introduced. Few believed that the paramilitaries were going to completely disarm prior to talks. An acceptance of this concept allowed the peace process to move ahead.

The IRA unilaterally ends a 16-month cease fire. Even though complete cessation of militant attacks failed, intensive negotiations continue. So called all party talks began Monday, June 10, in Stormont without Sinn Fein.

Erskine Childers III died suddenly of a heart attack after delivering a speech at the 50th anniversary congress of the World Federation of United Nations Associations. He began his career in academia and ended with 22 years in service in various roles in the United Nations. He was the son of Eire president Erskine Hamilton Childers and the grandson of Robert Erskine Childers.

1997 AD

Tony Blair, British Labour Party leader, became Prime Minister on May 2, and continued peace efforts while still challenged by failed efforts to commission paramilitaries.

On May 28, the White House held discussions with Tony Blair and subsequently issued a harsh statement to the PIRA.

By August 29, an international group called the International Commission of Decommissioning was formed.

On September 9, Sinn Fein entered the peace process formally. This encouraged supporters who propounded that only majority consent would resolve the issues. They would later be expelled for their involvement in two Belfast murders. Subsequently, on September 13, the Democratic Unionist Party (DUP) asked George Mitchell to remove Sinn Fein from the peace talks. The Ulster Unionist Council executive decided to grant David Trimble authority to decide tactics in the peace talks.

Finally, on October 7, substantive talks with delegates from eight parties and two governments commenced.

December 3. A list of topics and format for their resolution was proposed by George Mitchell. A deadline for submittal was set for December 15.

By December 16, group leaders met on key issues under the chairmanship of George Mitchell. However, they failed to resolve all issues and broke up for Christmas. Tony Blair made the traditional Christmas visit to Northern Ireland.

Splinter groups and political prisoners engaged in violence. The list includes the Irish National Liberation Army (INLA), the Loyalist Volunteer Force (LVF), the Ulster Freedom Fighters (UFF) and the Ulster Defense Association (UDA).

1998 AD
The Mitchell led peace talks resume.

On January 30, a new judicial inquiry into the events of Bloody Sunday, 1972, is announced by Tony Blair.

Tony Blair meets with President Clinton and various U.S. Congressional groups on February 4, and conducts a briefing on peace negotiations.

On March 17, President Clinton meets with David Trimble and encourages him to meet with Gerry Adams. Trimble tells the President the Ulster Unionist Party (UUP) is not interested in a "stunt" meeting with Adams.

By March 25, George Mitchell proposed ending talks by April 9th.

April 3 – Friday - Of the three "Strands" of the agreement being drafted, "Strand Two" is behind schedule. Prime Minister Tony Blair and Irish Taoiseach Bernie Ahern telephone George Mitchell to inform him they need more time. Mitchell, after consultation with fellow commissioners and party representatives, gave the Blair and Ahern until Sunday evening to complete Strand Two.

Blair and Ahern hand in a draft of Strand Two and Mitchell immediately recognized that Nationalists will like it and Unionists won't. Further, Blair's and Ahern's staffs wanted the document included without any changes. Mitchell found this disturbing since that hadn't been the practice on Stands One and Three. Considering time was running out, Mitchell acceded to their demands although he could see the Irish felt more strongly about it than the British.

George Mitchell discovers that annexes to the Strand Two document were not yet negotiated. These annexes were crucial proposals on how to establish North-South institutions - the long term basis for a North-South relationship. He thought that when he had received the document the previous evening it was nearly complete. He could continue to wait for the annexes to be negotiated or distribute the document to the parties incomplete. He waited and by midnight they were handed to the Commission. Mitchell was surprised by their length and completeness; however, in Mitchell's mind this made their rejection by Unionists more certain.

April 7 – Tuesday - Unionist parties claimed the draft was nothing more than a Sinn Fein wish list. David Trimble wanted an assurance that the draft would be renegotiated by Ahern and Blair to more fairly recognize Unionist concerns. Mitchell believed there was a breakdown in communication between Trimble and Blair. This nearly caused the process to collapse.

Mitchell, Holkeri and de Chastelain basically agreed that Trimble would walk out and that they too believed Blair and Ahern needed to renegotiate Strand Two. British officials were willing to renegotiate but the Irish were concerned about keeping the Nationalists at the table as well.

Tony Blair flew to Belfast by evening. Before leaving London he made a statement that clarified his commitment, including a quote stating "I feel the hand of history upon our shoulders." He scheduled an early Wednesday morning breakfast meeting with Bernie Ahern.

Irish Taoiseach Bernie Ahern was committed to the peace process but he suffered an added difficulty at the worst time. His mother passed away suddenly only a few days earlier. Her funeral was scheduled for Wednesday.

April 8 – Wednesday - Bernie Ahern flew to Belfast to meet with Tony Blair and returned to Dublin by noon to attend his mother's funeral. Mitchell admired the incredible devotion Ahern demonstrated to both his mother and the frantic continuation of the peace process.

By late afternoon, Ahern flew back to Belfast to continue working on renegotiating Strand Two. Meetings lasted late into the night. Ahern, thought totally exhausted, kept telling Mitchell, "We've got to get this done, we've got to get this done." Mitchell admired his flexibility. In effect, he had already sold the first draft to the Nationalists and he could have simply said to Blair "I did my job, now you go sell it to the Unionists." He did not. He agreed to renegotiate.

He was a realist and understood that the Unionist would not have yielded, even to Blair.

April 9 – Thursday - Ahern's willingness to renegotiate put David Trimble in a position where he had to be reasonable or ultimately be chastised for not negotiating in good faith. There were clear signs that even though his party wanted what they wanted, the mass of society had been ground down by the fighting. In the last twenty-five years of sectarian fighting alone, there had been over 3,000 deaths and 36,000 injuries. Trimble also suffered severe criticism by Ian Paisley and Robert McCartney who saw the entire process as a "painful slide from a position of dominance to one of being besieged" according to Mitchell. Ironically, Trimble had once participated in the downfall of Brian Faulkner's Unionist government in 1974 because he felt they had conceded too much power sharing to the Nationalists. Now, as so often the case in Northern Ireland, fate had come full circle and as he attempted to craft a compromise, he came under attack by more conservative factions who believed he was selling them out.

Unionists, who wanted a strong assembly they believed they could control, feared that strong North-South institutions would overwhelm an assembly. Nationalists, as a minority, wanted strong North-South institutions because they were afraid an assembly would overwhelm them. The agreement included words that declared they were "mutually inter-dependent" and that "one cannot function without the other."

According to Mitchell, "The British and Irish governments made an absolute commitment to establish a North-South Ministerial Council and to create implementation bodies to carry out the councils decisions." The difficult issue of timing and authority was resolved by the creation of a "transitional" phase during which the ministerial council, the new Northern Ireland Assembly, and a new British/Irish Council would simultaneously and cooperatively begin to function.

Any expansion of these arrangements would have to be approved by the Assembly.

In addition to the question of the formation of North–South institutions there were extensive negotiations addressing the release of political prisoners and de-commissioning of paramilitaries.

Late Thursday evening, according to Mitchell, Dr. Ian Paisley, a conservative Protestant, Loyalist minister, made a last minute attempt to spoil the agreements when he led a few hundred supporters in a protest on the grounds of Stormont. He demanded he be allowed to hold a press conference. According to Mitchell, they decided to allow him to speak. He was interrupted by "loud, rude heckling."

Mitchell, in his memoir entitled *Making Peace*, goes on to say that some members of the loyalist parties, once among the most fervent of his supporters, savagely accused him of running away. They told him that earlier in their lives they had listened to him, but no more. He was a ghost of a violent past, now they wanted peace. "Go home," they chanted, "go home." It was a demeaning performance. Watching with us were several government officials with long experience in Northern Ireland. One of them said softly, "Once he would have brought thousands, tens of thousands with him. Now he has a few hundred. And look at those loyalists. Many of them thought him a god. They went out and killed, thinking they were saving the union. Now they have turned on him. It's the end of an era."

Midnight passed and the initial Mitchell deadline of April 9, was officially missed, but talks ground on. April 10, Friday - At 8:15 local time, President Clinton telephoned Mitchell (it was 3:15 am, Washington time) for a progress report. Mitchell asked why he was calling in the middle of his night. Clinton said he was anxious to hear what was taking place, couldn't sleep, and wanted to help. He did so by directly telephoning Trimble, Hume, Adams and others. He knew the issues and he knew the negotiators. They were impressed by his direct concern and interest.

Still, Unionist negotiators were concerned about prisoner release and decommissioning of paramilitaries. In a final effort to assuage their concerns, they persuaded Tony Blair to draft a letter effectively promising that these issues would be dealt with fairly.

On April 10, at 5:00 p.m., The "Good Friday Agreement" was signed and talks brought to an end. However, various groups waffled even though polling indicated 73 percent of the people of Northern Ireland were in favor of the agreement. President Clinton promised $100 million to support what was officially known as "The Belfast Agreement."

April 15. The Grand Orange Lodge met in Belfast and issued a statement that they could not recommend the agreement to its members without further clarification.

April 18. The Ulster Unionist Council delegates, who met in Belfast, voted 540 to 210 (72 percent) for the agreement.

April 30. The Provisional IRA states that the Belfast Agreement falls short of being a "solid basis for a lasting settlement." The Orange Order rejects the Belfast Agreement.

May 10. Sinn Fein reports 96 percent of delegates support the Belfast Agreement and agrees to permit members to sit in the Northern Ireland Assembly.

May 15. The LVF announces a cease fire but still rejects the Belfast Agreement by calling for a NO vote on the referendum.

May 21. A last minute application for an injunction by legal gadfly and college lecturer Denis Riordan of Limerick was rejected by the Dublin High Court.

Pop culture facilitated the "Yes Campaign" when Bono, lead singer of the group U2, joined Social Democratic Labour Party leader John Hume and the Ulster Unionist Party leader David Trimble on stage at a concert in Belfast.

May 22. The "All Island Referendum" passed in both the North and the South with an overall 85 percent yes and 15 percent no vote. It was the first all-island polling since 1918. An exit poll reported that 94 percent of Catholics favored the agreement while only 55 percent Protestants approved.

July 12. Three Catholic boys, Richard (11), Mark (10) and Quinn (9), were killed when their home was petrol-bombed by Loyalists. President Bill Clinton made a pledge to the fourth surviving boy, Lee (13), that he would do all he could to bring peace to Northern Ireland.

August 15. Twenty-nine people died in an explosion in Omagh, County Tyrone. The bomb had been planted by the "real" IRA, yet another dangerous splinter group. The dissidents later insisted they didn't mean to kill anyone. They claimed the Royal Ulster Constabulary had misunderstood a warning call and directed people toward the bomb rather than away from it.

August 18. Three days after the Omagh bombing the "real" IRA, in a telephone message to the Irish News, a Northern Ireland newspaper, claimed they were suspending all military operations.

September 3. U.S. President Bill Clinton made his second visit to Ireland delivering a speech at the Waterfront Hall in Belfast.

December 10. John Hume and David Tremble receive the Nobel Peace Prize at an awards ceremony in the City Hall of Oslo, Norway.

1999 AD

Decommissioning paramilitary weaponry remained a high priority and a condition to moving ahead with the peace process. A resulting document entitled "The Way Forward" emerged from talks and addressed decommissioning and the establishment of an inclusive executive.

In August, security forces investigated both the execution style Murder of Charles Bennett, a 22-year-old North Belfast taxi driver, and the attempt to import high-powered weapons by post from Florida. Both incidents raised questions over the IRA cease-fire and nearly stalled decommissioning talks.

November 18. U.S. Senator George Mitchell issued a report on his review of the Good Friday Agreement progress. Mitchell had been instrumental in brokering the agreement and continued to try to work through prisoner release and de-commissioning processes.

December 1. The end of Direct Rule as power shifted from Westminster to the Northern Ireland Assembly.

Decommissioning was still not accomplished and remained an open issue as the New Year arrived.

2000 AD

The IRA opened the New Year with a statement saying "you first" to reducing British military presence before they would decommission.

On Wednesday, January 12, Gerry Adams met Bill Clinton at the White House (coincidentally designed by an Irishman, based on an estate house in Ireland) urging the IRA to get on with decommissioning.

By February 11, no progress in decommissioning resulted in the suspension of the 72-day-old Direct Rule. This came after reports from the International Commission overseeing decommissioning indicated they were not seeing meaningful progress.

On February 15, the IRA announced it was withdrawing from talks with the International Commission on Decommissioning.

Fighting and deaths related to the conflict continued as the impasse on decommissioning continued. Tony Blair and Bertie Ahern, then Taoiseach (Republic of Ireland Prime Minister) continued talks.
By May 8, an offer was made by then Secretary of State of Northern Ireland Peter Mandelson, to reduce British military presence as a compromise towards decommissioning.

Arms inspectors arrived in Northern Ireland as international commission on decommissioning efforts appear to begin in earnest. David Trimble, leader of the Ulster Unionist Party, said IRA opening their arms dump to inspectors indicates the 30-year war is over.

On May 30th, the British government restored Direct Rule to the Northern Ireland Assembly.

On June 3, further British troop reductions were announced although 13,500 troops still remained in Northern Ireland—the lowest level since 1970.

The last of paramilitary prisoners in Maze prison were released bringing the total number of prisoners released as a result of the Good Friday Agreement to 428.

Feuding and in-fighting continued resulting in civilian casualties. On September 22, dissident Republican (Nationalist) paramilitaries fired an anti-tank rocket into the London Headquarters of MI6. No injuries were reported.

An argument broke out between David Trimble and Gerry Adams over decommissioning and power sharing.

Feuding continued and retaliatory assassinations reoccurred throughout the later months of October, November and December. On December 13, Bill Clinton traveled to Northern Ireland urging compromise and stating, "We have to keep going. I do not think reversal is an option."

On December 15, feuding Loyalists issued a statement announcing an "open-ended and all-encompassing cessation of hostilities."

However, the killing continues and the peace effort continues.